THE GIFT
THE STORY OF ANNIE LAURIE

By

Ta`Mara Hanscom

Sioux City, Iowa

The Gift: The Story of Annie Laurie

Published by Reata Publishing
2015 Indian Hills Boulevard
Sioux City, Iowa 51104
www.TaMaraHanscom.com

Edited by Kimberly J. Cotter

Cover design and concept by Laura Veronica Gibson
Back cover concept by Ta`Mara Hanscom
Cover and back cover layout by Jordan Thomas Gibson

Photography by Laura Gibson & James Hanscom

Printed in the United States of America
978-0-9844514-3-2

You may contact the author with comments at
TaMara@TaMaraHanscom.com

Cast of Characters

Joshua Hansen – married to Mona (Spencer) Hansen

Noah Hansen – brother of Joshua Hansen – was married to * Carrie (Miller) Hansen
Carrie passed away March, 1981

Ty Hansen – Carrie's son by Dr. Schneider Rauwolf a/k/a Roy Schneider, raised by Noah Hansen

Jake Hansen – Noah's son with wife, Carrie

Guiseppi Caselli – Married to Rosa (Rosa Matilde Rochelle) Caselli

Petrice Caselli – Eldest Caselli son, married to Ellie (Elaine Netherton) Caselli
Michael Petrice Caselli – son of Petrice & Ellie Caselli
Gabriella Elaine Caselli – daughter of Petrice & Ellie Caselli

Vincenzo Caselli – Second Caselli son, married to Kate (Katlin Martin) Caselli
Alyssa Katlin Caselli – daughter of Vincenzo & Kate Caselli
Angelo James Caselli – son of Vincenzo & Kate Caselli

Marquette Caselli – Youngest Caselli son, married to Tara (D`Annenci) Caselli

Tillie (Matilde Rosa Caselli) Martin – Only Caselli daughter – Nicknamed "Angel" by her brothers, married to Alex James Martin III

Angelo Caselli – brother of Guiseppi Caselli – passed away 1964

James Martin, Jr. – married to Frances (Dale) Martin

Sam Martin – Eldest Martin son – married to Becky-Lynn (Tucker) Martin

Katlin Martin – Only Martin daughter - married to Vincenzo Caselli

Alex James Martin III – Youngest Martin son - married to Tillie (Caselli) Martin
Alex James Martin IV – son of Alex & Tillie Martin
Laura Rose Martin – daughter of Alex & Tillie Martin

Burt Engleson – married to Diane Engleson

Rev. Andy Engleson – son of Burt & Diane Engleson – Pastor at Christ the King Church
Ginger (Engleson) Maxwell – daughter of Burt & Diane Engleson and life-long friend of Tillie (Caselli) Martin. She is married to Bobby Maxwell and they live in Las Vegas, Nevada.

Mario Ponerello a/k/a **Jack Nelson** – married to Della (Miller) Nelson – Carrie Hansen's mother

Mario is the arch nemesis of Marquette Caselli. Marquette has sought after Mario since The Great Palermo Diamond Heist of 1968

Antonio Ponerello – a/k/a Ben Simmons — Eldest son of Mario Ponerello

Charise Nelson – daughter of Mario Ponerello & Della Nelson

Salvatore Ponerello – brother of Mario Ponerello. Presumed dead.

Dr. Schneider Rauwolf a/k/a Roy Schneider – biological father of Ty Hansen

Reata—Ranch near Centerville, SD – Vincenzo Caselli inherited Reata from Uncle Angelo, the brother of his father, Guiseppi. Vincenzo and his family live there, and there are many events throughout the year that take place on Reata. Also, Uncle Angelo and his beloved wife, Penny, rest there.

To my Jim,

You were taught, with regard to your former way of life, to put off your old self, which is being corrupted by its deceitful desires; to be made new in the attitude of your minds; and to put on the new self, created to be like God in true righteousness and holiness…Ephesians 4:22-24 **NIV**

Thank you for your gracious and humble example. You inspire me, encourage me, and bless me. I love you.

— *Ta`Mara*

WHEN I WAS A CHILD I TALKED LIKE A CHILD, I THOUGHT LIKE A CHILD, I REASONED LIKE A CHILD. WHEN I BECAME A MAN, I PUT CHILDISH WAYS BEHIND ME. NOW WE SEE BUT A POOR REFLECTION AS IN A MIRROR; THEN WE SHALL SEE FACE TO FACE. NOW I KNOW IN PART; THEN I SHALL KNOW FULLY, EVEN AS I AM FULLY KNOWN...

I CORINTHIANS 13:11-12, NIV

Foreword

Noah reached for her hand, and to his surprise, she didn't try to get away. He felt the warmth and softness inside of his palm, and he smiled into her eyes. "I know *everything* about you. I know that you love white roses and brand new puppies. Your favorite story is *The Sound of Music*, and you get up before the sun. You make the best ravioli on the planet, and your brothers adore you. You wear Chanel No. 5…" Noah deeply inhaled, "and it still smells *great* on you. And sometimes when I look at you, it's like yesterday all over again — I *wish* it was yesterday and we could have another chance."

Noah Hansen, June 1987

Part I

Angel

Chapter 1

Easter Sunday, April, 1993
Sioux Falls, South Dakota

Guiseppi Caselli was nearly seventy-seven years old. There wasn't even a fringe of hair left around his bald head now, but his old black eyes still sparkled with delight when he looked at his Rosa. She had aged in the most graceful of ways. She didn't color her wavy silver hair, but kept it in a delicate modern bob just below her chin. Her black eyes were not heavily made up, nor were they lined with the age one would expect on a seventy-three-year-old woman.

Guiseppi sang the words in Italian, while the Dean Martin CD played in their new stereo system. He borrowed the idea from his daughter, installing the new system only a few weeks earlier. He did this so that his family would have wonderful music on Easter Sunday.

Guiseppi and Rosa's children and grandchildren watched them waltz around the living room, laughing at their "youthful" grandparents.

"It is *easy*!" Guiseppi encouraged with a smile. "Just watch me and Nonna. We are like the pros!"

"Oh, Guiseppi," Rosa giggled as she backed out of his arms. "I have had enough. You find another partner so that Tara and I may check on our dinner."

"Whatever you say, Rosa my love," Guiseppi smiled, allowing her to escape. He bowed politely before his granddaughter, Gabriella. She smiled as he took her hand and led her around the living room.

"She looks so much like Angel at this age," Petrice commented to his wife as they watched their teenage daughter waltz with her grandfather.

Soon the entire family had joined in the dancing, and Guiseppi chortled with delight, "We are 'The Dancing von Casellis!' Get it?"

His children and grandchildren smiled politely, nodding without remark.

Guiseppi frowned and whispered to his granddaughter, "Do they not get it, Gabby? After all, it was once my Angel's favorite story."

Gabriella laughed at her grandfather as they came to the end of the song and Guiseppi dashed back to his "magical" control box. Soon a familiar tune started to play and his eyes sparkled at Tillie. She was seated in the living room, content to watch everyone dance around her.

"Oh, my Angel!" he exclaimed as he held out his arms. "Certainly you remember this one? Let us have only one short dance."

Tillie smiled and shook her head as she replied, "I'm sorry, Papa. I just don't dance anymore."

Guiseppi's smiling eyes turned down but he covered his disappointment with a smile. Laura ran to her grandfather, slipping her tiny arms around his waist.

"I'll dance with you, Grandpa!" she offered excitedly.

"Well, all right then!" Guiseppi exclaimed as he took the little girl into his arms and waltzed her around the floor to the song he'd taught her mother to dance to: *Non Dimenticar*.

Alex and Sam were just a short distance from Tillie, and Sam saw the grieved look in his brother's eyes. He touched Alex on the sleeve and motioned for him to follow. Sam led him into the billiard room where it wasn't as loud.

Sam Martin was fifty-five years old and his black hair had silvered completely. He and Becky-Lynn were included in the Casellis' Easter celebration as Frances Martin had passed away soon after James's death. Becky-Lynn's ill mother passed away as well, leaving Sam and Becky-Lynn alone for the holidays. But Guiseppi and Rosa had known the Martins since 1956, and would not leave one of them to fend for themselves.

"How's things going, Alex?" Sam asked when he was alone with his brother. "I haven't heard from you in a long time."

Alex had just turned forty-three years old, but there was not a drop of age around his dark eyes or a line upon his beautiful face. His black hair was touched with soft silver at the temples now, but it only made him more handsome.

Alex shrugged as he answered, "I guess I've just been busy. I'm special counsel to the governor you know."

Sam nodded. "Still sticking around Rapid City, I hope?"

"Oh, yeah, I stay close to home."

"Tillie looks a little under the weather," Sam commented. "Everything okay with you guys?"

Alex glanced at his wife who was still seated in a chair in the living room. She was wearing a soft yellow dress, and had put her shoulder-length black curls in a bun atop her head. But her pretty black eyes didn't sparkle, and her smiles seemed forced. She looked older than her thirty-five years and she moved slowly, as if she was tired. She was still a very pretty lady, but she did look somewhat, "*under the weather*," as Sam had said.

"I think everything's okay," Alex replied. "She just *looks* like that now."

"Not that she looks *bad*," Sam added quickly. "Just different." He frowned at his brother. "You're still spending enough time with her and the kids, right?"

Alex nodded in response. "And I travel less than twice a month."

"What about this deal you're cookin' up with the Daniel Stahlheim Group? Is that keeping you away —" Sam's question was interrupted by Rosa's call.

"Come along now!" Rosa ushered everyone into the dining room for dinner.

"I'll tell you more about it later," Alex replied with a smile. "It's a great opportunity to put South Dakota on the map of corporate investment — did you see the article in the *Argus* the other day?"

Sam frowned curiously and shook his head, but decided to drop the matter until after dinner.

Guiseppi turned off his wonderful stereo and helped Rosa get everyone to the table. Twelve of them were seated at the main table but, as had become the custom, six more were seated at a table placed alongside the first so all eighteen of them could sit together. Guiseppi prayed and they began to eat and talk.

Petrice was excited to hear about Marquette's new offer from the University of Stanford on the Italian campus, and began to question his brother in that regard, "When will that position begin?"

"September," Marquette answered with a thoughtful expression. "However, I have yet to give them an answer. *Firenze* (Florence) is still very far from *Lago Di Como* (Como Lake) and Tara and I would have to find another residence for nine months out of the year. Of course it would require that we stay in *Italia* most of the time and I do not know if we are altogether comfortable with that either."

"It's an incredible offer, Marq," Sam said. "What would be your main focus?"

"Middle Eastern affairs," Marquette answered, "and I would oversee their programs with regard to regional policy and Arabic language."

"You'll have to grow your ponytail back to look the part of a professor," Elaine teased good-naturedly.

Everyone around the tables laughed, including Marquette. At the age of fifty-one Marquette was still a handsome man, but, much to the regret of his wife, he had cut off his ponytail on his fiftieth birthday. Silver had started to wind its way through the soft black waves and he felt it was time to take on a more dignified appearance.

Alex huffed inwardly because he knew the *real* reason Marquette would *never* take the position. He was afraid to leave his sister for too a long a time because of what had happened. It was as if it had become Marquette's duty in life to protect his little sister from that *fiendish* Alex Martin, no matter the cost to his own personal life. Alex wished he would just go away and leave them alone, but he'd never dare say anything to Tillie about it. He was determined to bite his tongue and mend whatever he could between himself and her family.

Kate cleared her throat and said, "Say, I saw an article in the *Argus* yesterday about the Daniel Stahlheim Group — and they have appointed Alex Martin III as their special counsel for their South Dakota interests."

The chatter around the tables fell silent at her words.

Oh dear, Alex thought as he slowly nodded his head, acknowledging his sister's words. He'd been wondering how his family would take the news. The Daniel Stahlheim Group was a "world-renowned" investment firm. The fact that Alex had attracted their attention was nothing short of genius. Hopefully his family would see it that way. But, judging by the way everyone's mouths were hanging open around the tables, he knew he had to proceed with caution.

"Well, as you know, they are very interested in investing in South Dakota," he began.

"The article said something about a pipeline?" Kate asked.

Alex nodded again, assessing the deafening silence around him, wanting to kick his sister for bringing it up…*she never could just let anything go*. He took a breath and answered, "As well as a refinery — possibly hydraulic fracturing."

"And the article said you've met with Mr. Stahlheim *himself*," Kate said.

Tillie rolled her eyes and focused on her mashed potatoes. She'd worried about their family's reaction, *especially Kate's*. Little did they know her husband had been courting Daniel Stahlheim for over a year.

Alex nodded again and answered, "Several times. He intends to produce over ten thousand jobs within South Dakota's borders."

Guiseppi smiled proudly at his son-in-law, but only for the sake of his daughter. Inwardly, his heart was breaking. It was a pattern he'd watched repeat itself too many times.

After dinner Kate became ill and asked Vincenzo to take her home. Tillie rolled her eyes again. The trouble that had started between Kate and Alex in 1987 had never completely mended. In fact, it seemed to have intensified after Frances's death.

It's too bad she can't let anything go, Tillie thought. *It's been six years. Good grief, let it die.*

Tillie was with her mother, Tara and Becky-Lynn, having afternoon tea. Petrice and Elaine, along with their children had gone back to Reata with Vincenzo and Kate, the twins were playing pool with Marquette and Guiseppi, and Sam and Alex had taken a walk.

And who knows what they're talking about, Tillie thought as the ladies chatted away about Becky-Lynn's hilarious clients (she always saved the best stories for Rosa) and Tara's possible move to Italy. Tillie smiled at them as she pretended to listen.

Don't worry, I've got everything handled, she wanted to say. She sighed inside…*then why am I still so afraid?*

*****

"The family is growing up so fast!" Rosa exclaimed as she and Guiseppi got ready for bed that night. "What with our Harvard students and our giant grandsons! Angelo must be a foot taller than Vincenzo, and he looks so handsome in his Air Force uniform. And I believe Alyssa is even taller than Frances ever was." Rosa chuckled with delight as she went on, "And Michael will already be seventeen next month! Guiseppi, can you believe it? It seems only yesterday Patty was bringing his young bride to Sioux Falls and Angel was so steamed." She sighed. "How the time has flown."

Guiseppi frowned as he sat down heavily on the bed. With a sigh he said, "My Angel would not dance with me this afternoon."

Rosa answered with a nod, wondering all day if he would mention the incident. "I noticed, but she *does* seem happier than when we visited at Christmastime," she said.

Guiseppi nodded and rubbed his bald head. "She just does not look well, Rosa."

"Guiseppi, all of Marquette's reports have been glowing with regard to Alex, and you know he has practically lived in Rapid City since the accident." The day Alex moved back in with his family six years ago, he agreed to Guiseppi's request that Guiseppi and Marquette be allowed to stay until Tillie was well again and more able to care for herself and the children. It was an awkward fifteen months, especially between Marquette and Alex. For more than a year they lived together, but spoke rarely. "What is it that you are worried about?" she asked.

Guiseppi shrugged as he answered, "I do not know, my Rosa, but something in my heart feels not quite right." He took a deep breath. "This position with Stahlheim, for instance, do you suppose he is away a lot again?"

"Marquette said that Alex is always home at the end of the day, and travels less than twice a month. And it would be out of character for Marquette to lie for Alex."

"I know. But the sadness in her eyes seems to grow every time I see her…" Guiseppi sighed heavily and whispered, "Has she spoken of him at all?"

"You mean Noah?" Rosa whispered, and Guiseppi nodded. "Never. She has not said his name since the day she sent him away."

Guiseppi continued, "Marquette told me this afternoon that he saw Noah last week."

"How is he doing?"

"Very well apparently."

"And what of Angel? Does she see him at all anymore?" Rosa questioned.

"No. Alex takes A.J. to the practices and Angel only attends the games, with Alex of course. Noah says he takes measures to keep himself out of her sight and that it has been more than three years since he last caught even a glimpse of her.

"Does Marquette believe him?" Rosa asked.

"Yes. Marquette claims that Noah has gotten over Angel and has moved on with his life. He says that Noah has spent these last six years repenting of his covetousness, has asked Alex for forgiveness, and it is a rare occasion when he even asks Marquette about her. And according to Marquette, all is very well between Noah and Alex. They do not talk about Angel, of course, but Alex has referred several projects Noah's way and has even asked him to accompany him on his trip to Denver next week when he visits Stahlheim."

"Is Noah going along then?"

"As far as I know, and hopefully they can talk a great game. Ten thousand new jobs in South Dakota is nothing to sneeze at."

Alex got into bed beside his sleepy wife, turned off the lamp and took her into his arms. "Are you feeling okay, honey?" He gave her a soft kiss on the top of her head.

"Fine. Why?" she answered as she snuggled closer to the warmth of his body and rested in his arms.

"You looked a little out of sorts today. Like maybe you didn't feel so good or something."

"I feel fine." Tillie smiled in the darkness. "I'm a little tired I guess. It always kind of wears me out to be with all of them. They're so loud you know."

Alex frowned. That had never bothered her before. In fact, she had always seemed to thrive on her family's loud banter.

"I think Papa felt bad when you wouldn't dance with him this afternoon," he whispered.

"Oh, Alex," Tillie scoffed with a smile, "he didn't care. He knows I don't do that anymore."

"Why not?" Alex blurted. He hadn't intended to ask the question, but there was a curiosity he had about it. She used to love to dance and her body was in perfect shape again. *Why doesn't she dance anymore?*

"I just don't like to," she answered with a yawn. "Shouldn't we be trying to fall asleep. We've got a long drive ahead of us tomorrow."

Alex gave the top of her head one more kiss and said, "Okay. I love you, Tillie. Goodnight."

"I love you, too," Tillie whispered as she yawned again and it was only minutes before Alex heard her breathing change and he knew she'd already fallen asleep.

As Alex held his sleeping wife in his arms his mind began to wander until it was back at the place it had been for so many years. What more could he do to somehow persuade his wife into believing he was there to stay? He knew Tillie loved him and she was happy to be together as a family, *but there is still something missing. Her eyes have lost their sparkle, and her easy laughter and quick wit are gone.* In the beginning he'd blamed the accident…*but she's made a tremendous recovery...and yet she's still not who she was when I married her. I wonder when, if ever, the old Tillie will come back.*

Alex sighed as he *again* went over his actions of the past. *She begged me to come home and I rejected her...why did I do that? She only wanted to be a family and I actually called her a nag.* He shuddered at the memories. Their reconciliation had sent her entire family, *and his*, into an uproar. They called him selfish and cruel, especially after several newspapers took turns rehashing the details of the dismissed divorce. In response to their families' anger Tillie said remarkable things in defense of her husband. She told them all to obey God's design in the matter. She and Alex would remain married and raise their children together.

Alex listened to Tillie's soft breathing as she slept in his arms. *How blessed I am. I can never do those things again....*

His heart pounded as he allowed his mind to wander to his thrilling new opportunity. After six years of painstakingly rebuilding relationships with colleagues he'd mistreated, Alex had won back his reputation. And because of his relationship with *the* Daniel Stahlheim, officials from the Conservative party in South Dakota had contacted him just the day before he took his family to Sioux Falls for Easter. It was their wish that he throw his hat into the ring for the United States Senate seat.

Alex had thought about it the entire four days they were in Sioux Falls, and had successfully skirted around Sam's questions. No one else knew. He probably wouldn't have the endorsement of Senator Caselli this time, but his relationship with Stahlheim promised a glowing recommendation. Alex was forty-three years old and he knew he was ready to handle this. In just the few days he'd considered it, he'd decided to find a place for his family to live in D.C. while the Senate was in session, just the way Petrice had handled it for the last seventeen years. He and Tillie could start a new life, close to her brothers and their wives and children, and he wouldn't have to worry about Noah losing control again.

*****

Jake heaved the heavy suitcase from the baggage claim and set it down in front of Mona. "There ya go, Auntie," he said, turning and reaching for another suitcase. He grabbed a matching bag and set that one by Joshua. "And there's yours, Uncle Josh."

"Oh you're so strong!" Mona exclaimed in her Southern accent — which had gotten even heavier during their family trip down south.

"You'd think Heidi Romanov was watching or something," Ty teased with a grin.

Noah laughed at his boys, reaching for his own suitcase.

Jake only grinned in return. Though Ty was nearly sixteen, and well over six feet tall, Jake was determined to best him in all tests of strength. Jake was only twelve years old, and nearly a foot shorter than his brother.

"Jake is a good boy," Mona said, reaching over to tousle his sandy colored hair. "And you both did such a wonderful job ushering at my cousin's wedding. We were so proud of you!"

Joshua wore an amused frown. "But, Jake, next time you seat the mother of the groom, don't do the moonwalk." Everyone laughed as they remembered the funny episode.

"But she was the *oldest* mother of the groom *ever*," Jake said with a half-smile. "I was just killin' time."

Noah raised his brows and added, "Well he was the *oldest groom* I've ever seen."

As they collected their bags and started for the door, Noah asked, "Mona, how old is your cousin, Bif, anyway?"

"Buford is fifty-seven years old," Mona answered. "And he certainly doesn't look that old to me."

"Buford Ignatious Franklin Spencer," Joshua said. "But we all call him Bif because it's shorter — but that's another story all by itself."

Ty laughed out loud, for he had heard many of Mona's dramatic stories over the weekend about her large Southern family, the Spencers. "And they're all from Atlanta," he added, mimicking Mona's southern accent. "Georgia, that is."

"So what was the deal with Bif?" Noah asked as he opened the RCRA terminal door for his family to pass through.

"Oh you know," Joshua reminded, "he was the one who met the love of his life at the library when he was something like twenty-four —"

"It was 1960," Mona corrected, "and Buford wasn't quite twenty-four."

"Yes, of course," Joshua went on. "Anyway, he met the love of his life at the library one Saturday morning. They spent the whole day talking and visiting, and she promised to come back to the library the following Saturday — but she never showed."

"Well, we all thought Buford was a confirmed bachelor," Mona continued, "until the story came out about Miss Betty desertin' him. Oh how I have prayed for my cousin."

"And God blessed," Joshua said. "Look at him now. Miss Betty finally came back and they tied the knot."

"Wow, what a story," Jake mused. "Good thing Bif became a librarian. No telling where he woulda been if he hadn't been working at that library the day she decided to come back."

Mona nodded with a wistful smile. "God delivered to Buford the delight of his life."

They had walked to Noah's pickup by now. Noah dropped the tailgate and the boys started loading the bags.

"What took Miss Betty so long to come back?" Ty asked, swinging a bag into the bed of the pickup.

"Just a terrible misunderstanding," Joshua answered.

Jake frowned. "Wow, that must have been some misunderstanding," he muttered.

Mona nodded. "Apparently Miss Betty saw Buford helping another girl over at the card catalogue and thought he'd found himself another gal."

Jake and Ty shook their heads with a groan as they loaded the last of the bags.

"I think we witnessed a miracle this weekend, boys," Noah said, watching them load the family's suitcases. "Don't forget to praise the Lord."

"We won't, Dad," Ty said.

"For sure," Jake agreed.

"Yes, praise Him indeed," Mona said with a smile. "He makes all things right in His own time."

*****

Maggie May West was nearly sixty-eight years young. She colored her silvered hair jet black and put it into the bee-hive style she'd worn for the last twenty-some years.

Estelle was sixty-three and Maggie colored her hair for her, too. *These days*, Maggie thought, *when there are so many good products on the shelves, there's no reason to go around looking like a gray-haired, old witch.*

It was early morning and Estelle was in her usual place at the bar as she read the paper, sipped coffee, and asked Maggie questions about what she had read in yesterday's news. Her memory hadn't slipped as quickly as their mother's, but the changes in Estelle were evident nonetheless.

"They're still trying to talk that guy out of his church in Waco," she muttered. "How long has that been going on now, Maggie?"

Maggie glanced at her calendar behind the bar as she reached for a cup for herself. "About six weeks," she replied.

Estelle shook her head as she asked, "Now, what's the deal with that, Maggie?"

Maggie poured herself some coffee as she answered, "Don't they have some guns or something?"

Estelle nodded. "That's right. Lots of guns," she replied.

Maggie frowned as she glanced at the loaded Remington she'd kept under the counter for the past thirty-some years...*everybody in town knows I have the thing...I can't believe they haven't reported me yet....*

The doorbell sounded and Maggie looked up, pleasantly surprised to see Noah stroll through the door. He smiled at her as he made his way to the counter and she pulled out another cup and filled it for him.

"You're an early bird today," Maggie greeted with a smile as Noah seated himself.

Noah had turned forty-one the December before and his sandy colored hair had grayed more on the sides. His blue eyes were lined with weather and grief and they seldom danced anymore.

"Hi, Estelle," Noah said as he gave her a gentle nudge.

"Hi, Noah," she replied, but was so engrossed in her paper she didn't look up to smile at him.

The separation from Angel was harder on Noah than he let on, but Maggie knew he missed her every day. He still glanced at the old portrait and the yellowed snapshot which hung near the bar, as it had for the last eighteen years. Sometimes the look in his expression made Maggie wish with all her heart she could do something to ease his pain.

"I've got a busy day today," he said as he reached for the cup. "Thanks, Maggie. McDarren's got me working my tail off on his new hotel project over there on Fifth Street."

"The new convention center?"

Noah nodded and answered, "He wants me to have the thing finished before Memorial Day weekend." He shook his head and rolled his eyes. "I don't know if the carpenters can get 'er all done. It's really a monster."

"So, how is ol' Scottie Boy? Still with Melinda?"

Noah answered with a grin, "I guess so."

"Ever see her anymore?"

"Never," Noah answered. "I guess she stays at their place in Texas. She sold that house out in Quartz Canyon. I know the realtor who listed it and the little battleaxe really made a fortune on the deal."

Maggie shook her head disgustedly and muttered, "She was such a gold digger."

Noah sipped at his coffee and said, "And then I've gotta get up to Angel's Place, sometime today. Viv says there's bats in the attic." He paused to roll his eyes. "She's getting *so old*, Maggie; she's gotta be at least a hundred by now and she still finds the time to torture me. There's no bats in that attic. She's just hearing things."

Maggie chuckled and added, "Viv's got bats all right. Bats in her belfry…oh, by the way, the paper did a nice little story about you and Alex this morning."

"No kidding? What about?"

"Just that you'll be traveling with him over to Denver to see Stahlheim next week," Maggie answered. She raised her eyebrows. "And you'll fly from Denver over to the Sioux Falls area in Stahlheim's *private* plane. Sounds pretty highfalutin." She winked. "So you guys must be calling him *Dan* by now."

Noah shrugged with a chuckle as he answered, "I guess. I put a proposal together for some developing and Ben drew out the specs on it. He did a really good job. I told Alex he oughta take Ben instead of me, but Ben claims he's afraid to get on those small planes Alex is always flying around in."

"I don't blame him," Maggie grumbled. "I wouldn't go near one."

"Oh they're perfectly safe, Maggie."

"When will you be back?"

"About suppertime that same day," Noah answered. "I guess we're just going over to eastern South Dakota for a look from above, and then we'll talk."

Maggie nodded. "And how's Angel. Do you know?" she asked.

"Marquette says she's doing really good," Noah answered, and he couldn't seem to help but look at the old yellowed snapshot in the corner of the portrait. He and Alex *never* talked about her but Noah thought of her and prayed for her every day. Noah took a sip of his coffee and sighed. "I sure miss her, Maggie."

Maggie let out a heavy breath as she replied, "Me, too, Noah."

*****

"Angel was not herself this weekend," Marquette commented as his father drove down Russell Avenue, on their way to the airport. Tara and Rosa rode in the back seat.

Guiseppi sighed and shook his head as he said, "She has not been herself for many years now. I feel as if I have lost my beautiful daughter forever."

"We have *not* lost our daughter," Rosa corrected from the back seat.

"Well," Guiseppi retorted, "she does not paint, she does not laugh and she does not dance. The daughter I used to know was drastically different from the woman who visited us this weekend."

"I cannot figure out what is wrong with her," Marquette said. "Alex behaves as the perfect husband. Even *I* cannot find fault with him."

"Which is remarkable," Tara mumbled, and Rosa giggled.

"Oh, ha, ha," Marquette mocked. "You are so funny."

"Do not tease my son." Guiseppi pretended a frown. "He has mellowed considerably in his old age."

Marquette humphed, "Old age?"

"Well, fifty-one hardly makes a spring chicken," Guiseppi replied.

"Will you take the position in *Firenze?*" Rosa asked, deciding to quickly change the subject. Marquette didn't like to talk about his age.

"Doubtfully," Marquette answered.

"And why not?" Guiseppi asked.

Marquette shrugged as he answered, "Something within in me does not want to be tied down for an entire year."

Guiseppi chuckled and said, "Though you have mellowed you still enjoy flitting about the globe."

Marquette rolled his eyes and nodded as he replied, "I suppose you are right, Papa."

*****

The Martins returned to Rapid City that afternoon and A.J. and Alex unloaded the back of Tillie's new Mercedes wagon. The interstate travel, as always, tired Tillie and she decided to lay down on their bed for just a few moments while Alex unpacked his things.

"Maybe we should take a charter next time," Alex suggested as he hung his suit into the closet.

"Na," Tillie answered, "I like the drive, but doesn't it make you a little tired?"

"Not really."

Tillie sighed and suggested, "Maybe it's just our family. Don't you think they were loud this weekend?"

Alex frowned with concern and looked at his wife who lay on their bed with her eyes closed.

"No, I don't think they were any different than they usually are."

"They drove me nuts," Tillie said with another sigh. "It's really good to be home and away from them."

Her statements were bizarre. She'd always enjoyed her family. *What's this all about?* He took a seat on the edge of the bed and reached for her hand.

She opened her eyes and smiled at him, noticing his concerned expression. "What?"

Alex shrugged and tried to smile as he asked, "Are you sure you're feeling okay, Tillie?"

"Just a little tired is all," but as she answered her smile faded and tears rolled from the corner of her eyes.

"Tillie," Alex whispered, taking her into his arms. "What's wrong, honey?"

She cried while he held her. "When are you going to tell me?" she whispered.

Alex felt his heart drop into his stomach. *How did she found out*? "I was going to tell you tonight," he lied. He hadn't planned to tell her until after his next meeting with Stahlheim — when he could be certain of the famous investor's recommendation. "When did you find out?"

"The Chairman called and left you a message on Thursday afternoon."

"Why didn't you just ask me about it then?"

"I thought I should give you the chance to tell me first," she cried. "I thought maybe it was a mistake or I was misunderstanding or something. Are you really going to do it?"

Alex swallowed hard and took a deep breath. "I'd like to," he answered.

"After everything we went through before?"

"Well," Alex began as he swallowed hard, searching for the perfect words, "I think it would be different now. A senator isn't nearly as busy as an attorney general. I think it'll be okay. We'll get a place in Washington and start a new life."

"And take the kids out of school?" she asked.

"We'll be closer to Patty and Marq."

"Unless Marq takes that position in Florence," she said. "I hope you'll pray about it a lot before you make your decision. I'm not comfortable with it all. What about the Stahlheim Group?"

"I will appoint Shondra to the position," he answered. "Tillie, I love you so much. I know that what I did back then was wrong and I promise not to make that mistake again."

"Our families will throw a fit," Tillie cried, *and that's not the half of it...there will probably be lots of "we told you so's."*

"They'll be okay," Alex assured. *It's none of their business anyway. Why can't they just leave us alone?*

Chapter 2

Kate waited patiently on the porch, bundled in a rain coat to protect her from the cold morning rain. Tracy trotted his horse up to the main house and handed her the newspaper, tipping his hat. The *Argus* was delivered as far as the front gate, so Vincenzo's hired hands took turns bringing up the newspaper every day.

"Thanks, Tracy." Kate smiled. "Would you tell Vincenzo breakfast is ready?"

"Sure thing, Mrs. Caselli," Tracy replied, and trotted off toward the barn.

Kate went back inside, tossed her coat over the hook by the door as she kicked off her shoes and headed for the kitchen. It was cold this morning, and already an entire week after Easter. *Will spring ever arrive this year?* She wondered. She poured herself a mug of hot coffee and relaxed at the small work table in the kitchen. She unrolled the front page of the paper and lifted her cup for a sip, nearly choking when she read the headline: *MARTIN SETS HIS EYE ON THE SENATE.*

"Is he kidding?" she whispered. With shock and disbelief, she read the article word for word.

The front door opened and she heard the familiar thuds as Vincenzo removed his boots.

"Hello, my love," he greeted her as he rounded the corner of the kitchen, heading for the coffee pot. "Anything interesting in the good ole *Argus Liar?*" He laughed at his attempted joke as he poured himself a cup. Kate did not respond with her usual chuckle so he looked at her, noticing her horrified expression. "What is the matter, my love?"

Kate shook her head as she held up the newspaper for her husband to see. "It wasn't enough that he killed our parents with this nonsense!" she barked. "Now he's gonna drag us back through the *same nightmare!* I don't think Angel should have to put up with this."

Vincenzo was quite stunned. No wonder Angel had looked so sad last week. "Perhaps we misunderstand," he offered.

"*We don't misunderstand!*" Kate snapped, reaching for the phone. "I'm calling him right now."

"No." Vincenzo shook his head and set down his cup. He put his hand on Kate's shoulder as he said, "Do not call right now. You are angry and may say things you will regret." Kate slowly nodded her head and hung up the phone. Vincenzo held Kate's hands and said, "Let us pray about this. Then we will give him a call and see what he says, but we should not attack him before we know *both* sides of the story."

Kate nodded again and they began to pray.

Guiseppi threw the paper onto the kitchen table and frowned at Rosa. "I begged her, *with tears*, not to return into that debacle! But would she listen even to her own father? *No!* She would *not!* And now we must start the entire disgrace all over again!" He took a breath and stormed, "This is *the last straw*, my Rosa! I will make a trip to Rapid City this afternoon, demand Angel pack up her things and her children, and they will come to live with us!"

Rosa swallowed hard and reached for one of her husband's hands. She took it lovingly into her own and placed a soft kiss upon it. "Guiseppi, my love, do not upset yourself so. We should pray for a time —"

"Prayer has done me no good in this matter!" Guiseppi interrupted with a shout. "Day in and day out I have returned to my knees!" He clenched his jaw in an effort to force away his tears of regret. The changes in Angel over the last six years were too marked to ignore. She didn't redecorate everything in her path anymore and the door of her studio remained closed. She had no desire to paint or sketch and she didn't want to look at any of the things that reminded her of those artistic gifts God had given her…and Guiseppi blamed Alex. The horrible things that man had said and done had obviously inflicted a wound that would never heal. Alex's actions had changed her forever.

Guiseppi drew in a deep breath and sighed heavily. "If only I would have intervened when I had the chance," he moaned with regret. "Oh, how I *hate* myself for what I did to my daughter's life."

*****

The scars of Tillie's physical injuries could not be seen, save for the dark purple marks covering her torso and left knee. But she wore her dresses just long enough to cover them, and clam diggers were a fashionable alternative to shorts. After nearly six years of intense rehabilitation, Tillie drove, cooked, and read to her children. She got around like a "normal" person, but Alex had insisted on hiring a lady named Diane to help out around the house. She limped if she became tired and still struggled with balance from time to time. However, if she stayed off ladders and descended the stairs slowly she was just fine. She didn't look up at the sky, and she didn't watch the ground pass beneath the car.

Older memories were confused at times, but for the most part Tillie remembered everything as it had happened, including her accident and the troubles within her marriage.

Tillie's children were twelve years old and seemed to have forgotten the horrible months of separation between their parents. Perhaps they were too young to understand what had happened, and for that Tillie was grateful. She wanted nothing more than to raise her children with their father and heal the life they'd enjoyed before Alex became the attorney general…but it was far more difficult than anticipated. Alex's actions left her unable to trust his promises or believe his words. Tillie's heart ached with a heavy load that seemed to increase with time. She carried her burden in what she thought to be secret, praying for God to soften the pain. But it grew in weight and sorrow as she feared every day Alex would leave them again.

Tillie picked up the *Rapid City Journal* off the front porch when she returned home after dropping A.J. and Laura off at school. She knew it was coming, but that didn't soften the horror she felt as she read the headline: *IS MARTIN BACK IN SOUTH DAKOTA POLITICS?* She sighed and tossed the paper onto the kitchen table, shaking her head as she fought away the tears burning her eyes…*Father, will this be okay?* she prayed, *Our families are gonna be so upset. Is there something more left to learn? I'm sorry for whatever I didn't learn the last time. Please forgive me and allow this cup to pass. Please soften his heart and help me change his mind.*

*****

Noah walked into the kitchen for a cup of coffee. He smiled at Ty and said, "Good morning."

Ty was at the kitchen table, looking at an old Post 22 program. He smiled at Noah and was about to reply when they heard Vera scolding Jake in his room.

"This room is a mess!" she admonished.

"I'll get it done," Jake replied, and it made Noah smile. Jake's room was a pit and it aggravated old Vera to no end.

"You *must* start picking up these dirty clothes," Vera continued. "It's Monday, Jake Hansen. Do you know what I do on Mondays? I wash your clothes, but I can't wash them if they're not in the laundry room, and I refuse to pick them up for you. You are plenty big now to understand this rule."

"Yes, ma'am," Jake answered, and Noah heard Vera sigh disgustedly and march away from Jake's room.

Noah smiled at Ty, who giggled.

"Is Jake giving Vera a hard time this morning?" Noah asked as he peered into the program Ty was reading.

"Nope," Ty chuckled. "She's got him totally under control." He looked up at his father. "Jake tried to pull the ole '*I'm sick this morning'* maneuver."

Noah shook his head as he walked over to the counter, poured himself a cup of coffee, and took a thoughtful sip. Vanilla meandered into the kitchen, and Noah was surprised at her size. She was just about ready to deliver. Her abdomen was swollen and lumpy.

"Maybe I'd better check him before I go," Noah said as he stooped to give Vanilla a soft pet. He looked at the dog and asked, "How are you doing girl? Just about ready to unload those pups?" In what seemed like an answer, Vanilla wagged her tail and licked Noah's face. "That's good," he said.

He made his way down the hall, stopping in Jake's doorway because he couldn't get any further. Vanilla followed, but she was brave enough to step gingerly through the mess on Jake's bedroom floor. She plopped down at the end of his bed.

"Wow," Noah said as he looked into the extremely messy bedroom, taking another careful sip of his coffee. "This place *is* a sty." He sniffed with a frown and asked, "What's that smell, Jake?"

"Dirty clothes, I s'pose," he answered as he threw some into the basket Vera had left for him. "I ran out of underwear and Miss Vera's totally ticked about it." He looked at his father and pouted, "And I don't feel good today, Dad. Can I just stay home?"

Noah stepped into the room, being careful not to crush anything beneath his feet, and put the palm of his hand on Jake's forehead. "You don't have a fever. And you're not pale or anything."

"Well, I'm *sick*," Jake muttered as he threw some more clothes into the basket.

"Well, here's the deal," Noah said as he made his way out of the bedroom and back to the doorway...*what in the world is that smell?* "If you stay home, you can't go to the Post practice tonight —"

"Oh, come on, Dad," Jake said with a scowl.

"And you've gotta get this little sty cleaned up *before* we go. And if I were you, I'd figure out what's stinking up the place before it makes you sick for real."

"Whatever," Jake muttered.

"I'm going out of town today with Mr. Martin so if you do get sick at school, call your Auntie Mona and she'll come and get you."

"Hey, Dad!" Ty called from the kitchen. "Mr. Martin's in the driveway."

"I gotta go. Be good today."

Jake rolled his eyes and replied, "I'm *always* good."

Noah nodded and smiled at his son, turned around and made his way back down the hall and into the kitchen. "Well," he said as he looked at Ty and reached for the coffee pot at the same time, "I think I'll be back about six or so. That gives us plenty of time to hit that first practice. Then we'll go out for pizza."

"Sounds great," Ty agreed with a smile. "Have a good day, Dad."

"Thanks, Ty."

Shondra Payne stood by the windows in her office watching the gloomy spring rain, wishing she was someplace else. *Is it just the crummy weather?* she wondered as she sipped her coffee. The uneasiness in her heart came upon her in another wave and she frowned. *Life is great, everything is swell...so what's my problem today?*

She had just celebrated her fifty-sixth birthday, and was, without regrets, still single. She came back to work for Alex in 1991, after finishing her stint as Deputy Attorney General. Alex called her after her public announcement that she would not be running for a second term with Robert, and asked her if she was interested in being a junior partner in his law firm. She took a few days to consider his offer and came back to Rapid City to accept the position.

She occasionally flirted with the idea of spending some time with Robert, but he was one of those men who loved his career even more than she loved her own. He'd called last night, *again*, said he was in town and wondered if they could have dinner sometime this week. She told him they could, but now she was having the strangest feeling about having committed to that.

The intercom next to her suddenly beeped and she jumped.

"Yes," she replied

"Sam Martin is trying to get a hold of Alex," Lori's voice announced. "But Alex is already gone. Sam said he wants to talk to you then. He's on line three."

"Thanks, Lori," Shondra replied. She set down her cup and picked up the phone. "Hi, Sam. What's up?"

"Humph," Sam replied, and from the tone of his voice she could tell that he was angry. "I wonder, Shondra. Why don't *you* tell *me*?"

"What are you talking about?" she asked as the hair on the back of her neck prickled.

"Oh, come on, Shondra," Sam snapped. "It's on the front page of the *Argus* this morning. Don't protect him."

"*What's* on the front page, Sam?"

Lori appeared suddenly in the doorway of Shondra's office. She grimaced as she stood there, holding what appeared to be the *Rapid City Journal*. She bit her lip and made her way to Shondra's desk. She set down the paper and hurried out of the office.

"Sam, Lori just brought me the paper..." Shondra said as she unfolded it, gasping when she saw the front page. "Sam, I *swear* I had no idea. Maybe it's just a misunderstanding."

"It's not a misunderstanding!" Sam raged. "I thought he acted weird last weekend, and obviously this is what he had up his sleeve!"

"Sam, let's give him a chance to explain —"

"I want to talk to him *right now*!" Sam growled.

"He went to Denver with Noah this morning. They're with Daniel Stahlheim. He won't be home until tonight."

Sam groaned and said, "Oh, brother. I suppose Tillie doesn't even have a clue."

"I'm sure he told her," Shondra assured. "Alex has changed a lot these last few years. Come on, Sam, let's give him a chance to explain this thing before we go off in a huff and say or do things we might regret."

*****

Tillie listened to A.J. brag about how he and Jake would be the next draftees for Post 22 as she drove her children home from school. It wouldn't be long, less than four years, and the two little leaguers would be eligible to try out for the team. They had played together since 1987 and Tillie could see A.J. and Jake playing for the American Legion. A.J. was an accomplished catcher, and Jake pitched, like his older brother.

"Mr. Hansen is sponsoring our team this year," A.J. went on. "We're calling ourselves The Builders."

"Oh, that is so stupid," Laura scoffed. "Who came up with that?"

"Me," A.J. answered. "And it is *not* stupid."

"Laura, don't call your brother stupid," Tillie admonished.

"Hey, by the way," A.J. said suddenly, "Jake got *really sick* in first period this morning. I wonder if he's feeling any better."

"No kidding?" Laura asked. "What's wrong with him?"

"He threw up in gym class —"

"Oh, gross!" Laura closed her eyes and shook her head.

A.J. laughed. "He told his dad he was sick this morning but he didn't have a fever so Mr. Hansen made him go to school. I guess they had to call his aunt to come and get him 'cause you know his dad went to Denver with Dad and the really rich dude."

"I wonder how all that went," Tillie said more to herself than to her children. Their meeting was over with by now, and Alex would be home in a couple of hours. They would have Alex's favorite — roast beef — for supper, and she would try to talk him out of running for the Senate seat. Her stomach felt like it was going over a hill. *Why does he want to leave again?*

As she neared their driveway she saw a South Dakota Highway Patrol car parked there.

"Hey, the cops are at our house," A.J. said.

Tillie's heart began to pound as she pulled in beside the trooper and parked her car. A tall patrolman exited his vehicle and waited for her.

"Are you in trouble, Mom?" Laura whispered, her eyes wide with curiosity.

"No," Tillie answered with a nervous laugh. "I don't think so." She and her children got out of the car.

The patrolman took off his hat as they approached, extending his hand to Tillie. "Mrs. Matilde Martin?" he asked, and Tillie nodded shaking his hand, and he continued, "I'm Officer Stan Taylor with the South Dakota Highway Patrol. Can we go inside and visit for a few minutes?"

"Of course," Tillie answered, feeling her legs go weak. Whatever news this man had wasn't good — she could tell by the grim expression on his face.

She and her suddenly quiet children led the officer into their home through the front door and into the formal living room.

"Please, have a seat, Ma'am," Officer Taylor said gently.

Tillie sat down on the couch with her children, one on either side.

The officer knelt in front of her and looked into her eyes. "Mrs. Martin, Daniel Stahlheim's plane went down this afternoon —"

Tillie gasped as her arms and legs started shaking.

"All aboard were killed," he continued, "including your husband. I am so very sorry."

"Dad too?" A.J. gasped in a whisper.

The officer nodded his head in silence.

A.J. and Laura looked at their mother, and then at each other as they began to cry.

Tillie put her arms around both of them, staring with disbelief into the eyes of the officer kneeling before her. "Are you sure?" she whispered.

"Yes, Ma'am," he answered.

"Oh," Tillie moaned as the tears left her eyes. *Just like that, Alex is gone? But we're supposed to have roast beef together tonight. This isn't right at all. There are too many things we have to talk about. Too many things we still have to figure out....*

The officer swallowed and said, "Mrs. Martin, we'll need your husband's dentist's name so that we can begin to transfer records to the medical examiner."

"Why?" Tillie whispered through her tears.

"For identification," he answered. "The plane went down just south of the Nebraska border. As soon as the medical examiner is finished they will bring the deceased to Sioux Falls. We'll take you there tonight."

Tillie nodded, praying she'd wake up and it would all be just a really bad dream.

"I can stay here while you contact your family," the officer offered. "We do need to take care of that fairly quickly. We're having a problem with the press."

Tillie nodded and said, "I understand."

"Mrs. Martin, I'm very sorry."

"Thank you," Tillie cried as she hung onto her children. They wept without words, holding tightly to their mother.

"Jake's dad was on the plane, too," A.J. cried.

The officer asked, "Did you know other people on the plane?"

Her chest tightened with pain at the realization...*Noah too*? *After all these years of forcing myself not to think of him and he's gone in the same instant that has taken Alex?* "My friend, Noah Hansen," she wept.

The officer let out a breath and said, "I'm going over to his brother's house as soon as you get your family called."

"No one that we're related to lives here," Tillie whispered. "How can I tell them *this* over the phone?"

"You *have* to, Mrs. Martin, before they see it on television," Officer Taylor reminded. "Your husband was with Daniel Stahlheim — the press is all over this already. I'm so sorry you have to do it this way."

"Okay," Tillie said with a nod, taking a breath through her sobs.

The officer stood and helped Tillie to her feet. A.J. and Laura stood up with her and they walked to the kitchen together, followed by the highway patrolman. Her children sat down at the small table in the corner and Tillie picked up the telephone.

Guiseppi and Rosa were watching the news with Burt and Diane Engleson when their telephone rang.

"I will answer," Guiseppi said as he hurried to the telephone in the kitchen. "Hello?" he greeted.

"Papa?"

"Angel?" Guiseppi heard the strangeness in her voice and his stomach turned.

"Papa," she whispered, her breath catching on a sob.

"What is it, my Angel?"

"Daniel Stahlheim's plane has gone down and all on board have died —" Her voice broke on a sob and she cried into the phone, "Papa, Alex and Noah were with them. I have to call Sam and Kate."

"Angel," Guiseppi gasped, stumbling into a kitchen chair. "I am so sorry. I will call Sam immediately. What can I do for you?"

"Just stay there," Tillie wept. "The kids and I....I guess they'll be bringing us to Sioux Falls tonight...they're bringing Alex to Sioux Falls —"

"Do your babies know?"

Rosa heard her husband's distressed tone and came into the kitchen.

"They're right here with me," Tillie answered. "There's a highway patrolman here with us, but he has to go to Noah's brother now."

Guiseppi thought he might fall from the chair...*Noah?*

"Guiseppi?" Rosa whispered as she took a seat across from her husband, reaching for his hand. "What is the matter?"

Guiseppi looked at Rosa and shook his head.

"Papa," Tillie cried, "I have to go. I'm gonna call Marq and Patty. You call Sam. Okay?"

Guiseppi took a deep breath, forcing away the sobs building inside of him, and said, "I will call your brothers. Do not put yourself through it. I can take care of this for you."

"Thanks, Papa. I have to hang up, now. We have to call the dentist."

"Okay," Guiseppi cried. "I love you, my Angel."

"I love you, too, Papa."

Guiseppi called Petrice at his new office in the Hart Senate Office Building. Petrice was stunned and promised his father he'd get permission to fly out of Washington within the hour. Petrice then called Elaine who said she would pack quickly, and Petrice drove to his brother's residence in Tyson's Corner. He couldn't deliver this message to Marquette over the telephone; it had to be given in person.

Marquette was on the telephone in his study, and glanced up when he heard his brother's footsteps in the hall. He was surprised to see Tara with him, tears streaming down her beautiful face.

Marquette hung up the phone, got to his feet and took his wife into his arms as he asked, "My Tara, whatever is the matter?"

Tara buried her head in Marquette's shoulder, so he looked to Petrice for an explanation.

"Daniel Stahlheim's plane went down this afternoon," Petrice said gently. "All aboard have perished."

"What did you say?" Marquette asked with a frown.

"Alex has gone Home this day," Petrice clarified as his eyes filled with tears, "And so has your dear friend, Noah Hansen."

Marquette clung to Tara as he took a very deep breath and stared at his brother with wide open eyes.

"We must leave quickly, Marquette," Petrice said, placing a hand on Marquette's shoulder. "Angel and Noah's brother will be coming to Sioux Falls tonight, and we must be there for them."

Officer Taylor called the dentist's office for Tillie and took care of the file transfer. Then he left, reminding Tillie he'd be back in a short time to take her and her children, along with the Hansen family, to Rapid City Regional Airport.

Tillie and her children attempted to pack some things before the officer returned. They'd probably be in Sioux Falls for at least the next week, if not longer. She went through the motions of packing, trying not to look at Alex's clothes hanging in the closet next to her own. She prayed she'd soon wake up...*this can't be real...the roast is nearly finished...he'll be home in a few minutes...A.J. and Laura are going to watch Ty's first practice —*

The sound of the front doorbell jarred her from her thoughts. The officer was back to reinforce the reality of the situation and Tillie began to cry again. She grabbed some tissues from the dresser and went down the steps and to the front door. She saw an unfamiliar white pickup truck out front, along with the officer's car…*That must be Joshua's,* she thought.

She opened the front door to find Officer Taylor and a man with Noah's boys.

"Mrs. Martin, can we come in?" Officer Taylor asked.

Tillie nodded and stepped back from the door.

"Where's A.J.?" Jake asked.

Tillie looked at him and saw that endearing expression in his eyes that reminded her so much of his father.

"He's in his room, Jake," she answered.

"Can we go up?" Ty asked politely.

"Go ahead, guys. I'll be right up."

The two hurried off into the house, and Tillie looked back at the stranger standing beside the highway patrolman. He was suddenly familiar, though she couldn't remember where she'd met him before.

"Tillie?" he said, and she could tell by his red and swollen eyes that he'd been crying. "I'm so sorry. I thought maybe me and the boys should come over."

"Noah?" she whispered as she studied his face. It had been nearly six years since the last time she saw him…*you're supposed to be with Alex today…I'm hallucinating*.... "How...?" She looked from Noah to the officer, and then back at Noah.

"Jake got sick this morning," Noah explained. "Mona reached me at the airport before I got on the plane."

The room began to spin and Tillie stumbled. Noah reached for her and held her close while she took deep breaths between her sudden sobs.

"I'll get her some water," Officer Taylor offered.

"The kids," Tillie cried. "Where are my kids?"

"They're upstairs," Noah reminded as he helped her to take a seat on the couch. Every bit of Tillie was shaking.

"Are you coming with us?" she asked.

"We can," Noah answered. "Do you want us there?"

Tillie nodded as she looked into his eyes and cried, "We thought you were with Alex today."

"I was." Noah's eyes filled with tears as he explained again, "Mona called me at the airport. She reached me on my beeper and Jake was so sick — I didn't think I should leave him. Alex said it would be okay if I stayed behind and he took Ben's file with him."

The officer knelt before them and offered Tillie a glass of water. She took the glass in her trembling hand, gulped down the cold water, and handed the officer the nearly emptied glass.

"Thanks," she said as she caught her breath and looked frantically into Noah's eyes. "I forgot to call Shondra. We should call her before the news comes on."

"I called her on our way over," Noah said gently.

"We need to be leaving," the officer said. "Do you want to get your children and your things together?"

Tillie and Noah nodded.

Kate sent a hand into the pasture to look for her husband. When Vincenzo came in he found his wife crying uncontrollably in the arms of her older brother. Sam told Vincenzo of the passing of his dear friend, Noah Hansen.

It took all the strength Vincenzo had to comfort his grieved wife while having to deal with the grief of losing Noah. He could not bring himself to believe God would take them both, and in his mind he determined that someone made a mistake.

Petrice and Marquette arrived in Sioux Falls shortly before Tillie. The South Dakota Highway Patrol gathered the family into a small boarding area and cordoned off the entire section for protection from the press. Soon the awaited flight arrived and two patrolmen escorted Tillie and her crying children, along with Noah and his boys, down the gangway.

"Praise God," Vincenzo breathed.

Marquette staggered with surprise and Tara took hold of his arm. He reacted so dramatically in these types of situations, and it seemed to have only intensified with his age.

"It is Noah," Marquette whispered.

Guiseppi and Rosa couldn't believe their eyes when they saw Noah with Tillie. They reached out to their daughter and their grandchildren, taking them into their arms and crying with them. Their surprise at seeing Noah alive and with Tillie had left them without words and they were only able to hold their daughter and her grief-stricken children.

Tillie's brothers and their wives were upon all of them. Marquette and Vincenzo expressed their relief to Noah, and he, in turn, attempted to explain the misunderstanding. He'd checked in for the flight at the Rapid City Regional Airport, and that's when Mona got a hold of him. He'd never made it as far as Denver, but apparently Stahlheim's passenger list had not been updated.

Noah and his boys went home with Vincenzo and the rest of them went home with Guiseppi and Rosa. Before he left, Noah promised A.J. that Jake would be around in the following days and that they could spend as much time together as he needed.

That night both of Tillie's children crawled into bed with their mother, in the room she'd shared with Alex only a week ago. She held them in her arms and they cried and cried.

"We'll be all alone now," Laura whispered in the darkness.

Tillie swallowed as hard as she could, but the tears kept coming.

"What will we do without Dad?" A.J. questioned.

"I don't know," Tillie sobbed in answer. "But I know that God loves us —"

"Pray for us, Mom," Laura wept.

"Okay," Tillie whispered, trying to swallow away her tears again, and then she began to pray.

Chapter 3

Tillie awakened the next morning still in bed with her children. They'd finally sobbed themselves to sleep. She looked around the old room where she'd slept while growing up, remembering why she was there. The aroma of brewing coffee floated in and she heard the soft drum of voices below. *There will be so much to do today*, she thought, shaking her head in disbelief. *Is he really gone? After all we went through and conquered he's not going to be here anymore? Unbelievable.* She looked at her sleeping children and clenched her jaw in anger. *What will they do without their father?*

She slipped from between them, found some jeans and an old gray sweatshirt and went into the bathroom. She looked out the window... *pouring rain...perfect.* She closed the blind and sighed.

She ran the water in the shower as hot as she could stand it, staying under the gentle spray for a long time. *I tried so hard to do the righteous thing*, she stormed at the Lord, *even when everyone else around me told me not to. Now my children are crushed again. Was that necessary? What can they possibly learn from this episode in their young lives?*

"I'm such an idiot," she mumbled as she dried herself off, then reached for the clean clothes on the bathroom counter. She got dressed and combed the snarls out of her wet hair. She opened the bathroom door, glancing over at A.J. and Laura, who were still asleep. Another pang of guilt pierced her heart. *I never deserved those babies.*

She pulled on a pair of thick socks and padded out of the room, closing the door behind her. The smell of coffee in the hallway was overwhelming. She made her way down the stairs and into the kitchen, where most of her family had already gathered.

"Hello, my Angel," Guiseppi said as took his beloved daughter into his arms.

Tillie put her arms around her father and rested her head on his shoulder.

"There is much we must talk about this morning," he said gently.

"I have coffee," Rosa said as she set a mug down at the table by an empty chair. "Sit here, Angel."

Tillie slid into a chair, and that's when she saw that Sam and Kate were there as well. Kate reached for one of Tillie's hands and Tillie's eyes gave way to thousands of tears.

"Kate, I'm so sorry," she said as she looked into the eyes of Alex's sister, and then she looked at Sam, who was the exact image of his brother. *Sam and Kate are all that's left of the Martins now. How strange.*

Sam tenderly placed his hand on Tillie's shoulder, "We are so sorry, Tillie."

She replied with a nod, "Thanks. What do I have to do first?"

"I've already talked to some people in Nebraska." Sam swallowed very hard before he could continue, "We can't have Alex until at least tomorrow —"

"Why not?" she interrupted with a frown.

"The medical examiner is...he...is..." Sam hesitated and swallowed again, then continued, "He's trying to make a positive identification with the dental records you had sent over yesterday."

"Dental records?"

Sam nodded and gave Tillie's shoulder a firm squeeze as he answer, "So...we thought..." and he looked at his sister, and then back at Tillie, "Kate and I...if it's okay with you, want to have a memorial service tomorrow for Alex, and then have another service, and internment on Thursday. I called Andy this morning."

"I brought a suit for him," Tillie offered.

Sam bit his lower lip and frowned at Tillie. He took a deep breath and looked at Kate, who was crying again. He then looked to Guiseppi, who was still near his daughter, hoping perhaps he could somehow explain it to her.

Guiseppi knelt beside Tillie and took one of her hands into his own as he said, "My Angel, there was a very bad fire and Alex will be placed into his casket in Nebraska. Sam has already had it sent there." He took a deep breath and swallowed his tears away, forcing himself to go on, "We will not be able to open it up after that."

"You mean I can't say good-bye?" Tillie whispered.

"Not in the way you would like, my Angel." Guiseppi's tears spilled onto his cheeks. "He has already departed us in spirit. His earthly body is of no consequence now —"

"But he's my husband, and I want to see him," Tillie insisted through tears.

"You cannot," Guiseppi said with gentle authority.

"Papa..." Tillie leaned toward her father and put her arms around his neck. Guiseppi put his arms around her and held her while she cried. "What will I tell the kids?" she whispered.

"We will tell them what I just told you," Guiseppi answered. "And they will have to understand. None of us have a choice in this matter, my Angel."

The front page of every South Dakota paper that day ran the tragic headlines. Tillie's family tried to hide the papers from her and her children by keeping them busy with making arrangements for Alex's return to Sioux Falls and the services to follow. Alex would be laid to rest with his parents and other ancestors there in Sioux Falls.

Kelley's Flowers on Minnesota Avenue made most of the floral arrangements that were taken to the Barnett Funeral Home. Tillie specifically requested they use as many white flowers as they could get a hold of. She wanted nothing dark in color placed around the closed casket that would arrive the next day. It was bad enough that they could never see him again, and the use of dark colored flowers would make things worse.

Tillie and Vincenzo told A.J. and Laura about the closed casket and they were devastated. It was difficult to explain why they couldn't see their dad when the casket arrived on Wednesday. Tillie wanted to hide in her old room and never have to come out again, and if it not for her children, that's what she would have done. She didn't want to say good-bye to Alex; she never had. Even when he was up to his most terrible of behavior she was never ready to end it. Now it was forced upon her. She asked God over and over, *Why? What good purpose can this possibly serve? What about my kids?*

"I want my dad back," Laura cried in the arms of her uncle.

"Why did he have to die?" A.J. clung to his mother, weeping most pitifully.

"I don't know," Tillie sobbed. She wished she had answers, but she didn't.

"Jesus has a plan for all of us," Vincenzo said as he swallowed away his own emotions and put forth an unusual sign of emotional strength. "It was your dad's time to go Home."

"He had a great home with us," A.J. argued between sobs.

Vincenzo nodded in understanding.

"Did it hurt?" Laura delicately inquired.

Tillie swallowed hard and looked to Vincenzo. That was something she'd wondered since finding out about the fire.

"No," Vincenzo answered firmly. "It does not hurt."

"How do you know for sure?" Laura asked.

Vincenzo took a deep breath and looked from his niece to his nephew as he explained, "Remember Stephen in the Bible? When he was very close to his death, he claimed, out loud, that he could see Heaven opening and that Jesus was standing there. Angry and belligerent people were stoning him but the Bible reports that Stephen simply *fell asleep*." Vincenzo paused and looked thoughtfully at his sister's children. "I am convinced in my faith and in my trust in Jesus that your dad did not hurt. He saw Jesus waiting and his spirit departed from his body, and his body, then, simply fell asleep."

At his words, A.J. and Laura and their mother broke into more sobs as they nodded their heads in understanding.

"Now listen to me, it is right to cry," Vincenzo comforted as he held his weeping niece. "It is right that our hearts ache for him. He is still a part of our lives and he is your dad and always will be no matter where he is. You will always love him and this is right. It is right to cry for him. But there is one more thing I wish you to know." He took a deep breath and tried to smile. "I was there the day your dad asked Jesus into his heart."

They stopped crying abruptly and stared at Vincenzo.

He nodded with a smile. "Your dad waited many, many years and was a grown man before he *finally* made his decision. But *I was there* and I *saw* him pray with Granddad Martin. He bowed his head, confessed his sins, and asked Jesus into his heart. It was a wonderful moment and I have cherished it for many years."

Tillie reached for Vincenzo's hand and whispered, "Thank you."

Vincenzo nodded and looked at her quiet children. "Your father chose the path to Jesus and *nothing* can snatch him from the Father's hand."

*****

Alex's children weren't the only ones struggling with his passing. His sister, Kate, had not been able to stop crying. Her tears alternated between anger and sorrow. She was angry with him the entire day before learning that he had died, and now she was torn between relief and regret.

"He never could just settle down," she cried as Vincenzo held her.

Vincenzo nodded as he brushed away some of Kate's tears with his gentle hands. "I know, my love," he said. "We are *all* having such a difficult time with this —"

"That's why the Lord took him," Kate sobbed. "So that he couldn't disobey anymore and we wouldn't have to watch it happen all over again. Now we just have to say good-bye and somehow try and get on with our lives. Nothing got resolved and now it never will."

Vincenzo swallowed hard. Things did *not* get resolved between Alex and his sister, and he wondered how Sam was dealing with the situation.

*****

The next two days were like a foggy dream for Tillie. She knew she was making decisions, and talking constantly with her children about the event, but other than that she tried to think of Alex's passing as little as possible. Her brothers and their wives surrounded her continuously, offering comfort, Scriptures and prayers. Even though she felt them right there with her, it was as if she was watching the whole episode from somewhere far away. It was like a very slow-motion play where everyone moved into their prewritten positions, said their lines, and set up for the next scene.

Noah was always in the background. It was unusual to see him there, yet a comfort at the same time. His presence was strangely familiar, as if he was *supposed* to be there with all of these people she was related to. Her brothers could not have done without him, that was plain to see, and even Guiseppi seemed to share a certain bond with Noah. Tillie's children gravitated to the comfort Noah and his sons offered just as they did their own cousins and uncles and aunts.

When Noah first arrived at Guiseppi and Rosa's house, he was taken aback by the familiar photo hanging in the entryway. It was the enlarged photograph of Rosa that Guiseppi had taken on the day they left Italy all those years ago. The very one Tillie had turned into Noah's favorite painting, *Obedience*. Marquette saw him looking at the old photograph when he brought Noah a cup of hot coffee.

"Thanks, Marq," he said as he took the coffee. He hadn't slept much in the last few days. He pointed at the photograph. "I have a friend in Rapid who bought that painting."

"It was always my father's very favorite," Marquette replied, looking thoughtful. "By the way, did you see this morning's paper?"

"I've been trying to avoid it."

"There was a nice little story in it about you," Marquette said. "They talked about how you were mistakenly listed on the passenger manifest, and then they went into great detail about your life — your parents, their affiliation with MacKenzie Dale, the death of your parents, your brother, his wife, your late wife, your alcoholism. It was a real rags-to-riches piece, and your picture was not half bad either."

"No kidding?" Noah mumbled as he sipped at his coffee...*wish they would have left out the part about the alcoholism....*

Marquette put his hand on Noah's shoulder and said, "I am so glad you were not on that plane and that you were there for Angel so that she did not have to make the trip alone."

Noah nodded. If it wouldn't have been for Jake and his little pigsty, and the resultant rotten pizza that had made him so sick, Noah *wouldn't* have been there.

It was nearly nine o'clock in the evening and people were *still* shuffling in and out of Guiseppi and Rosa's house. They shook Tillie's hand and offered their condolences. As Tillie's feet started to pulse with soreness from wearing high heels too long, she thought, *don't these people have families to go home to? Can't they just leave for a while so I can figure out what happened?*

She saw Jake, A.J. and Ty together near the fireplace in the living room. They were looking through old Post 22 programs. They talked quite a bit about baseball, but said hardly anything about A.J.'s dad being gone.

Laura, on the other hand, was inseparable from her mother. She wanted to talk about how sad she was that her dad wasn't going to be home when they got there. Tillie was patient and loving with the child, comforting her while she bided her time, planning to escape the madness and overgrown group of mourners who wouldn't leave her alone.

Alyssa was suddenly there and soon she and Laura walked off together with an album of photographs. Tillie smelled pipe tobacco, but Ma`ma didn't allow that in the house. *Vincenzo's really gonna get it....*

All at once Tillie realized that she was standing alone near the screen on the patio door while the crowd of mourners milled around silently between the kitchen and the living room. She slipped out the sliding door onto the cold dark patio and sat down on a lounge chair with a heavy sigh. Thankfully the rain had finally stopped, but it was still very cold. It was so warm inside of the house that she hardly noticed the drop in temperature. She looked at the ashtray to her right and saw Vincenzo's smoldering pipe.

She leaned back her head and looked up at the few stars that were beginning to show themselves from behind the heavy cloud cover. It was quiet out here and that was a relief. They could all comfort themselves until tomorrow morning if they wanted to but she was going to take a break.

She pulled her shoes off of her throbbing feet, dropped them onto the cement patio, and gave her sore toes a gentle rub. She glanced at the smoldering pipe and had the strangest compulsion to pick it up and have a puff. It had always looked so fun to smoke a pipe. The screen opened behind her and she groaned.

"Hello, my Angel," Rosa said as she took a seat next to Tillie. She had a folded afghan in her arms. "Because you may become cold."

"It's hotter than Hades in that house," Tillie mumbled.

"You sound like Papa," Rosa whispered with a gentle smile and a sigh. "I haven't had a chance to even speak with you, Angel."

"I've been so busy," Tillie apologized. "But we should be about done with everything tomorrow. The service begins at ten, and the interment will follow. The Martins have a big spot over in Wood Lawn and the whole family is over there, including Arturo. The will will be read in the afternoon. Sam is the executor." She shook her head and looked at her mother. "I just can't believe it, Ma`ma."

"I know."

Tillie's tears ran from her eyes and she attempted to brush them away while she shared her heart with her mother, "It was so hard to see that casket today and know that he was in there. I can't imagine how terrible it must have been for them. They must have known they would die."

Rosa reached for Tillie's hand and whispered, "God was with them, Angel."

"I know, but I saw the paper today. It said that the pilot had radioed for EMT service before the crash because someone had been burned, even though they won't tell us who it was."

"Perhaps it is better not to know."

Tillie swallowed and whispered, "Alex flew all over the country in those little planes and small jets. How in the world does something like this happen anyway, Ma`ma?"

"Things become old and worn out, my Angel," Rosa tried to explain. "You know, the things of this world are perishable, unlike the things in heaven — which will last forever, like Alex and his memory."

"I just wanted to raise my children with their dad and now he's gone. I can't hardly believe it, Ma`ma. This life has gotten *so hard*."

"I know it seems hard right now, Angel," Rosa agreed. "But it will get better somehow. We have hope."

"Hope in what?"

"Hope in Christ," Rosa answered. "The hope that only He can give us. That there is life everlasting and that we will, in time, see Alex again. We know that he is safe with Jesus now. His suffering, whatever it may have been, is over, and he rests in the arms of his Savior."

Tillie laid her head upon her mother's shoulder and Rosa put her arms around her daughter. Tillie sobbed while Rosa tried to comfort her, but even Rosa knew the loss of a husband would not heal easily. Thank God Guiseppi had lived this long, for Rosa could have never made it without him.

*****

Alex's childhood friend Andy Engleson spoke comforting words over the casket positioned just above the open ground at Wood Lawn Cemetery. A magnificent marble stone, standing higher than all the others, read MARTINEZ —the original name of the family when Alex's great grandfather, Arturo, came to America in the eighteen hundreds. Arturo and his wife Mabel rested side by side, as did Alex James Martin Sr. and his wife Daphne. Close to them were the two sons they lost to World War I, William and Matthew. James and Frances were laid a short distance from there and Alex would rest next to them.

" '*Do not let your hearts be troubled,' "* Andy said with a faint smile for the grieving crowd. *"Trust in God, trust also in Me*.' Jesus said those words to his own disciples before He died for us. He said, '*In my Father's house are many rooms; if it were not so, I would have told you. I am going there to prepare a place for you. I'll come back and take you to be with me that you also may be where I am. You know the way to the place where I am going*.' " Andy took a breath. "Alex knew the way to where Jesus was going and he is there with Him now, but oh how our hearts will ache until we see him again." He paused, and for the first time during the last two days the minister who'd been Alex's friend since 1957 had to swallow his tears away in order to keep his composure for the grieving family. "As you all know, I knew Alex quite well when we were younger. We did everything together from the time we were seven years old, including having the measles. Alex spoke at my ordination in 1975 and I'll always remember his words. He said, *no greater friend have I than the friend I have in you*, but he was wrong. Alex's greatest friend is Jesus and he's finally at peace with Him now."

*****

On Saturday, three days after Alex's funeral, Petrice offered to fly Noah and his boys back to Rapid City so they could resume school again on Monday. Tillie's children wanted to go home as well. They had been away from home for nearly a week and their little hearts desired to get back to a place where they had known their father. Even though A.J. and Laura couldn't understand what they were feeling, Petrice understood. He saw that it would be far harder on them if their mother were to keep them away from their Rapid City home much longer. They needed to be in the place where they had lived with their father, if only to see his things and be closer to his memory.

Petrice found her hiding beneath a tree in the backyard where she shivered and cried in the cold spring breeze. He covered her with the afghan his mother sent him out with and took a seat on the ground.

He pulled his heavy, denim jacket up around his neck and said, "It is very cold out here." He reached for her hand and gave it a tender kiss. "Why do you hide?"

"I'm not hiding. I'm thinking. "

"Thinking about what?"

"Trying to figure this nightmare out," she whispered. "I think I'll just make a new life here. We should have *never* moved to that God-forsaken Rapid City in the first place."

"Oo," Petrice pretended to grimace. "Strong words. You must have some strong feelings about that."

Tillie shrugged and sniffed as she answered, "Maybe. You know, he was headed back into politics."

Petrice nodded. "Papa showed me the headline."

"And he'd tried to keep it from me, but I found out by accident," she added. "And he was always scheming on the sidelines. He always had irons in the fire."

"Were you angry with him?"

Tillie bit her lip and looked away from Petrice as she admitted, "I am now. All his wheeling and dealing finally caught up to him. And everything was so *perfect* between Alex and I until we moved to Rapid City. We had a great life in Sioux Falls and then everything had to go straight down the tubes. Nothing was the same after he came back. He tried, really, really hard, but I was always so afraid that he'd leave again." She took a deep breath. "And now I don't have to be afraid anymore because he's finally gone for good."

"Oh, my Angel," Petrice whispered as he held her close. How could he possibly comfort her? He had no wise words to offer because even he had struggled with his feelings for Alex for the last six years.

"And how am I gonna raise those kids without a father?" She whispered through her sobs. "They loved their dad. They don't have any idea about the struggles we went through. You know the stats, Patty. Kids raised by a single mother suffer in all kinds of ways, sometimes they even wind up in trouble."

"There are many men in your family, Angel. Your brothers and your father, and of course, Sam —"

"Sam and Becky never had children. And, pardon me, but Sam doesn't have the first clue about what's it like to be a parent —"

"Well I do," Petrice interrupted her gently. "And Vincenzo and Papa know what it is like. We will help you."

"How can you help me, Patty?" Tillie snapped. "You sit in Washington *most* of the time, and Vincenzo lives three hundred and fifty miles away."

Petrice saw where this was leading, and that was the justification of keeping her children in Sioux Falls. *I nearly played into her hand.*

"Your babies call Rapid City their home," he reminded with tender authority. "It would be wrong to suddenly take them from that place while they grieve the loss of their father. Certainly you must understand this?"

"Doing the *right* thing has *not* blessed me. I thought that the *right* thing was making my marriage work with Alex, but he was bound and determined to start the whole battle all over again and wound up killing himself."

"Oh, Angel," Petrice admonished, "of course you have been blessed. Certainly, you cannot blame God for Alex's poor decisions. You are very strong in character and God knows this about you, and so He asks you to do the *right* thing again. You must return your children to their home, allow them to finish out the school year, and then we can see what happens after that."

Tillie clung to her brother and wept.

*****

In righteous but disgruntled obedience, Tillie and her children boarded Petrice's Learjet on Sunday morning, along with Noah and his boys and Guiseppi and Rosa. Her parents thought perhaps she should not return to Rapid City alone and that their presence with her for a short time might help to ease her desire to uproot her grieving children.

Sam and Becky-Lynn rode along because they would have much to reconcile with the cases Alex had left pending. And there was the matter of executing Alex's estate. Shondra had gone back to Rapid

City immediately following the funeral, promising to have a preliminary report by the time they arrived.

Petrice and Elaine and their children would fly back to Washington upon leaving everyone else in Rapid City. Petrice had some time left in the Senate before summer break and further hearings on Federal judges. They promised to visit Rapid City that summer and invited Tillie to visit New York if she wanted to get away for a time.

Noah drove over to Joshua and Mona's house where they took him into their arms and tried to offer him some comfort.

"The whole thing was really terrible," he cried when he was alone with his brother and sister-in-law, his sons watching television in the living room. "Alex's sister, and I think his brother, were both mad at Alex, and poor Angel walked around like she was half asleep."

Joshua took a deep, thoughtful breath and softly frowned. He was sixty years old and had been a minister for nearly two-thirds of his life. Nothing was more difficult for a family to have to go through than having to say good-bye to a family member with whom they were at odds.

Mona cleared her throat and reached for Noah's hand. He looked into her pretty, green eyes, and saw tears of compassion as she said, "Did you know, Noah, that Alex was planning on a run for the senate in November?"

Noah gulped at his sister-in-law's words, staring back at her in quiet horror. He shook his head but sat without words for response.

Joshua sighed as he said, "So that's probably why they were all a little angry with him, you know, considering what happened the last time he got caught up in politics."

Noah let out a heavy breath and shook his head in disbelief.

*****

Upon execution of Alex's estate, it was revealed that Alex had provided very well for the family he'd left behind. Not a bill was left unpaid, nor were there any debts to worry about. Many years before, Alex had set up a college trust for each child, along with a separate wedding trust for when they were married. He also left a trust for Tillie, which he requested be completely unsupervised. She could do with the funds as she saw fit. His partnership in the family's law firm was divided between Shondra Payne and Tillie. Tillie's share of the profits were to be paid directly to her on a quarterly basis. When and if either of his children decided to practice law, and upon passing the South Dakota Bar Exam, they could move into the law firm and take over the partnership at that time.

Alex left substantial gifts to the church Joshua Hansen pastored and also to the church that he and Tillie were currently attending. And he left a sizable donation to the new Rapid City Regional Hospital Rehabilitation Center.

His most beloved possession, the portrait of *Obedience*, he requested be returned to Tillie. The painting of his grandfather, Arturo, he requested be hung in the reception office of the Rapid City law firm, and the 1920 painting of Harvard Law, he gave to his son. To his daughter, he left the watch Tillie had given to him on their first Christmas together, which Laura had long admired.

Sam and Becky-Lynn and Shondra called and came over on numerous occasions within that first week. They had paper after paper requiring Tillie's signature and eventually the final business was completed. Alex's car was sold, and the proceeds were deposited into Tillie's trust. Shondra and Sam assured Tillie that she could call if she had any questions, or if she needed anything at all. Then Sam and Becky-Lynn left town and Shondra was put in charge of the Rapid City office indefinitely.

Everything was organized and in good order. Alex's family was provided for well beyond their futures, and there was absolutely nothing to ever have to worry about. But that was the easy part.

Tillie walked through the home she'd shared with Alex, seeing memories everywhere. He'd left a file on his desk in his office upstairs, and his favorite coffee cup was close by. His clothes still hung in the closet next to her own, and the soft scent of Polo hung in the air around them. His razor, toothbrush and the comb he'd used on his hair still waited in the small leather bag where he kept them just at the edge of the sink in their bathroom. Tillie had lived with Alex for nearly sixteen years. It was hardly believable that he was not coming home.

A.J. and Laura loved to look at their father's possessions and smell them, speaking fondly of the last things they'd done together. Then they'd dissolve into tears and Tillie would have to comfort them and talk to them about Jesus and Heaven and how happy their dad was to finally be Home. They spent many nights sleeping in the same bed with their mother, and Tillie didn't mind. She still remembered her nights alone in that big bed when Alex was the attorney general and she wasn't ready to face that just yet.

The twins were anxious to get back to school, see their friends and tell them what had happened. It seemed to Tillie they were concerned about seeing the friends they'd left behind just to make sure that nothing had happened to them while they were away. Early into their first week back A.J. and Laura asked to go back to school, and Guiseppi coaxed Tillie to allow it. If they became upset while they were away, school officials were instructed to call their mother to come and get them.

While the twins were in school, Guiseppi and Rosa helped Tillie get Alex's things out of the house, saving only a few reminders his children loved.

"This is so hard, Ma`ma," Tillie whispered the day the Salvation Army picked up Alex's clothes. Rosa put her arm around Tillie's waist, and Tillie laid her head on her mother's shoulder. "What am I gonna do now?"

"We are going to go on, my Angel," Rosa answered. "I do not know how, but my faith in God tells me that He will take care of us and lead us through this time."

"I want to go back to Sioux Falls," Tillie whispered.

"I know, but you must not. You must be strong for your children and give them a chance to grieve before you make such a change in their lives. They are already without their father, my Angel, do not take them from their home."

Chapter 4
June 1993

Maggie came around the corner of the back room and saw Noah in front of the old painting, staring at it as if he hadn't seen it in a lifetime. Estelle was peeking at him from the kitchen, concealing herself around the corner.

Maggie frowned with curiosity. "What are you doing?" she whispered.

"He's a gonna take my picture," Estelle whispered. "I'm gonna catch him."

Maggie smiled and shook her head. "He ain't gonna take your picture, Baby. He's just lookin' it over like he always does."

"He's lookin' at it a *whole lot* different today."

Maggie walked to the bar and barked, "What'll ya have, Noah?"

Noah startled and turned to look at Maggie. His blue eyes were downcast today and he looked like he hadn't slept in weeks. Maggie had read all about the crash in the paper, but she hadn't seen Noah since it happened.

"Whatcha got?" He asked, walking to the bar and taking a seat in front of Maggie.

"Meatloaf." Maggie pulled a bottle of Coke from beneath the counter, opened the old fashioned cap and set it before him.

"I'll take it," he said.

She scribbled the order down on her pad and put the slip on the wheel behind her.

"Ain't seen ya in a while," she began with a frown. "Sorry about what happened. You know…and everything."

“Thanks, Maggie,” Noah said as he lifted the bottle for a good, long drink. “And thanks for the flowers you and Estelle sent over to the funeral. That was sure nice of you.”

Maggie nodded. “How’s Angel doing?”

Noah shrugged. “Don’t know. Her parents are with her, but A.J. hasn’t been to practice so I can’t imagine they’re doing very good.”

“You mean you haven’t even gone over to say hi or anything?”

“No, I didn’t think I should. You know...” his voice trailed off as he took a breath and rolled his eyes.

Maggie’s black eyebrows knit themselves together in a most disapproving frown. “So you just let her sit over there all by herself?” she questioned.

“Well, she’s got her folks there,” he answered, looking into the top of his Coke bottle. “Besides, she doesn’t want to see me.”

“I’d bet you’re wrong about that.”

Noah suddenly frowned and said, “I’m not going over there, Maggie. It would be *too weird*.”

Maggie’s frown deepened. “Do you miss him?” she asked.

“Yeah,” he answered with a thoughtful expression. “You know, Maggie, I’m just so surprised about the whole thing. It just doesn’t seem right that God take Alex like this, you know, after everything Angel went through to keep the marriage together. It just doesn’t seem right that God let this happen to her.”

“I’ve *never* understood your God,” Maggie barked, “but I’ve sure seen Him screw lots of things up.”

“He doesn’t screw things up. I’m sure He knows what He’s doing, we just don’t understand it right now.”

“That’s a joke,” Maggie said with a scowl, and she stomped away to wait on another customer.

*****

Vincenzo held the hand of the woman he’d loved since that wonderful day in 1956 when he tried to catch snowflakes on his tongue on her front porch. She smiled so beautifully into his eyes that day, but today, and since the crash, her eyes did not smile at all. They walked through the apple orchard, which was in full, fragrant bloom, and she cried again about the unfinished business with her brother, Alex.

“You must forgive him, my love, and go on,” Vincenzo kindly encouraged.

“I’ve forgiven him, Vincenzo. It’s just so very hard to forget. There were so many things he didn’t make right that he should have.”

"He did what he could," Vincenzo defended in a gentle tone. "Perhaps he did not do things as you wish he would have, but he did them the best he could."

"I just don't understand. We were raised by the same parents. What happened to him? Why did he turn out so differently?"

"He did not turn out differently," Vincenzo answered. "He just *did* things differently. Holding it against him at this point will only hurt you and your good heart. You must remember, Alex is not the only one in this world that has had to deal with sin. You and I sin every day, my love."

"You've never tried to divorce me," Kate snapped.

"Kate Martin!" Vincenzo gasped. "He *dismissed* that action and it has been long forgotten. You must forget it as well."

Kate walked along in silence, going over and over in her mind her brother's sins of the past. Vincenzo would always defend Alex, especially now that he was gone, and it made her anger boil.

"I see how hot you are," Vincenzo said. "But Alex could not have brought back your parents. Just as it was with Alex, so it was with your mother and father — only God decides and ordains the days of our lives. We have nothing to do with it. You must blame Alex no more, my love, for it will only make you a bitter old woman."

Kate raised one eyebrow as she questioned, "Old?"

Vincenzo grinned and replied, "None of us are getting any younger, my love. The sooner you put this aside and praise the Lord for saving your brother, the sooner your bitter root will begin to heal."

*****

"You might as well start practice," Jake grumbled as he pulled on a batting helmet and looked at his father. "I guess he ain't gonna show."

"Are you seeing him in school?" Noah asked.

"Yeah," Jake answered, "but he never wants to talk about baseball anymore. Him and his grandpa have been *fishing*." He frowned and shook his head. "Who in the world would fish when they could play ball?"

Noah shrugged, obviously as perplexed as his son. "Okay then," he said with a sigh, "Let's go ahead and get started so we can catch some of your brother's practice over at Fitzgerald."

Jake nodded, trudging out of the dugout with his trusty bat in hand. Baseball was still fun, just not as fun as it was when A.J. played with them.

A few hours later Jake and Noah joined Joshua and Mona in the sparsely filled stands at Fitzgerald Stadium to watch their favorite pitcher practice his famous fastball. Jake took up his position behind the fence, shouting instructions and giving advice.

Joshua laughed and remarked, "That kid has really gotten bossy."

Noah took a seat beside his brother and sister-in-law.

Mona offered him a smile and asked, "How are ya doin', Noah?"

"Better," he answered with a heavy sigh. "A.J. didn't show up for practice again today. Guess he's gonna be done with it."

"How long has Alex been gone?" Joshua asked.

"Eight weeks."

"That's not very long," Joshua reminded. "Better give it some more time. He'll come around."

"Jake sure misses him," Noah said.

"Have you talked to Angel?" Mona asked.

"No," Noah answered, looking away from Mona to watch Ty throw a fastball. "Why?"

"Well, cuz," Mona said delicately, "maybe you should...ya know…."

"Her parents are there. Besides, she doesn't want me creeping around the place."

Mona chuckled and said, "I didn't say to go *creeping* around the place. I thought maybe just a *call*. You know, you and Alex were fairly close toward the end and you're with her brothers a great deal. It's gonna be strange if you *don't* call."

"I don't wanna call her, Mona," Noah mumbled.

Joshua raised an eyebrow and asked, "Why not?"

Noah's brows dipped into a deep furrow as he looked at the two of them and grumbled, "Let's use our heads here, people. I'll look like the *old* lecher coming in for the kill, and in case you guys haven't noticed, I'm not a young man anymore. I really *am* getting old."

Joshua and Mona chuckled at his analogy and Mona put a tender hand upon his shoulder. "I don't believe for one second she'll look at it like that. Come on, Noah, you guys go way back. You were her best friend when she had her accident."

"She hasn't seen me for nearly six years," Noah snapped abruptly. "We just don't know each other anymore."

"Well, I'm gonna pray that you do the *right* thing," Joshua said.

"Yeah," Noah said, taking a breath as he rose from his place on the bleachers. "You guys pray while I go and watch Ty pitch." And he stomped away.

"Well," Mona said with a sigh, "that didn't go as well as we'd hoped."

Joshua grinned. "Not exactly," he replied, "but I don't think it went as badly as it could have."

*****

Rosa watched Tillie sleep in the sun in a lounge chair on her stone patio. School would soon let out for the summer and it was nearing her birthday. Rosa wondered if Tillie would allow her to throw just a small party. Her brothers had called often to say they would be out, but Tillie had not expressed any desire to see them.

The associate pastor from the Martins' church family had called once since the accident. Other than that, not a soul contacted them. Certainly the family had received many cards and flowers, but there were no visits or phone calls and Tillie made the quiet decision to stop attending church. Mrs. Romanov, always a faithful friend to Tillie, stopped by several times a week, literally begging the Martins to at least return to Joshua's church, but Tillie refused. She was withdrawn and losing weight. She had dark circles under her eyes and her clothes hung off of her like those on a scarecrow. She rarely touched a meal. When she did Rosa thought perhaps she only consumed one small noodle or maybe a tiny piece of stew beef.

During the day, while the kids were in school, Tillie dragged herself around the house, took several naps, and said barely a word to either Rosa or Guiseppi. But when the kids came home in the afternoon she appeared to come alive, asking them about their day and if they wanted to do anything together, like go to a movie or out for ice cream. Her behavior was strange, to say the least, but Guiseppi and Rosa dismissed it as part of the grieving process — the grief of losing her husband as well as her "friends." It appeared to them that the Martins' old church had gotten what they wanted out of the Martins and were now done with them.

The cleaning lady, Diane, came around twice a week. She dusted, scrubbed and made the place sparkle. Tillie had no desire for grocery shopping or cooking, so Rosa took care of that. When Guiseppi threatened to do the laundry Tillie was alarmed enough to perform at least that housekeeping activity. Apparently the idea of her father hovering over the washing machine and dryer scared the daylights out of her.

Rosa took a seat beside a sleeping Tillie, gently touching her shoulder. Tillie nearly jumped out of the lounger with a start, but when she saw her mother she only frowned, laid back down and attempted to resume her nap.

"You know that scares me," she grumbled as she closed her eyes.

"I want to visit with my daughter."

"Sure. What's on your mind, Ma`ma?"

"Your brothers are coming to Rapid City for your birthday," Rosa sweetly announced. "I was wondering if I could cook up a little something special."

Tillie groaned. "Please don't," she said. "You don't need to be knocking yourself out for my birthday." If Tillie's eyes had been open, she would have seen the sad pout upon her mother's pretty lips.

"But I want to knock myself out," Rosa replied.

Tillie sighed. "It's just another birthday, Ma`ma, the same as I had last year, except this year I look like *the wrath*."

"Angel!" Rosa softly gasped. "Do not speak in such a way!"

"Well, it's the truth, and you can tell those brothers of mine that I'm not in the mood and they might as well stay put."

"But they have already made plans," Rosa persisted.

"Well that's fairly typical of them. They just go off and plan up a storm, and don't even bother to consider how somebody else might feel about it."

"Well," Rosa said with a sigh and a frown, "perhaps your babies would like to see their cousins —"

"Ma`ma." Tillie opened her eyes and frowned at her mother. "I don't want to have a bunch a people here that I have to cook for. I just don't want to do it right now. Surely you can understand *that*."

"I told you," Rosa admonished, narrowing her expression and pointing her index finger, "*I want to take care of the cooking*."

Tillie relented with a sigh, "Fine. Go ahead. Do whatever you want."

"I will," Rosa snapped as she got to her feet. She stomped back into the house through the sunroom doors, slamming them behind her.

Guiseppi was preparing to serve iced tea and he looked up with surprise as Rosa huffed into the kitchen.

"I would not take those out there if I were you," Rosa warned.

Guiseppi raised one of his eyebrows and asked, "She is cranky *again*?"

"*Very*. She does not want her brothers to come for her birthday."

"Well, she is grieving, my Rosa," Guiseppi explained with understanding. "Remember when Angelo went Home? I did not want any celebrations around me either."

"Shall we cancel it then?" Rosa suggested.

Guiseppi shook his head and answered, "I think not. Her children are looking forward to seeing their cousins. The birthday is still more than a week away. Perhaps she will feel just a little better by then —"

The telephone's ringing interrupted them, and Guiseppi reached for the cordless on the counter. "Hello."

"Mr. Caselli?"

"Yes. But if you are selling something I want nothing this day."

"No, it's Noah Hansen."

Guiseppi looked at Rosa, raising both of his eyebrows and smiling as he said, "Well, hello, Noah Hansen. How are you?"

Rosa's eyes were alight with surprise. They hadn't seen or heard from Noah since leaving Sioux Falls.

"Pretty good," Noah answered. "I thought maybe I should call and see how things are going. A.J. hasn't made a practice yet and Jake's getting pretty worried…and Mrs. Romanov told us about the situation with the church."

"Well," Guiseppi answered sadly, "that is a mess for certain, and Angel does not wish me to speak of it." He took a breath as he said, "A.J. suffers most grievously. He misses his father. But I will talk with him and see what he says."

"I understand…." Noah hesitated for a moment, then asked, "How's Angel doing?"

"Not very well," Guiseppi answered. "But I think better than most. She is of very strong faith and character."

"Well, if you guys need anything go ahead and give me a call. My office knows how to reach me and my home number is listed in the book."

"Actually," Guiseppi said with a curious expression, taking a gentle hold of Rosa's hand. "There is *one* thing you could do for us."

"Anything."

"We are having a birthday celebration for Angel one week from Saturday," Guiseppi said, and Rosa gasped. Guiseppi continued without missing a beat, "I was thinking of calling you and inviting you and your boys. Do you think you could make it?"

The line fell into silence for several seconds.

"Noah," Guiseppi asked, "are you still there?"

"Yeah." Noah cleared his throat. "I don't know. I can't imagine she'd want to see me right now."

"Well, why not?" Guiseppi asked with a frown. "Have you forgotten all that you once meant to her?"

"No, but it just doesn't seem right —"

Noah was interrupted by Guiseppi's soft, but pretended, moan into the phone.

"Mr. Caselli, are you okay?" he asked.

"Oh," Guiseppi moaned softly, and Rosa looked at him questioningly. "I am sorry, Noah," he breathed into the phone. "But I must cut this phone call short, as much as I enjoy visiting with you. I am aged, you know."

Rosa gave him a disapproving frown. He had not played *this* particular trick in a long time.

"Are you sick?" Noah asked with concern.

"No," Guiseppi answered in a soft, feeble breath. "Just a little chest pain. Think nothing of it."

"Is anybody there to help you, Mr. Caselli?"

"Oh, my Rosa is here, but it is already passing. I will not be needing any help."

"Are you sure?"

"Oh, quite sure," Guiseppi replied. "Anyway, I should go and lay down for a moment. Will you be able to make it?"

"I'll see what I can swing."

"Thank you, Noah, and have a good day." Guiseppi quickly turned off the phone and looked at his very disapproving wife.

"That is a most *dreadful* trick you play," she scolded. "And to do it to someone as tenderhearted as Noah —" She shook her head and said, "Tsk, tsk, tsk, tsk, tsk."

Guiseppi smiled mischievously and put his arms around his wife. "It is also most effective in times of emergency. Why, the boy was about to refuse me."

"What if Angel is not comfortable?" Rosa worried.

"She *will* be comfortable," Guiseppi encouraged with a confident smile.

"It seems too soon, Guiseppi —"

"I am not attempting to send them off together, only a mere reintroduction —"

"I am not comfortable with this, Guiseppi. By the time of her birthday, and your little *reintroduction*, Alex will have been gone for only a few months."

Guiseppi rolled his eyes and said, "Listen to me, my Rosa, no one is getting any younger around here. For thirty-three years you have diligently prayed for this man, Noah. You were actually *younger* than he is now when you began. Do not tell me now that you are suddenly *uncomfortable* in his presence."

"It is not his presence that causes the discomfort," Rosa replied. "But our Angel has dealt him not only one, but *two* severe blows. He may not be as willing to put his heart at risk for her anymore."

"A knight thinks only of those he loves."

"And you are confident he loves her still?"

Guiseppi nodded. "I am as sure of it as I am the nose upon my face. When I watched him give up Angel without a fight nearly six years ago now, and only for the cause of what she saw to be the right thing to do, I knew then what he felt for her was profound and long lasting." He smiled and gave Rosa a squeeze as he reassured, "This will be all right. You will see."

*****

Noah stopped at Joshua's church on his way home, thankful to find his brother still in his office on a Friday night. It was the day before Tillie's birthday party and he had already received several calls from Marquette and Vincenzo, making sure he'd be over. Obviously they were looking forward to seeing him, but Noah still didn't feel right about the whole thing.

"I don't know," he worried to Joshua, "I'm not sure."

"Not sure about what?" Joshua asked with a frown. "They've been your buddies for years."

"Yeah, but I haven't been able to see their sister in a *very long time*. It's like everybody forgot about that or something. Don't they know how awkward this will be for me? And if I say anything to Mr. Caselli I'm afraid he'll have a heart attack or something."

"Do you *want* to go over?"

"Of course I do," Noah answered. "I want to see her again. Nothing has changed for me, but her husband had to die to make that possible. Am I the only one in the world that's bothered by that?"

"You're overreacting, Noah." Joshua smiled and shook his head. "It's not like they've set up a date or something. It's just a birthday party and you and Angel have quite a past. Why is this such a strange thing for you? You're so close to her brothers that it's gonna look weird if you *don't* go."

"I don't know." Noah sighed, shaking his head.

"Let me tell you something," Joshua said, removing his glasses and leaning back in his chair. "You have lived quite a remarkable life, Noah. I've been a minister for nearly forty years, so I know a remarkable life when I see one. I hate to have to break the news to you, but I don't think God's quite through with you yet. You are a dependable servant."

"What are you talking about?" Noah asked with a frown.

"Well," Joshua began, "first there was Vietnam. You returned from a place few survived. Then you meet up with some girl named Angel, fall madly in love and quit your drinking. Then you marry Carrie and raise someone else's child as your own. And need I even mention the ordeal you overcame when Angel sent you away six years ago?" He shook his head. "I wouldn't have been able to do that. You've got remarkable strength and character, Noah. You're a dependable servant."

Noah shook his head and scoffed, "Those things were no big deal. I just did what anybody would have done."

"Not *anybody*," Joshua argued. "Listen, Noah, you get over there to that birthday party. Say hello to one of your oldest friends, *because that's what she is*, have some cake, visit with her brothers and try to enjoy yourself. Did you pick her up a little something?"

"No," Noah moaned, shaking his head and frowning. "What could I possibly drag over there that wouldn't make me look so lecherous."

Joshua laughed. "Get one of those rubber tree plants Mona bought for the church. They're having a big sale on 'em over at Flowers by LeRoy. Put a big bow on it and take it over."

"A plant?"

Joshua nodded and answered, "Plants are impersonal and non-threatening. It's a good, generic gift and she'll really like it. What's her favorite color?"

"Pink."

"Well, then, get the pinkest bow you can find and put it around that shiny stuff at the bottom of the pot. She'll *love* it."

*****

Vincenzo puffed agitatedly at his pipe as he watched his two brothers attempt a fire in the charcoal grill. *Those two have never cooked anything for themselves, let alone over an outdoor fire. This situation is rapidly spiraling out of control.*

"It probably needs more of that lighter fluid," Petrice suggested as he reached for the can. Marquette nodded his head in agreement.

Vincenzo frowned, grabbing the can of fluid before Petrice could get a hold of it. "It does *not* need more fluid," he growled. "You have placed the briquettes into the grill in a most unorganized fashion. That is why your fire will not light."

"The expert speaks," Marquette quipped, raising one eyebrow and glaring at his brother.

"Yes, I *am* an expert," Vincenzo agreed. "I have cooked outside for *many years* and the two of you are inexperienced. Perhaps you should allow me to start the fire before you burn Angel's home to the ground."

Marquette and Petrice raised their hands, taking a step backward as if thinking, *go ahead then, fix this thing.*

"They are seriously into it," Elaine said, watching the three brothers from the kitchen window.

Tara peeked out the window and couldn't help giggling at the three of them. "I knew there would be trouble with that fire," she said. "Why did they not just ask Vincenzo to start it in the first place?"

Kate laughed from her place at the counter, where she was mixing lemonade. Even though Alex was absent, it was comforting to have everyone getting together again. She wished, however, that Sam and Becky-Lynn would have joined them. Instead, they'd flown to Paris to celebrate their thirtieth wedding anniversary.

Angelo, Michael and A.J. came through the garage door with several sacks and looked to the ladies for direction.

"Hey, we got the stuff you said you needed," Angelo said. "Where do you want it?"

"How about on the table in the corner," Kate answered. "You did get the *good* plates?"

"Whatever was written on your list, Ma`ma," Angelo answered.

"Thanks, guys," Elaine said as she went to the bags. "Perfect. These work the best."

"Well, we'll be out back if you need anything else," Michael said as he and his cousins headed for the sunroom doors. "We're gonna throw a few balls for A.J."

Tillie was coming down the steps at just that moment and heard *throw a few balls for A.J.* Her heart jumped with excitement and she smiled.

"Happy birthday, Angel!" Kate exclaimed when she saw Tillie.

"Thanks, Kate," Tillie replied.

Kate embraced her sister-in-law, holding her for just a few seconds and then letting her go to take a look at her. Tillie was dressed in a sleeveless, white blouse and had tucked it into a pair of soft blue capris. Her curly hair was in a neat pony tail and Kate saw the delicate pearls on her earlobes.

"Oh my goodness!" she exclaimed with a smile. "Are those the pearls Vincenzo and I gave you, like a hundred years ago?"

Tillie nodded and answered with a smile, "Yep."

"They still look *great*," Kate said, and then she pretended to frown. "But you look *thin*. Is Ma`ma giving you enough noodles?"

Tillie actually laughed and her sisters-in-law were surprised. Tillie had brooded from the time they'd arrived the day before and Guiseppi and Rosa had expressed concern that perhaps they'd made a mistake in forcing this birthday celebration upon her.

"Yes," Tillie answered. "Ma`ma makes *plenty* of noodles."

"Well eat more of them," Kate admonished, sounding *exactly* like a Caselli.

"Okay," Tillie said with a chuckle. "Where's Papa and Ma`ma?"

"They are out back with the girls," Tara answered, pointing toward the place where they were congregated under a tree. "Look."

Tillie saw them beneath the tree on a blanket. Laura was sketching something.

"She's drawing everyone," Elaine said with a smile. "And she's quite a little artist."

Tillie nodded. Laura had been sketching things like crazy lately and was becoming especially good at faces. "She's really talented," she said.

"I suppose she gets the best tips from her mother," Tara commented.

"I don't really like to do that anymore," Tillie replied.

The other ladies fell quiet so Elaine quickly offered, "Kate's been making your favorite lemonade. Want a glass?"

"Sure," Tillie answered, looking around the kitchen at all of the food being prepared. "Wow, you guys didn't have to do all of this."

"Of course we did," Kate said, handing Tillie a glass of the lemonade. "It's your birthday."

"And another *big* Caselli anniversary," Tara added.

Tillie frowned curiously and asked, "Which one? There are so many I can hardly keep track of them."

"I was there," Kate said with a smile, looking at Tillie. "And it was your fifth birthday. You were *so cute* that day."

Tillie shook her head. "I can't remember."

"The Swearing In Ceremony," Kate reminded.

"Oh my goodness," Tillie gasped with a soft smile. "I *do* remember. I got that little, black patent leather purse that day —"

They were interrupted by a soft knock on the garage door. Elaine hurried over to open it up and there werer Noah and his boys with a huge rubber tree plant, complete with a pink bow fastened sloppily around the bottom. Ty and Jake stepped into the house and Noah followed.

Tillie's eyes showed her surprise. "Noah?" she greeted with a soft smile.

"Hi, Noah," Kate greeted.

"Hi," Noah said with a hesitant smile, realizing that Tillie was obviously surprised by his arrival. "Your father invited us. Is it okay?"

"Oh, my goodness!" Elaine exclaimed, throwing her arms around Noah. "Of course it's okay! We're so glad to see you!"

"Hello, Noah!" Tara greeted him with an enthusiastic hug. "It is good to see you."

"Thanks," Noah replied, noticing that his sons had already made it across the kitchen and were greeting a very surprised Tillie.

"Happy birthday, Mrs. Martin," Ty said, reaching for her hand and giving it a polite shake. "You look very nice today."

Noah glowed with pride at the actions of his polite son. What a wonderful job he'd done with that young man.

"Thanks, Ty," Tillie replied.

"Yeah," Jake said, reaching for her hand in the same way his brother had. "You do look good. Happy birthday, and look," he said, pointing at the rubber tree, "we bought you a present."

"Thanks, Jake," Tillie said, smiling at the handsome young boy and then she smiled at his father.

"Happy birthday, Tillie," Noah said. "Where can I put this?"

"How about just over there by the door for now."

Noah nodded and set the plant down.

"Vanilla had her puppies," Jake reported. "I wanted to bring you one of them, but Dad said that was a *stupid* idea, and that we should bring something more impersonal and non-threatening."

Tillie smiled and her sisters-in-law giggled.

"I didn't say it was a *stupid* idea," Noah said, moaning under his breath. *That kid...what will he say next?* "What I said was that it would probably be a *handful*."

"You remember Vanilla, don'tcha?" Jake went on.

"Of course I remember Vanilla," Tillie answered. "How many puppies did you get?"

"Eight," Ty answered. "And they all look just like Vanilla."

Tillie nodded. "Let's see, she's a golden retriever?"

"Yep," Jake affirmed.

"Did you breed her then?" Tillie asked politely.

"No." Jake snickered and shook his head. "Dad says the puppies are half golden retriever and half sneaky neighbor dog."

Tillie laughed at Jake, as did her sisters-in-law, and Noah turned a wonderful shade of red.

Ty laughed and asked, "Hey, where's A.J.?"

"They are in the back, throwing some balls," Tara answered with a smile.

"Thanks," Ty said as he put his hand on Jake's shoulder. "Come on."

"Okay," Jake nodded with a smile and started to back away. "Well, happy birthday, Mrs. Martin."

"Thanks, Jake," she replied.

Tillie's brothers, along with Noah, took care of the grilling while the ladies remained inside, visiting as they finished the rest of their preparations. Baked beans were pulled from the oven and a huge macaroni salad was taken from the refrigerator. Along with fresh vegetables and a delicious dip, prepared by Tara, were sliced cheese on a wooden platter, and caramel apples Elaine had brought all the way from Washington.

When the hamburgers and hot dogs were finished, they set everything out on the counter in the kitchen and told everyone to help themselves. The ladies had spread blankets and set the picnic table in the backyard, and everyone was told to take their food outside. Soon they were all eating and talking.

"She looks better today," Rosa whispered to Guiseppi, watching their daughter sit down with her brothers and Noah.

As he watched her, Guiseppi couldn't help but notice the difference in his daughter. She didn't seem uncomfortable to be with Noah, yet she hadn't had too many words for him, either. But she hadn't looked this chipper on Easter Sunday, which was only two months before. Guiseppi was struck with a surprised thought. *That was a week before Alex's death....*

"And she is into the macaroni salad," he murmured.

"She does not seem to be uneasy with Noah being here," Rosa commented.

"It is strange without Alex, but *easier*." Guiseppi raised a silvered brow and looked at Rosa.

"Do not say it, Guiseppi," Rosa warned.

"Do not say what, my Rosa?"

"I know what you are thinking, and you will be struck in your sleep if you do not stop pondering in such a way."

Guiseppi frowned as he replied, "Then it is amazing I still live."

Rosa huffed.

Guiseppi rolled his eyes and whispered, "Please do not be so unwilling to say what you see with your own eyes. Angel was in darker spirits *before* Alex died. He brought us much heartache, while Noah brings us blessing. Certainly you see the difference."

Rosa glanced at Tillie, noticing her smiling at Noah for the briefest of moments. Rosa's heart softened then and she said, "I see it, Guiseppi."

Noah was watching A.J. and his own boys practice pitching and catching.

"Hey, A.J.," he said with a friendly smile, "I saw you catch Ty's fast ball over there. Lookin' pretty good."

"Thanks, Mr. Hansen," A.J. replied.

"Man," Noah went on, "we could *really* use a good catcher this year —"

"Yeah," Jake interrupted. "That dork, Chip Davis, can't catch *anything*."

A.J. snickered. "Catching is a superior skill," he joked.

Noah laughed. "So are you interested, A.J.?" he asked.

"Maybe," A.J. answered. "Me and Grandpa been praying about it."

Noah nodded, pleasantly surprised with A.J.'s response. "Well, good. We've got a game on Monday night, you know, if you've decided by then. And Grandpa can come."

"Thanks, Mr. Hansen."

Jake elbowed A.J. and his blue eyes danced with mischief as he said, "And make sure you tell Laura to come, too — and her friend, Heidi."

Everyone laughed and Noah rolled his eyes.

Later in the day Rosa served the delicious chocolate cake she'd made especially for the celebration.

Noah couldn't help smiling as he watched the Casellis together, telling their old stories, laughing at one another. They had started to heal. Tillie was still very quiet, but she looked better than when they returned to Rapid City, and A.J. and Laura were interacting more with their cousins and their other relatives. The Casellis were a people with remarkable faith and character, and it was showing in the way they held each other up.

"Do you love my cake, Noah Hansen?" Rosa questioned with a mischievous smile.

Noah pulled himself from his thoughts, drawing his attention to the tiny lady before him. "It's the best, Mrs. Caselli," he said.

"I know," Rosa agreed, reaching for a nearby chair and dragging it closer to Noah. She took a seat and patted his knee. "Are you having a nice day, Noah?"

Noah smiled and answered, "I'm having a *great* day, Mrs. Caselli."

Rosa looked intently into Noah's expression. "You know, I must say that you have aged rather well, Noah," she said. "You have hardly the gray for a man of your age, and you appear to be as fit as a fiddle."

"Well, thanks, Mrs. Caselli," he said, blushing.

"It was very kind of you to come this day." Rosa smiled and patted his knee again. "Please know that Guiseppi and I appreciate your good heart."

"Oh, it's nothing," Noah scoffed.

Rosa winked and said, "But it is everything to us."

Chapter 5

Noah paced the dugout anxiously, wondering what A.J. would decide. Everyone else on the team was already there, warming up their batting on Ty's fast ball while Noah pondered the past weekend's events. After so many years of sneaking around with Vincenzo and Marquette, never daring to breathe a word of it to Alex, Noah had really enjoyed being with them out in the open — and it was *great* to see her again.

Jake ran into the dugout and started rummaging through the equipment bag. "So, do you think A.J. will show?" he asked.

Noah took a seat on the bench. "Don't know," he replied. "Did he say anything on Saturday?"

"Not really. But he seemed better than before school got out."

Noah agreed. They had all seemed remarkably *better*, if that's what you could call it, and Tillie had even laughed at Jake's description of Vanilla's puppies.

Jake looked curiously at his father's stressed-out expression and asked, "What's the matter, Dad? You look worried about something."

Noah shrugged. "I'm just thinking about stuff," he answered. "Big people stuff."

"Don't worry," Jake said. He finally emptied the bag and set it aside. He looked at his father and smiled. "It's all gonna work out just fine. Look at me and Ty, for instance. I bet you thought we'd be really screwed up with no mom, but look at how great we turned out."

Noah smiled and gave the bill on Jake's baseball cap a soft flick. "That's right," he replied. "You guys turned out really great."

"And A.J. and Laura are gonna be okay, too, 'cause they've got cool relatives."

Noah nodded with a smile and a sigh, looking toward the parking lot just in time to see the black, Mercedes wagon. "By golly, they're here," he said, getting to his feet.

"Hey, great!" Jake exclaimed, sprinting for the parking lot.

Noah followed him all the way, his stomach tying into unexplainable knots. He was so disappointed when he reached them that he couldn't hide it. Guiseppi had driven the kids over; Laura and Heidi in the back, and A.J. in the front. Heidi and Laura gave Jake a friendly wave when they got out of the car, and then the two of them hurried over to the stands to find themselves a seat.

"Hey, A.J.," Jake said with a smile. "Glad you could make it."

A.J. laughed and slapped Jake's back. "You're just glad *Heidi* could make it," he said.

"No," Jake scoffed, shaking his head. "Come on, we're already set up. Me and you bat last." And they hurried away.

Noah and Guiseppi were left standing alone by the car. Guiseppi saw the disappointment in Noah's friendly expression. He shuffled closer to the younger man, putting his old hand on Noah's strong shoulder. "She will come to the game tonight," he said with a twinkle in his eyes. "She and Ma`ma are putting a small garden in this afternoon."

Noah sighed and looked away.

"Noah," Guiseppi said, his black eyes sparkling with the same light Noah saw in the eyes of his children and grandchildren, "wait for the Lord, be *strong* and take heart. Wait on the Lord and be of good courage. I cannot imagine that this will take very long."

"But there are children now," Noah whispered with dismay. "They'll never understand."

"Be not afraid," Guiseppi reminded. "Jesus goes with you always and He will tell you when all is ready for His perfect plan to finish its course."

While Guiseppi and the children were at practice, Rosa and Tillie put on wide-brimmed straw hats and gardening gloves, to begin working in the small patch in the backyard. Tillie had always wanted just a tiny vegetable garden in the backyard, but for some reason had never gotten around to it. As long as Ma`ma was there for the summer, now seemed as good a time as any to get the job done.

"You loved to be with Papa in his gardens when you were small," Rosa reminisced as she worked beside her daughter.

"I remember. And I don't know why I never got around to doing this. I had a little garden in Sioux Falls."

Rosa nodded and looked at her daughter curiously. The last week had brought so many changes within Angel; Rosa wondered if she even noticed. Though sadness and grief were tugging at the corners of Angel's expression, a soft light was glowing behind her countenance. What the light could be Rosa was not certain, but it was there, faint and soft, and probably seen only by her parents. Rosa looked back into the dirt, stuffing a tomato plant into the ground. "Have you thought about your painting lately?" she asked.

"No," Tillie answered with a laugh. "I don't fool around with that anymore. You know that, Ma`ma."

Rosa nodded. "Laura certainly seems to have your talent for sketching."

"More than I ever had."

Rosa pursed her lips together tightly.

"Don't be angry with me, Ma`ma," Tillie said with a faint smile. "It's just that it reminded me of so many things I needed to forget about for a while."

Rosa nearly dropped her gardening trowel, looking at her daughter with surprise. The first honest words on the subject she'd heard out of Tillie in nearly six years. Rosa had convinced herself, along with Guiseppi, that Angel had very little, if any, memory at all of why she had stopped painting and sketching. After all, Tillie never once mentioned her past with Noah to any of her family members after her accident, and was suspiciously quiet on the subject.

"I must ask you a question, my Angel," Rosa whispered.

"Sure, Ma`ma."

"Have you thought of him these past years?" Rosa whispered again.

Tillie shrugged, but didn't answer.

"Please tell me," Rosa pleaded.

Tillie paused from her digging and looked to the hills in the distance as she answered, "Sometimes."

Rosa swallowed hard and asked, "What do you remember of that? Of the two of you?"

"Everything, Ma`ma."

Rosa took a deep breath. "Then why have you not spoken of him?"

Tillie looked at her mother with a clever expression and answered, "Ma`ma, I was trying to make my marriage work. I couldn't be thinking of someone else."

"Did you love Alex?"

"Yes," Tillie answered without hesitation. "But it changed, you know, after he stayed away for so long." She paused and continued, "I can still remember how I felt the day I married him, how exciting it was and how handsome he was. I *loved* Alex, but it changed and I think I resented him for that."

"Do you miss him?"

"Of course, but there's relief too. I don't know, Ma`ma, it's hard to explain. Alex was so driven and the kids and I held him back from what he *really* wanted to do. I think Alex is finally at peace now."

Rosa nodded. "I think so, too."

"He struggled every day," Tillie said with a wistful expression. "He tried so hard, but I could almost see what he was thinking in the back of his mind. He loved us, but he wanted politics *more*. He stayed with us because it was the *right* thing to do."

"Doing the righteous thing is *always* a good thing," Rosa said with a nod.

Tillie's eyes were suddenly surprised and she gave her mother a sly smile. "But you disagreed with me when I made the decision to do the righteous thing," she gently pointed out.

"*That was different*!" Rosa bristled.

Tillie laughed at her mother's reaction. "It was no different, Ma`ma."

"Noah *loved* you, no matter the circumstances! He would have *never* felt held back taking care of you and helping you through your rehabilitation. He would have sacrificed his own needs as a man in order that your needs be met."

Tillie was taken aback by her mother's strong response and opinion, but this was one of the reasons that Tillie had decided to never speak with her mother about it. She knew that it was a delicate issue with her mother six years ago, and obviously it still was now.

"We'd better not talk about this," Tillie said as she turned back toward her chore at hand, digging out another place for a plant.

"Do not attempt to brush me off, young lady!" Rosa admonished with parental authority. "Look at me when I talk to you! We will have this discussion *once and for all!*"

Tillie's mouth hung open in surprise. "Please, Ma`ma —" she began.

"Do not *please Ma`ma* me!" Rosa shook her index finger at Tillie as she scolded, "I did not want you to return to Alex and you did so under the guise of righteousness, while you were in love with another man!"

"Ma`ma!" Tillie gasped with an astonished expression. "I had to do the righteous thing for my children, no matter what my *feelings* were! A.J. and Laura were much happier when their father came home and I *don't* regret my decision at all. You wanted me to make a decision based on my *feelings* for Noah, and even in my own dilapidated little head I could see that it wasn't right —"

"Can you *blame* me! Can you really, truly blame me for wanting Noah, of all men in this world, for my daughter?"

"You wanted Alex for me, too!" Tillie argued.

"He was *different* when he was a younger man!" Rosa exclaimed, stabbing her gardening trowel into the dirt.

"That *doesn't* matter!" Tillie replied, raising her voice. "And that's not what I was raised to believe! I couldn't just simply trade in my old husband for a new one!"

"Oh, Angel!" Rosa gasped as she shook her head in disapproval. "Do you not recall that Alex was the one who left?"

Tillie had to swallow very hard and take a calming breath before she continued, "But he asked for my forgiveness. Please, Ma`ma, Alex and I had far more good years than we had bad years, and that's gotta count for something." She paused and tried to smile at her mother. She reached over and softly touched Rosa's shoulder. "Ma`ma, what happened with Noah was *not* Alex's fault, nor was it his responsibility. Ultimately, *I'm* the one responsible for the decision to marry Alex."

Rosa took a deep breath, looking into her daughter's eyes with a frown.

"I love you, Ma`ma."

Rosa's old, black eyes filled with tears, spilling wetness onto her cheeks as she said, "I love you, too, Angel."

Tillie put her arms around her mother and held her close.

"Please tell me, child," Rosa wept, "can you *ever* love Noah again?"

Tillie swallowed very hard and answered, "I've never stopped loving Noah. I always have and I always will, but I'm not gonna confuse my kids by starting that whole thing up again. They've just lost their father, and they loved him. They don't know anything about what happened and they don't remember Alex leaving us at all —"

"But, Angel —"

"No." Tillie shook her head. "Don't you think I've hurt Noah enough?"

Rosa bit her lip and nodded. "But he loves you, Angel."

"Maybe, but I screwed that up years ago."

"You were but a babe," Rosa defended.

"I was a disobedient child," Tillie reminded. "And you need to stop making excuses for me."

"You repented."

Tillie sighed with a smile. "Yes, I did repent."

"Why do you not forgive yourself?"

Tillie swallowed hard and took a deep breath as she answered, "I have, I just feel bad about what happened to Noah."

"I understand," Rosa relented. "But perhaps you could at least be his friend?"

"We'll pray about it, okay?"

"Okay," Rosa replied. "We will pray." Why *not* pray? Rosa had prayed for Noah for more than thirty years, and she'd *almost* told her daughter.

After a very quick supper of sandwiches and some leftover macaroni salad, Guiseppi drove everyone over to the ball diamonds at the Timberline Little League Complex for A.J.'s first game of the season. The early evening was cool in the Black Hills, a gentle breeze wafting pine fragrance into town.

A.J., along with a very curious Guiseppi, joined the team in the dugout, and they all huddled together.

Rosa brought along an afghan for her and Tillie to cover up with if the temperature dropped further and she adjusted it over Tillie and Laura after they had taken seats on the bleachers.

"Please, Ma`ma," Tillie chuckled as her mother perfectly positioned the afghan. "This is embarrassing."

"Laura does not seem to mind," Rosa said, taking a seat beside her daughter to wiggle in under some of the warm afghan.

Laura giggled, "Yeah, Mom."

Tillie smiled and shook her head. "By the way, where's Heidi?"

"She couldn't come," Laura answered. "They were having company tonight." She frowned curiously at the huddle in the dugout. "Is that Grandpa in there?"

Tillie and Rosa narrowed their eyes for a better look. Guiseppi's figure hovered close to the huddle. He shook his index finger, obviously giving some instructions of his own.

"That old rascal," Rosa said with a laugh. "What does he know of baseball?"

"Grandpa knows everything," Laura said with a smile.

Rosa laughed again. "Well, all right then. If you say so."

A tall man and his petite red-headed wife walked up to them, smiling and stretching out their hands in greeting. "Remember us?" the man asked with a friendly smile as he took Rosa's hand into his own. Tillie watched him carefully. He *was* familiar, and so was the woman with him.

"The brother of Noah!" Rosa softly gasped with a smile. "How are you, Joshua?" And then she reached for Mona's hand. "And beautiful Mona! How delightful you still are!"

"Oh, my goodness," Mona said with a blush. "You always were such a sweet lady."

Joshua offered Tillie his hand and looked into her expression as he said, "And you *didn't* remember me the last time we talked."

"Well I do now," Tillie replied with a smile, giving his hand a gentle shake. "It's good to see you." She indicated her daughter, "This is my Laura."

"I know, Laura," Joshua said. "She and Heidi *never* miss a practice or a game!"

Laura laughed and nodded.

Mona offered Tillie her hand. "How have you been?"

"Pretty good," Tillie answered. "And I got your card. Thanks."

"Just give me a call if you need anything." Mona gave Tillie's hand a gentle squeeze.

"Thanks," Tillie said.

"Can we sit with you ladies?" Joshua asked. "We brought our own blanket."

"Of course," Rosa answered.

The bleachers around them filled with people and the game began.

Guiseppi could be seen checking Noah's clipboard and pacing back and forth, like Noah, especially during batting and then again when Jake was on the pitcher's mound. Guiseppi rubbed his bald head as he paced along, obviously saying things no one but the team in the dugout could hear. Several little boys waiting on the bench were cracking up into uproarious giggles. Ty seemed to think Guiseppi was incredibly funny, because he hadn't *stopped* laughing since Guiseppi had joined them.

"I guess your father's gonna be the assistant coach this year," Joshua commented with a smile.

"I hope he's not bothering anyone in there," Tillie replied.

Jake was a most awesome pitcher, and A.J. didn't let a single fly ball get past him. The two of them together were unstoppable.

Their hands and fingers flew out coded messages to one another, producing one strikeout after the next. The Builders quickly racked up the runs, leaving the other team in their dust.

At one point, near the end of the game, the umpire made a bad call, and Guiseppi shouted something in Italian from the dugout. The umpire looked extremely confused, and so did everyone else. Noah laughed hysterically. He put his coach's cap on Guiseppi's bald head, and the old man smiled up at him. Laura laughed and cheered for her grandfather, giving him a "thumbs up" sign, and blowing him a kiss. Guiseppi was quite flattered by the attentions of his granddaughter. He took a graceful bow, tipping the newly acquired hat.

"Oh, Papa," Tillie moaned, rolling her eyes. "You're out of control." She looked at her mother, who was frowning in her husband's direction, and whispered, "What did he say, Ma`ma?"

"I do not speak in such a way," Rosa replied in an aghast tone, which only made Joshua and Mona laugh all the more.

"Grandpa's funny!" Laura laughed, and obviously everyone in the stands agreed with her as they began to applaud the old man.

"I hope no one here speaks Italian," Rosa groaned.

Tillie tried to suppress her smile, but the scene was too comical, and she thanked God for her father.

The Builders won an astounding victory and they were very happy when they finally emerged from the dugout to join their waiting families.

"Great job," Tillie said, hugging A.J., kissing his cheek. "You guys were awesome."

"How 'bout that coaching?" A.J. raised one eyebrow and smiled at his mother.

"Wow." Tillie looked at her father, who was still wearing Noah's hat and speaking enthusiastically with him near the edge of the dugout.

"He's great, Mom." A.J. smiled. "And I think Mr. Hansen really likes him. It was okay."

"He's hilarious," Ty added. "And really good for team morale."

Rosa raised both of her eyebrows and looked questioningly at Noah's red headed son as she said, "Team morale? You do not know what he said." She gasped softly, "Unless, but I pray not, he translated it for you."

"No," Ty laughed and shook his head. "It's his *tone* more than anything."

Guiseppi took off the hat and handed it back to Noah, who accepted it with a smile and they walked to where the rest of their families waited.

"Great job, Grandpa!" Laura exclaimed, throwing her arms around him.

"Well, thank you, my Laura."

Noah gave Tillie a soft smile. "Hi. Glad you could make it," he said.

"Me, too," she replied.

"Here's a schedule of the games this summer," Noah said, handing her a folded piece of paper. "And the practices are listed on there also."

"Okay."

"We play until July first," Noah continued. "Then there'll be an All-Star game around the middle of July. We'll be completely done before August."

"Thanks, Noah," Tillie said with a smile.

"I can pick up A.J. if you need to me to," he offered.

"Sure...that would be great."

"I gotta get going," Noah said. "I've got an early morning up in Deadwood." He looked at his sons, "Do we got all our gear, boys?"

"Yep," Ty answered as he picked up a bag of equipment and Jake grabbed the other one.

"See you guys tomorrow," Jake said to A.J. "Practice is at the same time."

"Great," A.J. acknowledged. "I'll be there."

"I guess I'll stop by and get you then?" Noah asked.

"And I will ride along?" Guiseppi asked with a curious sparkle in his eyes.

"Yes," Noah answered, "you're always welcome."

"Thank you." Guiseppi looked very satisfied.

Noah looked at Tillie one last time and said, "See you later." Tillie smiled in return and Noah and his sons walked away.

Rosa took Guiseppi's hand into her own, leading him toward the parking lot as she said, "We need to talk about something, my love."

"Oh?" Guiseppi pretended to be curious.

Tillie watched her little parents walking along ahead of them, hand in hand, having a quiet conversation between just the two of them. *How wonderful it must be to grow old with someone,* she thought.

*****

When Noah was done in Deadwood, Ben called him with a message to check in with Vivian Olson over at Angel's Place. Noah headed for Rimrock and the house he'd built for Tillie nearly seventeen years ago.

He parked out front and, looking at the place, was suddenly taken by surprise. For a building of its age it was still in extraordinary shape. Noah had made sure it was maintained properly over the years. He didn't allow just anybody to take care of it. Noah was the only one who made repairs and performed maintenance on Angel's Place.

An older, red Cadillac pulled in next to him. It was Vivian. She didn't drive anymore. She hired a young man named Dan for that duty. Dan helped her out of the backseat. Vivian was quite aged and extremely thin and frail. She styled her grey-bluish hair the same as when Noah first met her in 1976. Her eyebrows were penciled-in black and her red lipstick matched the color of her car.

Noah got out of his pickup and went to the passenger side door of the Cadillac where Dan was helping Vivian to her feet.

"Hansen," she barked in her familiar gravelly voice.

"Hello, Viv," Noah greeted her politely. "Looks like you waxed the Caddy."

"Had Dan take care of that for me." She frowned at her old car as she added, "Does a nice job, doesn't he?"

Noah smiled at the young man, who always looked uncomfortable. Noah reached for Vivian's arm and began escorting her toward the house. Dan always stayed with car. The escort was Noah's job.

"I was sorry to hear about your friend," she grumbled.

"Thanks, Viv. And thanks for the flowers you had sent over to the funeral. That was really nice."

"Ah, they were hardly nothing. How is his family?"

"I think better," Noah answered.

Vivian nodded. "Well, that's good. Now about my bats."

Noah rolled his eyes. He had just checked for bats a couple of months ago, and there hadn't been *anything* in that attic.

As they neared the front door Noah saw the familiar face of the lady Vivian hired to manage Angel's Place. She held the door open for them.

"Hi, Mavis," Noah greeted, helping Vivian up the steps on the porch. "I hear you're having some trouble with bats."

Mavis was a younger lady in her mid-thirties. She was tall and slender, and wore her blond hair up in a bun on the top of her head. She always looked a little nervous when Vivian was around, not unlike most of the help. She did a good job, obviously, because Angel's Place had done a great business under her direction.

"Well, we're not sure what it is," she replied, reaching for Vivian and helping her through the front door. She looked at Vivian and smiled. "Why don't you come with me, Viv, I'll get you a cup of coffee and Noah can check the attic."

Vivian nodded. "Sounds fine to me."

Noah headed up the winding staircase in the foyer, down the hall, and toward the small passage to the attic.

"There's no bats in this attic," he grumbled, unlatching the door. He pulled down the ladder and went up the narrow steps. When he reached the top rung, he felt around in the darkness for the string and turned on the light. He looked all around the empty attic, listening for whatever Vivian thought she might be hearing. Slowly and carefully he stepped along the rafters. Whatever noise he made should cause any bats to rustle and squeak around, but he heard nothing.

"She's crazy," Noah mumbled, and then he froze in his tracks. He *did* hear a soft squeaking noise coming from the dormer on the south side. He swallowed hard, stepping closer to where he thought the sound was coming from. Kneeling beside the dormer he lifted a piece of insulation for a peek. Nothing. He frowned thoughtfully and listened as the soft squeaking continued. He sighed with relief, realizing the problem. One of the shutters on the dormer had come loose. He opened the window on the dormer for a better look and saw the hinge needed repair.

"I'll have to pick one up in town," he said to himself as he closed the window and went back across the attic. He turned off the light, descended the ladder and closed the door latch.

As he started down the familiar hall he paused to look out the window at the very end facing west. He smiled as he gazed into the hills she loved...*that paned glass was for her....*

The door to the master suite was open and Noah peeked inside, suddenly drawn into the room he'd planned to share with her. Floor to ceiling windows faced the west in this room as well, but the smaller room just adjacent had windows facing the east...*so she wouldn't miss the sunrise if she was with the baby...*

He smiled as he walked through the room, passing the bathroom with the old-fashioned claw-foot tub he thought she might love and then stepping into what was supposed to have been the nursery. Noah frowned. While Vivian had put furniture in the main room, this room was strangely empty. *Well, Vivian's always been eccentric*, he thought.

He walked slowly back through the room, noticing that there wasn't a speck of dust on the light fixtures or even a cobweb in the corner. Vivian's employees took excellent care of the place and Noah was pleased. She had allowed no one to smoke in the house so it smelled only of the pine trees surrounding it.

Noah sighed with a melancholy smile as he left the room and went back down the hall. He laughed at himself as he descended the stairs, heading for the kitchen. *It's far too soon to be making these plans.*

Noah found Vivian perched in some Victorian furniture in the studio just off the kitchen. She was gazing out the paned window facing the west while sipping her coffee. She wore a thoughtful expression.

"I found the problem," Noah said, taking a seat across from her. "There's a shutter that's come loose on the dormer. I'll have to pick up a hinge but I can have it fixed by tomorrow."

Vivian shifted her gaze from the hills to Noah. "Very good." She frowned. "Ya know, Hansen, I always wondered why you built this place," she murmured.

"It was just a little experiment."

Vivian raised one of her penciled eyebrows. "A *little* experiment?" she quipped.

"Well..." Noah sighed with a smile as he looked out the window...*this was supposed to have been Angel's studio...she would have loved the view.*

"I noticed the woodwork had been done by hand," Vivian grumbled. "And after about ten years at the place I figured that you must have intended this house for something other than a bed and breakfast. Why didn't you ever live here, Hansen?"

Noah shrugged. "Guess I just never got around to it, Viv."

"Humph." Vivian set down her cup on the table and reached for Noah's hand. "Help me up, Hansen. It's time for me to go."

Noah got to his feet and helped Vivian out of the chair. They shuffled into the kitchen where Mavis was making a list.

"Hansen says it's just a shutter," Vivian barked at her manager. "He'll be up to fix it tomorrow."

Mavis acknowledged with a smile, "Thanks, Noah. See ya tomorrow."

Noah nodded and he and Vivian went through the foyer and out the front door, where Dan was waiting beside the car.

“I’m getting *old*, Hansen,” Vivian announced as he helped her manage the steps on the porch. “I don’t know how much longer I’ll be able to lease this place from you.”

“Whenever you’re ready to leave it, you just let me know,” Noah said, opening her car door.

Vivian looked at Noah with surprise, pausing before she got into the car. “Would you be willing to let me out of my lease, without all of those penalties Martin wrote in?” she asked.

Noah nodded and smiled. “However you want to do it, Viv. You just let me know.”

Vivian narrowed her eyes with mirth and cackled out a scratchy laugh. “You want the old place back for yourself, don’tcha Hansen.”

“I’m thinkin’ I just might get around to livin’ up here after all, Viv.”

Vivian cackled again and sat down in the car. She looked up at Noah one more time. “Is she nice?”

“She’s wonderful, Viv.”

“She’s not like that dreadful Melinda woman you took up with years ago is she?”

Noah shook his head and chuckled. “She’s not *anything* like Melinda.”

“Well,” Vivian sighed, “you probably never knew this about me, Hansen, but I pray. I’ll pray for you, and this gal.”

“Thanks, Viv.”

Vivian gave Dan a nod and said, “Let’s get out of here, Dan. I’ve got a golf game with my grandson this afternoon.”

“Yes, Ma’am,” Dan said. He closed her car door and hurried over to the driver’s side.

Vivian gave Noah a wave and he smiled and waved back. *Wow,* he thought with a chuckle, *Vivian prays. That’s amazing....*

Chapter 6

As spring turned into summer in the Black Hills, the season's heat forced leaves from their tiny buds. Flowers bloomed in abundance, and Tillie's vegetable garden came to life, even sprouting a few weeds between the rows. She donned her wide-brimmed straw hat and headed out back. Laura soon appeared with her sketch book.

A.J. and his grandfather visited on the front porch as they waited for Noah. The Builders had won all of their games and were well on their way to qualifying for the All-Stars game.

A.J. and Laura were slowly healing from their father's death. Even though they spoke of him often, there weren't as many tears as there were in the beginning. They loved looking at the things Alex left behind and the many photographs that were taken over the years. They spoke of memorable vacations, fondly reminiscing of the time he'd spent with them.

They still preferred staying very close to their mother, especially Laura, unless it was to attend a baseball practice with Guiseppi. In just the few weeks that he'd *joined* the team, Guiseppi had become a legend. The Little League players were very attached to the old man, and Guiseppi was having the time of his life.

"How long will they stay with us?" Laura asked as she sketched her mother beside the garden.

"Nonna says Labor Day," Tillie replied. She sighed as she pulled the weeds. "I wish they could stay forever."

"Me too — hey, Mr. Hansen is here."

Tillie looked up and saw Noah walking into the backyard with two icey glasses of something, and a smile on his face. She smiled in return, wondering why they hadn't left for practice yet. She dusted off her gloved hands and started to get to her feet as Noah approached, but he shook his head.

"No, you don't have to get up," he said, kneeling down to hand them each a glass of iced tea. "Mrs. Caselli told me to bring these out."

"Thanks." Tillie accepted the cold drink and took a couple of good gulps of her favorite orange and spice flavor. "That hits the spot. Guess I was warmer than I realized."

"Mmm," Laura said after taking a drink. "Nonna makes the best tea." She looked curiously at Noah. "Aren't you guys goin' to practice?"

"We're on our way," Noah answered. "I was wondering if we're supposed to pick up Heidi today."

Laura rolled her eyes and giggled. "But it's been so many days in a row now — she didn't want to look too obvious."

Noah raised an eyebrow. "Really now? Why don't you just give her a call? We can be over there in a couple of minutes."

"Okay," Laura said as she got to her feet. She hurried into the house.

Noah took a comfortable seat in the grass across from Tillie and took a ticket out of his shirt pocket. "This is a family pass to the Post 22 games this season," he explained. "I had an extra one and A.J. and your father were interested. Ty will be their starting pitcher and he's pretty excited about that."

"Thanks, Noah. I appreciate that."

He took a deep breath before beginning again, "Listen, Ty's turning sixteen tomorrow, and I know how hard the next few days will be for you."

Tillie swallowed hard, surprised he remembered. Ty was born the day before she and Alex were married. Friday would be their sixteenth wedding anniversary and she was already thinking about it.

"I've been through this myself, you know," Noah said gently. "The first time those dates start rolling around is kind of hard. It goes better if you can find something to do, or spend the time with the kids. I did a lot of hiking with the boys, and stuff like that."

Tillie took a breath and looked into Noah's concerned eyes. The sincerity and goodness she saw in them eighteen years ago was still there. "Thank you for being so kind," she said. "It means a lot to us."

"Sure."

"We'll be there," she promised. "We'll be there for Ty's birthday and to watch him start. He's such a nice boy."

Noah blushed. "Yeah, he really is."

"Where does he get all of that red hair?"

"Carrie had kind of strawberry, blond hair," Noah answered. "He's got her eyes, too."

"Do you still miss her? Can I ask you that?"

"You can ask," Noah answered. "Sometimes I think about her, but she's been gone for so long now, more than twelve years, and Ty hasn't asked about her since he was really little. Jake was only a few months old when it happened and so he never asks about her."

"Is it hard by yourself? You know, with the kids?"

Noah shrugged. "It's not too bad," he answered. He rolled his eyes and smiled. "We probably could have used some feminine influence over the years, but I think for the most part we turned out okay."

Tillie smiled and nodded her head.

"I really need to get going. But we'll see you on Thursday?"

"Yes," Tillie answered. "Can we pick up something for Ty's birthday?"

"Anything with Steve Avery on it."

Tillie nodded with a knowing smile. "Atlanta Braves fan?"

Noah looked surprised.

"Throws left, bats left. Too bad about last year's world series," Tillie went on. "Especially since they had to lose to a team based outside of the United States — first time that's ever happened.

Noah looked surprised again.

Tillie chuckled. "Didn't you know about that?"

Noah nodded. Of course he knew about it. He swallowed and asked, "How'd *you* know about that?"

Tillie smiled. "A.J.'s been obsessed with baseball for quite some time. I just keep track."

Noah smiled and nodded. *Beauty, brains and baseball. She's amazing.*

*****

Over the summer the humidity in Rapid City soared, which was unusual for the Black Hills of South Dakota. The climate normally was much drier and more temperate. The strange swing in the weather pattern caused thunderstorms in abundance, keeping lawns and gardens green and growing — and A.J. and his grandfather cutting the grass.

Tillie's garden came along at a phenomenal rate. While she dug away in her vegetable patch, Laura borrowed one of her old easels.

She set the easel up on the stone patio where she could watch her mother do her gardening.

Laura's first painting was of her mother. She based it on the sketch she had made of Tillie kneeling beside her small garden patch, dressed in her favorite yellow sundress. Her hair was tucked up under her straw hat, with only stray curls dangling from beneath. Laura painted only a side view of Tillie's face, but the likeness in the portrait was amazing. Everyone who saw it knew it was Tillie. Laura named the painting *Thinking*.

A.J., Jake and Ty were forming quite a bond, as they had games nearly every night of the week between the three of them. The two families lived on delicious sandwiches prepared by Rosa, smuggled into the games in her trusty cooler. Occasionally they broke down and had hot dogs or nachos at the concession stands, but those fun snacks didn't agree with Guiseppi, so he put a stop to it.

"Besides," he reasoned, "Good ball players require good food, and if hot dogs and nachos make a body that ill, then we should not eat them!"

Guiseppi was named honorary mascot to the Little League team. Noah gave him his own *COACH* hat, which he wore proudly to each game, including Ty's games at Fitzgerald Stadium. Guiseppi and Joshua were becoming good friends as well. They co-coached Noah's team when Noah was with Ty at his games or practices.

Noah took A.J. and Guiseppi, along with his sons and Joshua and Mona for rides on his pontoon boat on the Pactola Reservoir. They asked Rosa and Tillie to come along, but Tillie declined with a smile.

"No thanks," she said. "I like my cookies right where they are." She was afraid she would lose her balance and get sick in front of everyone on the boat.

As the end of summer approached, Tillie became more and more apprehensive about her parents going home to Sioux Falls. They had been with her all summer, and she knew she couldn't very well ask them to stay any longer. Being without them would be so hard, especially knowing that Alex wouldn't be coming home ever again.

Tillie wanted to move back to Sioux Falls more than ever, but she didn't speak of it to anyone but the Lord. Her brothers weren't able to make their promised trips to Rapid City, and she was more homesick than when she left Sioux Falls in 1986. She tossed around the idea of going to Italy with Marquette and Tara and hiring an American tutor for her children. She knew Petrice would probably oppose.

Even though A.J. and Laura missed their dad, they were recovering from his death better than their mother. They had friends and activities to rely on, but Tillie really had nothing, except for the small garden. She refused to paint, leaving her without a creative outlet once the garden was harvested, and she had decided against going back to church. Save for the associate pastor's one visit, not one of the Martins' professed "friends" had contacted Tillie. As a result, her '*hermitism*,' as Guiseppi had so affectionately referred to it, was a very convenient excuse for her withdrawal.

*****

Noah and his boys gave away all but one of Vanilla's puppies. The last puppy was infinitely different from all of the others. While all of Vanilla's puppies were long-legged and quite large, the last puppy was very short. She developed solid legs and feet that pounded the floor when she ran through the house. Her fur was the same creamy color as Vanilla's, but instead of smooth it was feathery and scruffy around her face and eyes. Sometimes she ran into things because she couldn't see where she was going through all of the fur on her face. Noah said that her feet looked like those of a Clydesdale because of their solid shape and the feathery fur hanging over them.

The puppy had other problems as well. The worst was that she was up between four thirty and five o'clock, every morning, or as Jake had put it, *the pre-crack of dawn*. Jake was convinced that no one in the world, not even his own father, got up that early. She howled and barked insistently from the garage where she and Vanilla slept. Noah or one of his boys would rush out to get her before she awakened the neighborhood. They would bring her into the kitchen where she'd fill up on a giant bowl of Dog Chow while Noah started a pot of coffee.

"So, does the little maniac sleep all day then?" Noah asked as he and the boys sat around the kitchen table at five o'clock one morning.

"Nope," Ty answered, holding his head in his hand. Post 22 had played late the night before because of a rainout and he was exhausted. It was impossible to fall asleep again after the puppy's howling and screeching. "She's up all day, Dad."

"Why doesn't she need to sleep?" Jake moaned, laying his head on the table. "What's *wrong* with that dog."

"I don't know," Noah grumbled. "But if we don't find a home for her pretty soon I'm gonna take her to the pound."

"No, Dad," Ty and Jake said at the same time, looking horrified at their father's suggestion.

"Maybe we can find someone," Ty offered as he looked at the scruffy little puppy, chomping through her morning ritual.

"The neighbors are gonna call the cops one of these days." Noah frowned. "Besides, I'm too old for this nonsense. I need my sleep."

"I'll ask some of the parents on our team," Jake volunteered. "Just give us a couple more weeks."

Noah sighed. If they didn't find someone to take the rotten little thing immediately, he was going to lose his mind.

*****

Ty had practice for the last game of the season. He and Noah went to Fitzgerald Stadium by themselves. Post 22 was scheduled to play Bismarck that evening for the championship title, marking the end of the greatest summer yet in Ty Hansen's life.

Noah watched from the bleachers as his tall and handsome son pitched strike after strike. It amazed Noah how Ty had grown up so quickly. It seemed like only a few weeks ago Ty was a tiny boy, running around with his inflatable bat and ball, trying to coerce anyone into playing with him. Noah smiled and shook his head. Things had really turned around for Ty. Now everyone else was begging *him* to play with *them*!

"Mr. Hansen?" An unfamiliar voice next to Noah drew his attention away from the practice and he looked into the expression of a slender man with blue eyes.

"That's me." Noah half-smiled as he looked at the man's familiar features. He tried not to frown, but he felt as if he knew the man before him. "I'm sorry, but do we know each other?" he asked.

The man nodded and swallowed hard as he took a seat near Noah, explaining, "I never miss a practice. I used to always wait at the park, when your housekeeper would take them out, and I wished that I would have done things differently."

Noah's heart pounded as he recognized the blackguard in the bleachers beside him. He'd all but forgotten the man who'd fathered his oldest son — the man he knew only as Roy Schneider. His half-smile went to a deep scowl.

"What do *you* want?" Noah growled.

"I want to spend some time with my son," he answered.

Noah grabbed a hold of his shirt front. "Well you *can't!*" He snapped. "Ty's *my* son. Carrie put *my* name on the birth certificate!" He let go of him and gave him a shove.

"I made a mistake," Rauwolf continued.

"Well that's just tough, Roy." Noah retorted, remembering their last altercation. Ty was about two or three when Roy had called him a little bastard. "You can't possibly think you can just drop back into the kid's life now. He's sixteen years old."

Rauwolf looked at Noah and took an astonished breath. "You never told him did you?"

"No," Noah scoffed. "Why would I? I'm the only father that he's ever known —"

"But I'm his *real* father —"

"No, you're *not!*" Noah shouted. "I'm the one who raised the boy! You just slept with his mother and then ditched her when she got pregnant! *That* does not make you a father and it doesn't give you the right to mess with his life now!"

"I just want to get to know my son," Rauwolf persisted.

"Well, *that's* not gonna happen. I oughta just beat you to a pulp right here. What on earth gives you the right to come around now?"

"I'm sure that if we had some blood tests done —"

Noah grabbed Rauwolf's shirt front again and growled, "Don't think for a minute you can start something here." He clenched his teeth. "If you're under the impression that you can drag this through court, you'd better be ready for a battle, because I'll fight you with everything I own, and that's quite a bit. And if that's not enough, I'll fight you with everything I know, like a body that's been buried for the last eighteen years." Noah roughly shoved him away, letting go of his shirt.

Rauwolf's eyes were wide as he whispered, "You wouldn't."

"Try me," Noah threatened. He shook his head and frowned. "You don't even know where they put the body, but *I* do, and I'll dig it up the *moment* you go near Ty."

Rauwolf swallowed hard. "Well, maybe we could just tell Ty that I'm an old family friend —"

"No!" Noah barked. "If you want to watch him play ball, that's fine, but don't walk up to him and don't talk to him, or the body comes up and that's final."

With that Noah jumped from his seat on the bleachers and left Rauwolf sitting alone. He didn't look back and he didn't feel guilty. *Roy had his chance,* Noah thought. *When Carrie thought she loved him and would have married him in an instant — the old blackguard didn't do the right thing then, and he's not getting a second chance from me. Ty's mine. It doesn't matter how that happened, just that it did. God gave him to me, and I'm not sharing him with Roy.*

*****

Fitzgerald Stadium was packed that night. The late August weather was warm but the humidity had dropped and it was comfortable in the stands. Guiseppi enjoyed Rosa's sandwiches, but everyone else splurged and went for the hot dogs and nachos at the concession. The Martins as well as the Romanovs were seated with Joshua and Mona and Jake. Jake wanted to be closer to Heidi, but Dmitri took an obvious seat beside his daughter and Laura. Noah paced nervously back and forth near the dugout.

"They're just so delicious, Papa," Tillie said, chomping a mouthful of hot dog. "I couldn't help myself."

"Just wait," Guiseppi warned with a soft frown, "later on tonight, when you are rummaging around for a Rolaid, you will wish that you had listened to your papa."

Tillie giggled and pretended to toast her cherry slushy at him. Guiseppi rolled his eyes and shook his head.

Joshua was worried about Noah as he watched him pace by the dugout. From where they sat, Noah appeared to be just an excited parent, but Joshua knew better. Noah had stopped by the church office after practice and told him that Roy had made an appearance that afternoon.

"I don't see the old blackguard anywhere," Mona whispered to her husband, using the term she'd learned from Rosa over the summer months. Mona had miniature binoculars, as most of the players' families did, so she didn't worry about looking suspicious as she scanned the crowds for the infamous Roy Schneider.

"You look like a spy," Joshua groaned. "Stop that."

"Everyone has binocs, Josh."

"But they look at the *players*, not *into the crowd*."

"Nobody notices," Mona whispered. "Besides, I wanna see the old blackguard if he shows up."

"Noah says he hardly recognized him," Joshua said. "He looked old and sick."

Mona glanced at her husband and replied dryly, "Maybe he died this afternoon, because he's not here."

Joshua chuckled and shook his head. "Here comes Noah. The coach must have finally thrown him out."

"Hello, Noah," Guiseppi happily greeted. "We saved a seat for you."

"Thanks, Mr. Caselli," Noah replied, sitting down in the vacant seat between Guiseppi and Joshua.

"You look a little nervous this evening," Guiseppi said. He gave Noah a reassuring smile. "Do not fret, Ty will be amazing as always."

"Want a hot dog?" Tillie asked, from the other side of her father. "A.J. got some extras."

"I'd love one," he replied, smiling at Tillie.

Tillie passed him the small tray of snacks and Guiseppi frowned. "I wonder if they sell Rolaids at the concession," he murmured.

Noah grinned and said, "This is just the first course, Mr. Caselli. I told Ty I'm taking the whole team over to Shakey's Pizza after the game."

Guiseppi moaned, "You are not getting any younger, Noah Hansen. You need to take better care of yourself."

Noah laughed. "Well, you guys are coming along, aren't you?"

Guiseppi sighed with pretended regret. "I suppose. Pray I live through this extravaganza."

Noah laughed again.

Mona leaned over and whispered to Noah, "I can't see the old blackguard anywhere, and I came early just to look for him. I don't think he's here."

"Good," Noah replied with a nod, and he let himself relax.

Ty threw strike after strike. The crowd from Bismarck 'booed' him regularly when he took the pitcher's mound. Post 22 shut out the team from Bismarck, winning their championship. The entire team and most of their family members assembled at Shakey's Pizza. Ty held ice on his shoulder and forearm, but smiled as he sat at the table with his family and the Martins and the Romanovs. He gracefully accepted compliments from other team members and fans that made it a point to come over and talk to him. He was the life of the party, and Noah forgot his altercation with Roy Schneider.

As the party began to wind down Joshua and Tillie were lured into the arcade with the kids, and Mona and Rosa were deeply engrossed in the finer points of canning and gardening. Noah was bored to tears, but he *hated* video games and pinball machines, so he ordered himself a hot fudge sundae and waited for Guiseppi to finish visiting with Dimitri.

After a few moments Dimitri left and Guiseppi took a seat directly across from Noah. "You have a wonderful family, Noah," he complimented.

"Thanks, Mr. Caselli."

"Your boys are so polite and behave as perfect gentlemen," Guiseppi went on. "Certainly you have done well with them."

Noah smiled and blushed at Guiseppi's kind words.

"Do not be embarrassed, Noah," Guiseppi said with a chuckle. Then he took a breath. "I need somewhat of a favor from you, Noah."

"Anything."

"Next weekend will be the Labor Day holiday and my Rosa and I wish to return to our home. Angel is planning on driving us back, but..." Guiseppi hesitated and took a breath. "But then she will have to return to Rapid City by herself, and I am not comfortable with her traveling back across the state with two children all alone."

Noah understood Guiseppi's request. He wanted Noah to take them *all* to Sioux Falls, and then bring Angel and her children back to Rapid City. "Have you asked Angel about this?" he asked.

Guiseppi shook his head. "I thought I would just spring it on her," he admitted. "Otherwise..." he rolled his eyes. "You know."

Noah took a deep breath. He frowned thoughtfully and replied, "I don't know. I think she needs some more time. It might make her uncomfortable to be with me, *alone*, for six hours."

"I am not asking you to take her on a date, for Pete's sake," Guiseppi scoffed with a smile. "Her brothers think it is a fine idea. Why, Vincenzo has even asked me to invite you to stay on Reata for the weekend. Can you imagine how your sons would enjoy the ranch, not to mention the 32nd Annual Apple Picking Party. Have you ever been to one?"

"No." Noah smiled nervously and shook his head.

"They are very fun," Guiseppi went on. "We have a story telling contest, a pie contest and Old Doria and Georgie make the most delicious sandwiches from fresh roasted meat you will ever taste. I order the *ristorante* closed for the entire day, and all of southeastern South Dakota turns out for the event."

"I don't know." Noah smiled hesitantly. "You know, she and I and our past and everything. I don't want to make her think that I expect anything other than just a friendship. It's only been —"

"Nearly five months. Noah," Guiseppi interrupted. "I truly do not want my daughter traveling alone. Certainly, as a father, you can understand. She has already been through enough this year, and I think she would look forward to your company on the ride back. I know that my sons would love to see you again."

Noah swallowed very hard and looked away.

Guiseppi got the feeling he was getting ready to refuse him...*but why*? He slowly reached for his chest and gave himself a gentle pat. "Oh," he pretended to moan. "I may need a Rolaid. I do not know what I have gotten myself into this evening. I abstained from all bad foods this day."

Noah looked back at Guiseppi and his eyes filled with concern. He reached for the old man's shoulder and asked, "Are you okay, Mr. Caselli?"

Guiseppi nodded. "I think so. Perhaps just a little too much excitement for my old heart this evening." He raised both of his eyebrows and looked seriously at Noah. "I am nearly seventy-seven you know. I should probably be getting home to my bed."

"Do you want me to find Angel?" Noah offered quickly.

Guiseppi nodded. "But do not tell her that I am so tired this night. She will only worry."

"Are you sure?"

"It is already passing." Guiseppi gave his chest another soft pat.

Noah started to get to his feet. "I'll go and find her," he said.

"Oh, Noah," Guiseppi reached for Noah's hand as he looked into his eyes. "About that favor —"

"No problem. I just bought a new Suburban for my business. We'll use that. We can all ride comfortably in it and there'll be plenty of room for our luggage."

"Oh, thank you, Noah."

"I'll go and get Angel and tell her that you need to be getting home."

Guiseppi nodded as he watched Noah hurry toward the arcade. He felt a small measure of guilt for what he'd done to dear Noah, but it could not be helped. He sighed and shook his head. *Sometimes, when a knight allows his gentlemanly qualities to overshadow the needs of a lady's heart, it is the duty of another knight to step in and gently urge him into the right direction. Noah's direction has always been along a path with Angel, and I created an unfortunate detour. Now it is time to help Noah back to where he belongs...and that is with us.*

Chapter 7

Tillie's mouth hung open with surprise.

"That's a great idea, Grandpa!" A.J. exclaimed with delight. "Jake and Ty are gonna love Reata!" He turned quickly toward his mother. "Hey, can I stay on Reata with them?"

Tillie swallowed and slowly nodded her head. "Sure," was all she could say.

"Thanks, Mom. You're the best!" A.J. hugged Tillie and dashed off to his room.

"This will be fun," Laura agreed with a smile as she started for the stairs. "I'm goin' to bed. I'll see everybody in the morning."

When she was alone with her parents, Tillie frowned and turned toward her father. "I think you could have better prepared me for that," she said.

Rosa had been taken by surprise as well, but remained silent.

Guiseppi rolled his eyes. "Preparation for what?" he asked with a scowl. "Certainly you did not expect me to allow you to drive clear across this vast state with my grandchildren *alone?*"

Tillie huffed and shook her head. "Papa, I know what you're trying to do, but it's too soon. It will only confuse the kids —"

"They do not seem at all confused to me," Guiseppi interrupted.

Tillie sighed. "Papa, *please*, we just need some more time."

Guiseppi frowned. "I have made my decision, Angel. You are a grown woman now, so if you want to make other plans I shall stand aside." He hesitantly reached for his chest.

Rosa looked away.

Tillie groaned. “Papa, don’t do that — your plan is fine, I was just a little surprised.”

Guiseppi’s frown melted into a smile. “There. This will be fun. We will make a day of it.”

Tillie nodded as she turned toward the steps. “I’m going to bed. We can talk about this more in the morning.”

“Goodnight my Angel,” Rosa said.

“Goodnight, Ma`ma.”

“I love you my Angel,” Guiseppi said.

“I love you, too, Papa.”

After Tillie rounded the corner at the top of the stairs, Rosa turned toward her husband with a disappointed glare. “That was uncalled for, Guiseppi,” she admonished.

Guiseppi appeared aghast. “But she was about to refuse me!”

“Why do you not just tell her the truth? Tell her of our prayers for Noah since before she met the man.”

“Not yet, Rosa. But when the Lord tells me that the time is right, I will tell her everything.”

Rosa sighed and shook her head. “And when do you suppose that will be?”

“Very soon now, Rosa. Very soon.”

*****

Early Friday morning the Hansens loaded everyone’s luggage into Noah’s new, navy blue Suburban and started for the Eastern part of the state. Guiseppi appointed himself copilot, taking the passenger seat in front.

“Why am I *not* surprised?” Rosa muttered as she crawled into the middle seats with Tillie and Laura.

Laura giggled and whispered, “He really likes to visit with Mr. Hansen, Nonna.”

Guiseppi made them stop several times along the way. He wanted to visit all the tourist traps, like Wall Drug where he tasted and purchased the “most delicious fudge” he’d ever had.

The Pioneer Auto Museum at Murdo advertised on an interstate billboard that Elvis Presley’s motorcycle was on display. They stopped and Guiseppi had his photo taken beside the glass case — and bought a round of ice cream cones at the lunch counter.

It was time for lunch by the time they reached Al’s Oasis on the Missouri River.

“They have sold a cup of coffee for five cents for as long as I can remember,” Guiseppi said as the waitress showed them to their seats. He opened his menu and his eyes lit up. "We *must* have the buffalo burger," he added.

Guiseppi's last hurrah was the corn palace in Mitchell, where he purchased straw cowboy hats for everyone.

"You will need one beneath the hot sun on Reata," he said.

Noah's boys, along with A.J. and Laura, posed in front of the world's oldest corn palace. Guiseppi took their photograph.

"Now you look like *real* South Dakota farmers in your smart hats," he said with a satisfied smile.

Noah's boys and A.J. and Laura chuckled.

"Your Grandpa's *the best*," Jake whispered.

The six hour drive turned into a ten hour journey. Shortly before the supper hour, Noah pulled into Guiseppi and Rosa's driveway in Sioux Falls. Marquette and Tara were waiting on the front porch and they hurried to the vehicle to greet everyone.

"Papa had to make a thousand stops," Tillie whispered as her brother embraced her and kissed her cheek. "I didn't think we were *ever* going to make it."

As Marquette smiled into his sister's eyes he noticed the drastic change in her expression. He hadn't seen her since her birthday, nearly three months ago, and while she looked very tired from the long and drawn out trip, there was something intensely different about her.

"Angel, you look so beautiful!" he exclaimed. "Have you put on some weight?"

Tillie smiled and shrugged. "Maybe."

Noah and Tillie's children laughed as they told their own versions of the ten-hour adventure Guiseppi had led across the state. While they visited, they quickly ate the sandwiches Tara had prepared before Noah and his boys, along with A.J., headed for Reata.

"Thanks, Noah," Tillie said with a tired smile as they stood beside his Suburban in her parents' driveway. "Thanks for giving Papa such a wonderful day. He loves to do things like this."

"It was fun," Noah replied. "He's really a great guy."

"Yes, he really is," she agreed.

"So, what time are you guys coming tomorrow?"

"Probably early," Tillie answered. "I promised the ladies I'd help. It's quite an event; just wait until you see everything. You'll be glad you came, and you probably won't want to ever miss another one."

Noah nodded, wanting to linger for a moment longer with her in the relaxed silence of the moment, but unable to think of anything else to say. "Well, I'll see ya tomorrow," he stammered.

Tillie nodded and backed away.

Noah got into his vehicle, the boys waved from inside, and Tillie waved in return.

Marquette, Tara, Rosa and Guiseppi watched the sweet farewell from the front porch.

Marquette nodded with a smile. "Excellent, Papa. Things seem to be coming along rather well."

Guiseppi nodded.

"When will you tell her, Papa?" Tara whispered.

"Very soon now. Very soon."

"Mark my words," Rosa interjected, "by this time next year, Noah and Angel will be making this trip as a family."

*****

Petrice and his family were also staying with Vincenzo. Kate assured them that there was plenty of room, especially if the boys were allowed to camp out in the loft. Bright and early, Noah and Petrice arose with Vincenzo and Angelo to help finish chores before the festivities of the day began.

"Now, we all have certain duties this day," Vincenzo instructed as the four of them trudged toward the main house as the sun rose. The chores were finished and Kate had sent a hand out to retrieve them for their breakfast.

"I'm keeping track of the water barrels," Angelo said.

"And we must be sure to assign a hand to that hog confinement," Vincenzo said. "I have several very ill-tempered mama sows and we do not want anyone wandering in and getting attacked."

"I'll send Tracey over," Angelo said.

"Patty, you will collect the money at the gate." Vincenzo smiled at his brother. "Because it is so fun for the community to see Senator Caselli when they arrive."

"Yes, my brother."

"I will have Marquette serve the cake this year because Angel has been stuck there for several years in a row now." Vincenzo smiled at Noah. "And you may carry things for the ladies."

"Carry things?" Noah raised an eyebrow.

"Yes," Vincenzo affirmed. "They prepare things from the kitchen, and they need someone to take them out to the party — someone with stamina and endurance."

"By the way, Vincenzo," Petrice began, "have you told Angel of her surprise yet?"

Vincenzo shook his head and smiled. "I thought it would be more fun if we saved it until she finally gets here."

"What's goin' on?" Angelo asked.

"We have invited Ginger and she arrived a few days ago," Vincenzo replied. He sighed with a smile. "We thought it might help to distract her a little."

"Who's Ginger?" Noah asked.

"She has been Angel's best friend since they were born," Petrice answered.

"Through thick and thin," Vincenzo added.

"Ginger and her husband moved to Las Vegas in 1980," Petrice said. "However, she and Angel have always stayed in touch. Ginger was not able to make it for Alex's funeral because she was about to give birth to her fourth child."

"It will surprise Angel to no end," Vincenzo chortled. "And it will be good for her."

*****

Since September of 1962 Vincenzo and Kate had hosted Reata's Annual Apple Picking Party. This year would make the thirty-second time the event had been scheduled. Preparations proceeded as they always had.

Rosa, Kate, Alyssa, and Barbara, the foreman's wife, prepared homemade buns for Old Doria's and Georgie's roasted meat sandwiches. They baked nearly one hundred apple pies, and Kate was impressed with the skills of her Harvard daughter. She lovingly joked that if she ever changed her mind about a legal career she could take up pie making.

Diane Engleson, Ginger and Andy's mother, along with Frances Martin, had always prepared the famous chocolate sheet cakes, but Diane and Ginger prepared them alone this year.

Old Doria and Georgie made huge tubs of their traditional coleslaw, and great roasters filled with baked beans. They came early in the morning, shortly after sunrise, and began the fire in the pit out by the barn. They put on two hogs and a side of beef for the meat sandwiches.

The traditional story telling contest for the gentlemen and a pie contest for the women were still among the favorite activities. Alyssa and Angelo offered short pony rides to the little children, and this year, Laura and Gabriella were assigned to help families with small children find places to sit and eat.

In 1962 the entrance fee into Reata was fifty cents, and each family could have all of the apples they could carry out of the orchard. In 1970 Vincenzo raised the fee to two dollars, and in 1990 he raised it to three dollars. No one balked a bit at the higher price, still considering it the best deal in the state. Reata's entire orchard was opened for everyone, except for the special place beneath some smaller trees on the west end. That place was carefully roped off and no one was allowed there, for that was where Uncle Angelo and Aunt Penny rested.

Hundreds of apple pickers from Centerville, SD, and the surrounding counties descended upon the ranch. Two young hands were mounted on prancing geldings at Reata's entrance gate, directing the large amount of traffic winding its way in and out of the ranch.

Noah looked around at the hundreds of buzzing people and was overwhelmed with the event at hand. His own boys fit in like they had done it for years, enjoying the many festivities with A.J. and Laura's cousins. Marquette was serving the cake, while Old Doria and Georgie worked their faithful post at the pit. Guiseppi and Rosa stood nearby awaiting their signal that all was ready.

Noah saw Tillie and Ginger laughing and visiting beneath a tree near the main house and he had to smile. They cried and cried when they first saw each other, and then they started to laugh and share stories. Tillie was gently rocking Ginger's new baby in her arms, cooing and smiling. Ginger had four children and had announced that she was pregnant again. Noah saw the fleeting look of disappointment in Tillie's eyes when Ginger made her announcement. She quickly smiled it away to congratulate her friend. It was obvious that Tillie would like to have had more children, but, for now, she seemed content to just hold Ginger's new baby.

Tillie happened to look up and catch Noah's glance. At first, he was embarrassed, but she smiled and waved him to come over.

"Do you remember Ginger?" she asked.

Noah stretched out his hand and smiled. "Of course I remember you. You were the dancer."

"Yes," Ginger answered. "Well, I don't dance so much anymore. And you are Noah?"

Noah nodded.

"Wow," Ginger went on with a dreamy look in her eyes. "That was the *best* trip we ever took, wasn't it Tillie?"

Tillie couldn't help but smile as she replied, "Remember how drunk Melissa and Sara got?"

"Oh, my goodness." Ginger rolled her eyes and shook her head. "Tillie was so mean to them the next morning."

"I can't imagine Tillie having a mean bone in her body," Noah said.

"Oh, she was mean all right," Ginger affirmed. "They were so hung over and Tillie didn't pity them one bit."

Tillie laughed. "I was so mad at those two. Just think, we had to go and fish 'em out of the bar. I was scared to death."

"Remember," Ginger went on, "you had to smack that guy in the face?" She looked playfully suspicious at Noah. "Wasn't he your friend or something?"

"Well…" Noah hesitated, clearly caught off-guard. He blushed with embarrassment. "He was *sort* of a friend. He's *not a friend anymore*. In fact, I haven't seen him since he went to the pen."

"He went to the pen?" Tillie gasped. "What for?"

"Robbery I think."

"Betchyer glad you quit bein' *his* friend," Ginger said.

Noah started to say something, when Elaine called him from the front porch. "Gotta go," he said with a smile. "My job is carrying things out for the ladies."

"And I'm supposed to be helping them," Tillie said with a mischievous look in her eyes. "Tell Kate I'll be right in."

"Okay." Noah smiled again at Tillie, then he looked at Ginger. "Good to see you again."

"You too." Ginger smiled in return, and Noah hurried into the house.

"Wow," Ginger mused as she watched him trot up to the porch, "he's still quite a looker."

"Ginger!" Tillie admonished with a giggle — it was as if they were in high school again.

"Oh, come on." Ginger rolled her eyes. "He *has* aged rather nicely, don'tcha think? I mean, whew! All those muscles and almost *no* gray. He's a *hottie*."

Tillie laughed. "He's really been good to my kids, and Papa."

"I'll bet," Ginger said with a sly grin.

Tillie shook her head and tried to force her smile away. "Don't think like that, Ging."

"Like what?"

"Like, *you know*. It's too soon. I still really miss Alex a lot and I don't want to hurt Noah again."

Ginger nodded. "I understand. I'm sorry."

"It's okay." Tillie sighed with a faint smile. "Maybe someday…I don't know."

"Oh, *definitely*, someday," Ginger stated with certainty. "You were *so crazy* about him. Remember?"

Tillie nodded. "How could I ever forget?"

Old Doria had worked for Uncle Angelo since *before* the Casellis arrived in America, and no one was ever quite sure of his age. Georgie came along in December of 1956 and became his assistant. Georgie was now in his mid-sixties, but it was assumed that Old Doria was even older than Guiseppi. However, Doria declined to retire and continued to work in Guiseppi's restaurant, even after Guiseppi left in 1987. And he still made it out to Reata every year to prepare the traditional roasted meat sandwiches.

Smoke billowed from the great fire below the pit. While Doria and Georgie sliced and frowned, Guiseppi and Rosa worked beside them. They handed the sliced buns to the cooks and then passed them out to the eager people waiting in line. As usual, Doria grumbled incessantly, which entertained Rosa and Guiseppi to no end, and they laughed heartily as they worked.

"That is the gay cook I was telling you about," Marquette whispered to Noah as they waited in line for a sandwich. Noah nodded, and Marquette continued, "He was saved in 1986, and apparently has not seen a man in several years, according to Vincenzo." He laughed and shook his head. "I tried to save him myself once. I set up this young lady I found in a grocery store. Long, beautiful legs, perfectly red lips, hair as black as could be. I thought she could pull it off, but…they were already acquainted."

Noah laughed at Marquette's story. "When was that?"

"Oh, years ago, now, before I found Tara. Let me think…it was Vincenzo's big Spring Celebration. Patty and Angel had recently survived the measles and I had gone to Baltimore on my *first* case. Hmm, when was that?" He looked thoughtfully at Noah. "Did I do that in 1960?"

"I don't know," Noah chuckled.

Marquette smiled and nodded as he recalled, "Yes, it was 1960…a kidnapping." His eyes narrowed. "And that was the same year I met Luigi Andreotti in Chicago. Just think, Noah, he had Tara with him that night at the theater and would not tell me."

"What a blackguard." Noah shook his head. He had heard the story many times from Marquette. Tara D`Annenci and Marquette had been friends from the time of their birth in the same valley in *Italia*, and were tragically separated during their fifteenth year when the Casellis moved to America. Tara's family was killed in a train crash in Rome just a few days later and it was assumed she'd died along with them. However, twelve years later, Marquette unraveled the greatest mystery of his lifetime and found her, alive and well, living with her aunt and uncle in Chicago.

Old 'friends' from *Italia*, Luigi Andreotti and his father, conspired to hide the truth from Marquette in order that Luigi might have Tara às his bride. They hid Marquette's location from Tara, but the Lord Himself saw to it their plans be foiled. Marquette and Tara married less than two weeks after he found her,

"I cannot believe I was so deceived," Marquette said.

Noah looked curious. "So, have you always solved all of your cases?" he asked.

Marquette narrowed his eyes and replied, "There is one that eludes me still.

"Really? A new one?"

Marquette shook his head. "One of my *oldest*. A very notorious crime family escaped Italian and Sicilian authorities in 1964, and has managed to hide even from me. I chased them as far as Rapid City in 1975, then caught a lead in Wyoming in 1980, but everything dried up after that."

"Who are they?"

"The most powerful Mafia family in Sicily," Marquette answered. "And with the help of a murderous German blackguard, two of their members, a father and his son, escaped the family in 1964, which was four years before I even began my search. However, I led the capture of more than thirty of them in August of 1968. One of them committed suicide that day, and the old patriarch cursed me." He chuckled. "Apparently, the curse did not take because it was only a few days after that that I found my dear Tara." He sighed with sadness. "And in 1975, the German murdered my dear friend and associate, Jon Peters. I did catch up to him in 1980 but was forced to let him go. I have not seen him since."

"Do you think you'll ever find any of them?"

"Perhaps," Marquette answered. "I pray about it every day, and, if God is willing, He will lead me to them."

Vincenzo and Petrice watched their sister visit with Sam under the tree. She was wearing a pink, western cut blouse, and her curly hair was in a messy ponytail behind her head. Loose curls were flying all around in the humidity and the wind.

"She looks like Angel again," Petrice said with a thoughtful frown. "She is still very sad, but she looks like Angel again."

Vincenzo bit his lip, hesitating, and then finally said, "And she walks differently. Did you notice that Patty?"

He nodded. "And she looks younger, but that is not possible."

Vincenzo shrugged. "How long has Alex been gone?"

"Nearly five months."

Vincenzo nodded again. "And I have not seen her wear that particular color in many years. Did it not used to be her favorite?"

Petrice hesitated, took a deep breath, and then he said, "I want to say something, Vincenzo, but I am afraid I will be misunderstood."

"I know what you want to say. We were all so uncomfortable these past years whenever Alex was around. We should have let the thing go, because it made Angel uncomfortable as well —"

"She is the one who made the decision to take him back," Petrice reminded him. "Even after all of those horrible things he did to her, and knowing how he accused Marquette, how could we *not* forget that?" Petrice frowned, "No, Vincenzo, *we* did not cause the discomfort. That is something Alex did —"

"But he was the brother of my wife. Perhaps we should have tried harder for Angel."

"Maybe this and maybe that," Petrice replied. "We cannot go back and second guess ourselves now. What is done is done."

Tillie went into the main house to help with further preparations. She and her sisters-in-law talked and laughed as they remembered the past Apple Picking Parties.

"There were always baby pigs in the barn," Tillie said, slicing buns for Kate.

"We have a hog confinement now," Kate said, stirring another pitcher of lemonade.

"The boys wouldn't be able to sleep in the barn if there were pigs in there," Elaine chuckled, and the other ladies laughed as well.

"Hey." Kate turned from her duties with a smile. "I've got a ton of photographs upstairs. Should we drag 'em down?"

"I can get them," Tillie offered. "I'm done with this tray anyway."

"They're up in your room," Kate said. "Toward the back of the closet — middle shelf I think."

Tillie left the kitchen, hurried upstairs and down the hall to the room she stayed in every time she came to Reata. The door was open, and she saw one of Petrice's hats on the old radiator.

She made her way to the closet, opened the door and pulled the familiar string. Old boxes and large, plastic bins were stacked neatly on the shelves. She spied the photograph albums on the second shelf in the back. Reaching for one of the albums, a familiar object caught her eye and she saw the old camera that had been missing for many years now. It was her most prized possession at one time.

Tillie picked up the dusty old camera and looked it over. *It's was probably still full of film,* she thought. *I remember leaving it behind on that horrible Thanksgiving in 1986...the one Alex decided not to show for.*

"I wonder what's in here?" she whispered. She bit her lower lip as she looked at the camera, wondering if any of the photographs inside could be developed...*but it's been nearly seven years....*

She reached for the photo albums and placed the camera on top of them.

Kate recognized the old camera on the top of the stack when Tillie returned to the kitchen."What else did you find?" she asked.

"Papa's old camera," Tillie answered. "There's still film in it."

"You used to develop the film yourself," Tara reminded as she walked over and looked at the camera. "Remember?"

"I had my own lab in the basement."

Kate raised an eyebrow mysteriously. "It would be interesting to see what comes out of there," she said.

*****

The meat sandwiches were gone and the water barrels drained. Not a single crumb of chocolate cake or apple pie remained, nor were there any baked beans or coleslaw. All of the apple pickers had gone home and Vincenzo's family and his hands cleaned up the mess.

"Only a few trees left to harvest," Vincenzo remarked as he and his brothers and his sister stood by themselves. He smiled at that, for it was not very often when it was just the four of them together.

"There were a lot more people this year," Tillie commented. "I think it's growing again."

"Probably the holiday weekend," Marquette offered. "There were perhaps more families visiting one another."

"When are you going back to Rapid City, Angel," Petrice asked.

"I guess we're driving back tomorrow," Tillie answered with a downcast expression. "School starts on Tuesday and I need to get a few things together for the kids."

Vincenzo put his arm around her and gave her a soft kiss on the top of her head. "How are you doing, Angel? We have not had a moment to visit since you arrived."

"Good. But it's still so strange without him."

Her brothers nodded.

"So, when will any of you be able to come out?" she asked.

They all inhaled deeply at the same time.

Tillie frowned at the three of them. "What's *that* supposed to mean?"

"I can make a trip in a month or so," Marquette answered quickly.

"I will be tied up until Thanksgiving," Petrice said.

"As will I," Vincenzo said. "I am adding to my herd again and really need to be here for the changes that are taking place."

Tillie shook her head. "Well, whatever," she muttered.

"Oh, come now, Angel," Vincenzo said, holding her close and giving her another kiss. "Do not be so hard on us."

"Well, I'm sure if I told you that I wanted to move closer to my family, you'd throw a fit," Tillie snapped.

"Tara and I will be out in October," Marquette offered. "You have my word."

"And what about Thanksgiving?" Tillie's eyes filled with tears. "What's happening for the holidays? Am I expected to just sit out there and watch 'em roll in? Because I don't want to. I know you guys didn't care much for Alex, but I loved him and I miss him."

"We understand," Petrice said, gently reaching for her hand and giving it a tender kiss. "I can make more of an effort. Let me check my calendar and then I will call with some plans. Okay?"

"Okay," Tillie relented. She laid her head against Vincenzo's chest and let her tears spill. "But I don't wanna go back without Ma`ma and Papa," she whispered.

"It will be all right," Vincenzo said, holding her close, wishing this hadn't happened to his little sister. Petrice quickly offered his handkerchief and she dried her tears as she looked around at them.

"I s'pose you expect me to just take it like a man or something," she grumbled.

"No, please do not do that," Petrice said with a smile. "You are far more graceful about the whole thing than I would have been."

"Yes," Vincenzo added, "By now, I would have kicked in several doors and done other destructive things."

"You, on the other hand," Marquette said, "have behaved as the perfect jewel you have always been. You are a faultless mother and have done everything that you can to help your babies through this time."

"We are very proud of you, Angel," Vincenzo said. "And we know that you will survive this —"

"Whether or not you want to," Petrice interjected.

Noah saw the four of them together and was pulled in their direction.

"Can I interrupt?" he asked politely.

"Of course," Marquette said, slapping his back. "What is up, Noah?"

"Hey," Noah began, looking at Tillie, "Laura was wondering if she could stay out here with Gabriella tonight. Is that okay?"

"Sure," Tillie answered. "We probably won't be seeing them again for a little while."

"We don't have to leave tomorrow," Noah offered kindly. "I can stay over another day if you need to."

Tillie sighed with a soft smile. "I just can't. I've got too many things to get ready for the kids…and didn't Jake say he needed a new backpack?"

"Oh, yeah," Noah remembered. "I almost forgot." He smiled at Vincenzo. "I guess I was having such a good time on the ranch that I forgot about my *real* life."

Tillie and her brothers laughed. Reata always made them feel that way.

"You should see it in the snow," Tillie said, and then her eyes looked surprised. "Well, maybe you will. I found my old camera here this afternoon and the last pictures I remember taking were during a heavy snow fall."

"Do you think they can still be developed?" Vincenzo asked.

"Won't know until I try," Tillie answered. "We have a specialty photo shop in Rapid City. I'll take it to them."

"Well," Marquette said with a yawn, "let us collect our parents and my wife. I have to go to bed." He smiled at Noah. "What time do you expect to be back in Sioux Falls?"

Noah shrugged and looked at Tillie. "What time do you guys get up?"

"She gets up before the sun," Petrice teased with a smile. "And no one will be ready *that* early."

Vincenzo laughed and looked at Tillie. "Why do you not let Noah and the children have breakfast here, and then we will send them up before noon. That way they do not have to be so rushed and you can still make it home by suppertime. Would that be all right?"

"Fine," Tillie agreed with a smile.

Noah nodded in agreement as well, but Petrice's comment continued to play over and over again in his mind... *"she gets up before the sun." ... Why didn't I think of that before?*

*****

It was nearly ten o'clock before Marquette pulled Guiseppi's Suburban into the driveway in Sioux Falls. The five of them made their way into the house.

"I need something cold to drink," Tillie said, setting her old camera down on one of the kitchen counters. She opened the door of the refrigerator.

"Marquette and I did do some shopping yesterday," Tara said, taking a seat on a kitchen chair. She reached behind her and pulled open the patio door. "It is hotter than Hades in this house. Rosa, did we forget to turn on the air conditioner?"

"Yes," Rosa yawned. "We were in such a hurry this morning."

"Ah ha." Tillie pulled out a bottle of club soda and a lemon. "My fave. Who wants one?"

"Oh, me for certain," Tara said.

"None for me." Marquette yawned, heading for the steps. "I will be sleeping in a few moments so try to keep your cackling to a minimum."

Tillie and Tara laughed.

"Do not stay up too late, Angel. You have a long trip tomorrow," Rosa reminded.

"Okay, Ma`ma," Tillie answered, searching through the drawer for a knife to cut the lemon.

Rosa followed Marquette up the steps, and only Guiseppi remained.

"How about a club soda with lemon, Papa?" Tillie offered her father.

"No, my Angel. I think I will be going to bed myself." He kissed her cheek and proceeded toward the steps.

"Goodnight, Papa."

"Goodnight, my Angel. Goodnight, dear Tara."

Tillie put ice into the glasses, squeezed lemon wedges over the cubes and added the refreshing club soda. She set a glass before Tara and seated herself across from her favorite sister-in-law.

"What a day!" she quietly exclaimed. "I don't think there have ever been that many people on Reata."

"I agree." Tara took a sip of the cool drink. "Mmm, Angel, this hits the spot."

Tillie took a sip and nodded in agreement. “Didn’t Ging look great?”

“Beautiful as ever. And what of all those babies? Does she have plans to stop anytime soon?”

Tillie grinned. “She says that this will be the last pregnancy. She’s almost thirty-six you know.”

“Ma`ma’s age when you were born.”

“You should have seen the look on her face when she saw that Noah was there. Tillie smiled wistfully. “She can’t believe he’s still in my life…” She hesitated and bit her lip. “And neither can I.” She shrugged and looked away, her eyes falling on the old camera.

Tara followed Tillie’s gaze and smiled at an old memory. “You took pictures of Noah with that very camera,” she said.

Tillie nodded and whispered, “I remember the last pictures I took with it. Wonder if they’ll turn out.” She frowned thoughtfully. “And I’m having the strangest compulsion to go down and look around in my old developing lab.” She chuckled at herself. “I don’t know what my problem is. There are no chemicals down there anymore. It’s not like I could develop anything tonight. But...” She shook her head and smiled faintly. “I haven’t been down there since I developed those photos of Noah eighteen years ago.”

“Really? I did not know that.”

“Come on,” Tillie said, getting to her feet. “I’ve gotta go down there. I can’t help it.”

“Angel,” Tara whispered with a smile, getting to her feet. “There won’t be anything down there anymore.”

“I know. I’m just having the oddest feeling. I *have* to go look.”

“Okay.” Tara followed her sister-in-law into the basement and to the door of her old developing lab.

Tillie opened the door and flicked on the light. They looked around the small empty room, noticing that the old tables Tillie had used were still in place. The pans had long been removed, but the wire line was still hanging just above them.

“How many photographs did I hang on that line?” she said with a melancholy smile.

“Thousands,” Tara replied, venturing further into the unused room. “I cannot believe the regular light still works.”

“Yeah...weird,” Tillie muttered. “Maybe Ma`ma and Papa use the room for storage or something.” And that’s when she noticed the large sheet-covered frames in the corner. Near them was a covered shoe box.

"What is that?" Tara asked as they moved at the same time toward the mysterious objects.

"Looks like some old canvases," Tillie said, kneeling down. She lifted the corner of the sheet.

"Tara!" she gasped. She sat down hard on the concrete floor, pulling the sheet from the old painting.

"Angel!" Tara exclaimed, sitting down beside her sister-in-law. She stared at the old painting of Noah beside Bridal Veil Falls.

"I'm fainting," Tillie whispered, reeling backwards from the anxious pounding in her chest. Trembling took over her entire body. "I see a painting of Noah…this is not here…I'm hallucinating. Help me, Tara. I must be finally losing it."

Tara put her arm around Tillie. "It is *real,* Angel," she said. "But where did it come from?"

"They told me they threw them away when I married Alex," Tillie said. She impulsively pulled the sheet from what she knew would be the other one. She gasped again. "They're both here. Why did they keep them —"

"Because they were your *best* work," Guiseppi's voice suddenly interrupted them, and they jumped.

He attempted a faint smile as he looked into their astonished expressions. "I thought perhaps I heard mice down here," he teased.

"Papa," Tillie whispered with wide-open eyes. "Why?"

Guiseppi took a shallow breath and said, "Tara, please allow me a moment with my daughter?"

"Of course," Tara whispered. She staggered to her feet and left the two of them alone.

Tillie could only stare at her old father. As he walked to where she sat on the concrete floor, she noticed that he was holding her mother's Bible. Two folding chairs were propped against the wall nearby. Guiseppi opened one for Tillie, and the other for himself.

"Have a seat my Angel," he offered.

Tillie nodded, standing up. She sat down on the chair and looked at her father. "Papa," she whispered. She had no voice. She could only stare with confused eyes at her father.

Guiseppi sat down beside her. "Angel," he said, taking her hand into his own. "Ma`ma and I could never part with them, for you see, we had a secret." His eyes filled with tears, but he swallowed hard and began again, "And I have regretted keeping it from you for many years." He kissed her hand and put it upon his knee. He opened Rosa's Bible, pulling out the old photographs. He handed them to Tillie.

"You took only one of those photographs. The other was taken by Joshua in the summer of '72."

Tillie looked at the photographs. She remembered the one taken in Maggie's bar in 1975, but she'd never seen the one of Noah with his motorcycle.

"But we knew about Noah *long* before that," Guiseppi continued. He held the open pages of the Bible before Tillie so that she could see the faded ink written in the margin.

"Twenty-one, twelve, sixty. Noah," Tillie read aloud. She looked at her father. "But, how?"

"Frances Martin's brother, Uncle Mac. He was friends with Joshua for many years, and on that date in 1960, he told us of a little boy struggling with the death of his parents and the authority of his older brother. Your Ma`ma made a commitment to pray for him and has diligently done so for more than thirty years." Guiseppi's tears fell from his eyes as he looked at his daughter. "It was no accident that you met him, Angel."

"Why didn't you tell me?" she whispered in astonishment.

"Many reasons, and none of them were right. You had been so desperately hurt and I was unwilling to risk your tender heart again. I feared, at first, that Noah was truly a blackguard and that if I sought him out for an explanation there was the possibility of making you hurt even more. It wasn't until you were graduating from college, and had been married nearly three years, that I met Noah and had the opportunity for a conversation with Uncle Mac. It was then that I realized Noah's true nature. I was heartsick over what I had done, and have remained stricken since that day."

"But, Papa," Tillie whispered with disbelief, "didn't it ever dawn on you that you had prayed for this man for fifteen years before I *accidentally* ran into him?"

"Of course it *dawned* on me," Guiseppi admitted as he swallowed hard, more tears spilling upon his cheeks. "Angel, I made a disobedient and reckless decision and I am more sorry than you can ever know. Please forgive me."

"Oh, Papa," Tillie cried, putting her arms around his neck.

Guiseppi took his daughter into his arms and held her close.

"It's not your fault," she whispered. "Please don't blame yourself. You've always been so good to me and I love you so much."

"I could have never guessed in a million years that things would happen the way that they have," Guiseppi said through his tears. "And you should know that your brothers all know, and that…" he hesitated for the longest moment.

Tillie lifted her head from his shoulder to look into his eyes. "Know what, Papa?" she asked.

"I told Noah. While you were having your surgery and we feared that you were dying. I told him everything. He loved you so much and I felt he deserved to at least know before you died."

Tillie stared at her father. "Wow. Why didn't you tell me then?"

"I was afraid to confuse you. I was not sure what you remembered and things were so terrible with Alex." He sighed heavily. "I have been such an old fool —"

"Oh, no, Papa," Tillie interrupted with a smile. She touched the tears on her father's face and looked into his eyes. "You've *never* been a fool and I will not allow you to speak of my father in such a way." She looked back at the paintings and glanced at the old shoe box next to them. "I can just about imagine what's in there." She picked it up and hesitantly lifted the lid, smiling with melancholy delight as she looked inside. They were there, all of the photos she'd taken of Noah and the beautiful Black Hills during their brief romance eighteen years ago.

"Is it all right that I have told you?" Guiseppi asked.

Tillie smiled into his eyes. "Yes, Papa. Thank you."

Chapter 8

The next morning Tillie wrapped her old paintings in brown packaging paper. "Are you sure it's okay that I take them?" she asked, as her parents watched the beloved paintings prepare for departure.

They nodded sadly, trying to offer their daughter smiles at the same time.

"They have always belonged to you, Angel," Rosa said.

"I can't believe you saved them," Tillie said, looking at her parents. "But I'm so glad you did." They nodded and Tillie saw tears in their eyes. She put her arms around them, and their arms folded over her. "I'll miss you so much," she whispered. "Do I really have to go back?"

"Yes," Guiseppi chuckled, sniffing away some of his tears. He looked into his daughter's eyes and promised, "A wonderful adventure has yet to begin for you."

Rosa looked at her daughter and asked, "Angel, will you look at him differently now?"

Tillie raised an eyebrow with a smile and asked, "Really, Ma`ma, how could I not?"

"Do not be afraid of whatever begins," Guiseppi said. "God watches over you, Angel. He always has."

Marquette came down the stairs with Tillie's luggage and set it in the foyer. "Is this all you have, Angel? Besides the paintings?" he asked.

"That's it," she answered.

"Noah and the children should be here shortly," he said. He took his sister into his arms. "It will all be fine," he reassured. "Do not be afraid; just believe. Jesus goes with you always."

"I know, Marq," Tillie replied, looking up into his eyes, "but it's all *so strange* now."

"Perhaps," Marquette acknowledged with a smile. "And even I am sometimes confused and afraid when God sends me onto a new path. But you must never forget that He has ordained each one of our days before we even live them. He knows what He is doing…as well as what *you* are doing."

Tara came down the steps and stood beside her husband and Tillie. She smiled at Tillie, then looked at Guiseppi and Rosa. "I am very happy this day. It is a great burden that has been lifted from my heart," she said.

"Ours as well," Guiseppi agreed.

"Will you think about your painting?" Rosa asked, looking at her daughter with hope in her eyes.

"Maybe," Tillie answered. "I'll see what happens."

From where they stood they saw Noah's Suburban pull into the driveway. Tillie suddenly caught her breath.

"It will be all right, Angel," Marquette encouraged.

Tillie took a deep breath, reaching for her brother's hand. "I don't know what to do."

"Wait on the Lord and be of good courage," Guiseppi said with a smile, his black eyes suddenly filling with tears. "This time will be different. *I promise*."

"Okay, Papa," Tillie said as she watched Noah and all of their children pile out of the vehicle, laughing and talking on their way up to the door.

"Dry up, Guiseppi," Rosa whispered. She pulled his handkerchief out of his back pocket and handed it to him. "We do not want him to think that anything is wrong." Guiseppi nodded, laughing at himself. He took the handkerchief and quickly dried his tears.

"Get the door, Marquette," Rosa instructed, and she looked at Tillie who was still looking a little frantic. "What will you tell him about the paintings?"

"Nothing yet," she answered. "Hopefully there will be enough room."

Marquette opened the door and Guiseppi and Rosa's foyer quickly filled. Everyone hurried to greet them, embracing all of the children and giving them kisses.

"You are such a handsome little fellow," Rosa said, kissing Jake, who blushed. "You look just like your father!"

"And you are wonderfully tall," Guiseppi observed as he looked up at a very embarrassed Ty.

"We're really gonna miss you now," Laura said as she hung onto her grandmother. "When can you come out for a visit?"

"I do not know, my sweet Laura," Rosa replied. "Perhaps at Thanksgiving?"

"That's more than two months away," Laura pouted.

Rosa laughed as she held the little girl in her arms. She gave her a kiss on the top of her head. "Tell you what, my little Laura, you draw and paint me some things to look at, and work on that mother of yours to do something as well. That will keep you busy while I am away. Can you do that for me?"

Laura nodded.

"I'm gonna miss you, Grandpa," A.J. said, holding his grandfather in his arms one last time. "I can't wait until you come back."

"Me too," Jake added. His dancing, blue eyes filled with tears. "Are you coming for baseball next spring?"

Guiseppi pretended to scoff, "You do not want such an old devil in your way." Then he raised an old, black eyebrow with hope. "Do you?"

"Yes," they answered at the same time.

"Okay, everybody," Noah announced. "We gotta get going if we're gonna make it back by suppertime."

Everyone moaned in objection, but Guiseppi and Rosa coaxed them out through the front door. They followed along behind, giving last minute kisses and hugs. Tillie and Marquette retrieved the two paintings from the kitchen table, then followed the meandering crowd outside.

"What's that?" Noah asked when he saw them with the wrapped paintings.

"Just some old stuff," Tillie answered with a soft smile. "Is there room to take them back?"

"I think so." Noah scratched his chin. "We can put 'em in the back."

"Great," Tillie said, and Noah and Marquette took the paintings to the back of the Suburban where they opened the cargo doors and began to figure out a way to fit everything in.

"All right!" Guiseppi said with as much enthusiasm as he could muster, clapping his hands together. "Everybody in!" The children had more last minute hugs and kisses as they reluctantly said goodbye and got into the back of the vehicle.

"Be good," Guiseppi instructed, wagging his index finger. "And do not beg for candy when Noah stops for gas."

They all laughed at Guiseppi, even though their eyes were filled with tears.

Noah and Marquette closed the cargo doors and walked to where Tillie stood with her mother and Tara and Guiseppi.

Tara looked at Tillie and her eyes revealed the ache in her heart. "I will miss you very much. *Please paint*," she begged.

"I'll try," Tillie whispered, feeling her own eyes burning.

"Goodbye, my Angel," Rosa said, holding her daughter in her arms. "I will call each day for a while."

"Me, too," Tillie cried.

Guiseppi took her into his arms. He placed a delicate kiss upon her cheek and whispered, "Be not afraid, my Angel. Jesus is with you always."

"I know, Papa,"

Marquette held her then. He kissed her cheek softly and looked into her eyes. "I will come in October," he promised.

"Okay," she answered, attempting to dry her face with her hands. Marquette walked her to the passenger door of the Suburban, where Noah was already standing. Noah held the door for her, looking more than just a little uncomfortable at their very emotional goodbye. Tillie chuckled at him through her tears, "It's the Italian in us that makes us behave this way. Sometimes we get a little carried away."

Noah nodded with an understanding smile. Tillie got into the truck and he closed the door.

"Good-bye my friend," Marquette said. He suddenly embraced Noah and held him close. Then he surprised Noah by kissing his cheek. Noah blushed. Marquette laughed and slapped Noah's back. "Drive safely, and have a good trip."

"Thanks, Marq," Noah managed to stammer. That was the first time in his life that another man had ever given him a kiss…*that's gonna take some getting used to,* he thought.

As they walked around the front of the vehicle, Guiseppi and Rosa grabbed Noah to hug him one last time, and Tara gave him a hug as well. They finally released him and he crawled into the truck with everyone else, barely able to keep his own sorrow under control. He looked over at Tillie, who was quietly crying in the passenger seat. He handed her his handkerchief, hoping he wouldn't have to use it himself.

"The kids wanna stop at Al's Oasis for a buffalo burger," he said, trying to smile. "Is that gonna be okay?"

Tillie nodded, trying to dry her eyes, but every time she looked at her family in the driveway they started up again. To make matters even worse, there was an abundance of sniffles in the back seat. She turned around and saw the wet faces of all four children. She smiled and encouraged, "It's gonna be okay. They'll come for a visit around Thanksgiving and we'll plan something for them. Okay?" All four heads only nodded as they held their sad mouths tightly closed in order to keep their sobs from bawling out of them.

They waved one last time at the wonderful grandparents in the driveway and Noah put the truck into gear and backed out.

"They will be fine," Guiseppi said, taking Rosa's hand into his own as they watched Noah drive away.

"Yes," Rosa agreed with a smile. "Everything will be okay now."

For the two hours required to reach Al's Oasis, Noah's and Tillie's children talked of nothing but how much fun they'd had at the ranch, and how great it was to have Guiseppi during the baseball season.

"We have to plan something really cool for when they visit," Ty said.

"But what?" Jake asked with a frown. "Compared to the things Mr. Caselli plans, we're *totally* lame."

Tillie laughed out loud. "You are *not totally lame,*" she said.

Jake gave Tillie a sideways grin, then he smiled into her eyes, looking so much like his father that it almost took her breath her away.

"Your dad is really fun," Jake said. "Was he always like this? Or just when he got old?"

"Hmm," Tillie smiled thoughtfully as she looked at the children in the back of the Suburban. "Papa has *always* been very fun."

"Why do you call him 'Papa?'" Ty asked.

"Because in Italy, where they came from, fathers are called 'Papa.' "

"He likes kids," Jake said with a smile. "I can tell."

"He loves children, and I think he would have liked to have had more," Tillie replied.

"How old is Grandpa?" A.J. asked. " 'Cuz, he doesn't have any hair or anything."

"He will be seventy-seven in October," Tillie answered.

"How long did his parents live?" Ty asked.

"They were killed in World War Two," Tillie answered. "I don't think they were very old. Maybe in their forties, or a little older."

"Was your papa in that war?" Jake asked.

Tillie nodded. "And his brother, Angelo."

"And they were powerful warriors," Noah said, more to himself than anybody else in the vehicle.

Tillie looked at him with surprise. *He remembered.*

"How'd you know that, Dad?" Ty asked.

"Mrs. Martin told me," Noah answered, keeping his eyes on the road, wishing he'd kept his mouth shut. *That was weird. Why did I just add that to the conversation. Like I know what I'm talking about or something.*

"Grandpa always says that," Laura said. She mimicked Guiseppi's accent, "*We were powerful warriors*."

"I love the way they talk," Noah said, glancing at Tillie. "Especially your father."

"Me, too," Tillie agreed.

"They must all speak Italian then," Jake said, "because they all have an accent."

"Uncle Marq speaks lots of different languages," Laura proudly bragged. "Even Arabic."

"Wow." Jake was obviously awestruck with the information. Then he frowned thoughtfully at Tillie and said, "See, we really are *lame*."

"No, you're not!" Tillie laughed again.

Their banter went on until they reached Al's Oasis. They all sat quietly around the big wooden table in the restaurant as they ate their buffalo burgers and fries, remembering the jolly Italian they'd shared the time with just a few days before.

Noah told everyone to use the bathroom before they left while he went to fill up the gas tank. Tillie was waiting just outside of the restaurant when he returned and he frowned curiously when he saw there weren't any children with her. He hopped out and opened the passenger door for her.

"Thanks," she said, getting into the truck.

"Where's the kids?" he asked.

"They just wanted to look in the gift shop for a minute," Tillie answered. "They're trying to find some postcards for my parents."

Noah nodded, closed her door and got in on his side. "Hope they don't take too long," he commented, pretending to be agitated. He hoped they'd take their time so that he could have a few minutes with Tillie. He glanced at the old shoe box she'd placed on the floor by her feet. "By the way, what's that?"

Tillie picked up the shoebox, and set it in her lap. "Papa saved these for me. I didn't even know he still had them," she said. She looked up, peered into the windows of the gift shop to make sure no one was coming, and then she took off the lid. She reached inside and pulled one of the old photos out and handed it to Noah. "Remember this?"

Noah took the old photograph and looked into the image of his younger self. "Oh, boy. I looked terrible back then!" he gasped in a whisper.

"Oh, you did not!" Tillie chuckled. She looked back into the box and pulled out another one, handing it to him as well.

Noah took the photo, looking it over with a frown. "This is getting embarrassing. I look like a hippie."

"Weren't you?" Tillie asked with a surprised expression.

"No…I was a biker. There's a *big* difference."

"Oh." Tillie looked back into the box for another, glancing quickly through the window of the gift shop.

Noah shook his head as he looked at the photos. "If I was a hippie, I would have worn a headband and some beads or something," he pretended to grumble. Tillie laughed. He looked at her and finished, "And tie-dyed stuff. Peace signs, you know, junk like that."

"I'm sorry," Tillie giggled.

Noah looked into her eyes and got the most amazing case of butterflies in his life. He nervously cleared his throat, looking back at the photos in his hands. "And I never saw no limp-wristed hippie ever handle a *Harley*," he added.

Tillie laughed again. "I'm *really* sorry. I won't make that mistake again."

"Good." He laughed in spite of himself. He saw the kids at the checkout stand in the gift shop and he handed Tillie the photos. He swallowed hard as he watched her put them away.

Their children were making their way out of the building now and heading for the vehicle. They got into the back of the Suburban, announcing their purchases.

"Just don't forget to buckle up," Noah instructed with a smile. He put the truck into gear and they headed for Rapid City.

Shortly before six o'clock, Noah and his sons and A.J. unloaded the Martins' luggage from the back of the truck and carried it into the house. Tillie stood alone in her kitchen, listening to everyone tromping around. Last time she'd returned from Sioux Falls it had been with her parents and they'd done what they could to help her make the transition to life without Alex. However, as she stood alone in that kitchen, listening to the same sounds Alex and A.J. used to make when they carried in the luggage, it started hurting all over again.

Alex wasn't going to be here anymore, and there wasn't anybody to distract her this time. She had to face it like a grownup.

"I can't do this," she whispered to herself as the tears began in her eyes.

"Tillie?" Noah's voice said from behind her, and she turned to see that he had come in through the garage. "Is everything okay?" he asked. Tillie shook her head and the tears flowed from her eyes. Noah impulsively took her into his arms and held her close while she cried.

"I can't do this," she wept. "I've never liked being alone and I don't know what I'm gonna do."

"I know," Noah said tenderly. "But you *can* do it, Angel. You're the strongest person I know."

"I'm *not*," she cried. "And I don't even want to try. I wanna go back home to my parents. I wish I was young again."

"No," Noah whispered, shaking his head. "You don't wanna do that to the kids. They need you, Angel." Tillie's body shook with sobs as Noah held her in his strong arms. "Shh…it's gonna be okay. You can do it." He swallowed hard as he knew the despair of having lost a spouse himself. How he wished more than anything that God hadn't seen fit to allow this trial upon Angel. In the silence of his mind Noah scolded the Lord, *of all people, Lord Jesus, You should have spared her of this. How could You*? Then, back behind the scolding, Noah started to hear Guiseppi sing that chorus he sang all summer long. He tried to squelch it away, but it was getting louder and stronger until Noah started to sing softly, "Wait on the Lord and be of good courage, and He will strengthen your heart."

Tillie took a soft breath and swallowed some sobs as she looked up into Noah's eyes. He fished out his handkerchief, dabbed softly at her tears, offering her a sad smile. "Wait on the Lord and be of good courage, and He will strengthen your heart," he sang. "Wait, I say wait...wait upon the Lord...Wait, I say wait...wait upon the Lord." He took a breath and said nothing as she looked at him with surprise.

"Papa's favorite," she whispered.

"I know," Noah admitted with a grin. "He sang it to me practically all summer." He held her close again and whispered, "It's gonna be okay. You're a faithful woman, Angel. I can't even *imagine* you not getting through this."

Tillie swallowed hard, trying to keep her sobs under control as she said, "You're very kind to me, Noah. Thank you."

He let her out of his arms and looked into her eyes. "Whatever you need, if something should come up, call me. Okay?"

"Okay."

"I mean it," he insisted. "And don't think I expect anything in return. I just want to be sure that you're all right over here, you know, by yourself."

Tillie nodded and Noah started to back toward the door. She looked like she was pulling herself together again and he was worried that he'd overstepped his boundaries. He could never help himself where she was concerned. "Hey, I'm gonna call ya," he offered. "Tomorrow after I'm done at the mall with the boys. Can I?"

"Yes," Tillie answered with a smile.

"Are you okay now?"

She nodded and forced a faint smile. "Thanks, Noah. I'll try not to get so hysterical."

"It's okay," he smiled. "I was a mess when I lost Carrie. It just takes a while —"

They were interrupted when the back door burst open and all four children clamored in.

"You okay, Mom?" A.J. and Laura rushed to her.

"I'm okay," Tillie said with a nod and a sad smile.

"Hey, we gotta go," Noah said, looking at his boys and then back at Tillie and her children. "See ya later."

"Thanks for the ride," Tillie said.

"No problem."

Their children said good-bye to each other and Noah and his boys left.

Tillie and her children stood alone in their quiet kitchen.

"We're alone now," Laura whispered.

A.J. swallowed so hard that it sounded like a gulp.

"Not completely alone," Tillie said, forcing a smile for them. "Jesus is with us…but, just the same, I say we all sleep in the same bed tonight."

"I say I agree," A.J. affirmed. Laura nodded, and they all put their arms around each other and cried for a very long time.

*****

Vanilla's unusual little puppy chomped happily at her dish, while Noah and his boys sat at the kitchen table, waiting for the coffee to finish perking.

"I slept so good at the ranch," Jake muttered.

"Even with the roosters crowing," Ty moaned.

Noah frowned as he looked at the note Joshua and Mona had left concerning the puppy's behavior while they were gone. Joshua and Mona were over to feed and exercise the dogs daily, but apparently hadn't arrived soon enough for the neighbors one morning. Dated for

Saturday was a bright, yellow nuisance ticket and Joshua explained in his note that it had been stuck to the back door. A neighbor had called the police because of the dreadful barking and howling of Vanilla's puppy.

"We just can't find anybody that wants a rotten dog," Ty said with a sigh. "I don't know what we're gonna do, Dad."

"Yeah." Jake shook his head. "Who in the world gets up *this* early?"

Noah smiled and began to nod. "I think I got an idea," he said.

*****

Not far from where Noah and his boys suffered with yet another early morning, Tillie was already up, showered and dressed. She curled up in the love seat in her sunroom to watch the glass windows for the sunrise, sipping at a cup of coffee. This used to be her favorite part of the day. She had always done it this way; get up early, talk to the Lord, wake up Alex...

"Please help me," she whispered in the early dawn. "I don't want to do this." She took another sip of her coffee as she watched the colors of the morning begin above the Black Hills.

A ray from the first light of dawn fell across the cover of Tillie's faded leather Bible, which was resting by itself on the coffee table before her. She deliberately looked away.

"I can't imagine what You could possibly have to say to me this morning," she whispered. "You took him away from me before I could get the thing figured out." Tears welled up in her eyes and she took a deliberate sip of her coffee, attempting to swallow away the emotion.

The morning sun moved further above the Black Hills, casting an even brighter glow on Tillie's old Bible. She frowned as she looked at the cover, thinking, *it's just a coincidence....* She spontaneously reached for the Bible, opening it to where she'd left her marker the last time she'd spent time with the Lord — last April, the morning Alex's plane had crashed.

She had highlighted a verse in Isaiah 43, and her eyes were drawn there. "I, even I, am He who blots out your transgressions, for My own sake, and *remembers your sins no more*," she read aloud. She took a deep breath and whispered, "I remembered Alex's sin, but You forgot it." She felt the tears burning again, but this time she didn't will them away. "He tried *so hard*," she cried quietly, not wanting her children to know of the bitterness that was still within her, "and still I just couldn't let the thing go. But You forgave him and even *forgot* about his sin. Father, what is wrong with me?" And in the quiet of her mind, Tillie heard the Father's reply…*you must forgive, Alex. He's with Me now, and I don't give one thought to his sins. He was made perfect in My Son….*

"But why, Father?" she whispered.

Because I love you and I want what is best for you…You will never be able to put the past behind you and get on with My pleasing and perfect will unless you forgive your husband and move on….

It started out faint, and she attempted to force it away. "No," she said aloud, trying to continue her brooding. But then she could almost hear Noah singing her father's favorite chorus, and the urge within her to sing along was stronger than she could fight.

"Wait on the Lord and be of good courage," she began as more light came into the morning sky. "And He will strengthen my heart." She sighed and closed her eyes, took a deep breath and listened to the memory of Noah's voice. "Okay," she whispered to the Lord as the sun came up over the Black Hills, "I release Alex and all that happened between us…forgive me, Father, for not doing it sooner."

A.J. and Laura mowed the lawn and watered Guiseppi's flowers, while Tillie finished the laundry and made a grocery list.

"I'm going over to Safeway," she announced. "Can I pick you up anything?"

"Blue Powerade," A.J. said, and Laura agreed.

"Okay," Tillie answered. "I'll be right back, and then we'll start some supper. You want me to make some burgers on the grill?"

"Yeah," Laura answered with a smile and a nod. Tillie smiled and waved, and left for the nearby grocery store.

When she returned less than an hour later, Noah's familiar white pickup was in the driveway and she frowned. She'd only been gone for a short time. Hopefully nothing had gone wrong.

She parked her car in the garage, took one of the bags out of the trunk, and went in through the kitchen. The house was empty. She set down the bag and glanced out of the kitchen window into the backyard, where she saw them all…*and they were playing with a scruffy little, cream-colored puppy.* Tillie smiled as she wondered what was going on, and went out to the backyard.

Noah looked up when he heard the door and he smiled bashfully as he started to walk toward her. "Hi. I should have called," he greeted.

"It's okay," she replied, looking from Noah's smiling eyes to the little puppy as it chased a ball. "What's going on?"

"Oh, the boys thought you guys might like to meet Vanilla's last puppy," Noah explained hesitantly.

"I thought you guys got rid of those puppies."

"All but this one," Noah answered, and then he swallowed hard...*please take the rotten, little thing.*

At that moment the puppy's ball bounced over by Tillie and the puppy happily galloped over to retrieve it. Tillie knelt down to greet the little dog. She reached for the puppy's feathery face, giving her a soft pat.

"Hi, there," she said with a smile. "What's your name?"

"The boys call her 'Sparky,' " Noah answered as he knelt down beside her.

"Hello, Sparky." Tillie lovingly stroked the little puppy's head. Sparky jumped on her short, hind legs and gave Tillie a lick right in the face, and Tillie laughed. "She's really short for a retriever, Noah."

"I know. The rest of the puppies looked more like Vanilla. You know, tall and slender, but this one, I don't know. Maybe she'll never grow."

"Look at this cute face," Tillie said, receiving another appreciative lick from Sparky. She laughed again and looked at Noah. "Haven't you been able to find a home for her?"

"Well," Noah began, and Tillie saw the hesitant expression in his eyes.

"Noah! Are you trying to get me to take this dog?"

"No." Noah shook his head. He rolled his eyes and guiltily looked away. "Okay. The little fiend gets up at five o'clock in the morning, and she barks like a maniac if you don't feed her before *five-o-five*. I've already gotten one nuisance ticket, and she's driving us crazy —" Tillie's quiet laughter interrupted him and he looked back at her with a sheepish smile. "Come on," he begged. "You get up early. You guys will get along famously."

"Noah, I don't have one thing in this house to take care of a dog with," Tillie explained. "Like food, for instance. I'm totally unprepared for this."

"About that..." Noah took a deep breath, and from the look in his eyes, Tillie saw that preparations had already been made.

"Oh, dear," she groaned as she looked back at the pretty little puppy at her feet. "I suppose you brought along all the gear I'll ever need."

"I bought her a really nice kennel, with a bed, some food, some dishes, a leash, and I can put up a fence tomorrow, anywhere you want it, so that she can be outside. She's already house trained so you don't have to worry about accidents. She has all her shots, and there isn't a flea on this dog. She's as healthy as a horse, she's just short."

Tillie chuckled. "Wow." She stroked the puppy's soft fur and looked back at Noah. "I've never had a dog before."

"I know," Noah said, smiling into her eyes. "And she'll be nice company, you know, now that your folks are back in Sioux Falls and the kids are starting school."

Tillie took a breath and looked at the little dog. She noticed that their children watched the introduction from a distance. They looked hopeful, and she sighed. "Okay, I'll take her," she finally agreed. She looked into Noah's eyes and saw an old, familiar sparkle.

"Thank you!" Jake shouted with exaggerated relief.

"Thanks, Mom!" A.J. and Laura shouted at the same time.

Tillie laughed again as she looked at the scruffy little dog. *Sparky. What a cute name.*

Chapter 9

Tillie woke the next morning at her usual time and hurried to the kitchen to see how the puppy had done during the night. She was surprised to find her still asleep in the kennel Noah had placed by the back door. The little puppy had been played with until well after dark, and passed out when Noah put her into the kennel before he left. Tillie turned on the soft light above the stove and bent over to peer inside the wire door.

"Hey, Sparky, wanna get up and have some breakfast? It's just about five-o-five." She opened the door to the kennel, reached inside and lifted out the sleepy little bundle.

Sparky wagged and wagged, making soft crying noises as Tillie snuggled her in her lap. She stroked her soft head and looked into her chocolate brown eyes. The puppy suddenly licked her on the face.

"Oh, goodness," Tillie said with a giggle. "Why don't we take you outside and then come back in for some chow." She sat the puppy on the floor and reached for the leash that was on top of the kennel. She clipped it to Sparky's collar and led her through the sunroom door and into the backyard.

Sparky took care of her business in just a matter of minutes, and was soon happily chomping a bowl of dog food while Tillie started her coffee maker.

"Now, I shower while the coffee brews. Are you gonna be good or are you gonna get into trouble if I leave you alone?"

The puppy stopped eating momentarily and looked up at Tillie with the sweetest face and wagged her tail.

"Hmm." Tillie thoughtfully looked at the puppy. "Well, there really isn't much you can get into I guess." The little dog dropped its head back into the dish as Tillie hurried upstairs to shower.

A few minutes later, as Tillie turned off the water, she heard very loud, frantic barking in the upstairs hallway. She hurriedly dried herself off, put on her robe and rushed out of her room to see what was happening. To her surprise, there stood Sparky, surrounded by shreds of what had apparently been a magazine, barking at the top of her little dog lungs. As soon as she saw Tillie she scampered to her and rolled over on her back.

"Sparky!" Tillie scolded softly. "Did you do this?"

A.J.'s bedroom door opened and he peeked out. "Is the dog barking?" he asked.

Laura's door opened almost at the same time, but she only yawned and looked at the mess in the hallway.

"Sorry guys," Tillie said as she stooped over to give Sparky a pat. "You don't have to get up yet. It's still early."

"Why are you playing with the dog this early, Mom?" A.J. asked with a frown.

Tillie almost laughed. "I'm not *playing* with the dog. I didn't think she'd get into anything while I showered." She bit her lip and looked at the puppy at her feet. "Guess she'll have to go back into the kennel when I shower."

"Who made this big mess?" Laura asked with another yawn.

"Sparky," Tillie answered.

Laura grinned. "I'm gonna lay down for a few more minutes, but I'll help you pick it up before I go to school."

"Okay," Tillie said as she scooped up Sparky and headed back into her room. "She'll have to come with me for now." She playfully frowned at the little dog. "Apparently you can't be trusted by yourself."

When Tillie took her children to school, she put Sparky back into the kennel, where she cried woefully. Tillie felt terrible, but she couldn't leave the little nut to destroy the house while she was gone. Hopefully Noah would make good on his promise to get that fence up so that she could put Sparky outside in the mornings while she showered.

Tillie dropped her children off at the junior high, the beginning of their second year. *It's amazing they're already in the seventh grade,* she thought as she watched them walk into Southwest Middle School. A.J. had grown so much this past summer, and Laura was turning into a wonderful artist. Even without Alex, their lives continued to march along.

She swallowed away her tears, turned her car around, and headed for the empty house she didn't want to face. She remembered Sparky, and that brought a small smile to her lips. *And Diane,* she remembered, *will be over today, and perhaps Noah....*

Diane's car was already in the driveway when Tillie got home.

"I'm a little early today," Diane said with a smile as Tillie let them in through the garage. The dreadful cries of the puppy rang in the kitchen. "Oh, my goodness!" Diane laughed. "Did you get a puppy?"

Tillie chuckled and nodded as she went to the kennel door and let Sparky out. The crying stopped instantly and she pawed at Tillie's feet. Tillie laughed and knelt down to pet the puppy. Sparky jumped on her hind legs and gave Tillie's chin a kiss. "Oh, you!" She smiled and stroked the puppy's face. She tried to move some of the feathers out of her pretty eyes and said, "I don't know how she can see a thing with all of this hair in her face! I think I'm going to take her to the groomer and see if they can cut her into the shape of a dog."

Diane laughed. "Where did you get her?"

"Noah Hansen brought her over last night. His dog had puppies this past summer and this was the only one they couldn't get rid of."

"Short little thing. What kind of dog is she?"

"Noah doesn't know," Tillie answered with a chuckle. "She's part stray I guess."

Diane laughed again. "Oh, dear!" She took a breath and said, "Well, I'm gonna start upstairs. Anything in particular you need me to get done today?"

"No."

"Okay." Diane headed into the upstairs to begin her chores.

"You know," Tillie whispered to her little dog, "I really don't *need* a cleaning lady anymore — but she's such a nice lady."

Tillie heard a knock at the garage door and opened it up to see that Noah was there with a pencil and small notebook.

"Good morning," he smiled, and he looked at the dog. "What time did she get you up this morning?"

"I was up before she was."

Noah looked surprised. "I came over to see where you want the fence."

"Come on in," she offered.

She led him through the kitchen and out through the sunroom doors, Sparky following on Noah's heels, pouncing at Noah's feet and snapping at the bottoms of his jeans. When Noah stopped to look at the dog, she pranced behind Tillie and growled at him as if he were a stranger.

"Oh, brother," Noah moaned, rolling his eyes. "You know me. You've lived with me for the past five months."

Tillie smiled as she watched the puppy's antics. "She's just playing," she said.

Noah shook his head. "Where do you want the fence?" he asked.

"Over here," Tillie instructed, pointing to the side of the house. "That way, I can just let her out through the sunroom door." She looked at Noah, and raised one eyebrow. "She has a problem with paper, doesn't she."

Noah *almost* laughed at Tillie's comical expression, but thought better of it. He bit his lip as he answered, "I thought maybe she was over that."

"I see. Well, she's *not*. She took care of my brand new *Good Housekeeping* at about five-fifteen this morning. I thought I could leave her alone for just a few minutes while I showered."

Noah's eyes became hugely surprised. "Don't ever leave her alone. *Ever*."

"Okay," Tillie agreed with a suspicious smile. "Is there anything else I should know about this dog?"

"She gets car sick," Noah answered, turning from Tillie as he pulled out his measuring tape to hold it up against the side of the house. "Here, hold this."

Tillie took hold of the end of the tape while Noah slowly walked a short distance out into the yard. "Car sick?" she asked.

"She just erps a little," Noah answered in a nonchalant tone, as if it wasn't a big deal. "But you really don't have to take her in the car that much anyway."

Tillie nodded as she watched Noah write down his measurements and move the tape in a different direction.

"And she doesn't like thunder," Noah went on, making the next measurement. "If you can't find her and it's storming, check under the beds, that's where she'll be."

Tillie tried to smile as she realized, *he's saddled me with a neurotic dog*.

*****

That first day by herself, Tillie wasn't alone at all. While Noah put up the chain-link fence in the backyard, Diane whistled through the house, dusting and cleaning. Tillie walked her little dog, watered her father's flowers in the front yard, her own garden in the back, and absorbed herself in a decorating magazine. She hadn't looked at one in forever, but, for some reason, she was suddenly engrossed in the ideas it had to offer.

Her parents called, as did each of her brothers, and they were all pleased to hear that she had a pet to keep her company. Marquette promised, again, to visit in October, and Petrice said he'd be able to get away on the same weekend.

Diane finished her chores in the early afternoon and stopped in the kitchen as she was leaving. Tillie was putting together something for dinner.

"You start early," Diane commented with a smile. "The kids aren't even home from school yet."

"It's a slow-baked recipe," Tillie answered as she covered the casserole dish and slid it into the oven. "It's one of my kids' favorites."

"Well, I'm gonna get goin', but I wanted to ask you about that room upstairs?"

"Which one?" Tillie asked

"The one that's always been closed," Diane replied. "The door was open this morning, and I noticed that the windows were really dirty. I could get those cleaned up for you next week if you want me to."

Tillie nodded...*she must be talking about the studio.* "I'll think about it," she answered.

"Well, okay," Diane said in her friendly way. "Let me know next week." With that, she smiled and left through the garage door.

Tillie stood in her kitchen listening to Noah's pounding noises out back, and the occasionally bark or growl of the puppy torturing him while he worked. She glanced upstairs…*the one that's always been closed...The door must have been left open on Sunday when Noah carried up the paintings.* She remembered the shoe box of photographs she'd stashed on top of the refrigerator and reached for it. With a soft smile she made her way across the kitchen, through the sunroom and up the stairs.

Her heart pounded with anticipation as she headed for the small sunroom at the end of the hall. She paused in the doorway and looked inside. A dusty haze floated throughout, and the windows were fogged with years of neglect. She stepped into the room, overwhelmed with the smell of dust, and went to the window. She looked down on the creek, remembering her first days in the house. She smiled. *There was Papa and the twins...and they were so little...he was teaching them how to fish...*

Tillie set her shoe box down on the floor, and, with some effort, opened the window. A fresh breeze of Black Hills pine blew into the room. She inhaled it deeply, indulging herself in the reminiscent fragrance. The dust and dirt was thick in the sill, and she noticed it was already all over the front of her jeans.

She turned from the window, looking around the room that was supposed to have been her studio. *I haven't been up here since before Christmas of 1986.* Laura had been up this past summer to get an easel, but everything else was still in the same place she'd left it. Her sketch table sat on the other side of the window, while a covered easel waited patiently in the corner. *Wonder what project that was,* she thought.

The two wrapped paintings leaned against the closet where Noah had put them a few nights before. The wicker furniture was more gray than white, covered in a thick layer of dust, and the table where she'd mixed her paints was bare, except for the red, tattered book.

Tillie frowned, picked up the book, and blew the dust from the top of it. She had told Ma`ma to put it away after Alex had returned it that day in the hospital.

"How could he have done that to me?" She whispered, slowly shaking her head at the horrible memory. She slowly opened the book to the old, familiar poem and the beloved photo still tucked inside. She smiled when she saw her younger self in Noah's arms looking up into his eyes.

Tillie smiled and shook her head as she closed the book and set it down on the table. She took the shoe box and sat down in a wicker chair that seemed to be just waiting for her. She still hadn't had the chance to go through all of the photographs yet, and now seemed like the perfect time.

For nearly an hour Tillie was lost in the memories of a young girl who fell in love with a biker and followed him into the most romantic adventure of her life. They'd gone everywhere that day, and she'd captured all of it in the photographs her parents were never able to part with.

"You see, we had a secret," Tillie whispered, mimicking her father's soft accent. She laughed softly, "Wow, Papa, that was *some secret.*"

"Angel!" Noah's voice called from the kitchen below, and Tillie jumped with surprise as she glanced at her watch. *Oh goodness! I have to get to the school to pick up the kids! Enough of memory lane.* She put the lid on the shoe box, hid it inside of the closet, and hurried downstairs.

"Hey, I'm done with that fence," Noah said when he saw her on the steps. "The little nut is still out there."

"That was fast," Tillie said, looking out at a very happy Sparky who was running around the safely enclosed area of the backyard. "Thanks, Noah. That'll help me a lot."

"No problem," Noah replied, hesitantly backing toward the door. "I gotta go. Ty's busy this afternoon so I gotta pick up Jake."

"Yeah, I gotta get going too," Tillie said, feeling the urge to ask him if he could stick around for a while.

"I'll see ya later."

"Okay." she smiled. "Thanks again."

Noah nodded and left, closing the door behind him.

Tillie sighed with a smile. *He called me 'Angel.'*

*****

The rest of September passed uneventfully. Sparky got a great haircut and a bath, at the Pet Grooming Center. Sparky's groomer, Mandy, recognized Tillie the moment she walked into the establishment and was delighted to serve the famous Senator Caselli's sister. She expressed her sincerest regrets at the recent loss of Tillie's husband, and went on to say that her brother was getting into politics.

Mandy's brother was Jack Goldstein and he lived in Sioux City, Iowa, where their mother lived. He planned on running for Congress on the Conservative ticket in 1994, and his favorite senator in the whole United States was Petrice Caselli. Mandy had come to the Rapid City area with her husband, Frank, who was stationed at Ellsworth Air Force Base.

Also that month, Mrs. Romanov began calling on Tillie more frequently, asking her over for tea, and sometimes just showing up on Tillie's front porch. It always made Tillie smile to see Mrs. Romanov with her basket of yarn and different projects. Her English was very good now, but she so enjoyed speaking with Tillie in Russian, and Tillie had to admit that it was fun for her as well.

Tillie and Diane together cleaned the studio, and Tillie started thinking about different projects she'd left on the back burner eighteen years before. Every day, after dropping the kids off at school, she and Sparky stole into the studio upstairs, took the old box of photographs out of its hiding place, and looked at each and every one of them.

"It won't be long now," she promised Sparky, "and I'll try a *new* project."

Tillie's parents and her brothers called every day to pray with her and to make sure that she was maintaining a good spirit. Sometimes Tillie felt like she talked on the telephone all day long, and those were her best days. The constant communication with her family held her up and encouraged her.

It stayed warm until the very end of September, temperatures hitting over one hundred degrees on the last day of the month. School was dismissed early that day due to the heat. It was on that day Tillie went to the Sherwin-Williams store on Main Street to choose a wallpaper border for her living room.

She wrestled a ladder from the garage into the living room, wondering if she'd be able to keep her balance as she climbed to the top. She perched herself sturdily on the top and looked around. *No nausea...maybe I can actually pull this off...* She heard Diane's whistling upstairs, and it made her smile. Everyone had something to do, except for Tillie, but that was changing *today*. Sparky looked up at Tillie from where she sat on the floor at the bottom of the ladder. Tillie smiled down at her faithful little dog. *That's funny — everywhere I go, Sparky goes.*

She climbed down the ladder and draped the furniture and floor with plastic drop cloths. Sparky wanted to shred them, and Tillie had to snap her fingers at the little dog to get her to leave them alone.

It was terribly hot in the house so she changed into a pair of old cut offs and a t-shirt. Nobody would be around to see how awful she looked anyway, except for Diane, who probably wouldn't notice — or at least she wouldn't say anything. She hesitated in front of the mirror when she saw the purple scars on her knee. She bit her lower lip and took a deep breath...*It doesn't matter,* she told herself, *I am who I am, and that stuff just doesn't matter anymore.* She reached for a hair tie and put her curly hair into a ponytail.

She climbed up the ladder, took a careful seat, waiting to see if she would lose her balance. *Okay, so far so good*, and she started her work.

After a short time, Diane came downstairs. When she saw Tillie on the ladder she gasped. "Are you supposed to be on ladders?!" she questioned with alarm.

Sparky had been sleeping in the corner by the couch, but at the sound of Diane's voice, she lurched at her, pouncing at her feet and biting at the bottoms of her pant legs.

"Stop that, Sparky!" Tillie scolded. "And I think I'm totally cured," she said to Diane. She pressed a piece of border to the wall, then glanced down at Diane. "What do you think?" At that moment, Tillie nearly lost her balance, but she managed to grab a hold of the top of the ladder with one hand and steady herself with her other against the wall.

"I think I'm going to faint," Diane whispered, patting her chest. "Now come down from that ladder and we'll call somebody to do this."

Tillie giggled mischievously. "I'm okay," she reassured. "It just takes a little getting used to."

Before Diane could admonish Tillie further, she saw Noah's pickup in the driveway. She frowned as she watched Tillie's children and Jake, along with Noah, get out of it. Tillie turned back to her papering, unaware that someone had arrived.

Diane stomped quietly out through the garage and into the driveway. Sparky was happy to see Diane leave and she retreated back to her corner by the couch.

"What is everybody doing home already?" Diane asked, looking at her watch.

"School got out early for heat," A.J. answered, noticing Diane's concerned expression. "What's wrong?"

"She's on a ladder in there," Diane announced. She looked at Noah. "She's already nearly fallen once that I know of."

Noah looked at A.J. and Laura curiously. "Is your mom supposed to be on ladders?" he asked.

"No!" Laura exclaimed, shaking her head. "She can *barely* keep her balance at the top of the steps!"

"What's she up to?" Noah asked as he walked toward the house.

"She's got a bee in her bonnet about that living room," Diane chirped, leading the march to the house. "She's hanging wallpaper border in there."

"Now, don't scare her, Mr. Hansen," A.J. warned as they neared the kitchen door. "She still startles you know."

"Okay," Noah promised, following Diane into the living room. Sure enough, there sat a tatteredly dressed Tillie on the top of the ladder, pressing a picce of border to the wall.

"Now don't be mad at me, Diane," she said without turning around. "This is a cinch. I could do this all day. And it's gonna look great!"

Sparky flew into Noah the moment her little brown eyes saw him. She barked and growled as she bit at his boots. Noah shook his head as he took several quiet steps to where Tillie was perched. She glanced down at him and appeared to be a little startled, but she took a tight hold of the ladder and steadied herself.

"What are *you* doing here?" she asked.

"The kids got out early today due to the heat," Noah explained. "And are you supposed to be on ladders?"

"Oh, heavens, yes," Tillie answered with a smile. Then she saw her children. They frowned at her, along with Diane and Jake. She waved and said sweetly, "Hi guys. Sorry, I didn't know you got out early today." She looked back at Noah, "How'd you find out?"

"They announced it on the radio," he answered. "And you're making us really nervous. Do you think you should get down and we could call somebody to do this? You know, Mona hangs paper all the time. She'd be happy to help you out."

"No," Tillie answered, shaking her head with a smile. "*I'm* gonna do this." She looked down at her little dog still attacking Noah's boots. She snapped her fingers and scolded, "Stop that, Sparky!" Immediately the little dog obeyed and went back to the corner, where she continued to growl and glare at Noah.

"I swear that little dog *hates* me," Noah said with a sigh and a shake of his head. "Well, do you think you'll be okay up there?"

"Oh yeah," Tillie assured with a nod.

"Mom," Laura protested, "what if you fall?"

"I don't think I will, sweetie," she answered her daughter with a smile, then let out a heavy breath. "I guess I could get down for awhile and we could cool off with some iced tea. Anybody want tea?"

"Love some," Diane grumbled, and everybody chimed in with her.

Tillie carefully backed down the ladder while Noah stood beside her, sweating profusely. He wanted more than anything to just reach over and *take* her off of the ladder, but it was as if she really wanted to do it this way, and he couldn't bring himself to interrupt whatever stride she felt she'd reached. They all let out an audible sigh of relief when her bare feet finally touched the floor.

"I'm not a baby, you know," she joked, tousling her children's heads on her way past them to the kitchen.

Noah smiled as he watched her walk away. She was still such a beautiful woman, and *something* was happening inside of her, making her shine like radiance. He didn't know what it was, or what was causing it, but it was *changing* her. He watched the mean, little dog trot along behind her and he shook his head. *That's not it — it's something else.*

*****

The nice weather in the Black Hills held out through October, so Joshua asked Noah to help him replace the old porch on the back of his farmhouse.

"How long have you lived on the place now, Josh?" Noah asked as they hammered away on what they had left of the railing.

"Oh, let's see now..." Joshua paused to rub his forehead thoughtfully. "1955."

"Wow, thirty-eight years in the same place." Noah smiled and looked around. "You've sure taken good care of it, Josh."

"Oh, that's Mona." Joshua smiled. "She keeps track of everything that needs to be done."

"How long have you guys been married?"

"The same year we bought the house."

Noah's eyes were thoughtful, briefly dancing with excitement. Joshua was surprised. He hadn't seen an expression in Noah's eyes like that in longer than he cared to remember.

"What are you thinking about, Noah?"

Noah blushed as he shook his head and looked away from Joshua. "What it must be like to grow old with someone," he answered. "You know, be with that same person forever."

"It's wonderful," Joshua admitted.

Noah looked at Joshua with a curious smile. "It's all I can do to stay away from her, Josh. I just wanna go over there and say, '*Hey, let's just get married because I can't stand it another minute —* '"

Noah was interrupted by Joshua's laughter.

"Do you think she's ready for that?" Joshua asked.

"No," Noah answered with a soft smile. "But *I* am."

Joshua laughed again and nodded his head. "I know *you* are, but how about the kids? How are they doing?"

"I think pretty good," Noah answered. "I don't see 'em as much now as I did during the summer, but A.J. comes over after school sometimes and he seems happy. He doesn't cry anymore when he talks about his dad, but I can tell that he still misses him."

"I still miss Dad," Joshua said with a sigh. "And I think I always will. Of course, Dad was nothing like Alex. For one thing, he wasn't a Christian and so there was a lot of unfinished business there with Dad. A.J., on the other hand, doesn't have to deal with any of that junk that Mona and I had to go through. At least A.J. *knows* that his father is with the Lord, and he's had a lot of wonderful relatives around to hold him up. And he's got a really great mom to help him, too. By the way, I saw her the other day. I was down at the post office and she was mailing a birthday card to her father. She looks really different. Did she change her hair or something?"

"I don't think so," Noah answered.

"Well, she looks different than she did this past summer," Joshua went on. "I don't know — younger or something."

"I've noticed it, too," Noah said. "But..." he hesitated. "I caught her on a ladder hanging wallpaper border a few weeks ago, and from what Marq told me, she hasn't done anything like that since before her accident." He hesitated again, leaning closer to his brother, whispering, "It's like she's *changing* somehow."

"Is that what her brother said, or is that just what *you* think?"

"Me and Marq talked about it a couple of days ago," Noah whispered for fear that if anyone else overheard his words, he might be misunderstood. "He says that it appears to him she even walks differently now —"

"And what about what *you* think, Noah?"

Noah shrugged. "I hadn't seen her in more than three years by the time we all went to Sioux Falls together for the funeral. She was in bad shape then, and I don't know *what* she was like before that. All I remember is what she was like after the accident, and she was very sad about what was happening in her marriage." Noah sighed. "Josh, I think — and I think Marq thinks it too but he's afraid to say — she never *really* got over what Alex did to her and now that's he's gone she's starting to come out of it."

Joshua let out a soft sigh. "Well, he was certainly cruel, that's for sure. I was always amazed that she took him back."

"If she was mine, Josh, I would never do something like that. Did he just stop loving her or what?"

Joshua shrugged. "I don't know, Noah, but he did come back and he did ask for forgiveness, and the rest is probably none of our business."

Noah nodded. "How much longer do you think I have to wait?"

"As long as the Lord tells you to wait, Noah."

*****

Tillie took her old camera to 1st Photo on West Main, where they carefully removed the seven year old film and said they would attempt to develop it. Later on that day, they called to say that several of the photos inside had developed nicely and that she should come down and take a look for herself. Tillie returned to the photo shop, where they excitedly presented her with the photos she'd taken on Reata, Thanksgiving 1986. The twins were only six years old, so little and so sweet, tucked into the blankets of Vincenzo's new sleigh; A photo of Vincenzo standing in the sleigh, tipping his hat and smiling into the camera, and a shot of the barn against a snowy fence line where a ranch hand paused. She had wanted to put that image into a charcoal sketch the moment she'd snapped the lens.

Tillie hurried home with her new treasures, pinning the newly developed photograph onto the corkboard above the sketch table in her studio. Ty and Jake picked up A.J. for a day at the movies, so Tillie told Laura to set up her easel in the studio so they could work together. While Laura worked on a new painting of A.J. in his baseball uniform, and Sparky napped in the corner, Tillie began to sketch her favorite scene on oversized paper.

Laura was surprised at her mother's sudden interest in drawing, but excited at the same time. She'd wanted to share her love for art with her mother for a very long time. However, Tillie had been adamantly opposed to drawing or painting since Laura was little. But things had changed — and for the better.

"I'm so glad you changed your mind," Laura said as they worked together in Tillie's studio upstairs.

"Changed my mind about what?"

"About drawing," Laura answered, chuckling. "What changed your mind?"

"I don't know," Tillie answered, concentrating on the image before her. "I guess I wasn't in the mood until now."

"So what's under the sheet in the corner?"

"I don't remember."

"Can we look at it?"

"Not yet, I want to finish this one first."

Laura nodded. "How about those paintings you brought home from Nonna and Grandpa's house?" she asked.

Tillie took in a surprised breath. "How do you know that they're paintings?" she asked.

Laura laughed and answered, "They *look* like paintings."

"I guess I'm not ready to look at those yet, either," Tillie replied with a smile. "I just want us to work on these for a little while first."

"Okay." Laura smiled at her mysterious mother. She took a breath and asked, "Is everybody coming for Thanksgiving this year?"

"Yes. They're all coming here — do you think we can handle it?"

Laura nodded and then sadly sighed. "You know, Mom, me and A.J. are gonna be thirteen two weeks from today." She paused and looked at her mother. Tillie saw the sad expression in her daughter's eyes. Laura bit her lip as she tried to hold back tears, continuing, "It's our first birthday without Dad."

Tillie set down her charcoal and reached for her daughter's hand. Laura put down her brush and Tillie pulled her into her lap, putting her arms around her.

"I miss him, Mom. Do you still miss him?"

"Yes," Tillie admitted, swallowing hard.

"Remember when he stayed away for that really long time? You know, when me and A.J. were little?"

Tillie couldn't hide her surprise. "You remember that?" she asked. All this time Tillie had assumed they didn't remember it, and yet, obviously, Laura did.

Laura nodded. "I remember how sad you were. How did you finally get him to come home?"

Tillie took a breath and answered honestly, "I just prayed a lot and he finally came back."

"Me and A.J. were really happy when he came home. Wish he was here now. He'd be so surprised to see you this way."

Tillie was floored by her daughter's words. "What do you mean?" she asked.

Laura looked into her mother's eyes and tried to smile. "You're so pretty now," she answered. Tillie stared back at her daughter in utter confusion. Laura couldn't help but chuckle at her mother's expression. "I don't know how to explain it, Mom, but *you look different*. You must have just been ready to finish getting better or something. Dad would be so surprised. It's sad that he's not here to see you like this."

"But I've been better for a long time, Laura."

"No." Laura shook her head. "You never really got *better*, Mom, not until just now."

"I'm sorry, Laura," Tillie said, holding her daughter close.

"It's okay, Mom. It wasn't your fault. Your accident was really hard on you."

Tillie slowly nodded her head as her tears fell, holding her daughter as close as she could. *I'm sorry, Father*, she silently prayed, *I will never carry unforgiveness and bitterness in my heart again.*

Chapter 10

October 1993

The Caselli brothers arrived early in the morning on the day *before* Tillie expected them.

"Well, *where* could she be?" Petrice pondered, peering into the garage windows, noticing that her car was gone.

"I cannot even imagine," Vincenzo said. "She is *always* home."

"Perhaps she is just running some errands and will be back in no time," Marquette offered with a hesitant smile. "We should just wait here."

"Do you still have a key to the place?" Petrice asked.

"I am afraid that I lost it," Marquette replied.

Vincenzo shook his head with obvious disapproval.

Marquette narrowed his eyes. "Do not look at me in such a way," he warned.

"Comc along, my brothers," Petrice said, starting for the rental car they'd parked in the driveway. "Let us find your friend, Noah. Perhaps he knows where she is."

When they arrived at Noah's office, a young lady informed them that Noah was working on-site at the hospital that day. She sent them to Rapid City Regional's newest specialized care center.

"I am starting to feel like that rat in the maze," Vincenzo mumbled as he and his brothers walked the many corridors of the hospital. "Hopefully they will give us a little piece of cheese when we get to the end."

Marquette laughed, and then he saw Noah. "There he is," he said, pointing at Noah. He was wearing a yellow hardhat, holding rolled up blueprints in his left hand, barking orders while directing with his right.

Noah caught a glimpse of the dark suited men walking toward him, and he startled momentarily. Upon recognition, he smiled and extended his hand in greeting.

"Hello, my friend," Vincenzo said, taking a firm grip on Noah's hand. "You are looking well."

"Thanks," Noah greeted in return, smiling as he reached for Marquette's hand, and then Petrice's. "Senator."

Petrice laughed at Noah's formal greeting, and so did his brothers.

Noah grabbed three hardhats from the nearby stack. "Put these on or I'll get a fine," he said.

They removed their stylish hats, replacing them with the beaten-up hard hats Noah offered.

"What are you guys doing in town already?" Noah asked. "I thought you weren't coming until tomorrow."

"We thought we'd surprise Angel and come today," Petrice said. He shook his head. "But she has surprised us. She is nowhere to be found."

"We thought perhaps you would help us," Marquette suggested.

Noah raised a brow. "*I* don't know where she's at," he said. "Did you try the paint store? Or maybe she's getting art supplies. Or Albertson's or Safeway? Depends on who's having the best sales. She might be getting groceries."

"We cannot drive to all those places," Vincenzo said with a frown, scratching his chin. "And when did she start this running around business? I thought she *stayed at home* during the day."

"She does...most of the time," Noah answered. "But she's been kinda busy lately. She's been trying to get a couple of things done."

The three brothers looked extremely perplexed at Noah's words.

"What are we supposed to do with ourselves until she happens back to her home?" Marquette asked.

Noah almost laughed at them. They'd been thrown a loop by their sister's unexpected unavailability.

"I can take you to a late breakfast, or an early lunch if you wanna kill some time," he offered. "There's a great place to eat up here on 8th Street."

They collectively sighed and submitted to Noah's suggestion.

*****

It was still too early for Maggie May's to be open, but Maggie and Estelle were inside, as usual, with their morning paper and coffee. Maggie had noticed the black Mercedes wagon in the parking lot out front, but when its driver didn't come in, she forgot about it, absorbing herself in the latest news with Estelle.

Out front, Tillie sat in the driver's seat of her car with her old camera. She took a deep breath as she opened her car door. "Okay, you wanna do this, now just do it, it's gonna be fun," she encouraged herself. "Just go inside and look around. They're never gonna remember you anyway." With that, she stepped out of the car.

Maggie heard the bell, and she looked up expecting to see Noah. He was the only person who ever visited them this early in the day. Instead, there stood a slender woman, dressed in jeans, a soft, pink sweater, and a light, white wind breaker. Her black, curly hair was pulled into a ponytail behind her head, and her black eyes sparkled when she smiled at Maggie. Maggie's jaw just about hit the bar, and her heart skipped a beat. She tried to take enough breaths to keep herself from fainting.

"Hi," Tillie greeted casually.

"Hi," Maggie whispered. She cleared her throat and repeated in an aloud voice, "Hi." She reached for Estelle's hand and gave it a soft squeeze.

"Whatcha want, Maggie," Estelle murmured, not even looking up from her paper.

Tillie's eyes fell to the portrait hanging on the other side of the bar, and she saw the yellowed snap shot in its corner. She softly gasped, covered her mouth with her hand, and looked at Maggie with a smile.

Estelle looked up when Maggie didn't answer. When she caught sight of Tillie, she gasped, "Angel!" She stumbled to her feet, staggering to where Tillie stood. She touched Tillie's arm and looked into her eyes with delight. "Is it really *you?!*"

Tillie smiled with surprise as she looked at the aged woman before her. "You remember me?" she asked.

"Of course!" Estelle exclaimed, stomping her foot. She turned around to look at a very amazed Maggie. "Look, Maggie! I been tellin' you she'd be back!" She threw her arms around Tillie and hugged her as tight as she could. She laughed and cried at the same time, then took Tillie gently by the hand and led her to a stool at the bar.

"Take a seat, young lady," Estelle commanded, and she looked at Maggie. "Get her some coffee. We got lots to talk about."

Maggie nodded as tears of joy filled her eyes. She placed a ceramic cup on a saucer, her hands shaking as she poured the coffee, and then set it before Angel. "*Man*, it's good to see you," she breathed, her eyes giving way to a million tears she'd held back for the last eighteen years.

"You can't imagine what it's been like without you," Estelle cried, pausing only to blow her nose into a napkin. She smiled at Tillie.

"Whatever made you come here?" Maggie asked, dabbing away at her tears with her apron.

Tillie looked at the two elated women, and she was moved by their overt display of emotion. Tears fell from her own eyes as she answered, "I can't believe you remembered me. I just wanted to see this place again. Things have been really strange for me this year...and... I...don't know why I'm even here."

Estelle laughed and sniffed away some tears. "We've been waiting so long for you to come back," she said. She smiled at Maggie and then grabbed a hold of Tillie's hand, looking into her eyes. "He's missed you so much."

"He has?" Tillie whispered.

"Every day," Maggie answered in her gruff voice, wiping away more of her tears. "How long can you stay?"

"A little while," Tillie answered.

Maggie smiled at Tillie. She put her hand tenderly to Tillie's cheek and said, "Well then, we got lots to tell ya, girl."

The Caselli brothers paced Tillie's driveway. They glanced at their watches, shaking their heads in disbelief. After their meal, Noah had gone back to work, and Tillie's brothers searched the grocery stores, art supply store, and the paint store, only to find that *no one* had seen her *at all that morning*. They paged Noah and requested that he meet them at her home to discuss whatever other possibilities remained. Noah met them in Tillie's driveway after receiving their frantic page.

"It is just not like her at all…especially after the accident. I fear she has gotten lost," Vincenzo declared, shaking his head with remorse. He reached for the tobacco pouch in his shirt pocket.

"I cannot even *begin* to imagine what has happened to her," Petrice lamented, his tone becoming more desperate with every moment that passed.

"It is nearly noon," Marquette moaned. "Wherever could she be?"

"Perhaps we should call the police," Vincenzo suggested.

Noah suppressed a smile. "Guys, I'm telling you, sometimes she gets a little busy," he reminded. She'll be home for sure around three because that's when she brings the kids home."

"And by that time, she will be missing *another three hours*," Petrice argued.

"I just cannot believe she is not here," Marquette grumbled.

Vincenzo put his pipe between his teeth and frowned. "This is unreal."

At that moment, Tillie's car pulled into the driveway. She parked behind the rental car as it blocked her way into the garage. She smiled excitedly at her brothers, obviously surprised they were there, and jumped out of the car.

"Hi, guys!" She greeted, walking to where they stood. Her smile faded as she approached them. She looked at Noah, who gave her the smallest hint of a smile, but nothing even resembling a happy expression came from her brothers. "What's goin' on?" she asked.

"Where have you been?" Petrice demanded, and for that moment he looked *exactly* like their father.

"We have been here for *nearly four hours*," Marquette admonished, shaking his index finger. "And we were worried sick about you."

"You're not supposed to be here until tomorrow," Tillie said with surprise. She bit her lower lip nervously. She was absolutely *not* going to tell them where she had been that morning, and Maggie and Estelle had promised to keep it a secret for a little while as well.

"Well," Vincenzo sighed, smiling as he went to her. He put his arms around her and said, "You are safe and sound and that is all that matters." He kissed her cheek and looked into her eyes, noticing the new sparkle. "My goodness, Angel, but you look radiant this day!" he exclaimed.

"Thanks, Vincenzo." She smiled mischievously at the other two. "You should have called," she said.

"Then it would not have been a surprise," Petrice said, allowing a small smile. He took her into his arms. "How wonderful you are looking. Have you gained weight?"

"A little," she answered.

Marquette sighed with obvious relief, putting his arms around her. He kissed her cheek and held her close. "It is so very good to see you again," he greeted.

"I gotta get back to work," Noah said with a smile, backing away from them. "I'll call the cops and tell 'em to cancel that all points bulletin."

Tillie and her brothers laughed.

"You can stay for lunch," Tillie offered with a smile.

"Wish I could, but I just ate with your brothers and I'm already way behind," Noah replied.

"Can we see you tomorrow?" Marquette asked.

"Sure," Noah answered. "See you guys later." With that he turned and left, and Tillie led her brothers into her home.

As they entered the kitchen, Sparky began whining and crying, and Tillie laughed.

"That's my rotten dog," she said. She opened the wire door of the kennel and a bundle of cream-colored fur raced out to greet the strange guests. She barked, growled and pounced at their feet for bites at their wing tipped shoes.

"Feisty little beast," Vincenzo commented, afraid to reach down for a pat.

"She's just playing," Tillie defended with a smile.

"I think *not*," Petrice noted with alarm, hesitating to pet the thing for fear of being bitten.

"Heavens, what is *wrong* with it?" Marquette questioned.

"Oh, she's just a puppy," Tillie said sweetly, kneeling down to stroke the puppy's soft face and head. She led the little dog over to the sunroom doors, where she let her out and said, "Go and take care of your business, Sparky." Sparky obeyed, jumping out the open door into her fenced-in area.

"Yuck," Petrice murmured with a shake of his head. "I cannot believe you have livestock in the house."

Tillie closed the sunroom door and turned to her brothers with a smile. "So whose bright idea was it to come early?" she asked.

"Mine," Vincenzo answered. "And when did you start leaving home without telling anyone where you were going?"

Tillie laughed and shook her head. She turned and started toward the living room. "Come on, I got lots of stuff to show you," she said.

They all looked at each other in total bewilderment. *How not typical of Angel.*

They were most impressed with the border and fresh paint she had applied to the living room walls.

"I've been thinking of getting some new furniture, too," she explained. "But I haven't found anything I really like yet." She paused for a breath and continued, "My next project is going to be that sunroom. I'm going to paint it yellow — 'cause it's a *sunroom* — get it? *Sunroom?*" She laughed at her own humor.

"But there is only one wall in the sunroom," Vincenzo pointed out. "The others are all glass."

Tillie smiled and rolled her eyes. "I know that, but it should still be yellow," she insisted.

She led them upstairs to her studio, showing them the new charcoal sketch she'd entitled, simply, *Reata.* They were most impressed again, and expressed their pleasure in the renewal of interest in her talent.

What they noticed the most, however, was the way she spoke with them. Her voice was soft and soothingly happy, she paused to smile and her arms and hands gestured while she spoke….*as she had many years before.* They'd not seen their sister behave in such a way for longer than they cared to remember. It was like watching a dream as she entertained them with her plans and schemes. They were overwhelmed with the change that had occurred within her since their last visit two months before. She was more like Angel now, the Angel they'd known and loved before that horrible accident took her away.

She told them to have a seat at the small table in the kitchen while she prepared a light lunch.

"I haven't eaten like you guys did," she explained, "and I'm starved!"

They watched her slender body move gracefully around the cupboards as she prepared them lunch…no limping, no stumbling, no hesitation. She was sure on her feet, and they cast one another glances of confusion. She finally seated herself with them. Petrice prayed and they began their meal.

"I think I'm going to sketch the photo of Vincenzo in his sleigh," she began as they ate. Her eyes were animated with the plans swirling about in her head. "I'm hoping to have that one done by Thanksgiving — you guys are coming for Thanksgiving, right?" They all nodded in reply, and she continued, "Great! I'm pretty excited about it."

Her brothers found themselves unable to respond. *Excited about it?* How atypical of the Angel they'd gotten used to.

"Wow," she commented between bites, "you guys must really be tired. You've hardly said anything all day."

They all attempted a few excuses and finished their lunch in amazed silence. Whatever had happened to Angel was very good, but it was quite surprising at the same time.

Shortly before three o'clock, Tillie left to get her children from school. She was humming a tune on her way out the door, and her brothers looked at one another, shaking their heads.

"I need a smoke," Vincenzo announced, heading for the sunroom door. He slid it open, looking at his brothers. "Is anyone coming with me?"

Marquette and Petrice followed him out onto the stone patio, where they were greeted by the furry lunatic Angel affectionately called her pet. Sparky growled and barked at them, biting at their shoes and the bottoms of their pants.

"Now, stop that!" Vincenzo scolded, snapping his fingers.

Sparky barked in retaliation, making his brothers laugh. She finally retreated into the grass and left them alone.

The weather was still very comfortable in Rapid City, and the brothers seated themselves in Angel's patio furniture. Vincenzo took out his pipe and began the ritual preparations.

"Does anyone see what I see?" Marquette asked. "And I want to talk about this, so please do not sit there and say nothing."

"I see it, Marquette," Vincenzo said, putting the light into his pipe, taking a deep draw. "Angel is Angel again. I do not know what else to say."

"I find myself without words," Petrice said. "I have not seen this side of our sister for many years."

"I did not realize how much I *missed* her," Vincenzo said. He blew smoke into the air and frowned.

"What is causing this?" Petrice asked quietly.

Vincenzo blew another cloud of smoke and replied, "Could it be Noah?"

Petrice shrugged. "She obviously cares for him, but I do not think *he* is causing this change."

"The two of you lack the courage to say what you truly believe it to be," Marquette grumbled.

Vincenzo raised one eyebrow. "And that is?" he asked.

"That is," Marquette admitted, "that perhaps Angel has finally been able to *forgive* her husband and heal."

"What a dreadful thing to say, Marquette." Petrice looked away from his younger brother, staring at the creek in the distance.

"What a dreadful thing Alex did," Vincenzo said, taking another deep draw from his pipe. He let out the smoke and looked thoughtfully at Marquette. "I imagine you are right, brother. My Kate has only recently forgiven Alex."

Petrice looked at his two younger brothers. While he'd had the same thought himself, he always found it difficult to speak of their sister's faults.

Marquette pointed his index finger at Petrice and admonished, "Do not be afraid to speak the truth, Patty. Our Angel is not without sin. She has finally forgiven Alex, and we should rejoice for her."

*****

The next day was Saturday, and Tillie prepared a feast for her brothers and her children. Tillie's brothers asked if Noah and his sons could be invited to share in the meal so they might celebrate the twins' birthday. Even though their birthday was still a week away, they had brought along some gifts. Tillie agreed *reluctantly*, and A.J. excitedly made the call.

It wasn't that Tillie didn't like to spend time with Noah, but she was afraid she enjoyed it far too much. She felt deeply for Noah, but her children would never understand if something happened between them this soon after their father's death. *And* she was determined not to lead Noah along. After her conversation with Maggie and Estelle, Tillie resolved that Noah did not deserve one more heartbreak. He was a good man and she would not allow his feelings to be trampled by her again.

She set her table with her very best china and crystal, completely wowing Noah and his sons. Only Auntie Mona knew how to do this, and she did it only on *special holidays*. Tillie smiled at their sweet apprehension, pretending not to notice when A.J. coached Jake and Ty on the uses of the different sized forks. Noah pleasantly surprised Tillie by sliding out her chair for her. She smiled into his dancing, blue eyes, her heart skipping a beat.

Everyone fit comfortably around Tillie's table, dining on delicious ravioli, zucchini salad, focaccia, and cannoli for dessert. The children took turns telling hillarious stories about their summer with Guiseppi, and how they hoped for his return in the spring.

After dinner, Tillie's brothers brought down the gifts they'd hidden upstairs. The twins were more than a little overwhelmed at the sheer number of things their relatives had sent. Tillie was amazed at their generosity as well, but thankful for the distraction from their sadness. While A.J. and Laura ripped open their presents, Tillie's dog pounced on the papers, tearing through the ribbons and bows.

"Maybe Dad can take us skiing next weekend," Jake offered with excitement. He looked to his father with a hopeful expression, "I hear Terry Peak already has an awesome base."

"Next Saturday is the *actual* day of our birthday," A.J. said, looking to his mother.

"We don't know how to ski," Laura blurted out quickly.

Noah sensed what the problem was going to be. While A.J. would have loved to avoid the situation by going skiing, Laura probably would have rather sat at home and thought about how much she missed her father on her first birthday away from him.

"I could teach you," he offered with a smile, and Laura looked at him with surprise.

"You ski?" she asked.

Jake raised one eyebrow and looked at Laura curiously. "Doesn't *everybody*?" he asked.

"I do not," Marquette said with a wink at Jake. "And neither do my brothers."

Jake laughed and shook his head.

"Well," Noah went on, "I could teach you if you want to go. Might be kinda fun."

"Can you go, too, Mom?" Laura asked.

Tillie smiled nervously and admitted, "Well, I probably can't get up on the skis, but I could come and watch. How would that be?"

Laura smiled hesitantly, shrugging her shoulders. "Well, I'll pray about it," she said.

Tillie nodded, quietly thanking God for the distraction coming their way. This would be the hardest day of the year for A.J. and Laura, but if they could find something really fun to do, maybe it would be a little easier to bear. The day was coming whether or not they wanted it to, and Jake's idea was the best yet.

As the evening began to wind down, Noah announced that he and his boys had to get going because of church in the morning.

"You guys could join us if you wanted to," Noah suggested as he looked more at Tillie's brothers than at her. He knew that she'd soured on church, but he really wanted to see her and the kids there nonetheless.

"Wonderful," Petrice agreed immediately. "I am not scheduled to fly out until shortly after noon."

Vincenzo and Marquette were both in agreement, but Tillie felt like she wanted to faint. She didn't want to go back there! Some of the church members had gossiped about her and Noah six years before, and she wasn't comfortable with having to face all of that again. She squelched her desire to flat-out refuse the invitation, allowing her brothers to make the agreement to attend.

Noah and his boys left the house, while Tillie and her brothers and the twins stayed in the family room to go through the gifts.

Tillie stood suddenly from where she had taken a seat with them. Her brothers stood politely, and she looked at them with surprise. "Please, wait here for just a minute," she said. "I'll be right back." She hurried out into the dark driveway where Noah's boys were already climbing into the pickup.

"Noah."

He turned around, smiling with surprise when he saw her. "Yeah," he replied, stepping in her direction.

"I...um..." Tillie stammered and swallowed as she tried to somehow find the words to make him understand.

Noah saw the apprehension in her eyes and he smiled with concern as he took a few more steps. "What's the matter?" he asked.

Tillie swallowed again, took a deep breath and whispered, "I'm afraid to go back to your brother's church."

"Why?"

"*Because*," she whispered. She took a breath and rolled her eyes. "*The gossip.* I *know* there was gossip...you know...*after*...."

"Oh," Noah said, laughing softly. He nodded his head, and in the darkness she saw him blush. He took a soft breath and whispered, "Yeah, there was *some* gossip, but most of those old biddies are dead now."

Tillie couldn't help but smile at his explanation, still she questioned further, "But what about younger people? If anything ever got back to my kids, they'd feel terrible." She hesitated as she looked into Noah's understanding eyes. "Alex and I never told them what he'd done, and I don't want them to ever know."

Noah smiled and tenderly reached for one of her hands. "Nobody talks about it anymore, Angel," he said. "I think it'll be okay, but you do what you feel is best for your children."

The warmth of his callused hand drew her back into a time when she had wanted to hold those hands forever. She smiled into his blue eyes. "I suppose, if you think it's okay —" she began.

"No." Noah smiled and shook his head. "Only if *you* think it's okay. I don't want you to do anything that you're not comfortable with."

Tillie took a soft breath and nodded. "Okay, I'll pray about it tonight," she promised.

Noah let go of her hand and began backing toward the truck. "Maybe we'll see you tomorrow," he said.

Tillie smiled, and he got into his truck. Noah gave her one last wave from inside of the cab as he left the driveway.

From behind the drapes in the living room, Tillie's brothers were watching secretly, accusing one another of spying. A.J. and Laura were still in the family room, thankfully, busy checking out all of their gifts. They hadn't noticed their uncles steal away.

"More than fifty years old are the three of us," Petrice whispered, "and *still* we have not learned the grace of privacy."

"He is so crazy for our little sister that he is just about ready to lose it," Marquette whispered as he watched Noah take Tillie's hand gently into his own.

"Lose what?" Vincenzo asked with a frown.

"Any self-control he *might* possess," Petrice answered dryly.

Marquette sighed with a smile as he glanced at his two brothers and then back through the small gap in the drapes. "He loves her and I believe she loves him," he said. "How long do you think they will wait?"

"Hopefully they do not elope tomorrow," Vincenzo replied. He bit his lip nervously. "Should we have a talk with him?"

Marquette huffed, "He is nearly forty-two years old. He does not require our direction and neither does Angel."

When they saw Tillie turn from the driveway, they jumped away from the window. They hurried to the sunroom where they were standing when she came back inside. She smiled at them, and they noticed the sparkle in her black eyes.

"Oh, *Angel*," Vincenzo groaned.

His brothers glared at him, wishing he could have hidden his feelings.

"What?" Tillie asked with a smile.

They shrugged in unison as they stared down at their shoes.

Tillie chuckled. "What's up, guys?" she asked.

"Nothing," Petrice offered.

"Are we going to church together before we leave?" Marquette blurted.

"Sure," Tillie answered with a smile and a nod, starting for the family room. "Come on. I wanna get a better look at the kids' stuff."

Chapter 11

A.J. and Laura decided to take Noah up on his offer to ski on their birthday. Early Saturday morning, Noah picked up the Martins in his white pickup. Snow started falling as they left town, and it was heavy by the time they reached Terry Peak.

The ski summit and lodge were located just west of the Lead-Deadwood area, in the Black Hills of South Dakota. Noah brought along all kinds of ski equipment, as he and his boys had skied for years. He outfitted A.J. and Laura with skis, pants and boots, then took them to the ski lift. Tillie followed with her old camera, but she startled when she saw the drop-off near the ski lift.

"I pertnear lost my balance," she joked, backing away to a safe distance. "I'll just take my pictures from over here."

A.J. and Laura were so excited they could hardly wait for their turn on the lift. Tillie was thankful for Jake's idea. The twins had talked *some* about their dad that morning, and there were tears again. However, by the time Noah and his boys arrived, they were determined to get on with the planned event.

Jake and Ty were accomplished skiers, and they went down the hills like pros. Noah helped A.J. and Laura figure out how to make it down the easiest of the slopes without hurting themselves. At first Tillie was nervous about it, but the activity was taking their minds off of their father's absence, and for that Tillie would have overlooked *almost* anything.

At noon, Noah announced that it was time for lunch and a cup of coffee. He found Tillie shivering by the ski lift, pretending to enjoy herself.

"How are you holding up?" he asked as they trudged toward the lodge.

"Good," she chattered.

"I could use some hot coffee," Noah suggested. He looked at the four children walking ahead of them. "Your kids are doing really well. Regular naturals."

"Really?"

"They'll be professional skiers before sunset," Noah said proudly.

Tillie looked at him with surprise and said, "Please don't tell me we're staying out here *that late*."

Noah laughed, impulsively putting his arm over her shoulders. "I won't keep you out here *that late*," he replied.

Tillie's most natural inclination was to snuggle even deeper into his arm. Instead, she looked at him curiously.

"Is this okay?" he whispered.

She nodded with a hesitant smile. "As long as the kids don't mind," she whispered in return.

"They won't hurt me, will they?" he teased.

Tillie laughed and shook her head.

When they reached the restaurant in the lodge, they were seated at a table near the fireplace. Noah was sure to sit next to Tillie. The kids didn't appear to mind, in fact, they didn't even seem to notice. They took their seats and started removing a few layers of clothing.

"This is really fun," Laura said to Noah. "Thanks."

"You're welcome, Laura," Noah replied. "And happy birthday." A.J. loudly cleared his throat and Noah laughed as he looked at Tillie's son. "Happy birthday to you, too, A.J. Are you having a good time?"

"This is great," A.J. answered. "Can we do it every weekend?"

"We ski almost every weekend in the winter," Jake announced with a smile.

"And Mrs. Martin," Ty added sweetly, "you don't have to stand outside the whole time. You can see us from those windows over there." He pointed across the lodge to the floor-to-ceiling windows.

Tillie nodded and smiled.

The waitress appeared with mugs of coffee for Noah and Tillie, and hot chocolate for their children. Then she asked for their order and was gone again.

"So when are your parents coming?" Ty asked Tillie.

"They will arrive, along with the rest of my family, the day before Thanksgiving," she replied.

"We've got a *great* plan for them," Jake said excitedly, and Tillie saw Noah almost wince. Obviously, they had already talked about it.

She laughed. "What plan?"

"We always cut down our own Christmas tree the day after Thanksgiving," Jake went on, "and Dad thought they might like to come along and get one for you."

"Oh, yeah!" A.J. said enthusiastically. "I've *always* wanted to do that."

Noah quietly cleared his throat and smiled at Tillie. "That is, if it's okay with you," he added.

Tillie found herself looking into Noah's dancing, blue eyes. "I think my parents would love that."

After they'd eaten their lunch, they hit the slopes again. Tillie alternated between being outside to take photographs, and warming up behind the lodge's magnificent windows. Occasionally Noah came inside to 'check' on her, giving her one of his handsome smiles, and then he was off again to be with their children.

Shortly before dark, which was only about five o'clock in the afternoon, they started back for Rapid City in the falling snow. The roads were fairly slippery and snow packed, but Noah's pickup handled them with ease.

A few hours later they were back in Rapid City, where it had snowed all day, covering the town with a thick blanket of white frosting. Tillie's driveway had drifted shut and they had to walk to the house from the road. They heard Sparky cry woefully the moment they entered the garage.

"I'll let her out for you, Mom," A.J. offered, and he and Jake picked up their pace, letting themselves into the house to let Sparky out of her kennel.

"I have some soup in my crock-pot," Tillie said to Noah as they walked along behind their children. "Do you guys wanna stay for supper?"

Noah couldn't believe she was actually inviting them. "That sounds great, we'd love to stay," he answered, trying to sound as excited as he felt.

While the kids watched Sparky scamper through her first snowfall, taking bites out of the cold fluffiness, Noah helped Tillie get their supper together. Obviously she had planned on doing this. She had sliced cheese and placed vegetables on a tray in the refrigerator. And she had popped homemade cinnamon rolls into the oven.

Noah glanced into the backyard and watched their children play with the puppy in the snow. He laughed and said, "I can't believe that little dog never grew."

Tillie watched Sparky play with their children. "I really love her. Thanks, Noah," she said.

"You do?" Noah asked, quite amazed. "How can you *stand* her?"

"She's a good little dog."

Noah raised a brow. "She bites. *And* she gets up too early."

"I'm up before she is."

Noah smiled as he looked from the little, pouncing dog, back into Tillie's eyes. He wanted more than anything at that moment to take her into his arms, ask her to marry him, and then run for the Justice of the Peace. Instead, he gently reached for one of her pretty hands, the hands that hadn't aged a bit since he first held them more than eighteen years before. He smiled into her eyes and said, "I want to spend some more time with you."

Tillie caught her breath as she looked back into his handsome expression, feeling that familiar tug in her heart. She bit her lip nervously and whispered, "Me too...but the kids."

"I know," he replied. He looked down at the hand he held, noticing that she still wore her wedding ring. "I promise not to do anything crazy. Let's just spend some time together, *with* our kids, and see what happens."

Tillie smiled back at him and slowly nodded in agreement. *See what happens?* She knew what would happen with Noah…*it's always what happens with Noah...because Ma`ma prayed....*

*****

The month of November passed all too quickly, with ski trips to Terry Peak nearly every Saturday, supper with Tillie on Saturday evenings, and church on Sunday mornings. Card games and homemade nachos were added to the event calendar for Friday nights.

Tillie brought along her sketch pad on Saturdays, and her drawings were breathtaking. She worked from behind the glass windows at the lodge while Noah skied with their children until they were soaking wet.

Laura forsook her newly discovered sport a few times in order to join her mother in the lodge with her own sketch pad. Some of Laura's sketches had even turned into paintings, and Noah coerced the manager of the lodge to allow her to bring her easel and paints inside. That way she could do her work from the windows of the lodge. She turned out a magnificent painting of the view of the snowy Black Hills and gave it to the lodge manager as a thank you. The manager was most impressed and had the portrait framed and hung above the fireplace in the lodge.

Thanksgiving was upon them in no time at all. Tillie hadn't realized it, but she hadn't contacted her family in nearly a month. She wanted Noah and his sons to share the holiday with her and her family, but Kate and Sam would be along and she wasn't sure how they were doing. A.J. and Laura were disappointed when they learned that Noah and his sons were spending the day with Joshua and Mona. Ty and Jake were equally dismayed. They'd become very accustomed to spending time together, and were less than willing to break it off for the holiday.

"But, Mom," A.J. complained as the twins sat on the edge of Tillie's bed one night, attempting to talk their mother into changing her mind. "Mr. Hansen is really fun. Why can't they come over?"

"Because he needs to spend some time with Joshua and Auntie Mona," Tillie answered with a patient smile.

Laura frowned. "Can't you just invite Pastor Hansen and Mrs. Hansen," she suggested. "They *like* us."

Tillie sighed. Their first holiday without Alex was scaring them all to death, and Noah and his sons were more than mere distractions. They were comical, sweet and considerate, and seemed to live for the time they spent with Tillie and her children. Tillie didn't want to go through the day without them either, but there were other people to consider in this delicate situation. She took the hand of each child.

"I don't know how to explain this so that you'll understand," she began, "but your Uncle Sam and Aunt Kate are still having a really tough time. They might not understand if we fill up the house with people they don't really know on this very special holiday. We'll have all the day after Thanksgiving to look for a tree, just like we planned. *Please* understand."

A.J. and Laura nodded in reluctant agreement, convinced their mother was making a big mistake.

*****

Right on schedule, the day before Thanksgiving, Petrice Caselli's plane landed at Rapid City Regional Airport. He brought with him their entire family, plus Sam and Becky-Lynn. Guiseppi and Rosa, along with Marquette and Tara, stayed at Tillie's house, and for everyone else, Tillie made arrangements at the Howard Johnson's. She rented two four-wheel drive Suburbans to get them around in the heavy snowfall. To transport her own house guests, she borrowed Noah's Suburban for the weekend.

After their weekend in October, Petrice, Vincenzo and Marquette, told their family of the changes in their Angel, but everyone was surprised when they saw it for themselves. Her open and sweet smile had returned, as had her outgoing personality and gracious demeanor. No longer did she attempt to fade into the walls around her, but, instead, interacted with her family members and their children.

They were amazed when she shared her sketches with them, and even more impressed when they learned that she'd helped Laura with her painting. Angel was Angel again.

Everyone attempted to become acquainted with Sparky, but she was overwhelmed with all of the unfamiliar people. Her behavior was worse than ever. She barked and growled and snapped at everyone, including sweet Rosa, until Tillie finally put her in her kennel and Vincenzo took it upstairs to the studio.

Thanksgiving Day itself was as difficult as Tillie and her children had feared it would be. They cried during the meal as everyone remembered the Thanksgiving before, when Alex was with them, and then the Thanksgivings of the past. Sam and Kate wanted to talk about their parents, and Guiseppi and Rosa broke down several times. Their first Thanksgiving in America had been spent with the Martin family. Guiseppi's brother, Angelo, and his wife, Penny were there. They'd all been so excited to start a new adventure. It was a lifetime ago, and yet it felt as if only a few months had passed. How had time gone by so quickly? Thirty-seven years ago, Rosa pointed out, she was Tillie's age, pregnant with a baby girl and had just left the country where she'd been born and raised.

It was a sorrowfully reminiscent day, and Tillie was thankful when it was over. She'd comforted her children, her parents, her brothers, their wives and poor, pitiful Sam, whose grief had remained the same as it was on that horrible day last April. Tillie's heart went out to him as it was apparent he still grieved deeply.

That night, after everyone had returned to their hotel rooms, and everyone at Tillie's house had gone to bed, A.J. and Laura crept down the hall and into their mother's room. Her light was still on, and she was sitting up in bed with a book. She smiled at them when she saw them in the doorway.

"What's up guys?" she asked.

They sat down on the edge of her bed and Laura began to cry.

A.J. rolled his eyes and pointed a thumb in his sister's direction. "*This* is why we wanted the Hansens to be here today."

Tillie took them into her arms and whispered, "I know, but we'll see them tomorrow. Come on guys, let's just hang in there. We're gonna be okay. We'll get a tree tomorrow and do some hiking in the snow..." She swallowed and looked at her sad children, and they slowly nodded.

"Can we sleep with you tonight, Mom?" A.J. asked.

"Of course," Tillie answered with a nod. She tucked them in, one on either side, and they all cried themselves to sleep.

*****

Shortly after noon, Noah and his sons arrived at Tillie's house. Since no one had arrived from the hotel yet, Tillie allowed Sparky to be free for a while. The rambunctious dog immediately tore into Noah when he came into the kitchen, pouncing upon his boots and biting at the bottoms of his pants.

Guiseppi frowned at the spectacle. "I cannot believe that you gave my daughter this beast," he groaned.

Noah watched the horrible attack at the bottom of his pants, and then he looked at Guiseppi. "I thought she might be lonely after you guys left, and Sparky could keep her company," he said.

"No one becomes *that* lonely."

At that moment, Tillie came through the sunroom, snapped her fingers at the dog and scolded, "Stop that, Sparky!"

Sparky went to Tillie, and she stooped to give her a soft pat.

"She only minds Angel," Noah pondered with a perplexed expression.

Tillie stood and smiled at Noah. "Hi. When did you guys get here?" she asked.

"Just a couple of minutes ago."

Guiseppi wondered if he was suddenly invisible. Tillie was looking at Noah as if he was the only person on the planet, and Noah returned his own star-struck gaze. Guiseppi couldn't help but smile as he realized that whatever happened between them eighteen and half years ago, was still very much alive. *They are still in love...how long can they wait before they suddenly turn up married...?*

Guiseppi cleared his throat to get their attention and said, "Ma`ma has filled thermoses with coffee and hot chocolate, in case we become cold."

"Okay," Tillie replied, smiling at her father, then looking around. "By the way, where is everybody?"

"The kids are outside," Noah answered. "They're discussing seating arrangements. We've got twenty people going on this trip."

Tillie looked surprised. "How are we going to transport everyone?" she asked.

"The Suburbans can each hold eight passengers," Noah answered. "We'll need to take mine, plus the ones you rented."

"Did you remember the permits?" she asked.

"Yep. I think we're all set."

"How about a saw?" Guiseppi asked curiously.

Noah looked at Guiseppi and comically raised one eyebrow as he replied, "I'm a professional, Mr. Caselli."

Tillie giggled like a little girl. Guiseppi smiled and shook his head. *They are nearly out of control.*

After a day of hiking through the snow near Rochford, South Dakota, and cutting down trees for the Hansens and the Martins, everyone returned to Tillie's where the ladies made sandwiches with the leftover turkey. Sam seemed a little better, even laughing at Sparky's terrible antics.

Noah and his sons stayed late, and Jake and Ty, along with Laura and A.J., taught their cousins a new card game. Tillie noticed the eight young people around her dining room table that evening and was surprised at how well they all got along, especially considering the difference in their ages. It was odd to watch them as they joked and laughed as if they'd known one another for years. Even Alyssa and Angelo, who were well on their way to becoming Harvard graduates, couldn't resist Jake's dry sense of humor.

Tillie watched her brothers visit boisterously with Noah. They, too, were so comfortable with one another. The difference in her brothers and how they spoke with Noah amazed her. They were always *friendly* with Alex, but barely tolerated him toward the end, and that was difficult. The difference in the way they felt about Noah was strangely open and bigger than life. *It's because of Ma`ma's prayers*, Tillie thought as she watched Noah's dancing, blue eyes glance about the room and find hers. She smiled in return, and he looked back to her brothers to continue whatever conversation they were into.

God is a perfect God, Tillie thought as she watched her family, *and He knows exactly what He's doing. Forgive me, Lord, for ever thinking otherwise....*

"Oh, we *will* stay on until Christmas," Guiseppi whispered as he paced the familiar floor in one of Tillie's guest rooms. He frowned as he rubbed his bald head with purpose. "Petrice will take everyone home, as planned tomorrow, but we will stay behind. I will feign illness."

Rosa's black eyes were more wide open than Guiseppi had ever seen them. "I am so surprised," she said. "Guiseppi, perhaps you should have *not* pushed so hard to get the thing going again. They are so very taken with one another."

"It is quiet unbelievable. I am afraid neither of them have the self-control it requires to..." he hesitated and looked at Rosa, rolled his eyes and shook his head. "*You know.*"

"They should wait. It is too soon for the children."

"Shall I speak with them?"

Rosa shrugged her tiny shoulders. "I do not know. They are adults, and they are good, Christian people —"

"Rosa, they could barely control themselves when she was married. How do you think it will go now?"

Rosa smiled nervously. "But they do not kiss, and very rarely did I even see them touch," she said. "He did not hold her hand or do anything lewd. I think there is some control there, Guiseppi, and let us not forget, we know Noah to be a knight. He has qualities that we have never known in other men. Do not forget about his beautiful son, Ty, and all that he has done for the child. How many men do that?"

Guiseppi relented with a sigh as he sat down on the bed beside Rosa. "I guess that if I had been kept away from you for so many years, my beautiful Rosa, my own heart would beat the same way as Noah's beats for Angel."

"But we will still be staying?"

Guiseppi nodded. "I am her father, just the same, and that will never change, no matter what her age. We will watch them just a little, my love. Okay?"

Rosa giggled. "You are *the best*, Guiseppi, and I love you so."

*****

December passed as quickly as November, and Tillie's parents rejoiced at the changes they saw in their daughter. For the past six

Christmases Tillie hadn't decorated for the holidays as she had before the accident, but this year was different. She and her children decorated the tree cut from the Black Hills National Forest with lights and their favorite bulbs. She hung garland from the railing on the steps, adding a string of dried cranberries and popcorn.

Noah hung lights on the front of the house, and in the bushes out front, while the snow in Rapid City continued to pile. It was the heaviest snowfall anyone in the area could remember, and Noah was over on a regular basis to clear Tillie's driveway with a snowblower.

Tillie baked gingerbread men, made divinity and fudge, and frosted hundreds of vanilla and almond Christmas cookies. Ma`ma was delighted to help. Tillie hadn't been so animated about Christmas in such a long time that Rosa nearly cried as each day unfolded. Years were erased from Tillie's expression and her graceful movements returned. Angel was Angel again, but even more beautiful than Rosa ever remembered.

Noah and his sons came over on Friday nights for cards, and now Guiseppi and Rosa wanted to be included. Jake taught them all a new game requiring two decks and four partners, and they played late into the night. Guiseppi found Jake's dry sense of humor irresistible, and he laughed so hard Tillie feared he might have a *real* heart attack. The two partnered up in the new game, winning nearly every hand.

No matter how late it was the night before, Noah was there early on Saturday morning for their ski trips to Terry Peak. Sometimes Guiseppi and Rosa went along. They watched Tillie's sketches come out of her pretty hands, reminding them of when she was young and had entertained them with her talents. Noah wandered in and out of the lodge 'checking' on everyone, but it was obvious he just wanted to see Tillie. He'd look into her eyes, tell her how beautiful her latest sketch was coming along, and then reluctantly rejoin their children on the slopes.

*****

Tillie and Rosa tried to keep their time in the crowded Rushmore Mall to a minimum, but they did have to do some Christmas shopping, so they bravely ventured out. As they walked along the midway of the mall, Tillie put her arm around her tiny mother and gave her a hug and a kiss upon the cheek.

"What was that for?" Rosa asked with a soft smile as she looked up at Tillie.

"I'm just so happy that you and Papa decided to stay this month. Me and the kids were really afraid to be alone, you know, for the holidays."

"You would have hardly been *alone*," Rosa tittered. She noticed they were approaching a coffee shop. "Let us have a short rest, my Angel," she suggested.

Tillie agreed, and they went inside the aromatic shop, ordered some coffees and sat down to rest their weary feet.

Rosa sipped at her hot coffee, smiling at her daughter. "What is happening between you and Noah, my Angel?"

Tillie smiled and her black eyes sparkled as she answered, "Something, but he promised not to do anything crazy."

Rosa raised her brows. "Have you talked about it?" she asked.

"Only that we wanted to spend some time together *with* our kids, because, you know, Ma`ma, we can't just forget about them. We're not so young anymore and we can't do as we please — or as we would like to."

Rosa nodded. "He loves you, Angel, and he is very good to your children. How long will you wait?"

Tillie's smile faded into a confused expression. "Wait for what?" she asked.

"Oh, Angel," Rosa chortled. "*Wait for marriage.* How long will you wait?"

"Oh, goodness, Ma`ma, we haven't even talked about that, but I'm praying everyday about this, and I don't want him to talk to me about it until God has everything worked out, you know, for the kids."

Rosa smiled. "You are the perfect Angel, and God is going to bless you, I just know it," she said.

Guiseppi refused to take another trip to the mall that season. He stayed home with Sparky in the safety of Tillie's quiet house. Over the course of the last month, the two had become friends. Sparky followed Guiseppi everywhere. It was a relief for Guiseppi not to be attacked, as he was irritated with being bitten on the leg every time he turned around. And while Angel had insisted that Sparky was only playing, Guiseppi had been convinced that Sparky wanted to kill him, beginning at his ankles and working her way from there.

He saw Noah's pick up pull into the drive, and he hurried to open the front door. It was snowing, as usual, and Noah was covered in wet flakes by the time he reached the door.

"Happy birthday, Noah!" Guiseppi greeted excitedly, as he opened the door and Noah stepped inside.

Noah smiled with surprise. "You remembered."

"How old are you this day?"

"Forty-two," Noah answered with a shake of his head. "I can hardly believe it."

Guiseppi laughed. "Oh, to be forty-two again…Angel and her mother have gone shopping."

"I know. I came over to see you, Mr. Caselli. Do you have time for a ride?"

Guiseppi caught his breath. "Of course," he answered. "Let me get my coat."

Noah drove them up a snowy Rimrock Highway, past the fish hatchery, and into the driveway with a sign that said Angel's Place. They visited along the way, but only about safe things, such as the weather, how awesomely Laura skied the weekend before, and whether or not Vincenzo would have any luck with his winter wheat. Guiseppi was fairly certain he knew what Noah wanted to talk about, and yet he was stumped by his hesitation.

As they rounded the corner of the long driveway, the beautiful Victorian house came into view. Guiseppi could only wonder what was going on as Noah parked the truck.

"Come on," Noah said with a smile. "I gotta show you something."

Guiseppi followed Noah up the porch steps. They were greeted in the elegant foyer by a smiling woman.

"Hey, Mavis," Noah greeted.

"Hello, Noah," she replied with a polite smile.

"This is Guiseppi Caselli," Noah introduced. "Mr. Caselli, this is Mavis Olson. She manages this place. It's a bed and breakfast right now."

Guiseppi smiled curiously at the woman, extending his hand. "How very nice to meet you," he said.

"Thank you." She smiled at Guiseppi, and then she looked back at Noah and said, "I made you guys some coffee, whenever you're ready."

"Thanks, Mavis," Noah replied. "I'm gonna show him around really quick and then we'll come down."

Guiseppi got the most peculiar feeling in his stomach as he watched Mavis walk away, and he and Noah were left alone in the foyer.

"That's my favorite light," Noah said, pointing above them at the crystal chandelier sparkling in the high ceiling. He looked toward what appeared to be a formal dining room, with floor to ceiling windows, and he sighed wistfully. "But what I really love is the way the sun comes up in the mornings. It hits the front porch first, and then slowly moves over the glass in the dining room and then into the hall, and when it catches in the chandelier above, it makes this whole entryway sparkle." He sighed again and looked at a very quiet Guiseppi. He turned to the winding staircase. "I'll show you the upstairs first."

Guiseppi nodded and followed Noah up the steps.

"I did all of the woodwork by hand," Noah said as they walked along the hall upstairs. He led Guiseppi to the paned glass window, bathing the entire hall in snowy brightness.

"You what?" Guiseppi asked curiously.

"I did all of the woodwork by hand," Noah replied, stopping at the window to look out over the hills in the distance. "And I made sure there were plenty of views of the Black Hills, because she loved them so much."

"Oh, Noah," Guiseppi gasped in a whisper. "*You* built this house?"

"Yep. And when I couldn't find Angel, I leased it to a lady who turned it into a bed and breakfast. She's getting really old now, and says she wants out of her lease before spring." He chuckled and shook his head. "There are six bedrooms up here." He turned around to lead Guiseppi back down the hall, pausing in the doorway of the master suite. "This one would have been ours." He led Guiseppi into the room, stopping at the bathroom with its claw-foot tub.

Guiseppi gasped again. "Angel had one of those in Sioux Falls," he whispered.

"And there's a little room over there," Noah went on, pointing in the direction of the small, empty room. "It was supposed to be the nursery." He turned again, leading Guiseppi from the room and into the hall, where he continued, "I put a bathroom between the other rooms up here, so there wouldn't be any fights in the mornings." Noah laughed quietly as he and Guiseppi walked along. "I planned for everything. I thought we'd have a bunch of kids."

Guiseppi was without words as he walked along next to Noah in stunned silence. The house was a literal mansion, and Noah had built it especially for his daughter. Guiseppi was overwhelmed.

"It is beautiful," he finally managed to say as they descended the winding staircase.

Noah faintly smiled. "Thanks. I really enjoyed building it."

Noah led Guiseppi through the kitchen and into the studio, where Mavis had already placed a pot of coffee and two cups. Noah reached for one, filled it for Guiseppi and handed it to him. Then he filled one for himself.

"Sit here," Noah suggested, indicating the chair facing the west window. Guiseppi took a seat. Noah sat down across from him and sipped at his coffee. "I made sure that this window faced the west because I wanted her to be able to see the hills when she painted. This is the studio."

Guiseppi's eyes filled with tears. "You are an amazing man, Noah Hansen," he said.

Noah smiled and raised his brows. "I was hoping you'd say something like that." He set his cup down and took two felt boxes out of his pocket. He set one down beside his coffee cup, and opened the other for Guiseppi. Guiseppi hesitantly reached for the small diamond ring inside.

"It was all I could afford," Noah explained. "Read the inscription."

Guiseppi squinted, peering at the inner circle of the band. He softly gasped, "*For Angel, 4/75.*"

"I would have given her the ring that night, had she showed," Noah went on, reaching for the other box. "Of course, now, I've got some money so I picked this one out for her…" He opened the box, " 'Cause she's not a girl anymore."

Guiseppi gasped softly again as he looked at the much larger diamond, set into a plain gold band, and then he looked at Noah's.

"Mr. Caselli, can I marry your daughter?"

Guiseppi gulped. "When?" he asked.

"When the time is right. Please know that I am praying all day long, every day about this. I won't do anything until the Lord tells me it's okay."

"Then why ask me now?" Guiseppi whispered.

"You'll be leaving after Christmas and if God should allow while you're away, I'll ask her…but I wanted to be sure that I had your blessing." Noah took a deep breath. "I promise not to elope with her or anything like that. I'll make sure we have a proper wedding and that everyone has plenty of time to be here for it."

Tears spilled onto Guiseppi's dark cheeks. He quickly wiped them away and faintly smiled as he apologized "Forgive me for being so *Italiano*…she was always meant to be *your* gift, Noah, but I do worry about her children. They are still missing their father."

"I know. And the only reason I've waited this long is for them. Mr. Caselli, I love her and I always have. I can't explain it; I just have to be with her."

Guiseppi slowly nodded. “You have my blessing, Noah Hansen, and from this day, you will call me Guiseppi.”

“Thank you.” Noah’s blue eyes danced and sparkled. “Thank you, Guiseppi.”

PART II

NOAH

Chapter 12

April, 1994

Being with Noah and his sons for the entire winter was very good for A.J. and Laura. The four children bonded in a way Noah and Tillie never imagined, and it was a blessing to watch the four of them together. They rarely argued, and when they did, they were quick to settle things.

Every Friday night over the long, Black Hills winter, they partnered up and played cards viciously around Tillie's dining room table: Noah and A.J., Laura and Ty, and Tillie and Jake. Joshua and Mona were known to join these card-playing sessions as well, and became very good at Jake's two-decked game

On Saturday mornings they went to Terry Peak and skied the entire day away. They returned to Rapid City before dark to have supper with Angel. On Sundays they attended church together, and the long wait for Friday began again.

Noah's weeks were longer than he could stand. He couldn't wait for Friday night after work. He zoomed home to change his clothes, pick up his boys, and head over to see Angel. He tried not to be too obvious in front of the children, but sometimes he couldn't resist at least a touch of her hand or a smile into her pretty eyes. She *always* laughed at all of his jokes, even when they were corny, and she *always* smiled back whenever he smiled first. Even though she didn't say it, he knew she still loved him by the way she looked at him, and in the way she said his name. He didn't tell her that he had Guiseppi's blessing because he didn't think A.J. and Laura were ready. But things were getting better and better for the children, and he doubted God would make him wait much longer. He prayed for a *specific sign* from God for when the time was right, promising to act immediately when the sign was revealed.

Over the winter months Tillie regularly 'sneaked' over to have coffee with Maggie and Estelle. Noah caught them one morning in February, and the three of them giggled like schoolgirls. Noah wondered about how much Maggie had told Angel, and later, when they had a chance to be alone, Maggie assured Noah that they'd kept the house a secret. After all, it was always intended to be a surprise for Angel. However, they did tell her about Ty and how Noah and Carrie had gotten together. According to Maggie, Tillie cried the day she was told the story. A few weeks later, Noah asked Tillie if she had any questions about that, and if she would please not tell anyone. Because, after all, Ty was truly Noah's son, and it really didn't matter where he had come from, just that he had come to Noah. Tillie agreed to always keep his secret.

An extremely early and warm spring in the Black Hills melted all of the decent snow from Terry Peak. This prompted Noah to ask if they could go on an early picnic. It was near a date he never forgot — the day he and Tillie had gone hiking in the Black Hills in April, 1975. He wondered if she would remember, and thought about asking her.

Noah and Tillie spoke very briefly about how they could let their children know of their *acquaintance* many years ago. Naturally, they wouldn't share all of the emotional details, however, they wanted their children to know *something* of their past. They ended the short conversation by deciding to pray about it, promising to follow wherever the Lord led them.

Tillie hadn't been to Spearfish Canyon since 1975, but she recognized the drive when Noah turned off the highway at Cheyenne Crossing, heading north into the Canyon. She smiled from her place in the passenger seat of the Suburban, and Noah glanced her way with a grin.

"So, when was the last time you were up here?" he murmured.

Tillie giggled softly, shook her head and turned from him to look out of her window. "You know," she quietly replied.

Noah laughed at her silly response.

From the back seat, Jake and Laura saw the mysterious, but loving glance Tillie and Noah had shared, but they didn't hear Tillie's muffled response. They'd noticed several of these particular looks, and had even discussed the possibility that something *might* be going on. *But then again, maybe not.* They never held hands, they never kissed, and they didn't go out on dates. Just the same, Laura and Jake watched for little signs like the one they'd just witnessed.

Jake raised his eyebrow and looked at Laura, nodded his head, and hoped she got his message. It was his own personal, coded sign that he'd seen something.

Laura gave him her code, a double blink, and nodded in return. She glanced over her shoulder at her brother and Ty who were seated in the third seat of the Suburban. She sighed disgustedly. As usual, they'd missed it. The two of them were engrossed in an old Post 22 program and probably hadn't looked up since they'd left Rapid City.

Laura and Jake sighed and shook their heads. Well, at least *they* paid attention to what was going on around here.

As it had nineteen years before, the Black Hills had warmed the day to unexpectedly high temperatures. The buds on the hardwood trees were forced open by the early, spring heat, and the fresh smell of pine was drawn out of the trees. Noah parked in a designated area, and everyone got out. A.J. and Ty collected the picnic basket and cooler, while Laura carried a blanket.

"Did you bring your camera?" Noah asked Tillie.

"I did," Tillie answered with a smile, giving the bag on her shoulder a pat.

"Good," Noah said, reaching for her hand as they walked along a rocky trail. "I don't want you to trip."

Jake rolled his eyes and looked at Laura, who gave him the double blink sign as they walked behind them.

They had to hike up a slight incline, and Tillie did get a little off balance, which made Noah's handholding look *almost* legitimate. After all, she would always have a problem with her balance.

Soon they reached an area close to Bridal Veil Falls. Tillie had to swallow hard to keep from crying. It was as if they'd stepped back into a time left in perfect condition, just for them. It was *exactly* the way she remembered it...the filmy, foamy water flowing over the rocks, giving it the appearance of a long, taffeta bridal veil as it trailed gracefully down the aisle of a church. Tillie caught her breath and gave Noah's hand a gentle squeeze. He looked at her and smiled.

"Wow," Laura gasped with wide-open eyes. "This is incredible. You gotta get a picture of this, Mom."

Tillie could only nod.

"There's a nice little place closer to the pond," Noah said as he tightened his grip on Tillie's hand. "We can picnic down there."

The decline was nearly straight down, but Tillie leaned on Noah's strong arm as he led them down the rocky path. The soft roar of the waterfall made Tillie's heart pound with sentimental reminiscence. She glanced at Noah and saw him smiling. *Thank you, God,* she prayed, *for this wonderful moment...and thank you for the beautiful memory.*

Noah showed them to a dry area near the pond. Jake took the blanket from Laura and spread it out on the ground.

"Haven't you ever seen this before, Laura?" he asked curiously. " 'Cause me and Ty and Dad have been up here like about a bazillion times." He frowned mischievously at his father. "Must be your *favorite* place."

"It is," Noah replied, looking away from the eyes of his probing son.

"It's really cool up here," A.J. said, setting down the picnic basket. "But let's eat. I'm starved."

Ty set down the cooler next to the picnic basket and opened it. He pulled out a Coke, then rummaged through the picnic basket. "Did you bring any of those little cookie thingies." He looked at Tillie.

"What's a little cookie thingie?" Tillie questioned as she took a seat on the blanket next to the picnic basket, looking inside.

"You know," Ty said, "those little round things that you put the white stuff into."

"Cannoli?"

"Yeah. Cannoli. Did you bring any?"

"Yes," Tillie answered, "The filling is in the cooler."

Noah sat down next to Tillie, maybe a little closer than usual, and Jake and Laura briefly exchanged another coded look.

Well, the blanket is pretty small for all six of us, Jake thought, *maybe they're just trying not to hog it up.*

"So," Jake said, taking a bite out of sandwich, "what are we gonna do after we eat?"

"I thought we'd hike around here for a while," Noah answered.

Jake raised an eyebrow...*my perfect opportunity,* "Mrs. Martin can't hike, can you?"

"I can give it a try. Maybe if you guys help me, I won't fall."

"We can help you, Mom," A.J. volunteered.

Jake shook his head. *Shut up, A.J. I'm tryin' to get Dad to hang himself here.*

Noah noticed Tillie's long gaze at the waterfall, and he leaned close to her ear and whispered, "What are you thinking about?"

Tillie turned her head and smiled into his eyes, and then she looked back at the water fall. "I was just remembering that story."

"What story?" Jake asked quickly, before A.J. had a chance to ruin it. *Something is going on with those two today and I'm going to get to the bottom of it!*

Tillie smiled at Jake and began, "Those falls weren't always there. It all started when an Indian Warrior became engaged to a girl who had a white mother and a Sioux Indian Chief for her father. One day, the Warrior had to leave to fight a great battle and when he returned to his tribe, his betrothed had taken ill and was dying from a fever. Her parents took the only thing of value they had, which was the bridal veil worn by the Chief's wife on their wedding day, gave it to the Warrior and sent him to buy medicine with it. The Warrior did as he was told, taking the veil to the nearest settlement. He bought medicine and returned as quickly as he could to his dying bride. She took the medicine and soon was well again.

"Now, the bride had nothing to wear on her head because it had been sold for medicine, but they went ahead with the wedding anyway, right here, on this very spot. And when the Warrior kissed his bride, God broke open the rocks above and let a veil run through for her. The old Chief said that it was God's affirmation of the Warrior's noble and pure heart and that the waters would flow here forever."

"Oh," Laura breathed with a smile. She placed her hand over her heart and closed her eyes. "That is the *most* romantic story I've ever heard."

"Oh, brother," Jake moaned, rolling his eyes. He looked at Ty and A.J., who also seemed quite thrown by the sickening story.

Ty laughed at his little brother. He politely asked Tillie, "Where did you hear that story?"

"From your dad," Tillie answered.

Laura's black eyes flew open in amazement, and Jake's jaw hung open.

"When?" Jake whispered. *Dad's not the romantic type...never has been.*

"Oh, let's see now." Tillie took a breath and pretended to think. "About nineteen years ago." She playfully frowned at Noah. "Right?"

"Right," Noah answered with a smile and a nod.

A.J. almost choked on his Coke. He looked seriously at his mother and asked, "How did you guys know each other back then?"

"I had a motorcycle," Noah volunteered with a smile, "and she wanted a ride real bad."

A.J. and Laura's eyes flew open with surprise again. They stared at their mother in disbelief.

"You actually rode a motorcycle?" Laura asked.

"Yes," Tillie laughed.

"Well," Noah added, "it was a Harley, so you could hardly blame the girl. I couldn't *beat* her away from the thing, so I finally just let her have a ride."

Noah's horrible untruth made Tillie and all of their children laugh out loud.

"Did you like Dad?" Jake asked with a curious smile.

Tillie nodded with a soft smile as she looked at Noah and confessed, "I liked him right away."

"No kidding?" Laura attempted to confirm with the same curious smile Jake had. "Then why didn't you guys ever get together?"

"Well, we lived too far apart," Noah answered with a smile. "I was too busy with stuff. I had to finish school and start my business."

Tillie nodded at the perfect explanation, and their children nodded as well.

Maybe that's all it is, Jake thought, *just a friendship that's been around for years...but, then again, maybe not.*

*****

Petrice was too busy to fly his parents to Rapid City that April, but Guiseppi was determined to make good on his promise to help coach A.J. and Jake's baseball team. So, much to the disapproval of their children, Guiseppi and Rosa set out in their new, gold Cadillac. Before leaving Sioux Falls, he announced that he was itching to spend some of the inheritance before he died, and his children shuddered at his poor choice of humor. They took turns telling him he was too old to make a drive from Sioux Falls to Rapid City, but Guiseppi disagreed heartily. After all, he was a very youthful seventy-seven and it was high time he and Rosa had a little vacation. They stopped along the way at Guiseppi's favorite places, picking up trinkets for Noah's and Tillie's children, as well as their other grandchildren. They finally made their way into Rapid City around suppertime on the last Friday in April, 1994.

Tillie jumped from her front porch when her parents pulled into the driveway. Noah and his boys had waited with them to make sure everyone arrived safely.

"Oh, I'm so glad you made it!" She exclaimed, throwing her arms around her mother and then her father. "We were so *worried* about you."

"Oh, please," Rosa scoffed. "We are as fit as two fiddles. Do not give us so much grief."

"It will take more than a twelve hour drive to kill this old bird," Guiseppi muttered.

Tillie laughed and hugged them again.

Everyone hugged and kissed like crazy, and then Tillie announced that supper was waiting if they were ready. They confessed that they'd snacked along the way, but could probably manage a few bites of whatever delectable treat was waiting in Angel's kitchen.

"She made this Sicilian stew stuff," Noah tried to describe to Guiseppi as they walked into the house. "It's really gonna be good."

Guiseppi smiled as he looked at his pretty Angel, seeing that all was right with her once again, and it filled his old heart with joy.

*****

After Noah and his sons left that evening, and Angel's children had wandered up to bed, Guiseppi found his daughter on her stone patio. She was alone at last, staring quietly into the stars of the Black Hills sky. He took a seat in a chair next to her lounger.

She smiled at her father and said, "Hi, Papa. Is everything okay with your room?"

"Perfect, as always. But I did notice that you have not painted your sunroom as you planned."

"Oh," she sighed and shook her head. "Well, we had such a snowy, old winter, and I couldn't get the windows open enough. I was afraid I'd fume myself, but I'm gonna get it done before everybody comes for Memorial Day weekend."

"Ma`ma and I will help."

"Sure," she replied as she gazed back up at the stars, and then happily sighed. "The boys are so excited about you being here for baseball."

"I know. And they are such wonderful treasures."

"Have you heard from Marquette?" she asked.

"No, but I expect to shortly. Whatever the two of them are working on must be very secretive. I believe them to be in the Middle East again."

"Oh," Tillie moaned. "I'll be glad when they're back. I haven't heard from them since Christmas."

Guiseppi nodded.

"Vincenzo told Noah that hogs are up."

"They are." Guiseppi took a deep breath. "My Angel, your children seem to have healed. How are they?"

"They're good, Papa." Tillie looked at her father. "They still miss him, but I think they always will."

Guiseppi nodded. "And how about you, my Angel?" He gently reached for her left hand. "Why do you still wear your ring?"

Tillie swallowed hard. "I don't know, Papa."

Guiseppi softly sighed. "Do you miss him?"

"Sometimes…but you know, Papa, Alex left me *long* before he ever died. What I really miss is what we had before…you know…all of that."

Guiseppi nodded again. "Are you afraid of a life with Noah? Is that why you still wear your ring?"

"I *am* afraid, Papa. What if he finds something else." She took a breath and shook her head. "Alex *always* found something else, right up until the horrible end."

"Noah is a *different* man," Guiseppi gently defended. "Do you love Noah?"

"More than anything. Sometimes I want to be with him so much that it scares me."

Guiseppi frowned. "And so you wear your ring?"

Tillie looked into her father's eyes, praying for an all profound answer that would completely melt her heart.

Guiseppi smiled as he held her left hand in his own. "There is an old tradition in *Italia*…well, some say it came from the French, but I heard of it in *Italia*…when a young lady is widowed before her time, and if her father is still living, it then becomes his responsibility to tell her when her tears have been enough." He reached for her ring with his other hand, carefully worked it off of her finger and laid it into her palm. He closed her fingers around it. "You may keep this ring, but only in a place where your Noah will never see it. Your tears have been enough, my Angel, *because they that wait upon the LORD shall renew their strength; they shall mount up with wings as eagles; they shall run, and not be weary; and they shall walk, and not faint.*"

Tears rolled down her cheeks as she looked at her wise and wonderful father. "Isaiah 40:31," she whispered.

Guiseppi nodded. "The Lord gave it to me when you were very small." Tillie looked confused, and her father laughed through his tears. "I was so afraid to become a father again at the age of forty…the boys were big, nearly ready to leave home…I had raised my family…I was so afraid to start over…but one night, as I prayed for strength and wisdom, God led me to that verse and it is what has helped me through so many trying times, because, my Angel, we *do* hope in the Lord, and now your heart flies like an eagle."

Tillie's eyes gave way to thousands of tears, and she went into her father's comforting arms.

Guiseppi smiled as he continued, "And just as God comforted His exiled people, telling them that their tears had been enough, He comforts you now and dries your tears of despair — because you have hope in Him." Guiseppi paused to smile. "Your tears have been enough, my Angel. Let us rejoice and move on."

Tillie nodded and whispered, "Thanks, Papa. You're the best, and you always have been."

*****

May began with a dreadful thunderstorm, darkening the sunny skies in the Black Hills. Poor Sparky couldn't stand the horrible thunder and lightning, and she hid herself beneath Tillie's bed. The first ball games of the season were canceled and rescheduled. The boys were beside themselves, but Guiseppi and Noah took them, along with Laura and Heidi, to the movies. Tillie and Rosa stayed at home to complete a list of things they needed before the rest of the family arrived for Memorial Day weekend.

Tillie and Rosa made a pot of hot tea, sat down together on the love seat in the sunroom, and enjoyed the pounding of the rain above them.

"Mmm." Tillie sipped the orange and spiced tea. "Only you can make it this way, Ma`ma."

"It was always your favorite."

"And we can't forget to pick up an extra cooler," Tillie said, quickly penciling it onto her list. "We never have enough cool drinks."

"If only we had Vincenzo's water barrels," Rosa giggled. "With some straws."

Tillie laughed. "And I have to find time to get this sunroom finished," she went on. "I want it to look perfect when everybody gets here. And what about that old furniture in the living room? What should I do about that? I haven't really been able to find anything that I like. Maybe I should try to clean it or something."

Rosa smiled as she sipped at her tea, looking at Tillie thoughtfully.

"What, Ma`ma?" Tillie questioned with a curious smile.

"So many changes in you…my old heart is so blessed."

Tillie smiled and whispered, "I've got a secret, Ma`ma."

"Oh?" Rosa raised one eyebrow. "What kind of a secret?"

"One that only *I* know about."

Rosa chuckled. "Well, are you going to tell me?"

Tillie hesitated for a moment. She finally nodded and stood. "It's upstairs, Ma`ma. Come on."

Rosa followed her daughter up the steps, down the hall, and into the studio. Tillie turned on the lights, and in the corner, Rosa saw the familiar, covered easel, one she knew that had waited for Tillie for several years.

"I still remember the day I stopped working on this painting," Tillie said with a smile, lifting the sheet to expose the painting beneath. "It was right before Christmas in 1986." She chuckled and added, "Melinda had been calling about her wedding plans on a weekly basis, and I was really ticked off."

The portrait was of Rosa and Delia walking along the floor of a canyon in the Black Hills. Tillie had used hues of purples, blues and grays, and Rosa gasped when she saw it.

"It is beautiful!" she whispered.

"Thank you." Tillie looked wistfully at the painting. "I had intended to give it to Alex, but...I could never finish it until just recently."

"You have been painting then?" Rosa asked with surprise.

"Painting requires a steadier hand, and I cannot paint unless all is right in my world." She shrugged, "I don't know, Ma`ma, it's hard to explain."

"It appears to be finished now," Rosa said.

"I finished it this winter."

"All is right in your world, my Angel?"

"Just about." Tillie winked at her mother. "We told the kids a couple of weeks back that we knew each other a long time ago."

"You did? How did that go?"

Tillie smiled and answered, "They really didn't say too much, but I think Laura and Jake suspect something. They have this funny, little sign with their eyes they think we don't know about."

Rosa smiled and looked into her daughter's sparkling black eyes. "Only once in your life do I remember seeing this expression upon your face."

"When, Ma`ma?" Tillie asked.

"When you returned from Rapid City the *first* time." Rosa raised her eyebrow, attempting a mysterious expression. "I thought to myself, *boy, that was some art show*."

Tillie laughed and said, "He makes me feel young again, Ma`ma. It's so different with Noah, and it *always* has been."

"The children. Are they ready?"

"I think so, but I'm still praying about it."

Rosa put her arms around her daughter and held her tight. "You are such a good girl, my Angel. God is blessing you and your children." Her own expression became sincerely curious. "How much fun it will be to plan a wedding again. Shall I start the cookies?"

"Oh, Ma`ma!" Tillie laughed. "I guess we'll just have to see."

*****

The children only had a few days left of school in Rapid City, South Dakota. Memorial Day weekend was nearly upon them, and Tillie's brothers and their families would arrive on Saturday. The sun was shining and the day was hot, prompting Tillie to use the good fortune of decent weather to open her windows and paint the sunroom. She covered everything in the sunroom with the heavy plastic drop cloth Sparky loved to chase.

"Stop that!" Tillie scolded Sparky as she bit at the plastic, attempting to run off with it in her mouth. "No! No! Bad dog!" Tillie snapped her fingers.

Sparky cowered away, taking her little self to a corner where she plopped down and watched Tillie move around the room with that wonderful plastic.

"What a terrible little beast," Guiseppi grumbled as he watched the scene from the doorway of the kitchen; it was his pretty daughter, dressed in a most dreadful pair of cut-off jeans and an oversized t-shirt. Her hair was tied up with what appeared to be an old rag. In Guiseppi's eyes, she looked about twelve years old as she attempted to correct her undisciplined little dog.

"She's just a puppy," Tillie defended with a smile.

"That dog is nearly a year old," Guiseppi pointed out, "and livestock does not belong in the house."

Tillie laughed. "It's not like I've got a cow in here, Papa! Besides, she keeps me company when you and Ma`ma are away." As she began to wrestle her ladder into place, she heard Guiseppi gasp. "What?" she turned and looked at her father.

"Let us call someone to do this," Guiseppi said. "I am so afraid that you will fall."

"I won't fall," Tillie assured with a determined expression. "How do you think I got the whole living room done. This is only one wall. I'll be done in a couple of hours."

Guiseppi put his hand over his heart, moaning. He looked pleadingly at his daughter and said, "I do not think I can take it if you go up on that ladder."

Tillie chuckled and begged, "Papa, please don't do that."

Rosa came down the steps with her purse in hand. She was dressed in nice slacks and a white blouse, and she looked at her husband."I need a ride to the store," she announced with a smile.

"Right now?!" Guiseppi gasped with disbelief. "And leave the child alone to kill herself?!"

"I'm not a child," Tillie scoffed with a grin. "I'll be thirty-seven years old next week. Good grief, I'm practically forty."

"Oh," Guiseppi moaned, clutching at his heart again. "Do you hear the way she speaks to me?"

Rosa tittered, "Come along, my love. I think she will be okay, and I must run a few errands for her party."

Guiseppi shook his index finger at his daughter and admonished, "When your brothers get here, I will tell them how unmanageable you have become —"

Tillie and Rosa laughed.

He shook his head with a frown. "The two of you have conspired behind my old back."

"Please, Guiseppi," Rosa said, tenderly rubbing his shoulder, "let us go. I wish to have my errands complete before the children get home from school."

Guiseppi sighed heavily and started for the door with his wife. He paused at the knob, looking back his daughter. "Please be careful, my Angel."

"I will, Papa," she promised.

Guiseppi left reluctantly, and Tillie ascended the ladder to begin her project.

A few hours later, as she predicted, the wall was nearly finished. She stood in the doorway of the kitchen, admiring her work. It had turned out *exactly* as she thought. The sunlight spilling in through the glass ceiling bounced off the pale yellow wall, lighting the whole room with radiant brightness. Only a few places near the ceiling required touch-ups, and she climbed the ladder again.

She heard a knock, and then the garage door creaking open in the kitchen. Sparky flew into a furry storm, dashing at whoever had entered the kitchen. She barked like a maniac, biting at the feet and pants of whoever had dared enter *her* kitchen.

"Stop that, you little demon," Tillie heard Noah admonish as he came into the sunroom. He must have just left a worksite because his shirt and jeans were dusty. Tillie smiled. She loved that part of him.

"Hi, what are you doing here?" she asked with surprise.

Noah couldn't hide his worried expression as he looked at her up there on that ladder. He attempted a soft smile as he answered, "I was on my way back from my job on Sheridan Lake Road and I thought I'd drop off that extra cooler…and what are you doing on that ladder *again*?"

"Painting. How do you like it?"

"I hate it when you get on the ladder. Did you do all of this by yourself?"

"Yes. And you can't tell me that you don't think it makes a difference, because I think it's beautiful."

Noah sighed. "It looks great, but it makes me nervous. You can hardly keep your balance when we go hiking."

"You mean, you're afraid I'll fall?" Tillie asked with a mischievous sparkle in her eyes.

"Yes, it scares me to death," Noah admitted.

Tillie pretended to lose her balance then, just long enough to make Noah gasp and reach out his arms beneath her. She quickly recovered, took a tight hold of the sides of the ladder, and laughed at the expression on his face.

"Don't do that!" Noah laughed nervously. "What if you *really* fall?"

Tillie laughed again. "I won't. I have this thing mastered. Watch." She pretended to reel backwards, but this time she really did lose her balance. She couldn't get a hold of the side of the ladder in time to catch herself. She let out a little scream as she fell directly into Noah's arms.

He laughed. "Now, *that* was funny."

"I feel really stupid," Tillie moaned, rolling her eyes.

Noah laughed again. "Say," he began, "this is incredibly convenient — kinda like manna from Heaven."

Tillie smiled as she looked at his handsome face and into his dancing, blue eyes. She could smell the soft scent of Old Spice and dust, and her heart skipped a beat. She touched his cheek as she said, "I love you, Noah."

Noah thought he might drop her when he heard her words, but he held on tightly. *That's the sign!* He lowered his lips to hers, kissed her tenderly and looked into her eyes. "I love you, Angel." He softly kissed her again as he held her close to himself. "You can't imagine how long I've waited to hear you say that."

Tillie smiled and touched the soft gray at his temples.

Noah sighed. "This is *not* at all how I planned it would go, but I've gotta ask you something, and I've gotta ask it *now*."

"Okay." Tillie nodded with a smile.

Noah sat her down on the plastic covered love seat and knelt in front of her. He took one of her pretty hands into his own, gave it a soft kiss and said, "Angel, I've had your father's blessing since December. Will you please marry me?"

"Yes, I want to marry you!" Her heart pounded as tears of joy fell from her eyes. She put her arms around Noah's neck, exclaiming, "I want to be married to you!"

"When?" he asked.

"Oh, this afternoon," she answered, and they both laughed.

"Well, we'd better talk to the kids after school, and see how everything goes. I can call Josh and see what he has available. We have to get a license you know."

Tillie nodded. "I know. I was just joking…sort of." If the Justice of the Peace would have been standing right there, she would have married Noah on the spot.

"I have something to show you right now." Noah got to his feet, noticing that she wasn't wearing shoes or socks.

"What? I can't go anywhere looking like this!" she protested.

"You look great," Noah said. "Just get your shoes. I have to show you something."

Tillie hesitated for a moment, biting her lip. "Okay," she relented, "give me just a second." She skipped up the stairs, grabbed an old pair of sandals, and hurried back to where Noah waited in the sunroom. "Come on Sparky." She picked up her little dog and hurried to the kennel. She tossed Sparky inside and quickly closed the door. "I have to leave a note for Papa and Ma`ma. They'll be back in a minute and I don't want them to worry."

"You are such a good kid," Noah said with smile as he watched her reach for the pad and pen by the phone. She scribbled a quick note, and turned back to him.

Noah led her from the kitchen through the garage and out to his pickup, where he opened the door for her and she got inside. He reached for the glove box just in front of her, pulling out the two felt boxes that had ridden around with him, *just in case*, for the last several months.

"I'm so funny," Noah chuckled with a shake of his head. "I should have given you this first."

Tillie gasped when she saw the obvious ring boxes, wondering why there were two of them. Noah opened the darker one first, and it was the new diamond that he bought for her last December. He plucked it from its safe nest inside, reached for her left hand, and slid it onto her finger.

"It's beautiful," she whispered. "Thank you, Noah."

He looked into her eyes, leaned close for another soft kiss on her lips, and opened the other box. "This was the first one," he explained. "I want to give you both of them."

Tillie gasped again as she looked at the tiny diamond in the other box, and then into Noah's eyes. "You mean, you had it with you that night?" she asked.

Noah nodded. "You would have come home with this ring on your finger and your father would have probably had me arrested." He chuckled, "But I wouldn't have cared. I'd been arrested before." They both laughed, and Noah took the old ring from its box. "Read the inscription."

Tillie peered into the inner circle of the ring. "*For Angel...4/75*." She looked at Noah and said, "Oh, Noah, I'm so sorry that it's taken us so long —"

"No, don't be sorry anymore. Don't *ever* look back, Angel. *Forget what is behind and strain toward what is ahead, press on toward the goal to win the prize for which God has called us heavenward in Jesus*." He took the ring from her hands, and slid it onto the middle finger of her right hand, next to the mother's ring that she wore. "There," he sighed with a smile. "Now we can go." He smiled into her eyes, and gave her lips one more delicate kiss. He closed her door, and hurried to the driver's side. He laughed out loud as he backed out of the driveway.

"What's so funny?" she asked.

"I just can't believe it." He laughed again. "We're actually getting married." He smiled and shook his head. "I have half a mind to camp out in your front yard so that I don't lose track of you again —" Noah was interrupted by Tillie's laughter, and he glanced over at her. "You are just gonna love this."

"What is it?"

"It's too hard to explain. You have to see it for yourself."

Tillie watched the road before them as they turned out of her neighborhood, onto Jackson Boulevard, and headed west.

"It's really close by," Noah said, reaching for her hand, then giving it a tender kiss as they drove along. They passed Canyon Lake and headed into Rimrock Canyon.

"Isn't the fish hatchery back here?" Tillie asked curiously.

"It sure is," Noah answered.

In less than fifteen minutes they passed the fish hatchery on the winding, gravel road, and through a cluster of pine trees. They passed a sign that said, Angel's Place, and Tillie got the strangest feeling in the pit of her stomach. Around a bend, and through a few more trees, the green meadow opened up before them. The magnificent Victorian mansion came into view against the Black Hills and a clear, blue sky.

"Wow," Tillie breathed, as they parked. "That's a *really* nice house."

"Think so?" Noah asked. He looked at Tillie, raising one eyebrow.

"Yes," Tillie chuckled at his mysterious expression.

"Well, let's go have a look," he said.

"No!" Tillie softly gasped. "What if somebody sees me?! I look like a bum!"

Noah laughed out loud. "You don't look like a bum. Besides, it's empty. There's nobody in there."

Tillie hesitantly nodded...he seemed to want to see it so much.

"Come on." Noah jumped out of the truck and hurried over to open the door for her. He walked her up to the porch and to the front door. She was surprised when he produced a key, unlocked the door, and opened it for her. She stepped inside, and was awestruck with the entrance. Noah turned on the light above her, filling the foyer with an elegant sparkle.

"Wow." Tillie looked around. "This is *awesome*." She glanced into the formal dining room, with its floor to ceiling, paned glass windows. "I *love* that dining room." She looked at Noah with a soft frown. "Is it the dining room?"

"Yes," Noah answered with a soft sigh and a smile. "And the kitchen is straight back through there. There's a little parlor over there."

"Look at this incredible wood work." Tillie gently reached out for a touch of the railing on the winding staircase. She looked at Noah and got the strangest feeling. "You built this, didn't you?"

"Yes," he answered, so satisfied with her reaction that he could have done back flips. He took her into his arms with a sigh. "I built it for you."

"You what?" She looked at him with a soft frown, waiting for further explanation.

"I built it for you," Noah repeated with a smile. "And when I didn't find you, I leased it to a lady who turned it into a bed and breakfast —"

"You built it for *me*?" Tillie looked so amazed that it made Noah laugh. While Maggie had shared many secrets with Tillie, this had certainly not been one of them. Tillie was completely taken aback.

"I thought you might like it. Do you want to see the rest of it?" he asked.

"Do you still own it?" Tillie asked, still so shocked at what she was hearing that she hadn't been able to put it all together.

"Sure do. I could never bring myself to part with it."

He led her up the winding staircase saying, "And lucky thing, too, because we're gonna need all six bedrooms — do you think the kids will go for that? I mean, all of us moving in together, after we're married, of course."

Tillie laughed nervously and shrugged. "Probably. I don't know. We'll have to ask them about that when we tell them about the wedding."

Noah took her all through the house, explaining every detail, and why he had chosen the materials he had. She loved the glass and the light fixtures, just as he knew she would, and she was excited about the claw-foot tub in the master suite. She complimented his woodwork several times, and then he led her downstairs to his favorite room.

"This is your studio," he announced.

She softly gasped, reaching for his hand. "It faces the west," she whispered. She went to the window, gazing out at the Black Hills. She looked at Noah, noticing the sweet dancing his eyes did when he was excited, remembering that expression that had so attracted her nineteen years ago. "It's perfect. Just like you."

Noah took her in his arms, and passionately kissed her lips. "I love you, Angel," he said, touching the soft skin on the side of her face, and inhaling the fragrance that had haunted his dreams forever. "I have always loved you, and I'll never stop."

Chapter 13

"Have gone *somewhere* with Noah," Guiseppi read aloud, while Rosa let Sparky out through the sunroom doors, "Will be right back. Love, Angel."

"Wonder where they are off to," Rosa murmured. She looked at Guiseppi with curiosity. "You do not suppose —"

"They have eloped?" Guiseppi raised one eyebrow.

Rosa smiled and shook her head. "Oh, they would not do that. He promised you a *regular* wedding."

They heard laughing in the garage, and Guiseppi opened the door to find Noah and Tillie just about to enter. Tillie threw her arms around her father and announced, "I just saw the house, Papa!" She held out her left hand. "Look! We're engaged!"

"Oh, congratulations, my Angel," Guiseppi said, beginning to tear up. "I am so happy for you!"

"Thanks, Papa!"

Rosa trotted into the kitchen, reaching for Tillie's hand. "Oh, let me see," she said. She smiled with approval and said, "It is lovely, Noah."

Tillie's eyes shined as she exclaimed, "I can't believe you guys kept the house a secret!"

"It was Noah's special gift," Rosa said, dabbing at her tears. "We did not want to spoil it for him."

"When will you tell the children?" Guiseppi asked.

"After school," Noah answered with a smile. "I'll have to go over to my place and pick up Jake and Ty, because they ride home together. Then we'll come over here."

"And I don't want to tell the rest of our family until they're all here on Saturday," Tillie said. "I want to tell everyone at the same time."

"Okay, Angel," Guiseppi agreed.

Rosa looked at Noah. "Have you told your brother yet?" she asked.

"We're going over there now," Noah answered.

"Let us have them over for dinner this night!" Rosa said excitedly. "It will be like a little celebration. We can make something on the grill —"

"How 'bout some burgers?" Tillie suggested. "And we'll pick up some salads at the Albertson's Deli."

"And some Cokes," Noah added.

"And some Rolaids." Guiseppi groaned.

Everyone laughed, and Tillie looked into Noah's eyes. After all these years, it was finally happening!

*****

Joshua was surprised, to say the least, when Noah showed up at the church *with Tillie.* He smiled at the two of them when they walked into his office, and then he shook his head.

"I can just about *guess* what the two of you have been up to today," he said.

Noah and Tillie laughed.

"We want to be married," Noah announced. "I asked her this morning, and she said yes."

Joshua grinned. "Finally." He offered each of them his hand, saying, "I'm really happy for you two."

"Thanks, Joshua," Tillie said.

Joshua gestured toward the chairs in front of his desk and said, "Well, have a seat." He picked up his calendar and began to page through it. "What kind of a date are we looking at?" He raised one eyebrow as he looked at the two of them holding hands. "I've already got a wedding this weekend."

Tillie chuckled. "We have to finish baseball, so we were thinking about mid-July. After the All-Stars game."

Joshua nodded, scanning his calendar. "I've got the third Saturday in July still open. That'll give you just a little over eight weeks to plan something." He smiled and teased, "Are you sure you can wait that long?"

Noah and Tillie laughed, looked into each other's eyes, and Noah said, "We'll be okay."

"Have you told your children yet?" Joshua asked.

"We're telling them this afternoon," Tillie answered. "Papa and Ma`ma want you and Mona to come over for a little celebration tonight. Can you make it?"

"We certainly can."

"We'll make more plans then," Noah said as he got to his feet. "But we gotta get goin'. We gotta get the kids." He smiled at his brother. "And please pray for us, Josh. We want this to be okay for A.J. and Laura, and Jake and Ty, too, but especially A.J. and Laura."

"I will," Joshua promised.

Noah's pickup was already in the driveway when Tillie returned home with her children.

"Hey, what are they doing here?" A.J. asked. "Do we have an extra practice or something?"

Tillie glanced at her children with a mysterious look in her eyes and shook her head.

"Well, what's up, Mom?" Laura asked as they pulled into the garage and parked the car.

Tillie giggled, "You'll see."

A.J. and Laura hopped out of the car, and went into the house through the kitchen, followed by their mother. Guiseppi and Rosa were in the kitchen, and they greeted their grandchildren with hugs and kisses. Just beyond them, they saw Noah and his sons in the sunroom.

"Hey the sunroom looks great, Mom," A.J. complimented.

"Yeah, that's bright," Laura added.

Noah and his sons rose from their seats when Laura entered the room, and she was impressed. They were starting to act like a bunch of regular Casellis.

"Come along now everyone," Guiseppi chortled. "Find a place to sit your little bodies. We have an important announcement."

Tillie smiled at Noah, taking a seat next to him on the loveseat. She looked into his eyes for a moment, and he blushed.

Laura sat next to Jake, raised one eyebrow and nodded. Jake gave her the double blink.

A.J. sat down next to Ty, but Guiseppi and Rosa remained standing.

"We have to ask you all about something," Noah began with a smile. He blushed profusely as he looked at Tillie. He took a deep breath and then he looked at their children. "We have been spending quite a bit of time together as families these past few months…" He swallowed and took another breath. "I...Mrs. Martin and I...we..." He stammered so terribly that it made Guiseppi chuckle.

"Can I help you a little, Noah?" He offered.

"Yes," Noah answered with an embarrassed smile.

Guiseppi smiled at the children, who looked back at him with curious frowns. "For several months now," he began, "the six of you have been spending a considerable amount of time together, and it seems to all of us that you children have become quite attached to one another. Would you agree?"

They all nodded.

"Well," Guiseppi began again, "your parents have also become quite attached to one another —"

Laura gasped and brought her hands together, "I *knew* it!" She exclaimed, looking at Jake. "We *knew* it, didn't we?"

Ty frowned. "Knew what?" he asked.

Guiseppi put his hand firmly upon Noah's shoulder and said, "Noah has to ask you all about something."

Noah cleared his throat. "I need to ask the four of you a very important question." He looked at Tillie, and then he looked back at their children. "If it's okay with everybody, and after we're done with baseball this season, we'd really like to be married."

While Ty and A.J. sat with surprised open mouths, Jake and Laura giggled and clapped. Laura got up from her seat, went to her mother and put her arms around her neck. "Will it be a *real* wedding?" she asked.

"Yes," Tillie answered as she held her daughter in her arms.

"I'm so happy for you." Laura looked at her mother and Noah. "And you too. For all of us."

"We *knew* it!" Jake laughed and slapped his knee. "You've been secretly dating or something, haven't you?"

"No," Tillie answered, surprised at their jubilant reaction.

A.J. smiled and shook his head. "If you haven't had any dates, how do you know that you want to be married?"

"We've been praying about this," Noah answered A.J. with a smile. "I love your mom very much, but it has to be okay with all of you."

"It's fine with me," A.J. said, raising both of his eyebrows. He smiled at his best friend. "This will be fun. We'll be able to live together."

Ty rolled his eyes and jokingly muttered, "What a mess. You can't put them into the same room together. It'll be a health hazard." Everyone laughed.

"How about you guys," Noah asked, looking at his sons. "Is it okay with you?"

"Fine," Jake agreed with a smile.

Ty chuckled. "Okay by me."

Laura giggled and hugged her mother again. "I'm *so* excited." She looked at Noah, reaching for his hand. "We can be a *real* family again."

Noah was touched at her words, and his eyes filled with tears. He quickly blinked them away and said, "Thanks, Laura. That makes me very happy."

"You make my mom very happy," Laura said. "I can tell."

Guiseppi and Rosa sighed with satisfaction.

"Now listen to me," Guiseppi said, looking from Ty to Jake. "My Rosa and I are very happy with this new arrangement, and we do not want to be called Mr. and Mrs. Caselli anymore. It has become too formal. So, from this day, Ty and Jake will call us Rosa and Guiseppi."

"Okay." Ty nodded with a smile.

"Yes, Sir." Jake smiled at Guiseppi.

"And," Tillie added, "Don't call me Mrs. Martin anymore. Call me Tillie or Angel."

"And, of course," Noah said with a mischievous expression, "everyone will still call me Mr. Hansen." Everyone laughed at him.

"Joshua and Mona will be coming over shortly," Guiseppi announced with a smile. "So let us get ready for a celebration!"

"Hey!" A.J. suddenly shot to his feet, looking as if he'd just had an epiphany. "Does this mean we'll spend all the holidays *together?*" he asked.

"Right, A.J.," Noah confirmed. "Every single one of 'em."

A.J. sighed with absolute contentment, nodding as he looked around the room. "That's *great*."

Noah smiled at Tillie and murmured, "Yes it is."

Joshua and Mona arrived and the planning began. Noah and Tillie told their children all about the house they wanted to live in after they were married, but left out the details of why the house was built. They wanted to keep that as their own, special secret for awhile. However, they told their children they wouldn't make a final decision until they had *all* looked at it first and were given an opportunity to see what they thought of it.

After dinner, they gathered in the sunroom, where Tillie and Noah sat together on the loveseat. He just didn't want to be away from her today, even after the boys, along with Guiseppi and Joshua went outside to play a little ball.

"We will have to figure out a way to set some time aside for the cookies," Rosa said. "Mark that down."

"Yes, Ma`ma." Tillie added one more thing to the growing list.

"The cookies?" Mona asked.

"It is tradition," Rosa smiled. "We bake many, many cookies, and serve them at the wedding reception. The leftovers are sent home with the guests."

"Maybe Tara and Marquette will stay over, or come back early, to help," Tillie suggested.

"We'll have to get the flowers ordered right away," Mona added. "Summers are always busy with weddings."

Tillie nodded. "We'll do that tomorrow, along with the invitations."

"And a cake," Rosa reminded. "We have to order a cake…how many guests do you think you will have?"

"Noah knows practically everybody," Tillie answered, and Noah and Mona nodded. Tillie went on, "And then there's our family, plus Ginger's, and I know that Marquette and Petrice will want to invite some of their friends from D.C. We thought maybe about two hundred or more."

"What kind of colors are you looking at, Mom?" Laura asked.

"I think *pink*. It's my favorite."

*****

Tillie was in her studio with her father when they heard Rosa laughing heartily in the kitchen below. Sparky was growling and barking.

Tillie giggled and said to Guiseppi, "Noah must be here."

"You vicious little brute," they heard him scold. "How am I ever gonna live with you?"

Tillie looked at the old paintings and said, "If you can carry this one, I'll carry that one."

Guiseppi took one, and Tillie the other.

"They'll be so surprised," she said as they made their way down the steps and into the sunroom.

When Noah saw Tillie, he smiled — though Sparky continued snapping at the bottom of his pants. Tillie was wearing in one of his favorite dresses — the soft pink tank.

Guiseppi and Tillie set the paintings down. "Good morning," she said to Noah.

"Good morning." Noah greeted, looking curiously at what appeared to be the backsides of large canvases. "What are these?"

"These are for Maggie and Estelle," Tillie answered, and she and her father turned the portraits around so he could see them. "Actually, they're more for Estelle. I did them when I came back from Rapid in '75."

Noah's mouth fell open with surprise as he looked at the images of himself, nineteen years before, pony tail and all. "Wow, Angel, those are really good," he said. Are you sure you wanna give 'em away."

"I'm sure," Tillie answered. "Papa and Ma`ma and I prayed about it this morning. They don't feel right taking them back to Sioux Falls, and I'm not too sure about letting the kids see them yet. And I hate to have to hide them in a closet somewhere."

"Well, Maggie and Estelle are gonna love 'em," Noah said.

*****

Maggie and Estelle were drinking their coffee and enjoying the morning paper, when the bell went off. Maggie looked up and smiled when she saw the two of them together holding the large canvases.

"All right, Noah," she grumbled with a smile. "What are you doing bringing a nice girl like that into a rat-trap like this?"

Noah laughed, and when Maggie looked into his eyes, she knew what had happened. She hadn't seen his eyes dance like *that* in years, and she laughed and shook her head.

"Hello, Angel," Estelle sweetly greeted as she reached for Tillie's hand. She gave her a soft kiss on the cheek. "Will you have some coffee?"

"Love some," Tillie answered.

Estelle nodded with a smile, leading the two toward the bar.

"Good morning, ladies," Noah said. "We've got a surprise."

"Thought you might want these for the bar," Tillie said with a hesitant smile. She and Noah showed them the paintings. "If you like them okay."

Maggie and Estelle gasped, and Maggie placed her hand over her heart. "Angel! Did you do those?" she whispered.

"Right after I left. They're of Noah," she answered.

"I can see that," Maggie nodded.

"They're beautiful, Angel!" Estelle gasped, reaching to touch of one of the portraits. "How can you part with them?"

Tillie raised a brow and answered, "Well, our kids don't know *everything*, and I thought maybe we shouldn't throw it at them all at once. Maybe when they're a little older —"

"Hey, we're getting married," Noah interjected, and the ladies gasped again.

Tears fell from Maggie's eyes. "When?" she asked.

Noah had never seen Maggie cry before. He swallowed hard, fighting his own emotions, as he handed her his handkerchief.

"Oh, brother, you actually carry one of these?" Maggie took the handkerchief from Noah, dabbing at her tears.

"We're getting married the third Saturday of July," Tillie answered.

Estelle put her arms around Tillie and began to cry, "I just knew it. I knew it would come true some day!"

"I knew it, too, Stellie," Noah said with a soft smile. He looked at Tillie, and then back at Maggie. "Because I prayed for a second chance —"

"Oh, don't start that up," Maggie scowled. "You been preachin' that nonsense to me for thirty years, Noah —"

"But it's true, Maggie May," Noah interrupted. "And I've been prayin' for you, too."

"You'll have to pray a lot longer to get me to go along with that phony-baloney stuff you're always spoutin'." Maggie frowned, and Tillie couldn't help but smile at the old woman.

"Maggie," Noah said with a smile, "God didn't say *no*, he just said, *wait*."

****

At The Little Print Shop, Noah and Tillie chose simple invitations. The manager promised they would be ready within less than a week. That gave them plenty of time to get them addressed and sent out. Then, they went to Flowers By LeRoy, which was the only flower shop in town that didn't have a wedding scheduled for the third Saturday in July. Together they chose white and soft pink orchids, delicate garlands of ivy, gold candelabras and silky cream and pink ribbons.

When they stopped at Albertson's grocery store to pick up a few things for Rosa, they ordered the largest wedding cake available, along with two full size sheet cakes.

"And how do you feel about wearing a tux?" Tillie asked as they drove back to her house.

Noah gave her a glance as he drove along, then answered, "Do we *really need* to wear tuxes?"

"It would look really nice."

Noah sighed. "What color?"

"I think black. Do you have one?"

Noah laughed. "No, but I suppose your brothers all do."

"Well, yes…but we have time to order you one. I'm thinking of getting our dresses over at Randall's. They have tuxes there."

"You know, I don't think I even own a suit. Well, maybe a really old one, but it probably doesn't even fit anymore."

Tillie grinned. "Well, you should at least wear a suit."

"You mean, I can't just get away with nice jeans and boots?"

Tillie laughed and shook her head. "You at least have to wear a suit."

"I'll get a tux," he groaned.

"Oh, good, I love tuxes."

"Oh? Are you wearing one?" Noah teased.

Tillie laughed again. "I saw a really pretty, cream colored, suit style dress over at Randall's a couple of weeks ago, and I almost bought it, but it was kind of formal and I didn't think I'd have anywhere to wear it. They actually have two of the same dress, and so when I ask Tara to be my Matron of Honor, I'm taking her down to try one on. That way, we'll match. By the way, who's gonna be your Best Man?"

"Marquette."

"It would be nice if we could get the kids into the wedding party somehow," Tillie said with a thoughtful expression. "Do you think it would be weird if Laura were a bridesmaid, and Ty a groomsman? We can have A.J. and Jake be ushers."

Noah shrugged. "I don't think it would be weird. They *should* be involved somehow."

"We can ask them tomorrow. You guys *are* coming over tomorrow?"

"Yep." Noah smiled and playfully "leered" at Tillie. "I'll be over every day now."

Tillie laughed and reached for Noah's hand. She couldn't wait until the day they were together forever.

*****

Petrice Caselli was cleared to land his Learjet at the Rapid City Regional Airport before noon, on the last Saturday in May, 1994. With him, were his brothers, and their wives and children, excited to be together for a holiday in Rapid City. Sam and Becky-Lynn had decided not to visit this time, explaining that their schedules were too hectic at present to be away from the office.

Angelo did not come along, nor did his sister. As part of his ROTC commitment, Angelo was serving his summer duty with the Air Force at Avian Air Base in Italy.

Alyssa had won the coveted intern's position at the United States Marshal's Office in Washington, D.C., and she would remain there for the entire summer.

Only Noah and Tillie met them at the airport that day, and the Casellis were surprised. Their pretty sister stood, in a soft, yellow summer dress, holding Noah's hand. Noah was wearing clean jeans and his usual cowboy boots, but today he also wore a white knit shirt. Normally, he dressed in sturdy working-man's clothes, and Vincenzo noticed the difference immediately.

"Just look at the shine on those boots," he teased as he embraced Noah, surprising him with a kiss upon his cheek. "I must say, Noah, you look absolutely stunning this day."

"Thanks." Noah blushed, wondering if they were going to start *that* with him. He'd always noticed they kissed each other quite a bit. He presumed he was safe because he wasn't Italian, but he'd gotten a couple of kisses from those ol' boys over the past few months. He suddenly wondered if there would be more.

"How beautiful you look this day," Marquette said as he held his little sister in his arms, giving her cheek a soft kiss. "And what a delight to see you with Noah."

"He brought his Suburban so that you guys don't have to rent a vehicle this time," Tillie said.

When Gabriella stepped into the greeting area of the terminal, Noah nearly fainted. "Well would you look at that," he whispered into Tillie's ear. "She looks just like you at that age, except for the blue eyes…and she might be a little taller."

Michael loped over to his aunt, and Tillie gasped with surprise. She hadn't seen the young man since December, and he'd grown considerably. "Oh, my goodness," she said, reaching up to put her arms around her nephew. "How tall are you, Michael?"

"Six feet, four inches," Michael answered proudly, and then he whispered, "*Ten inches taller* than Papa!"

Tillie laughed as she looked at her brother. "How did you get such tall children?" she asked.

Petrice rolled his eyes, avoiding the question. "Where are Ma`ma and Papa? And your children?" he asked.

"They're busy at home setting the table, and things like that," Tillie answered. "Jake and A.J. are helping Papa with the yard."

"We were hoping to see you today," Marquette said as he gave Noah's hand a firm shake. "But I never expected to see you here. I thought perhaps you would just appear later on."

Noah smiled and said, "Well, we wanted to meet you guys together, because we have something to tell you all."

"Oh, goodness!" Tara gasped, grabbing a tight hold of Elaine's hand.

"Angel?" Vincenzo asked with a curious smile, "What have you been up to?"

Tillie giggled, and had her skin been any lighter they would have seen the soft blush upon her cheeks. Noah stood beside her, took her hand into his own, his cheeks shining with delight.

"We're gettin' married," he said with a grin.

Everyone cheered.

Petrice and Vincenzo offered to man the grill, and Marquette and Noah went into the living room to start some music. The boys had already escaped into the backyard with a baseball and some gloves, but Laura and Gabriella, along with the rest of the ladies, were content to visit as they finished preparations for the meal.

Gabriella and Laura were at the sink, washing strawberries, and Tillie and her mother worked on a vegetable platter. Kate mixed up her practically famous lemonade. Guiseppi supervised.

"Oh, my goodness," Elaine heard her daughter whispering to Laura at the sink. "He's *so* cute.

"Oh, brother." Elaine rolled her eyes. "You're not talking about Jack Goldstein *again,* are you?"

"Oh," Gabriella sighed wistfully, "yes, Ma`ma, we are."

"Who's that?" Tara asked.

"A young man running for Congress," Elaine answered. "Petrice and I hosted a fundraiser for him last week."

"Wow." Kate glanced over at Gabriella, who couldn't seem to keep the silly smile off of her face, and said, "He must be quite a guy."

"He's *so* cool," Gabriella went on. "He has his master's in political science, *and* Divinity."

"But he's Jewish," Elaine grumbled.

"His sister is Sparky's groomer," Tillie added. "Really nice lady."

"Running for Congress?" Kate asked. "How *old* is this guy?"

"He's twenty-seven," Elaine answered without a smile, "and way too old for a seventeen-year-old."

Gabriella turned around and smiled at the ladies in the kitchen. "And I think he likes me."

Guiseppi groaned, clutching at his heart as he pretended to stagger.

"Stop that, Grandpa," Laura giggled.

Tillie laughed at her father, and then she whispered, "Hey, do you guys wanna hear some really good gossip?"

"Yes!" Guiseppi leaned toward his daughter.

Tillie gave Gabriella a sidelong glance. "And this has *everything* to do with you, Gabby, so be sure to listen. Remember Melinda?"

"Oh, how could we ever forget her?" Elaine admitted.

"What a gal," Kate said without expression.

"Well," Tillie whispered, "she's suing old McDarren for divorce. Noah says he's gonna lose his shirt."

"No kidding?" Tara whispered in a surprised gasp. "Whatever went wrong?"

"Apparently, she caught the old boy seeing someone on the side over in a retirement community in Florida," Tillie answered. "Can you believe it?"

Everyone laughed, and Kate said, "She was *too young* for him." She gave Gabriella a sly glance. "Just like this Goldstein character. You're *too young* for him, and he's liable to run off with someone from the nursing home when he gets a little older."

Everyone laughed again, except for Gabriella who only smiled and said, "Papa is ten years older than Ma`ma."

"Ouch." Elaine pretended to grimace. "I was wondering when you were gonna bring that up."

In the living room, Marquette and Noah had loaded all of their favorites into the CD player, except for the new one Noah was pulling from the plastic. "Here," he said with a clever expression, handing Marquette the CD. "Play this one first. It's Angel's favorite."

Marquette nodded with a smile, and loaded the CD.

Soft mandolin music was heard, coming from the living room, and Tillie took a soft breath as she listened. *Annie Laurie*? As the first few notes progressed, Tillie felt her eyes fill with tears she couldn't stop. She reached for the towel, dried off her hands, and made her way into the living room.

"Where are ya goin', Mom?" Laura asked as Tillie floated out of the kitchen.

Noah was beside the stereo with Marquette, and the moment he saw Tillie enter the living room, he whispered, "Told you it was her favorite." He smiled at Tillie as he watched her brush away her tears. He stretched out his hand, walking toward her. Tillie put her hand into his, and he folded her into his arms, holding her close while he led her into a waltz. "It's *our* song," he whispered, softly kissing her cheek.

Tillie nodded, unable to speak around the emotions in her throat. She hadn't danced since that night at The Sluice, on her thirtieth birthday, and had refused to dance ever since.

Noah touched the tears on her cheek with one of his rough thumbs. "Why are you crying? Everybody's gonna think I'm being mean to you or something."

Tillie chuckled through her tears and whispered, "Do you know why we cry when we're happy, Noah?" He shook his head, so she continued, "Ma`ma says that it is God's love and when there is so much of it, it leaks out in the drops of our tears so that He may make room for more in our hearts."

"Oh, dear," Noah whispered, "now I think I'm gonna cry."

Guiseppi and Rosa came around the corner and saw their daughter dancing with Noah.

Guiseppi frowned. "I thought she did not dance anymore," he muttered.

Rosa smiled and took Guiseppi's hand into her own, coaxing him into a few dance steps. "All is right in her world at last, Guiseppi" she said.

Guiseppi took Rosa into his arms with a sigh and a smile as they watched Noah hold their only daughter…*all is right in her world at last*…he felt the tremendous weight of years past fall from his shoulders. His eyes burned with tears of joy. "She has always loved him," he whispered to Rosa. "Perhaps even more than she has ever loved us."

Chapter 14

A.J. and Jake bragged incessantly when The Builders took home the trophy at the All-Star's game for the second season in a row. Post 22, with the help of their phenomenal pitcher, won its championship as well. No one could pitch like Ty Hansen, and he received state-wide attention in all of South Dakota's newspapers. Because of his amazing talent and popularity, *and his exceptional grades*, Lynchburg College offered Ty a scholarship.

Reporters bombarded him after his last game of the season, pushing their way into the dugout, begging for just a *short interview*. Ty politely obliged.

"Have you decided on Lynchburg?"

Ty shook his head and answered, "I still have to finish my senior year, and I haven't looked at any other colleges yet."

"So what are you doing with the rest of your summer?"

Ty smiled with a blush as he answered, "My dad is getting married and we're getting a bigger family."

The front page of *The Rapid City Journal* carried the story. They went into great detail about how Ty's mother had been killed when he was very small, and that his father, *the* Noah Hansen of Hansen Development, LLC, had raised him and his younger brother by himself. The article also explained, in detail, that Noah Hansen was marrying Tillie Caselli Martin, younger sister of Senior New York Senator Petrice Caselli and Marquette Caselli.

The Casellis laughed at the article and thanked Ty for making them famous.

Every spare minute Tillie and Noah had, which were not many, was spent looking at furniture for their new home. Together they picked out couches, chairs, tables, lamps, and a new bedroom set. Everything was elegant and traditional. Noah couldn't have been more pleased as he watched his bride choose the very furnishings he thought she'd choose nineteen years before.

Tillie didn't want to change one thing about the house, except to fill it with their family and have lots of company whenever they could. She loved the big kitchen and could hardly wait to prepare meals in it. She loved the dining room with its built-in hutch, and floor to ceiling glass windows. But her favorite room was the small room just off of the kitchen, facing the west; the room Noah intended for her studio. She hung all of her work in there, and Noah helped her move in the old white wicker furniture.

Tillie paused by the window facing the west and sighed with a smile. "This is perfect."

Noah smiled with satisfaction, reaching for her hand. "By the way," he began, "I was talking to Marquette the other day and he said that you've always wanted to visit Italy. Should we go there for our honeymoon?"

Tillie turned from the window and looked at Noah with surprise. "But we only have a few weeks before we're married. We need more time to plan something like that. And you need a passport."

Noah shrugged with a chuckle. "I got a wild hair last fall and applied for my passport, and Marquette says —"

"You applied for a passport?" Tillie was stunned.

Noah grinned. "Well, I figured you probably already had one, 'cause you guys are so *finesse*."

Tillie laughed and said, "I would *love* to go to *Italia* on our honeymoon. I've been trying to get there for years."

Noah nodded. "Marquette says he knows a guy with a small villa outside of a little town called Bellagio. He thinks we should stay there. He says Lake Como is real pretty this time of year."

Tillie smiled. "Marquette lives near there."

"And he says he'll take you over to see your family's old farm if you want to," Noah added. "It might be fun."

Tillie frowned with hesitation. "But what about the kids? With all of the publicity, and then us leaving town, wouldn't it make the perfect opportunity for Ol' Roy to come creeping around?"

"Vincenzo says he'll take the kids over to Reata," Noah said. He raised an eyebrow and added, "Ol' Roy will never find 'em there."

Tillie nodded and put her arms around Noah's neck. "Well, since you've already done so much planning, let's see what we can throw together."

Noah held her close and gave her a kiss on her cheek. "This is gonna be great. I think I'm gonna love *Italia*."

*****

It was the hottest day anyone could remember, and the air conditioning broke down at the church. Everyone was testy, especially the people preparing the wedding feast in the basement.

Old Doria and Georgie had traveled to Rapid City with great plans for the feast. Much to their chagrin, Maggie May and Estelle volunteered to help.

Old Doria was very set in his ways, as was Georgie, and when they got together with Maggie May and Estelle, their plans hit the fan.

Georgie huffed, "My dear lady, I was educated in *Roma*. Believe me, I know what I am doing." He continued to slice the crusts off the bread, in preparation of Angel's favorite sandwiches. *This will be an elegant reception, no matter what has happened to the air conditioning, and despite the unfortunate fact that I have been locked in a basement with a crazy woman.*

Maggie rolled her eyes and barked, "And I was educated in the school of hard knocks, pal." *It can still be a fun reception, even if old fancy pants wants to make it stuffy.*

While Maggie and Georgie quarreled, Estelle hovered near Old Doria as he placed another enticing pan of something into the oven. She didn't care if Georgie and Maggie May fought all day long, she really liked to watch this old man as he stirred his pots and put things together.

"Mmm...now what did you call that?" she asked

"Stromboli," Doria answered with a wink. "Have you ever tasted it before?"

Estelle shook her head.

Old Doria dipped a spoon into one of his pots and offered her a taste of the sauce.

"Thank you." Estelle took the spoon. "That's delicious." She looked curiously at Old Doria and whispered, "How old a fella are you?"

He gave her a coy smile and whispered, "*That*, my dear Madam, is my very own secret. No one knows my age, but me."

Estelle nodded. "Very clever of you." She looked sideways at Maggie May and Georgie, who were still bickering, and she whispered, "Maggie likes him, I can tell."

The church was decorated with ivy, orchids and baby's breath. Soft piano music played as the guests began to enter.

Guiseppi looked at his young comrade. He and Jake wore matching black tuxedos; it was their responsibility to light the tall candles lining the aisle. They'd finished with the last ones, and Guiseppi indicated that they should step outside for just a moment.

Guiseppi wiped the sweat from his bald head and moaned, "It is hotter than Hades in that church. Did someone call a repairman?" Jake erupted into giggles, and Guiseppi couldn't help but smile at the lighthearted young man. He pretended to frown. "You laugh at everything that I say."

" 'Cuz you're so funny. I wish you could live with us, too."

Guiseppi's old heart was so softened at Jake's words, his black eyes filled with tears and he put an arm around Jake's shoulder. "You are such a sweet boy. My Angel will be praising the Lord for you every day."

"Well," Mona began in her soft, Southern drawl as she adjusted the bowtie on Noah's tuxedo, "you're gonna finally do it. Tyin' the knot with Angel."

"Yes, Ma'am." Noah sighed and shook his head. "These last eight weeks have taken longer to get here than the last nineteen years."

Joshua smiled from where he sat on the other side of the small dressing room. "Noah, you are one remarkable man," he said.

Mona smiled as she touched the soft gray at Noah's temples. "And look at how handsome you still are. She's one lucky gal."

Noah laughed and said, "Sometimes I just can't believe it."

"Believe what?" Joshua asked with a smile.

"I can't believe that she *still* wants me. After all these years, and all that it's taken to get to this point, Angel still wants to be with *me*."

"She's a wonderful girl," Mona said. "And you'd better take extra special care of her."

"I will, Mona. I promise."

Joshua got to his feet, putting his hand on Noah's shoulder as he said, "You're getting everything you ever wanted today. Angel, and a whole bunch of kids." Joshua chuckled. "And two dogs. That must be a bonus."

"I thought you were crazy to go and build that giant house," Mona drawled with a smile. "But now it's gonna be plum full!"

Noah sighed with a contented smile, looking at the two people who'd *always* been there for him. He put his arms around them. "Thanks, you guys. You've always been there for me, and I can't imagine my life without the two of you. I would have never made it this far."

Mona dabbed at her tears. "You were our special gift, Noah, and we love you so much."

Upstairs in her dressing room, Tillie sat still while her mother wound white, shiny beads into her hair, piling it on top of her head. She was dressed in a sleeveless, cream-colored, suit-style dress that came nearly to her ankles. The neckline was a modest 'V', and she wore the pearls Vincenzo and Kate had given her so many years ago. Tara and Laura wore matching dresses, and Rosa had fixed their hair the very same way earlier that morning.

Tillie watched her mother in the mirror. Tara and Laura had left, and they finally had a few moments alone.

"You haven't fixed my hair in a long time," Tillie said as she watched her mother's fingers fly.

Rosa swallowed hard as she remembered the last time she'd fixed Tillie's hair — the day she'd married Alex. "Many years," she agreed.

"You're still very good at it," Tillie said.

Rosa's emotions were tender, but she didn't want to cry so she attempted to change the subject, "What of something old?"

Tillie held up her right hand, the ring Noah planned to give her more than nineteen years ago sparkled in the light.

Rosa nodded with approval. "Something new?" she asked.

Tillie reached for the photograph of their four children, holding it up for Rosa. "From the kids," she said. "They had it made at the mall a few days ago."

Rosa nodded. "Something borrowed?"

Tillie pointed to the pocket watch on the vanity before them. "From Papa." She sighed heavily, "But I don't have anything blue, Ma`ma."

Rosa stood back a short distance and admired her work. "I am finished. What do you think?"

"It's great, Ma`ma," Tillie said, patting the pretty hairdo.

Rosa took a seat beside her daughter. She reached for her purse and opened it, hunting around until she found her wallet and pulled it out. "When Papa and I were married," she began, "we were so very poor that my parents could scarcely afford to dress me. Of course, that would have been fine with Papa." Rosa giggled and continued, "Anyway, how things were done back then, was that the young lady was kept separate from the young man for an entire week before the wedding, and they were allowed no communication during that time. It was to be used for prayer and meditation. However, like you, I was fairly rebellious, and I dispatched a note to my betrothed. My twin sister, Edda, delivered it for me."

Rosa paused and smiled at her memories. "I wrote in the note how I loved him and how eager I was to be his wife, and would you not even guess it, but that young man secretly sent a letter back to me, through your Uncle Angelo." She opened her wallet and carefully removed a piece of pale blue paper covered in laminate, no bigger than a playing card. She handed it to Tillie. "I had it laminated many years ago, when I first learned of the procedure. That note you hold in your hand is now nearly fifty-eight years old, and I have always carried it with me." She took a breath, and whispered, "You must be very careful with it, my Angel."

Tillie took in a soft breath as she looked at the foreign writing on the small note. Her eyes filled with tears as she looked at the faded ink her own father had written to his bride so many years ago. "What does it say, Ma`ma?" she asked.

"He writes, *Il mio Rosa bello, non dimentica quanto ti amo e che la mia vita non sarà mai completa senza voi in esso* — my lovely Rosa, do not forget how much I love you, and that my life will never be complete without you in it." She sighed with a wistful smile, "We had quite a romance for two people with nothing but a pound of sugar and a half side of beef. He is all that I have ever wanted — nothing else."

"Oh, Ma`ma," Tillie breathed as her tears left her eyes.

Rosa smiled. "I love him, Angel, in a way I have never loved another person in my life. With your papa, it has always been different. Like with you and Noah."

"I love him so much, Ma`ma."

"You are so blessed to be getting this second chance." Rosa put her arms around her daughter. "And I am at last at peace with your future."

The wedding party, except for Tillie and Rosa, gathered in the lobby of the church. All of the men were dressed in identical black tuxedos, and they wore white orchids on their left lapels. Laura and Tara carried bouquets of white and pink orchids.

"You look smart this day," Marquette said to Noah. He suddenly embraced Noah, kissing his cheek. "Soon, I will call you *brother*."

Noah's face flushed and he smiled.

"Is everybody ready?" Joshua asked.

"Everybody's seated," A.J. announced, and he smiled, remembering how Jake had moon-walked Heidi Romanov and her parents to their seats.

"Where are my brothers?" Marquette asked.

A.J. smiled, and Jake snickered.

"They'll be right in," Ty answered with a wink.

Marquette frowned. "They are up to something?"

Guiseppi cleared his throat and said, "Do not trouble yourself with it now, my Marquette."

Joshua peeked inside of the church, assessed the crowd, then looked back at the small party with him. "Okay, it looks like everybody's here and it's a really hot day, so let's get this wedding going." He looked at Noah and asked, "Are you ready?"

"Ready as I'll ever be," he answered.

Joshua nodded. "Okay, Noah and I will get into place. Mona, you'll get Rosa and Angel. When they come downstairs, Jake, you'll seat Rosa and A.J. will seat Mona, and then the two of you will seat yourselves in the last row." He raised his eyebrow and looked at the two boys. "And you'll be good, *right?*"

"Like little angels," Jake said with a clever shine in his dancing, blue eyes.

Jake looked so much like his father at that moment, it struck Joshua with fear. He softly frowned and said, "Don't make me beg, Jake. Just be good."

Jake grinned and nodded.

Joshua took a deep breath, "Okay, let's get going." He and Noah went into the church, and Mona hurried to the dressing room upstairs. She knocked softly on the dressing room door, then let herself in.

Rosa's eyes filled with tears. "Is it time?" she asked.

Mona smiled, reaching for the older woman's hand as she looked at Tillie. "Are you ready?" she asked.

"Ready as I'll ever be," Tillie answered.

Mona laughed. "That's exactly what Noah said. Come on."

The three of them went downstairs and into the lobby, where they were greeted by the rest of the wedding party.

"It is nearly time," Guiseppi said, taking Tillie by the hand. He gave her cheek a soft kiss. "How are you feeling?" he asked.

"Like I'm floating or something," Tillie answered, smiling nervously at her father. She chattered on, "And I might be a little dizzy from coming down the steps too fast, so be sure to hang onto me. I don't want to fall down in front of everyone."

They all laughed, and Laura said, "You're gonna be fine, Mom."

"Ladies," A.J. said as he offered Mona his arm, and Jake offered Rosa his.

Rosa put her arms around Tillie and kissed her cheek. "I love you, my Angel."

"I love you, Ma`ma," Tillie whispered.

Jake and A.J. led Mona and Rosa into the church, and Tara brought Tillie her bouquet. "You do not want to forget this," she teased. She put the bouquet into Tillie's hands and gave her a soft kiss on the cheek.

The organ music started, and Marquette's eyes were wide with surprise. "Oh, my goodness it is time." He looked at Ty and Laura and said, "Come children. It is time." He and Tara ushered them into place, leaving Guiseppi and Tillie alone.

Guiseppi looked at his beautiful daughter, remembering the day he gave her away the first time. He couldn't keep the tears from dropping from his eyes. He took her left hand into his own and removed her engagement ring, placing it on her right hand. "To make room for Noah's ring," he said with a soft smile. "God is blessing you this day, Matilde Rosa Caselli, because He *delights* in you, the same way I have delighted in you your whole life." He took a soft breath. "It amazes me that we stand here about to give you to Noah Hansen. God is a good God, filled with love and holiness. He puts all things right this day."

Tillie put her arms around her father and whispered, "Thank you for everything."

"You are most welcome."

From the front of the church, Noah watched Ty and Laura come down the aisle. Ty was so handsome and tall, his strawberry-blond hair gleaming against the blackness of his tuxedo. He smiled at his father, and Noah smiled back. Laura was on his arm, so petite and perfect, a younger image of her mother.

Marquette had Tara on his arm, and Noah saw them look into each other's eyes just before they started down the aisle.

Guiseppi and Angel will be next...

Ty and Laura took their places on the platform with Joshua and Noah, and Marquette and Tara joined them. Noah's heart raced with expectancy as he watched the back of the church for her. She came around the corner with her father, and Noah let out an unexpected, but quiet, sigh of relief.

The congregation stood and Guiseppi started down the aisle with his daughter on his arm. She wore the same dress as Tara and Laura, and it fit the shape of her feminine body to perfection. With her hair up this way he could see the gentle curve of her face and neck, and the delicate outline of her jaw. In her pretty hands she carried the bouquet they'd chosen together. Noah thought she must be the most graceful creature ever created.

Tillie's heart pounded as she walked along with her father. She looked at Noah and saw that his eyes were dancing, as they always did now. He gave her a mischievous wink, taking her by surprise. Tillie smiled and bit her lip to keep from laughing. *Did he have to do that? Right here in front of everyone?* She heard the congregation laugh quietly. She held tightly to her father's arm until they reached the front of the church, where Noah waited.

The music stopped and Noah extended his hand. Guiseppi turned to face his daughter. He took her right hand into his own, bowed before her, then kissed it. He stood straight, smiling into her eyes, then placed her hand into Noah's. Noah and Tillie stepped up to the platform where Joshua waited, and Guiseppi took his place beside Rosa.

"Who gives this woman to this marriage?" Joshua asked with authority.

"We do," Guiseppi and Rosa answered together, and the congregation seated themselves.

Joshua smiled at the couple before him and then he looked out into the congregation as he said, "God tells us in the book of Jeremiah that he has plans for our *prosperity*, and not our calamity, so let us all rejoice in this prosperity, together with Noah and Tillie, and their children."

As Joshua spoke, Tillie looked into the dancing eyes she loved, wondering what he was thinking.

Noah silently mouthed the words, "I love you."

Tillie smiled. "Me too."

It seemed only a matter of moments and they were in the receiving line in the lobby.

Vincenzo and Petrice, along with their children and wives were the first through the line, and Tillie was surprised to see the tall soldier with them. It was Captain Angelo Caselli, in his dress uniform, and he looked so official that it set her back.

"Wow!" she laughed as he took her into his arms and congratulated her. "When did you get here?"

"Just this morning," Angelo answered. "I was able to get some leave and use military transport all the way from Avian to Ellsworth."

"You look so cool," Tillie said, winking. Alyssa came through the line behind Angelo, and Tillie was surprised again. "I didn't know you were coming!" she exclaimed. "I thought you were busy."

"We *are* really busy," Alyssa said with a smile. "But, I figured, what the hay. I jumped on a plane last night, got held up in Minneapolis, and finally made it here this morning." She leaned close to Tillie and whispered, "I couldn't miss my favorite Auntie's wedding."

"Thanks, Alyssa."

Ginger and Bobby, and their troop were just behind Alyssa. They had arrived in Rapid City the day before. Their new baby was nearly three months old, and Ginger was thankful that the nursery was available during the wedding. The two older ones were dressed in suits, and they obediently followed along with their parents.

"I stashed the three little ones in the nursery," Ginger whispered, embracing Tillie.

Tillie laughed and whispered in return, "Did you take the test this morning?"

Ginger nodded her head, and Tillie saw Bobby blush beet red when Ginger answered, "*Positive.*"

Tillie laughed out loud and gave Ginger another hug. "What *is* it with the two of you?"

"Somethin'," Ginger answered with a coy smile.

After everyone was through the receiving line, they went downstairs to the fellowship hall, where it was, thankfully, cooler. Somehow, Georgie and Maggie May had gotten the reception together with elegance and style, and everything was ready. The cookies Rosa, Tara, Tillie, and Laura had slaved over were set out on platters everywhere. The delicious aroma of Old Doria's Stromboli floated in the air, and Tillie's favorite ribbon sandwiches were piled on crystal plates. The cake Tillie and Noah had ordered was set up in the center of the hall, and on top of it someone had placed the traditional plastic bride and groom.

Noah laughed when he saw that. He whispered, "Aren't we kinda old for something like that?"

Tillie shook her head and smiled into his eyes. "We're *never* gonna be *too old*."

Joshua stood before the crowd and raised his hand. "Excuse me," he announced. "The father of the bride will pray."

Guiseppi stepped forward and stood beside Joshua. He bowed his head and raised his hands as he prayed, "Dearest Father, thank You for this day and the glory of Your might. Bless this meal that we are about to share, and bless this union You have brought together. We praise You for Your goodness and love. Lead us along Your Divine Path so that we may always glorify Your ways and give an example to others who watch that they may be drawn to Your Son, Jesus. In His wonderful name I pray, Amen."

Georgie ushered everyone into lines, encouraging them to take whatever they wanted, and then to find a seat. The fellowship hall in the church basement was significantly smaller than his restaurant back home, and he and that *grumpy old woman* had to make several adjustments to the seating arrangements in order to find places for everyone.

Vincenzo laughed as he watched Georgie argue with Maggie May. He elbowed his brothers and said, "Look at those two. I do not believe I have ever seen Georgie taken with a woman of any kind."

Petrice raised one brow. "Can it be?" he wondered aloud.

"How long has he been saved now?" Marquette asked.

"Let me think." Vincenzo scratched his head. "It will be eight years this October," he answered.

Petrice glanced at Marquette and asked, "Remember when you were going to *save* him with Marta?"

Marquette remembered with a chuckle, "And just think, rather than the voluptuous specimen I discovered, he required the wits of a mean old bartender. Wish I knew then what I know now."

Vincenzo laughed and slapped Marquette's back. "Do not we all, my brother?"

His brothers laughed and nodded.

While everyone ate and visited, Noah and Tillie moved throughout the crowd together, thanking everyone for coming. They finally connected with their children at a special table set for just the six of them. They took their seats, and began to share their first official meal together *as a family*.

"What *is* this?" Jake asked as he stuffed another delicious bite of the Stromboli into his mouth. He looked at Tillie. "And can you make it?"

Tillie giggled. "It's called Stromboli, and I can make it."

"Like once a week," Ty said through a mouth full of food, and Tillie laughed.

"Mom makes lots of Italian food." A.J. grinned.

"Mom used to work in the restaurant when she was a kid," Laura added.

Tillie nodded and smiled at the old memory. "Those were the days," she said.

Guiseppi clanged two knives together in front of the cake, and when everyone had quieted, he announced with a smile, "It is time to cut this cake. Noah and Angel, you must come now."

Noah stood and offered Tillie his hand, helping her to her feet. Jake and A.J. looked at each other with mischief, and began clanging their spoons loudly against their glasses. Soon, all of the guests were doing the same thing. Noah looked at his new bride. He gave her a soft kiss on the lips, and everyone applauded in response. Then he led her to the cake. Guiseppi placed the knife first into Tillie's hand, and covered her hand with Noah's.

"Okay, now," Guiseppi instructed, and Tillie and Noah cut the cake. The guests applauded again.

"And the Best Man shall make his toast now," Guiseppi commanded.

Marquette got to his feet and stood with the newly married couple. He took a bottle of sparkling cider and filled a glass for Tillie, one for Noah, and one for his father. He filled two more, stepped back to where he had been seated with Tara, giving one to her. He took the last one for himself and held it into the air.

"I do not believe I have ever made a toast with sparkling apple juice before —" he began, having to pause when the guests laughed. "However," he continued, "this day I will make an exception." He looked at Tillie and Noah, his black eyes filling with tears. "*La mia sorella bella*. My beautiful sister. I used to speak that way to you when you were very small, but Papa wanted that you be *Americano*, through and through, and we were told to speak only English to you. He said that you were God's special gift in our lives, and we believe him to this day." He looked at Noah, his tears spilling down his cheeks. He laughed at himself. "Forgive me, but I am *still Italiano* and it controls my very spirit at times." He took a breath and continued,

"With you, Noah, we share our greatest gift, and with you we know that her happiness is assured. Our hearts have peace in your union." He clanged his glass against Tillie's. "To you, *la mia sorella bella*." He clanged his glass against Noah's. "And to you, *blesid marito*. Blessed husband. May God pour his blessing upon you and give you the desires of your hearts."

Tillie smiled at her romantic brother, and then she looked at her new husband. They clanged their glasses together and took a sip of the sparkling juice.

"Mm," Marquette murmured with a smile, raising one eyebrow. "Not bad." The guests applauded again, and Georgie and Old Doria came to finish cutting the cake.

When Guiseppi felt that everyone had had their fill of wedding cake, he found the youngest and strongest-looking men in the fellowship hall. He asked them to please remove the tables and chairs so that the dancing could begin. On Guiseppi's signal, A.J., Jake and Ty set up the rented music equipment, and very soon, the first soft notes of Guiseppi's favorite Dean Martin song were heard.

"Now, my Angel," Guiseppi said as he took her by the hand, leading her away from her new husband and onto the dance floor. "If we were in *Italia* this day, I would have the first dance with you. Now, I am old and I wish my way."

Tillie laughed at her father as he took her into his arms and began to sing along with Dean Martin's voice as they danced.

"*Non dimenticar*, means do not forget your heart, my darling," Guiseppi sang quietly in English this time, and Tillie's eyes filled with sentimental tears as he continued, "Do not forget to be all you mean to me. *Non dimenticar*, my love is like a star, my darling, shining bright and clear, just because you are here..."

Tillie held tightly to her father as they danced. It felt so good to dance again, reliving the wonderful memories of her childhood with him and Ma`ma. They had revolved around her, and she prayed to leave the same mark upon her own children — and now Noah's children as well!

It wasn't long before everyone was dancing along with them. Guiseppi led his daughter back to her new husband. Noah took her by the hand, led her on to the dance floor and took her into his arms.

"I'm having the best day of my life," he whispered with a smile, kissing her cheek.

"Me, too." Tillie smiled at him, and then out of the corner of her eye, she saw the strangest thing. She gasped, "Noah, look at *that!*"

Noah followed her gaze, and to his surprise saw Maggie May dancing with Georgie. They were smiling sweetly into one another's eyes.

"I thought he was *gay!*" Noah gasped in a whisper.

"I think he has had a change of heart," Tillie suggested with a giggle.

Vincenzo and Kate danced close to Tillie and Noah, and Vincenzo chortled, "Can you stand a secret this day? Georgie and Estelle led Maggie May to the Lord shortly before your wedding began."

Noah laughed and shook his head. *God didn't say no — He just said wait!*

The dancing continued for some time and the church basement grew hot. Large amounts of ice water were consumed until finally the guests started to go home to their air conditioners.

Elaine found Tillie and reminded her, "You guys need to go. Petrice is scheduled to take off in about an hour." Petrice was flying them to Chicago for connection to their flight on *Al Italia*, which was taking them all the way to Milan. "Let's get you out to the parking lot so you can throw your bouquet."

Tillie and Noah followed everyone into the parking lot for their departure. Noah moaned when he saw his Suburban.

"Your new brothers-in-law did that," Elaine tattled. "They aren't really acting their age, *especially* not the Senator."

Tillie laughed.

Elaine and Kate gathered all of the single women together in a group.

"Okay, pay attention now," Kate said. "I'm anxious to see who catches this thing!"

The group of single ladies included many members of Joshua's congregation, along with Heidi Romanov, Laura, Maggie May, Estelle, Gabriella and Alyssa.

Kate turned Tillie around in front of them, and said, "Close your eyes!"

Tillie tossed the bouquet backwards into the crowd behind her. To everyone's surprise, the bouquet landed in Alyssa's hands. Everyone cheered.

Kate laughed out loud. Tillie turned around and saw her tall and beautiful niece holding the bouquet.

"I don't even have a boyfriend," Alyssa said with a dry smile. She winked at her mother. "It's just for fun anyway, Ma`ma."

Tillie and Noah's children surrounded them with hugs and kisses, and Tillie began to cry as she looked into their faces. It had been many years since she'd left her children.

"Oh, come on, Mom," A.J. said, giving her a hug. "You gotta have a honeymoon. Besides, we're gonna have fun on the ranch."

"I know," Tillie cried.

Laura scoffed, "It's only for ten days. Think about all the fun you're gonna have moving into our new house when we get back." Her black eyes sparkled with delight. "And Jake and Ty won't have to go home anymore. We're a *real* family now."

"I'll really miss you guys," Noah said as he took his own sons into his arms.

"We're really excited to go to Reata with Vincenzo and Kate," Ty said with a smile. "If it's not too hot, Vincenzo's gonna let us sleep in the barn —"

"Yeah," Jake interrupted, "like they used to when they were boys in Italy."

"And we'll help with chores," Ty added excitedly. "And we'll ride with the men in the mornings."

Soon the entire family was upon them, wishing them well one last time, and kissing them goodbye. Petrice and Ellie coaxed them toward the Suburban, and Noah and Tillie got into the back seat. They waved out the window at their children as Petrice pulled away.

They landed in Chicago shortly before sundown. Along the way, Elaine helped Tillie remove the tight knots and beads her mother had put into her hair and her soft curls rested on her dark shoulders. That was the way Noah liked her hair the best.

The plane taxied toward the terminal. Tillie saw a black limousine waiting on the Tarmac, and she smiled with surprise.

"Petrice and I have a friend," Elaine explained with a smile. "He will take you directly to The Drake, and then bring you back here at noon tomorrow, where you will catch your flight on *Al Italia.* That way, you won't have to try to find your way around Chicago."

"Thanks, Ellie," Tillie said. "I haven't had a limo ride in a *really long* time."

"I've never been in a limo," Noah said.

"Then you're in for a real treat," Elaine said. "Patty had some sparkling apple juice put on ice for you guys to enjoy on your way over." She rolled her eyes and added, "He thought it would be romantic."

The plane finally came to a stop and Petrice emerged from the cockpit. He smiled at Noah and Tillie and said, "Well, this is it!" He looked at his wife. "Did you tell them about the limo?"

"Yes, my love," she answered.

"Then you are all set," Petrice said. "Noah, will you help me with this door?"

Noah got to his feet and helped Petrice lower the steps onto the tarmac.

Petrice extended his hand, giving Noah's a hearty shake. "Say hello to *Italia* for me, for I have not seen her in a very long time," he said.

Noah nodded. "Will do."

Petrice took Tillie into his arms, holding her close as he said, "You will soon see where you come from, my Angel. You will feel home in your heart as you look upon her glorious beauty. There is something about that land no one understands until they see her for themselves."

Tillie nodded at her brother's words. They all said goodbye one last time, and Noah and Tillie went to their limousine.

"Alone at last," Noah said with mischief in his eyes, and he took Tillie into his arms.

The sun was already beginning to set when the bellhops left Tillie and Noah, along with their luggage, in their suite overlooking Lake Michigan.

"We stayed here when Marquette and Tara got married," Tillie said, looking around at the elegance of the room. The entire lakefront wall of the suite was glass. The softness of the setting sun glimmered through the tall windows, gliding its way across the floor, and lighting the room with a romantic glow.

"This is the nicest place I've ever been," Noah said as he put his arms around Tillie. He held her close and softly kissed her lips. He smiled into her eyes, scooped her up in his strong arms, and laid her on the bed. He passionately kissed her lips, and Tillie sighed as she nestled into his arms....

Chapter 15

Their plane took off from Chicago the next day. As they flew over the eastern United States and into an evening crossing over the Atlantic Ocean, Tillie snuggled close to Noah. He put his arms around her, enjoying her familiar scent, and feeling the delicate softness of her skin. They talked and planned their journey, not noticing the hours that passed.

Dinner was served as the sun began to set. While most of the passengers fell asleep after eating, Noah and Tillie continued visiting until their plane carried them into a sunrise on the other side of the world.

"But it's only midnight in Rapid City!" Tillie whispered, clutching Noah's hand as they watched the brilliance of the rising sun. They had been in the air about five hours.

Most of the passengers closed their windows against the brightness so they could sleep, but Tillie and Noah kept theirs open, watching the snow and ice of Greenland pass beneath them.

In a few hours they passed over Reykjavik, and finally the United Kingdom. As they glided over the English Channel and into Europe, the snow-covered Alps came into view. The Italian mountain range wound into the sea below, stretching back over the greenest lands they'd ever seen.

Tillie looked into the valleys under them. "Just think, Noah, my brothers were all born there — and I come from there, too!"

Noah smiled, seeing the wonder and amazement in his new bride. He was struck with awe as he realized that this was the place where God began His delicate creation of the person sitting next to him. Somewhere, in one of those valleys, God started the process of what was happening today. Noah could only take a deep breath and thank Him for His goodness and love.

"It's amazing," he whispered as he put his arm around his precious wife.

They landed at Milano Malpensa 1 without incident, and a tall, slender man with a sign that read HANSEN was waiting just inside the gate.

"Hey, that's us," Noah said.

"It must be Jonathon," Tillie said. Marquette had promised to send someone to help them get to their villa on Lake Como.

"*Buon giorno*," he greeted.

Noah extended his hand in friendly greeting, and the tall stranger accepted with a smile.

"I am Jonathon Miller," he said with a British accent.

"Noah Hansen."

Jonathon nodded, reaching for Tillie's hand. "And Angel, I presume?" He asked, and Tillie nodded. "It's a pleasure to finally meet you," he said with a smile. "Mr. Caselli has made arrangements for me to take you directly to your villa. Our helicopter is waiting."

Marquette had explained that it would be much easier to take the helicopter straight to their villa, rather than fight with the Italian traffic. He'd said that it was very difficult to get around, what with the narrow roads and impatient drivers. And many times there was nowhere to park. The village in which they would be staying was very small, and much easier to navigate on foot. Ferries ran between the small towns on the lake, so it would be no trouble to get from one place to the other without a car.

Jonathon helped them collect their luggage, then led them to the helicopter.

Tillie bit her lip nervously as they put on their seatbelts and prepared for departure.

"I've never been on a chopper," she moaned. "And I'm not that excited about it."

Noah grimaced as he remembered his last chopper ride — the day he left Saigon. Hopefully this ride would be better than his last. He reached for Tillie's hand and gave her an encouraging smile. "It'll be great. Don't worry," he said.

Though she was frightened, Tillie couldn't help but steal a glance at the landscape below as the chopper carried them northward. The sprawling city beneath them was much bigger than she'd imagined. In her mind, she'd always seen *Italia* as a country filled with tiny villages, vineyards and farms — the landscape her family had descriptively reminisced of for many years. But what she saw was heavily congested traffic. Inky black spots, she realized, were actually pedestrians — thousands of them. *Milano* was a huge city — bigger than Chicago — and that surprised her. *No wonder Marquette put us on a helicopter.*

As they flew away from the city, the landscape began changing. Small villages, farms and vineyards were dotting the rolling hills, and Como Lake gleamed in the morning sun. The helicopter engines slowed as they glided through a lush park surrounding a two-story, brilliant orange villa. Gleaming white shutters framed tall windows. The roof was made of terra cotta tile. Perfectly manicured trees and bushes concealed a floral garden. A helicopter pad came into view and the pilot signaled that he was landing.

Once on the pad, the villa fell from view behind a tall hedge. They waited for the pilot to shut down the blades, and then he signaled that everyone could get out.

"We will take care of the luggage," Jonathon announced as he helped Tillie and Noah from the helicopter. He nodded toward a young Italian woman waiting near a gate at the hedge. She was dressed in simple jeans, a white blouse, and Nike tennis shoes. "That is Sylvia. She will take you to the villa and show you around. She will also help to care for you this week. You won't see me again until I bring Mr. and Mrs. Caselli here next week."

Noah nodded as he reached for Jonathon's hand. "Thanks for everything," he said.

"You are quite welcome," Jonathon replied.

Tillie reached for Jonathon's hand as well as she said, "And tell my brother that we'll be so looking forward to seeing him."

Tillie and Noah joined Sylvia by the gate, and she introduced herself. "It is such a pleasure to meet Signor Caselli's sister," she said in heavily accented English. "He speaks of his family often."

"Have you met my other brothers and my parents?" Tillie asked as Sylvia led them through the gate and onto a cobblestone path. The villa came into view again.

"Yes, but not for a very long time," Sylvia answered. She took a breath and continued, "This is the back of the villa. I can show you to the road so that you may walk into *Bellagio* and shop, or catch a ferry to one of the other towns on the lake. From back here you cannot see *Lago di Como*, but from the veranda in your room, and from where you will eat your meals, you will have a nice view. It is not as busy in the country, nor as close to the lake as some like to get, but it is quiet."

Well-cared-for gardens surrounded the back of the villa, and there were two separate stone patios: one connected to the villa, and another further out. Flowers grew from every available pot — on tables, near chairs and on pedestals. Boxes beneath the windows of the villa were filled with geraniums, bougainvilleas, and azaleas.

Sylvia led them through a back door into the villa's kitchen. Tillie sighed…it was exactly what she'd expected an Italian kitchen to look like. Tall, wooden cupboards with glass doors housed brightly painted dishes and elegant stemware. Copper pots and pans hung above a gas stove. The floor was gray slate, and the countertops were orange tile.

A young man entered the kitchen with his hand extended.

"This is my brother, Gionni," Sylvia introduced. "Gionni, this is the new brother of Signor Caselli, and Angel."

Gionni shook hands with Noah first, and then Tillie. "I will cook for you this week," he said. His English was more heavily accented than his sister's.

"Whatever you need, you will tell us," Sylvia said with a smile. "Come along now and I will show you to your room. You should have a rest, and then we will prepare an afternoon meal."

Beyond the kitchen was a small, but elegant, formal dining room. Just off the dining room was a veranda, and the floor-to-ceiling doors were open. Como Lake was now visible and Noah and Tillie gasped at its beauty. Just to the left of the dining room was a living room with another veranda, and its doors were also open.

Sylvia led them up an open and winding staircase, stopping at the open door.

"Here is your room," she said as she took them inside. "There is an American bathroom." She opened a door just to the right, revealing a garden bathtub, sink, regular toilet, and a shower. "There is also a veranda." She pointed beyond the king-sized bed. "And you may have your *caffé* there in the mornings if you wish."

Tillie noticed that the doors of their veranda were open, and that no screens were visible.

"Can we close the screens?" she asked politely.

"If you wish," Sylvia answered. "But it may become hot and stuffy in your room." She hurried to the windows and began closing the heavy doors.

Tillie smiled and shook her head as she tried to explain, "Not the windows, just the screens."

Sylvia looked baffled. "I guess I do not understand."

Tillie went to the window, realizing there were no screens available.

By the expression on her face, Sylvia could tell something was amiss. "What is wrong, Angel?" she asked.

Tillie swallowed and smiled with embarrassment. "In America we have a sort of mesh covering for our window that lets in the air, but keeps out the bugs —"

"Bugs?" Sylvia frowned.

Noah chuckled. "I get it," he said. "There are no insects here, are there?"

Sylvia shook her head and smiled. "No insects. Correct. No *bugs*." She giggled and patted Tillie's arm. "Take a rest and then come down later for something delicious. Gionni will not disappoint you." She giggled again and scurried from the room, closing the door behind her.

Before them was the view of the still, blue Italian lake, the peaceful sky and the security of the close mountains.

Tillie sighed. "Wow, it's awesome here."

Noah nodded and reached for her hand. "Sylvia says we should rest," he said.

Tillie smiled into his dancing blue eyes.

Noah took her into his arms and placed a soft kiss upon her lips. He held her close and kissed her again….

*****

Sylvia was right, there were no bugs in *Bellagio*, and it amazed Noah and Tillie to no end. In their part of the world flies and gnats were a common problem, though the altitude in the Black Hills tended to wipe out most of the mosquitoes. *Bellagio*, on the other hand, had no such things. Everyone's windows and doors remained open, unless it rained.

*****

A short walk from the villa took them into the bustling town of *Bellagio*. As Sylvia explained before they left, "*Bellagio* looks the same today as it did one hundred years ago. And hopefully it will never change."

The small town on *Lago di Como* was built into a hill along the shoreline. Stone steps constructed the narrow streets, winding between immaculate buildings and storefronts. Above the stores were apartments with balconies decorated with bright flowers and green plants. Small inner courtyards were filled with flowering plants and leafy trees. The Italians took every opportunity to plant what they could, where they could, and Tillie was reminded of her father's flower gardens in Sioux Falls, South Dakota. For as long as she could remember, Papa had kept the most beautiful flowers in the neighborhood. As she looked at the way the Italians kept their homes and gardens, she swallowed away sentimental tears. *This is what's in Papa's heart, and it always will be.*

Every few steps was a different shop, market or bar. Tables with umbrellas lined the walkways where people gathered to either socialize or read the paper. To Noah's and Tillie's surprise, a "bar" in *Italia*, was far different from a bar in America. An Italian bar served espresso, or a glass of wine or beer. And drunks didn't linger in and out of Italian bars. Everyone was well-behaved. No one overindulged as they enjoyed an afternoon "siesta," which appeared to be all about visiting rather than an afternoon nap!

American coffee was impossible to find; even Gionni did not prepare coffee the way Noah liked it. Tillie was used to the strong espresso and steamed milk, but Noah was shocked that someone would "burn their coffee." Their first morning at the villa, Gionni presented them with *il caffé Americano*. A small cup was filled about two-thirds of the way with espresso, and a small pitcher of steamed milk was served on the side. Noah didn't want to hurt Gionni's feelings so he struggled through the bitter brew, and then went looking for a coffee shop in town. He found the same recipe, over and over again, which he eventually named "*caffé Americano disappointamento*."

Sylvia laughed when she heard about Noah's funny expression. With a smile she pointed out, "But if we compromise on just that one small thing, all of *Bellagio* will change." She giggled and shook her head. "You will understand when you see *Firenze*."

Tillie was curious about Sylvia's comments, but shrugged them off. Marquette had promised to take them to *Firenze* (Florence) when they visited the *Tuscano* region together. Perhaps he would explain what she meant.

Hand in hand, Noah and Tillie walked all over the romantic town of *Bellagio*. They explored the amazing gardens of *Villa Melzi*, along the shore of Como Lake, even finding an American Sequoia among the famous trees.

Navigazione Lago di Como, the ferry service on the lake, took them to the small town of Lenno, where they hiked the entire peninsula, and then toured the gardens of *Villa Balbianello*.

In the sleepy town of *Varenna* they walked along the shoreline, and had lunch on a patio overlooking the peaceful waters of the lake. *Varenna* was fairly void of all souvenir shops and had only a few hotels on the lake. Their streets were made of stone steps, like

Bellagio, and took them up and down between beautifully cared-for residences. Tillie took photos of the cityscape, and their majestic *Duomo*, (cathedral) in the town square, planning sketches and paintings for when she returned.

In *Menaggio* they listened to an accordion player, along with his tambourine man, play traditional Italian music on a street corner. They allowed Noah to take their photo, with an excited Tillie posed between them.

Their favorite place to eat was *Trattoria San Giocomo*, which was one of the restaurants located in *Bellagio*. They prepared a steak as well, or better, than any steak house in the Black Hills of South Dakota, and their traditional Italian dishes were superb.

And whether it was Sylvia and Gionni, or any of the Italians they met during their time in *Bellagio*, Noah and Tillie were impressed with their hospitality. The kindness of the people of *Italia* was overwhelming. More than once, Noah and Tillie were brought to tears by their tender overtures and true spirit of service.

On their last night together in *Bellagio*, they ate a traditional meal of pasta and fish prepared by Gionni on their romantic veranda overlooking a moonlit lake. They sipped sparkling water, reminiscing of their time in Italy until late into the evening. Later Noah held Tillie in his arms as they lay in their bed listening to the sounds of the water against the shore below. It had been a wonderful week, and the only thing Noah wished for was more time.

"My life is finally complete," he whispered in the dark as he held her. "I was always so *discontented*. I never thought I'd be with you, and now I am. God has been so good to me."

Tillie sighed. "I love you so much, Noah, and I'm never gonna stop."

*****

While Noah showered, Tillie took the opportunity to explore the rest of the villa. Sylvia had invited her many times to do so, but there hadn't been extra time that week. Marquette called to say they would be just a little late, and that gave Tillie some time to look around.

In all, there were five bedrooms upstairs. Two appeared to have their own bathrooms. A very lovely sitting area overlooked the livingroom below. Every bedroom was decorated with great care in its own bright color scheme, and loaded with old, black and white photographs and drawings. She only observed the bedrooms from the doorway, until she reached the small room at the very end of the hall. What appeared to be a crayon drawing encased in a frame hung on the wall near the windows. With a curious frown she went to the drawing, stopping in her tracks when she realized what it was. Tears flooded her eyes as she reached for a touch to make sure that it was real. It was a brown crayon drawing of the puppies on Uncle Angelo's farm, and at the bottom was a young child's chicken scratches…*Angel.*

"I remember this," she breathed. She'd drawn the picture for Marquette's birthday, and then had her mother send it to him wherever he was at the time. She looked at the left hand corner and smiled. Rosa had written Marquette's birthday and the year he received it: *14/02/1964.*

The room had many black and white photos, and a few color photos as well, and she decided to take a closer look. She had to laugh when she realized that most of them were old photos she'd seen in her parents' albums. They were mostly of the Casellis when they first came to America, and some taken shortly after Tillie was born.

This discovery made Tillie retrace her steps and she went back through the other bedrooms. Sure enough, all of the photos were of the Casellis, and some photos Tillie recognized as people from Tara's family. One of the bedrooms had only very old photographs, obviously taken in *Italia* before they came to America. All of the drawings bore Tillie's signature, though some she didn't remember doing.

On a dresser she found her father's favorite photograph — the one of Rosa leading Delia to the back of the D`Annenci's buggy. It sat next to the photo of Guiseppi and Angelo, wearing their Italian hats, on their way to the war. Tillie took the old photo into her hands and sat down on the bed.

"We were *powerful warriors*," she whispered.

"What's that?" Noah's voice came from the doorway, and Tillie jumped with surprise.

"Oh my goodness!" she breathed with excitement. She hurried to where he stood and showed him the photograph. "We were powerful warriors," she whispered as the tears spilled upon her cheeks. "This is the photo." She glanced around the room. "This must be Marquette's house because all of the pictures are of my family."

Noah smiled as he looked at the old photograph, and then he glanced around the room. "But Marquette doesn't *live* here," he said with a question in his voice. "You said once that he lives in a *pink castle*, and he said he was taking us there this morning for breakfast before he flies us over to Florence." Marquette had also promised a visit to the place where the Caselli brothers had been born and raised.

Tillie nodded. "Well, this must be his place because these things belong to him."

"Two houses in Italy, one in D.C. — he must be *so* loaded," Noah murmured. It was something he'd always suspected, but had admitted quite by accident. He blushed with embarrassment at his slip of the tongue.

Tillie giggled. "I think so, too….what with all of the helicopters and stuff —"

The helicopter was suddenly overhead, and the two of them laughed.

"Let's go meet the ol' rich guy and see what other secrets shake out of the trees," Noah teased, and they headed downstairs.

By the time they reached the landing area, Marquette and Tara were being helped from the helicopter. They waved and smiled as they hurried to Noah and Tillie.

Marquette hugged his little sister, kissed her cheek and then he moved on to her husband. Noah knew the kiss was probably coming, but it was becoming less and less strange.

"How were the kids when you left?" Tillie asked.

"They were well," Tara answered. "And I believe that Vincenzo and Kate are having the time of their lives with them."

"For it is a fun thing to spoil our nieces and nephews," Marquette added.

They started back inside and Tara smiled as she said, "We are so happy that you are finally visiting our home."

"I can hardly believe that you are here," Marquette said.

"I know," Tillie said, shaking her head. "I can hardly believe it either. I've talked about it for years, but I never made it until now. And by the way, is *this place* yours too?"

Marquette nodded with a grin. "Sylvia and Gionni live here most of the time, but I make it available for special guests."

"Do you love the lake, Angel?" Tara asked with a wistful smile.

"Yes," Tillie answered. "No wonder you guys live here."

"Let us get your things together so that we can continue your journey," Marquette said. "We will fly to *Cadenabbia*, have our breakfast, and then leave for *Tuscano* from there."

"And we get to see Florence?" Tillie reminded.

Marquette rolled his eyes. "Are you certain that you want to see that unholy debacle, Angel?"

Tillie giggled. "Why not?"

"It is not exactly the *Italia* of my childhood, but if you insist."

"I insist. It was the birthplace of the Renaissance," Tillie said.

Marquette shrugged. "Well, then, we must be on our way."

The helicopter carried them across the lake and into another park, where a *pink castle* came into view. Tillie softly gasped as they landed on the pad. The castle dropped from view behind the hedge.

In just a moment they were heading down a path and through a gate, where they saw a full three-story mansion, complete with turrets at each corner. It was situated perfectly upon the shore of the lake. The Italian flag flew next to the American flag at a covered dock. A wall of stone protected the castle from the water below. Hundreds of potted azaleas decorated its edge. Magnificent trees appeared to grow directly out of the stone, and lush green vines ascended the sides of the castle walls. Marquette's home was even more beautiful than the villa they'd just left, and Noah and Tillie looked around in quiet amazement.

"Come along, Angel," Tara coaxed, reaching for her sister-in-law's hand. "We have a brunch ready."

Tillie and Noah followed Marquette and Tara over a stone patio and into the entrance, where they were again taken by surprise. Just to the left of the entrance, was the parking garage, where a red Ferrari F355 Spider and a long, black, Rolls Royce waited.

They continued into an entrance of white and gray marble, shiny brass fixtures gleaming overhead. A set of double doors opened automatically as they approached.

A man in a black suit was waiting there, and he nodded with a serious expression. "Signor Caselli," he greeted.

"*Buon giorno*," Marquette acknowledged. "*Inglese, per favore*." He looked at Tillie and Noah and introduced, "My sister, *Signora* Hansen, and her husband, *Signor* Hansen. This is our *maggiordono*, Carmine."

"How do you do?" Carmine said, nodding at Tillie and Noah. Tillie and Noah smiled politely in return, wondering what in the world a *maggiordono* was. Carminc looked back at Marquette and said, "Your brunch is ready, *Signor*."

"Very good," Marquette acknowledged with a smile. He continued through the entrance, leading them into another incredible room. "This is our greeting area," he explained.

The greeting area was open to the third story. Noah quickly estimated the ceiling to be at least thirty feet high. The windows facing the lake reached to the top, and most of them were open today. The floors were the same gray and white marble that had greeted them, and columns of the matching marble were positioned throughout the open room. Oversized couches, chairs, love seats and tables were placed around the perimeter of the room, along with colorful potted plants and full-size trees. Above them, handsome black wrought iron railings lined an open balcony of doorways to other rooms. Beyond the windows on the lake, they saw the veranda Marquette had often spoke of, for it was his favorite place in all of his home. An elderly lady approached them with a smile, and Tara smiled in return.

"This is Hannah," Tara introduced. "Hannah, *Signora* Hansen, Marquette's sister, and her husband, *Signor* Hansen."

"It is a pleasure," Hannah replied in heavily accented English. She looked at Tara. "I have set your favorite table on the veranda whenever you are ready."

Tara nodded. "Thank you."

Hannah hurried away, Noah and Tillie watching in amazement. Obviously, Marquette and Tara lived very differently in Italy than they lived in America, and it was quite something to watch.

"Come along," Marquette said with a smile as he led the way to the veranda. "We have not had a chance to eat yet this morning."

They followed him through elegant glass doors and onto the marble veranda. The generous, cylinder-shaped railing was also made of the same marble they saw inside of the house. The veranda stretched out over the lake, and all around the north side. Its glass doors were open as well, leading into other rooms they'd not yet seen.

"This is so awesome," Tillie finally managed to croak out in a soft voice. "It looks like a real castle, Marquette. When was it built?"

"1625," Marquette answered. "It was originally intended to be the summer home for a wealthy *Milano* duke. When he passed, a cardinal bought the place and created the outer grounds and gardens. When the cardinal passed, there was not a buyer to be found, and the place fell into disrepair. It was empty until the late 1800s, when a British man purchased it. It remained in his family until Tara I bought the place in 1969. Of course, over the years, Tara and I have made many improvements. Electricity, for one, and we updated the water system back in the early seventies."

"How many bedrooms?" Noah asked.

"Eight upstairs," Tara answered, "and two more just off of the veranda. Here," she said as she stepped toward an elaborately set table. "Hannah has set our favorite table and we should be seated before she returns. Our Hannah prefers perfect etiquette."

The table was set with expensive china and crystal, and everyone took their seats.

Marquette smiled at his sister as he placed his napkin on his lap. "You are very quiet this day, Angel," he said.

"Sorry. I'm just a little overwhelmed by all of this. Your house is really awesome," she said.

Tara chuckled. "Oh, thank you, Angel. That pleases me to no end."

Marquette laughed. "Well, it is perhaps a bit overstated. However, it is a wonderful escape from our difficult assignments."

Hannah bustled in, along with a younger woman. They carried trays of food.

"Are you ready?" Hannah asked.

"Yes, Hannah," Tara answered.

Promptly, Hannah and her assistant set plates filled with eggs, sausages, fruit and cheese before them. She handed her empty tray to her assistant and poured the juice from the container sitting in the middle of the table.

"Anything else?" Hannah asked.

"We are fine," Tara answered with a smile. Hannah nodded, and she and her assistant left them alone.

"We had them prepare American," Tara said.

Marquette prayed and they all started on the delicious meal. As they ate, and visited, the shock of Marquette's elaborate home began to wear off, and Tillie and Noah were more comfortable. It was still just Marquette and Tara, no matter how fancy they did things at their place.

After they'd finished with their brunch, Marquette and Tara showed Tillie and Noah the guest room, which was a lovely suite located off of the veranda, overlooking the lake. Floor-to-ceiling windows indulged them with an uncompromised view of the lake. Plush carpeting beneath their feet, an oversized bathtub and a king-sized bed facing the lake and the mountains made them gasp. It was decorated in deep purples, blues and golds — bold colors of Italian decor that Noah and Tillie were getting used to.

They took them out onto the grounds, where they walked for what felt like acres through flowering gardens along the shore of the lake. Thousands of blossoms filled their senses. In the near distance were other homes and gardens, but nothing compared to Marquette and Tara's villa. Tillie took dozens of photos so that she could show their children what it had been like to visit such a magical place.

It wasn't long and they were back in the helicopter, heading for *Firenze*. Marquette had promised that after a few hours in the heart of the city, they would visit the hillside country where he and his brothers had been born and raised.

They landed at *Amerigo Vespucci* in the early afternoon and were met by yet another employee of Marquette's. He led them to a Mercedes wagon, and everyone climbed in.

"Take us to the *Piazza della Repubblica*," Marquette politely requested. "We will begin there."

The driver nodded, started the vehicle, and then suddenly lurched into traffic.

It took only a few moments to realize why Marquette had recommended helicopter travel. As their driver literally careened into Florence, Tillie's stomach began to wobble. In and out between cars, on a narrow road with no passing lane, the driver hit speeds of nearly 140 kilometers per hour. Noah saw how pale Tillie was becoming and he wondered if she'd spill before they reached their destination.

Tillie was horrified at what she saw as they sped along between the streets. Every sidewalk was crammed with people as far as the eye could see. She couldn't see the storefronts, or anything else for that matter, because of the tremendous amount of foot traffic. And the vehicle traffic before them and behind them was just as bad. She glanced at the speedometer, wondering what the miles-per-hour equivalency was...*and why is Marquette letting that guy drive so fast?!*

At last they came to sudden stop at what appeared to be a corner. Tillie looked around, realizing that they were in an intersection, but it was difficult to see because of the multitudes.

Marquette was the first to get out of the car. He opened the rear doors of the Mercedes. "We must hurry," he said with a smile. "Our driver cannot wait forever." And he was right. The honking had already started.

Noah, Tillie and Tara quickly exited the vehicle, joining Marquette on the sidewalk.

Piazza della Repubblica was a large square. Hotel Pendini was just to the west, several cafes were just to the north and south, and to the east were several narrow, winding streets. People filled every available square inch.

Marquette took Tara's hand in a firm grasp and shouted above the noise of the crowd, "Noah, you must hold Angel's hand, and we must stick together. It is very easy to be swept into the crowd!"

Marquette led them through the *piazza* on foot, and then north on *Via Roma*. They passed elegant shops Tillie had only seen in magazines, such as Louis Vuitton, Gucci, Georgio Armani and Valli. Marquette paused beside a Dolce Gabanna and rolled his eyes.

"I am afraid to report that *Firenze* has turned into a playground for the very wealthy and affluent."

And Tillie saw exactly what he was talking about. Women who'd been in tanning beds until their chests had wrinkled, whose bleached hair resembled broken straw, hurried in and out of these shops. Their fake laughs were heard above the roar of the crowd while they told one another of yet another great purchase they were taking home. Unassuming, and obviously bored, men tagged along behind them, carrying their packages.

Marquette shrugged. "But the architecture here is fantastic — hopefully you will be able to admire it through the crowds."

And the architecture was awesome — though some of it was hidden within the populous. The Cathedral of *Santa Maria del Fiore* was amazing. It had been carved from three different colors of marble: green, white and red. All of her statues were carved from marble, and the doors of the adjacent baptistery were gilded in bronze.

Marquette took them through the winding, narrow streets to visit the *Piazza della Signoria*, where stood a copy of the famous statue of David.

"The original *David* is in the *Galleria dell'Accademia*, but the lines are about four hours long." Tara explained. "However, this is the place where Michelangelo first put his most famous work."

They went past the Uffizi, and across the Arno Bridge. They took a short tour of the *Palazzo Pitti* and the Boboli Gardens. And everywhere were crowds of tourists and shoppers. Every street corner, and every available block was filled with souvenir stands, postcard kiosks, and t-shirt shops.

Tillie had to admit that the architecture and history were awesome, but what had become of the *Italia* her family had spoken of for nearly forty years? It was nowhere to be seen in this place. She shook her head and wiped tears from her eyes.

Marquette saw her distress and he put a tender hand on her shoulder as he said, "Let me take you to a place I know so that you may have something to eat, and so that we may rest and visit about these things we have seen."

Tillie nodded, and they followed him back through the winding town.

It seemed they'd been walking for hours when they came upon a run-down storefront with several tables outside. The sign read: *Osteria dell'Agnolo*, and Marquette took them inside.

An Italian man about Marquette's age dashed from the back of the restaurant and took him in a hearty embrace. "*Buon Giorno, Marquette*!" He exclaimed, kissing Marquette. "*Che cosa li porta a Firenze?!*"

Marquette returned his embrace and kiss. "*Alessandro! Inglese, per favore*. I am with my sister —"

"The Angel!" Alessandro exclaimed. "So many things I have heard! You have made it to *Italia* at last!" He embraced Tillie quite exuberantly, but before he kissed her, he glanced at Noah. "*Americano?* Husband?"

Noah frowned softly and nodded.

"Okay to kiss?" Alessandro questioned.

Noah's frown deepened, but he nodded.

Alessandro lifted Tillie's hand in a most delicate way, placing a polite kiss upon the top.

Noah smiled with relief, and Tillie couldn't help but giggle.

Marquette laughed. "Alessandro, allow me to introduce my sister, Angel, and her new husband, Noah. They have been on their honeymoon, and she wanted to see *Firenze*, if you can believe it."

Alessandro moaned and shook his head.

"And this is one of our oldest friends," Marquette introduced. "Alessandro Gionelli. We knew one another in *Chianti*, and have kept in touch over the years."

Alessandro nodded. "Now, please, take them to the back where the air conditioning works and I will bring you bread and water — sparkling or still?"

"Sparkling," Marquette answered. Alessandro nodded and rushed off. Marquette led them to the back.

Osteria dell'Agnolo was very old. The plaster on the walls was cracked in several places, exposing the original brick structure. In an attempt to spruce the place up a bit, they had painted over the damage. The booths were at least twenty-five year old vinyl, and the wooden tables were dark lacquered. The tile floor had cracked in places, and been repaired with cement. Soft accordion music played in the background. Tillie smiled as they seated themselves. She liked it.

"*Italia* was becoming very busy when we left in 1956," Marquette said with a sigh. "We did not come to town very often, but when we did we had started to have a most miserable time."

"On the hillside," Tara continued, "where we were all raised, it is still quiet, and truly enchanting — all of the things that makes one love *Italia.*"

"But the cities have succumbed to commercialism and greed," Marquette added. "Some of the wealthiest Americans and Europeans vacation here only because of the shopping. They do not come to see the beauty of the Renaissance, or our vineyards, or the hospitality of our people. They come to buy something that is available to them in their own cities, only to boast of buying it in *Italia*."

Alessandro had arrived with their water while Marquette was speaking, and he sighed as he set the bottles on the table. "It is because their hearts are empty," he said.

Everyone looked up at him with surprise, except for Marquette for they'd had this conversation many times.

Alessandro smiled, patting his chest as he said, "Without a Savior one grows a place that cannot be filled."

Later in the afternoon, a different driver met them with a Rolls Royce.

"For a more comfortable ride," Marquette explained as they were seated.

They headed south out of the city, taking a paved highway. After some time, they turned onto a gravel road and Tillie noticed that there were fewer and fewer houses and buildings. The expanse before them and all around was quickly changing to only vineyards, grassy rolling hills and perhaps a stone mansion or two.

"The area has remained fairly unsettled," Marquette said as they watched through the windows of the Rolls. He took a breath and pointed to the impressive stone mansion just to their left. "There is the Andreotti Winery, where we all stayed during the war."

"We must be getting closer," Tillie whispered.

Marquette nodded, holding his breath, wondering what she would feel when she at last saw the place. Their father's cousin, Giovanni Caselli, had vacationed on the place for many years, and kept the small property in excellent repair. Marquette had purchased several thousand acres surrounding the old farm many years ago, and secured a building prevention measure in order to keep the area as it was when they left in 1956. That is why the roads around it were still gravel.

Marquette reached for Tillie's hand and whispered, "Here we come, Angel. Just over this next hill." He'd been with all of his family members when they'd revisited the spot later on their lives, and their reactions had been quite dramatic. Petrice and Ellie visited during their honeymoon in 1975, and again when they brought their children for a visit in 1987. Guiseppi and Rosa came for their fiftieth wedding anniversary, in the early spring of 1986, and they had cried. Vincenzo and Kate came for their thirtieth wedding anniversary in July of 1992. Tillie was the last of the Casellis to come for a visit.

"There it is," Marquette whispered, pointing to the small cabin in the near distance.

Tillie took in a soft breath, watching the cabin, along with a barn, get closer and closer. The driver pulled the car into the dirt driveway, continuing the short distance to the house. The car came to a stop and their driver hurried around to the rear door, and opened it for them. They slowly stepped out, and Tillie looked at the tiny cabin before them. Just beyond it was the big barn in the photograph she'd turned into a portrait. She could almost see her mother leading the old, black horse to the back of the buggy.

It must have been parked right about there, she thought as she took in the scene. She bit her lip, trying to keep her composure intact, but the feelings within her were more intense than she'd ever imagined they would be. This was, undoubtedly, the place where she'd been conceived. She felt as if she belonged, the same as she felt when she was at her parents' home in Sioux Falls. That struck her as being quite odd, seeing as how they were standing in a valley in the middle of another country, where she'd never been before…*but I have been here before! This is the place I came from!*

The cabin had a simple roofline with a stone chimney. The small wooden porch was decorated with red and purple bougainvillea, and pink geraniums. The front door was plain wood, but there was a paned glass window to the side, and Tillie was startled when she saw an old woman's face peeking out at them. She jumped a little, and Marquette smiled.

"That is Anna," he said.

The front door opened, and an elderly man and his wife stepped out onto the porch. They smiled and reached for Tillie. She impulsively smiled and reached back.

"*A suo casa bevenuto, Matilde*," the old woman said with tears and a smile.

Tillie could only smile in response, because she hadn't understood anything the old woman had said, except for her name.

Marquette put his hand on his sister's shoulder and explained, "She says, welcome home, Matilde. Tell her *grazie*."

Tillie's eyes filled with tears as she looked at the old woman before her. "*Grazie*," she whispered.

"This is Papa's cousin, Giovanni and his wife, Anna," Marquette introduced. "They do not speak English, so I will have to interpret for you. They stay here when they want to get away from *Genova*, which is where they live."

Marquette said something in Italian, and Giovanni and Anna nodded with smiles, and led their guests into the cabin.

Noah was quite moved with emotion from the brief exchange on the front porch, but nothing could have prepared him for what happened *inside* of the cabin. They stepped inside, where the floors were made of wooden planks, and the old fireplace was built of stone. Comfortable looking, but old, furniture was around the room, and an oversized, braided rug covered the planks in front of the fireplace.

The tiny kitchen was just off to the right, and Tillie caught her breath. A table with four chairs around it drew her attention first. A very old cook stove, a model that would be extremely expensive in an American antique store, stood in the corner. An old fashioned icebox stood beside it, and the several wooden cupboards, without doors, held the dishes and bowls. Two open doors were just a few steps beyond the kitchen.

"Do you want to look around, Angel?" Marquette asked quietly.

Tillie swallowed and nodded with a faint smile, and Marquette led her through the house.

"We acquired running water and electricity here when I was about ten years of age," he said as they walked through the little cabin. He led her toward the open doors, stopping at the first one. "This is where your brothers used to sleep together, until we became big and then Papa put us in the loft above the barn." They took a few steps further, and he stopped by the next door. "This was Ma`ma's and Papa's room."

Then he turned and they looked into the larger, outer room. Marquette smiled at his memories as he said, "There was a fire burning there the night Papa told us we were leaving *Italia.*" He swallowed and shook his head. "I threw a brutish sort of fit and stomped from the house." He sighed with regret. "What a terrible spectacle I made of myself."

Tillie looked around the room, seeing the episode acted out for the first time before her very eyes. She had only heard stories about this place, but now she stood in the midst of it.

"How could they ever leave?" she whispered.

Marquette smiled with a nod. "It was time to go," he answered. "God wanted other things for us. The valley could only offer us poverty and wine, and God had begun your creation, obviously intending for you something different than what we could give you here in this land." He smiled at Noah. "And there was a little boy who desperately needed the prayers of our mother and the companionship of our Angel's dearest heart. It *was* a wonderful place to be, but God had so much *more* He wanted to give us."

Part III

Annie Laurie

Chapter 16
Rapid City, South Dakota
April, 1995

Noah's and Tillie's children adjusted to living together quickly. A few minor surprises did occur, but nothing they couldn't handle. Noah and his sons hadn't lived with a woman in more than thirteen years, and suddenly there were *two* of them to remember. For instance, they couldn't walk around in whatever clothing they felt appropriate anymore; they had to remember to cover themselves now. Thankfully, Laura had her own bathroom, which helped considerably.

Noah and his sons' favorite adjustment was suppertime. When they heard Tillie's singing from the kitchen, and the ensuing chopping and rattling of pots and pans, they knew another delectable meal was on deck. And Tillie's dinners were *not* served on the card table in front of the evening news. *No way*. Everyone reported to the dining room *promptly* at six o'clock p.m. The table was always set, and the meal was waiting. For A.J. and Laura, it was normal, but for Noah and his sons, it was like magic. For years, they'd fended for themselves — now there was someone who not only *prepared* the meals *for* them, but made it enjoyable to listen too as well.

Tillie's new studio was already packed with paintings, sketches and photographs. Noah often wandered home in the middle of the day to see what she was doing. He'd settle himself in the wicker furniture and watch the creativity flow from her pretty hands. It was a dream come true, and he thanked God every moment of every day.

Even Sparky was happier in her new surroundings. She pranced through the meadow around Angel's Place daily. The only time Tillie saw her little dog was either when it was very hot or very cold, otherwise Sparky didn't like to come inside much at all. Her mother, Vanilla, on the other hand, was quite content to lie on the kitchen floor and watch her family go to and from the house.

Noah's old housekeeper, Vera, and Tillie's cleaning lady, Diane, were more than happy to share the housekeeping duties at Angel's Place. Tillie felt she could take care of everything herself, but Noah insisted he wanted her to be able to enjoy the things she really cared about, and that was being a mom and a wife — and an artist. To have to keep up on the large home they'd moved into would rob her of the precious time she intended to spend with *all* of their children, and her artwork.

In was nearly May, but still windy and cold in the Black Hills of South Dakota. Guiseppi and Rosa had arrived in Rapid City for their summer visit, and for Guiseppi's favorite summer job. When Jake and A.J. played, he wore his blue COACH cap proudly, dancing around in the dugout with the same team players who found him so comically entertaining for the past two summers. It was the *best* part of Guiseppi's life.

Tillie was seated with her parents at the first game of the season between Post 22 and Bismarck. Laura and Heidi were up by the gate with Jake and A.J. Noah had gone into the dugout to see Ty just before the game, and Joshua and Mona brought a tray of hot dogs and cherry slushies down from the concession stand.

"So, what's Ty's thinking about that Lynchburg scholarship?" Joshua asked. "Think he can move that far away from home?"

"I don't know if Noah could stand it," Tillie answered. She swallowed a bite of hot dog, grimacing inwardly at the peculiar, but oddly *familiar*, sensation in her stomach.

Guiseppi raised a silvered brow and replied, "Perhaps Ty could attend the university in Spearfish."

"They don't have a baseball program there, Papa," Tillie said. She tried another bite of hot dog, wishing she hadn't.

"He really needs to play," Mona added with a smile. "He loves the game so much."

"He wants to learn architecture, too," Tillie said.

Guiseppi sighed, "Well, I am sure he is looking forward to graduation."

Tillie winked. "He's so excited, and he has a date for the prom." Mona gasped, and Tillie laughed. "She's really cute, too," she went on. "Ty had her over to the house last weekend. Sweet girl. She's planning on going to school here in town."

"Maybe that'll make him stick around," Joshua said.

"Maybe," Tillie agreed, taking a sip of a slushy. A bad wave of nausea made her grimace again, and she set down the slushy. "Hey, Papa, do you have any Rolaids?"

"Of course," Guiseppi said, fishing a roll out of his pocket. "I do not come to Rapid City without them." He frowned at his daughter. "Are you sick, Angel?"

"Laura had the stomach flu last week," she said, slipping a Rolaid into her mouth. "I think I may have caught it." Guiseppi pretended to slide a short distance away from her, and Tillie laughed. "Don't worry. I won't breathe on you."

Guiseppi's expression was disapproving. "It is probably that horrible food you feel you must eat," he admonished.

Tillie grinned at her father and shook her head.

Noah came out of the dugout, making his way into the bleachers where he took a seat beside Tillie and kissed her cheek.

"How's Ty doing?" she asked with a smile.

"Nervous," Noah answered. "He had to give a little interview over the radio, and he's kinda jumpy about it."

The players came onto the field for the playing of the *Star Spangled Banner*, and all of the fans got to their feet. When Tillie stood up, she lost her balance.

Noah caught hold of her and chuckled, "You okay?"

"Just a little dizzy. I must have stood up too fast."

Noah nodded, but he kept his arm around her during the singing of the national anthem, and then he helped her sit down on the bleachers.

Through the entire game, Tillie fought waves of nausea and dizziness. Noah brought her a 7-UP, but it didn't help. She was thankful when Post 22 had a sufficient enough run lead to call the game, and it ended early.

"I've caught Laura's flu," she whispered as Noah walked her and her parents to the Suburban in the parking lot. "I hope I make it home before I spill."

"Me, too," Noah said as he helped her into the front seat. "I'll get the kids, and you guys just wait right here."

As he hurried off to find their children he couldn't help but remember the last time he'd seen her this way. After her accident she'd struggled with balance and nausea.

Tillie had to lay her head back on the rest above her seat in order to keep the dizziness under control. By the time they reached Angel's Place, she was very sick. She made it to the front door on her own steam, but Noah had to pick her up and carry her to their room upstairs. Their children and Tillie's parents were alarmed, to say the least.

"Do you think we should call the doctor?" Noah asked as he sat on the edge of their bed.

Tillie smiled faintly. "No. I'll be fine in the morning," she assured. "Just pray I don't throw up. I really hate to throw up."

"Okay." Noah tucked the covers in around her and lay down beside her. He put his hand upon her shoulder and prayed.

*****

The next morning was worse. Not only had Tillie started to throw up, but she was doing so convulsively, and couldn't leave the bathroom for even a minute. Noah was beside himself with worry. He left their room for only a few moments to make sure their children were getting ready for school, and then to find Rosa and Guiseppi. He didn't tell the kids how sick Tillie was, but he told her parents.

"She can't even leave the bathroom," he whispered to Rosa. "I've never seen anyone get the stomach flu like *this* before."

Rosa nodded. "I will go and check on her. You keep the children busy for a few moments, and I will be back with a report."

Rosa made her way to Tillie and Noah's room, closing the door behind her. She found her poor daughter still in the bathroom, crouched before the stool. Rosa ran a washcloth under cold water and placed it on the back of Tillie's neck.

"You have put quite a scare into your new husband," Rosa said with a soft smile.

Tillie sat down carefully on the bathroom floor and smiled at her mother. "Ma`ma," she whispered, and Rosa could have sworn there was a sparkle of delight in Angel's black eyes.

Rosa frowned. "Angel?"

"Ma`ma, I can hardly stand up," she whispered. "The whole room spins, and then I have to throw up again. This has only happened to me one other time in my life."

"After your accident?" Rosa questioned with caution.

"Well, it came then, too, but —" Tillie swallowed very hard, attempting to force away the nausea. "Last week, I was queasy every day, and everything I put into my stomach just didn't feel right. I've been really tired, and I've been sneaking naps during the day that nobody knows about." She shrugged with a smile. "I don't know, Ma`ma, maybe it's just the flu."

Rosa softly gasped as she frowned into her daughter's eyes. "Angel, have you told Noah?" she asked.

"I thought maybe it was all in my head, you know, one of those hysterical things women go through at my age. But now, I'm *so sick*."

"How late is your cycle?" Rosa whispered.

"Almost four weeks."

Rosa gasped again. "But your womb has been closed for so many years. How could this even be possible?"

Tillie bit her lip. "I don't know," she replied. "I need to go to the doctor and find out, but I'm so afraid."

"Afraid of what, my Angel?"

"That it'll be something else," she admitted. "Come on, Ma`ma, what are the chances I could be pregnant? I even had surgery to help things along in there, and it didn't work. There's just no possible way, and I'm afraid to tell Noah, because he'll worry. And I don't want him excited about a new baby if it turns out to be a false alarm."

Rosa swallowed hard and took a deep breath. "We must take you to the doctor and find out, no matter what," she said. "You cannot sit here and wait to get better. That will only worry Noah further." She shook her head and frowned. "Perhaps you can get an appointment today."

Tillie nodded, and was suddenly hit with another wave of nausea that she couldn't fight off.

"Oh, my poor Angel," Rosa sighed, shaking her head. She gently rubbed her daughter's back while Tillie began to throw up once again.

Tillie managed to call her doctor between episodes, and was relieved to learn that she could get in to see him that morning. She didn't tell Noah what she suspected. She had yearned for another child for so many years, and had even prayed for more. She was under the impression that God had answered her prayers with Noah's sons, and was content with the large family they shared together.

Dr. Barnes was a Christian man, and Tillie started seeing him when she moved to Rapid City in 1986. He had all of her health and pregnancy records from Dr. Lewis in Sioux Falls, and he knew Tillie's case history well.

Tillie left Noah to pace the waiting room while she went into the examining room alone.

Dr. Barnes sighed and shook his head as he said, "Tillie, you know that it's just *not possible*. There is way too much scarring, and even *if* fertilization did take place in one of your fallopian tubes, the embryo would die once it reached your uterus. You *cannot* get pregnant, but I'll send a lab tech for a couple of samples. The quickest way, I guess, is to get a urine sample, so we'll do that too, and then I'll do an exam. We can always do an ultrasound."

Tillie nodded, but in the back of her mind she'd already started to make plans. That little room Noah had intended to be a nursery was quickly redecorated in Tillie's imagination. Would it be for a boy or a girl? Or, perhaps, one of each?

Noah continued his frantic pacing in the lobby out front. He glanced occasionally at the stomachs of what seemed like hundreds of pregnant women — they seemed to be everywhere that day — and his mind began to wander. *Why are we at the gynecologist's office about the flu or her old head injury?* Fragments of past conversations started to pop up in his memories, and he was soon lost in a time he hadn't thought of in years. Alex had said she was *so dizzy she couldn't even drive herself.*

Noah mentally slapped himself back into reality. *What in the world am I thinking? Angel can't have babies anymore — and I'm forty-three years old! I must be nuts!* He shook his head with a sigh. *It's just because things have been so perfect...I've gotten myself caught up in my old daydreams of having children with her—*

"Mr. Hansen?" A nurse was in the doorway of the waiting room.

Noah stopped his pacing just a short distance from where she stood. "Yes," he said.

She smiled and opened the door for him, saying, "The doctor would like to speak with you and your wife."

Noah's heart fell into his stomach. He nodded his head and followed the nurse back. She knocked on the examining room door and then let him in.

Tillie was sitting on the examination table looking extremely nauseous and tired. Noah went to her.

Dr. Barnes was on the small stool by the desk, absorbed in Tillie's records. He looked at the small piece of paper the nurse handed him, and then he frowned.

Noah looked at Tillie for an answer, but she only shrugged in confusion.

Dr. Barnes turned in his chair to face the two of them. His frown deepened as he said, "During the exam, I did find that the uterus is enlarged and firm. I did a pregnancy test and it shows *positive*. I really think you guys are pregnant."

Tillie gasped with a smile, and Noah's mouth fell open with shock.

Dr. Barnes nodded. "I know…I'm sort of having the same reaction, Hansen. I don't know how this happened —"

"Well *I* do," Noah murmured.

Tillie laughed out loud.

Dr. Barnes smiled and gave Noah a wink as he said, "I'm gonna give you December 15, 1995, for your due date." He tore off a prescription and handed it to Tillie. "Take these vitamins, if you can hold 'em down, and drink plenty of water. You're not a spring chicken anymore, so let's be careful."

Noah sighed heavily, hanging his head as he replied, "I guess I *am* sort of oldish —"

Tillie guffawed. "He's talking to *me*, Noah," she said.

Dr. Barnes laughed and slapped Noah on the back. "You'll be okay, Hansen — once the shock wears off."

Noah nodded with a smile, and then he looked into Tillie's eyes. "I don't know what to say," he murmured.

Tillie's black eyes filled with tears as she smiled at her husband. "Me neither. What will we tell the kids?"

Noah's mouth fell open again, and Dr. Barnes laughed.

"They are home!" Rosa yelled to Guiseppi from the door in the entry way. She hurried to open it as Noah helped his staggering wife up the steps.

"How are you feeling, Angel?" she asked as they came through the door.

"As well as can be expected," Tillie answered.

Guiseppi trotted into the foyer. "We have been so worried!" he exclaimed. "What did the doctor say?"

"Angel's pregnant," Noah blurted.

Rosa gasped and Guiseppi's mouth fell open in surprise.

Noah nodded with a grin as he put his hand on Guiseppi's shoulder and said, "I had the *same* reaction."

Guiseppi's eyes filled with tears, spilling onto his dark cheeks. He reached for his daughter, whispering, "How can this be?"

Tillie smiled as she answered, "God *really loves us*, Papa."

*****

When their children came home from school, Noah ushered them quickly into the family room.

"We have to have a family meeting," he explained.

Ty looked at his father, seeing the stress between his brows. "You look tense, Dad," he said with concern.

"I'm fine," Noah answered gruffly.

Jake rolled his eyes at A.J. and leaned over to whisper, "He found that hole you knocked through the shed wall —"

"I fixed that shed wall a week ago," Noah grumbled. "I wondered who did that."

Tillie was seated in Noah's easy chair, nibbling on a soda cracker and sipping at a glass of 7-Up.

Laura knelt beside her mother and asked, "Mom, are you still sick?" Tillie nodded with a smile. "Wow, I wasn't *this* sick."

Rosa and Guiseppi meandered into the family room, taking seats among the children.

Noah clapped his hands together as if he were getting ready to address his baseball team. "Okay, listen up," he instructed. "Me and Angel gotta tell you something, and it's *big*."

Everyone focused on Noah.

Noah took a deep breath and announced, "We're getting a new baby —"

"Are you guys adopting?" Ty asked.

Noah frowned and said, "Angel's pregnant."

Jake's eyes were wide with surprise. "Aren't you guys sort of…*old?*" he asked.

"Well the Lord doesn't think so," Noah replied.

Laura put her hand on her mother's. "You're pregnant?" she asked. "I thought that couldn't happen anymore."

Tillie half-smiled as she said, "You can't imagine how surprised we are."

A.J. laughed. "Wow, Mom, that's great. When will it come?"

"December 15," she answered. "And don't say *it*, try to say *the baby* instead."

A.J. nodded.

"Is that what's making you so sick?" Jake asked.

Tillie nodded. "But it should go away in a couple of months. I was pretty sick with the twins."

Ty chuckled and put his hand on Noah's shoulder. "That's great news, you guys. I'm really excited for you — for all of us."

Guiseppi pulled his handkerchief from his back pocket, dabbing at the fresh tears on his cheeks. He smiled at his family and said, "At the age of seventy-eight I have been privileged to see many miracles, but *this* has been the best by far."

Chapter 17

Noah dashed into the bedroom he shared with Tillie, only to find her on her knees in the bathroom…*again*. He sighed and handed her the package of crackers she'd asked for.

"Too late," she joked as she flushed, and then sat back against the wall. She smiled at her very worried-looking husband. Mornings had been the worst for the nausea and vomiting.

"Are you gonna be okay?" he asked, crouching down in front of her.

She fished out a cracker and took a nibble. "Someday — at about the twelve week mark — this part should go away."

Noah quickly tallied the time in his head. He suddenly frowned and exclaimed, "But that'll be *June!*"

Tillie giggled at the expression on his face, and then she set down the crackers quickly. "Oh no! Here I go again."

"Oh dear," Noah replied, helping her back into a kneeling position, and she began again.

Noah checked in with Ben in the mornings for any emergencies, and then he hurried back home to see how Tillie was feeling. He wanted to be with her, touch her, visit with her and plan with her. This was their only chance at having a child together, and he didn't want to miss a second of it.

During this exciting time, Ty was only two weeks away from graduation — and he still hadn't decided on a college. His graduation announcements, thankfully, were sent out before Tillie became so sick, but the Casellis would arrive very soon. Tillie began preparations in early spring, but there was still a significant amount of work to be done. She was determined not to ruin the event with her constant nausea as she remembered how important and exciting her own graduation had been. She gritted her teeth, and with the help of her parents and her husband, and their children, she was confident they could put it all together with the special perfection Ty deserved.

Every day she teetered around the house with her club soda and crackers, giving everyone loving instruction on how to *exactly* position and prepare things for the quickly approaching graduation festivities. And everyone *had* to pitch in. Tillie was thoroughly disabled by her morning sickness, though she pretended not to be. She swayed, stumbled and tripped, as she meandered around the place, hanging onto Noah's arm, checking on everyone's duties.

Laura and Heidi cleaned the windows, and Jake and A.J. mowed and trimmed the landscaping around the house. Mona helped Vera polish up the hardwood floors, while Diane made sure there was not a speck of dust to be found anywhere in the house.

Noah's job was to help Guiseppi with the elegant decorations, and those went up just a few days before the event. They coiled silk ivy from the winding staircase, while Tillie stood below and watched. If she looked up at them while they worked, she became dizzy, and had to rush off for the bathroom.

And though everyone felt sorry for Tillie, they couldn't help but laugh at her comical performances.

"Papa, that wreath doesn't look right above the kitchen entry…do you think we should put it someplace else?" she said, taking a sip of her club soda, then stifling a belch.

Guiseppi continued to adjust his work then looked down from the ladder with a smile. "I think it is just perfect," he said, lifting one eyebrow. "And you remind me of Dean Martin."

Noah laughed.

Tillie nodded and pretended to slur, "Well, then, I guess I'll go to the couch now."

Guiseppi and Noah guffawed.

Tillie chuckled at her own humor and took another sip from her drink. "Also, these must be wound through the ivy on the front porch railing," she insisted, holding up ribbons in Ty's school colors. "But it makes me too sick. Who will do this for me?"

Ty happened to walk into the room at that moment and he volunteered, "Me and Dad can do it just as soon as he's finished helping Guiseppi."

Tillie nodded. "I'll be waiting on the porch," she said as she turned to leave.

When Noah and Ty reported for duty, they found her fast asleep in one of the chairs on the porch, still holding the ribbons in her lap. Noah laughed and helped her to the couch.

*****

The food preparation was the *most* difficult. Tillie had asked Ty what kind of menu he wanted served for his graduation, and he chose Stromboli.

"I will make the sauce," Rosa volunteered. She looked hesitantly at Tillie and said, "But I will need your direction, Angel, because only you share Old Doria's recipe."

Tillie groaned, "Okay, Ma`ma."

"Do you think you can stand it, Angel?"

"Doubtfully," Tillie replied. "But this is important and I don't want to wreck it."

They set aside an entire day to prepare the food, and went to work. As cooking aromas engulfed the kitchen, Tillie gulped fresh air from an open window, praying she'd stay upright.

The bread baking went much better. And when they deep-fat fried the cylinder cookies for the cannoli, Tillie made it through the whole process without a single trip to the bathroom.

When Rosa dropped into bed beside Guiseppi that night, she sighed with relief, "I am so thankful to nearly be done with this graduation!"

"And I as well, Rosa," Guiseppi agreed. "I am exhausted just watching Angel's many trips to the bathroom! I scarcely have the energy for any more of her projects."

Rosa chuckled and said, "We will need a vacation on a desert island to recover."

Guiseppi laughed and held Rosa in his arms. "But does she not look beautiful?"

"More beautiful than ever," Rosa agreed. "In fact, for as sick as she is, I have never seen Angel look better."

*****

Ty decided to wear the black tuxedo he'd worn to the wedding the summer before. He ordered a beautiful corsage of soft, pink roses for his date, and Guiseppi loaned him the gold Cadillac. Ty was beside himself with excitement. Not only was it the night of the prom, but it was Ty's very first date. Though the young lady had visited their home for dinners a few times, they'd never been out *alone* together.

He put on the flashy suit, and stood in front of his bedroom mirror. He heard a soft knock at the door. "Come in," he said, adjusting the bow-tie to perfection.

"Hi, Ty," Tillie said as she and Noah came through the bedroom door, closing it behind them.

Ty smiled as he noticed Tillie's glass of club soda and nibbled-on cracker. "How are you feeling tonight?" he asked.

Tillie pretended to moan, "*Terrible*. But you look great. What a handsome man. That Marti Myers is one lucky gal."

Ty smiled. "Thanks. Are you sure I look okay?"

Tillie nodded with a smile and looked at Noah. "Doesn't he look wonderful in black?"

"You look great, son," Noah replied, admiring his tall, beautiful son, thanking God, again, for such a gift. *All of the years have passed so fast*, he thought. *Where did they all go?*

"I'm just about ready to go," Ty said, turning back to the mirror, making one last adjustment on his cummerbund. "Marti wants to know if you guys want to take some pictures, because if you do, we can come back here after I pick her up."

"That would be nice," Tillie said, taking a delicate sip of her club soda.

Noah cleared his throat. "Before you go, we wanted to talk to you for just a second."

"Okay." Ty turned from the mirror and looked at the two of them.

"Of course, by now you know the story of the Blackguard and the Knight pretty well," Noah began.

Ty chuckled. "Guiseppi has told it to us steadily for the last two years. I've got it memorized."

Noah and Tillic laughed.

"Well," Noah continued with a sigh and a smile, "We, Tillie and I, wanted to give you something special for your first date and everything." He handed Ty a black, velvet box. "Open that up and see if it fits."

Tillie had to squelch a giggle as she remembered receiving the same type of gift from her parents in 1975. Guiseppi and Rosa were very dramatic about the whole thing, but Noah just handed the kid the gift, without explanation.

Ty opened the box, puzzlement filling his expression.

Tillie smiled and put her hand on his shoulder. "It's a purity ring," she explained. "Because you may be tempted." She took the thin, gold band from the box, and held it before him. "And your dad and I would really like you to wear it."

"Why?" Ty swallowed hard, looking embarrassed.

Tillie took a soft breath and smiled at her stepson as she replied, "Sometimes when a young lady is as lovely and sweet as Miss Marti, a young knight can find it very difficult to keep his passions in check."

"I promise not be a blackguard with her," Ty stammered.

"Even knights can make a mistake," Noah said, reaching for Ty's left hand. "But if he has another, older and more experienced knight to help him through it, he's not as apt to fall off the wagon, so to speak."

"Please wear it," Tillie said with the sweet smile Ty had grown to love. "You don't have to tell anyone what it's for —"

"But what *is* it for?" Ty whispered.

"It's our secret pact," Tillie answered. "If you are tempted, and you don't know what to do, call your dad, or me, and we'll help you through it."

"And I won't be in trouble for that?" he asked.

Noah and Tillie laughed, shaking their heads.

"Being tempted isn't what causes the trouble," Noah said. "It's *giving in to the temptation* that turns your life upside down."

Ty hesitantly nodded, and Tillie slipped the band onto the ring finger of his left hand.

"Don't kiss her on the first date," Noah said. "Well, you know the rules. I've told them to you a million times."

"And so has Guiseppi," Ty added, blushing. He took a deep breath and looked from his dad, to Tillie, and then back to his dad. "I promise not be a blackguard, Dad."

Noah nodded with a smile, and put his arms around his son. "I love you, Ty," he breathed. "And I know you're gonna really impress this gal and her family." He let go of Ty and looked into his eyes. "I'm so proud you're mine."

Tillie stood on her toes, kissing Ty's cheek. "I know everything's gonna be okay because you're such a cool kid."

"Thanks." Ty smiled, looking at his watch. "I gotta go, but I'll hurry back for some pictures."

Tillie and Noah nodded as they watched him dash out the bedroom door, listening to his shoes click along the hard wood hallway and down the steps.

Noah sighed and put his arm around Tillie as he asked, "How did your parents handle your date to the prom?"

Tillie laughed heartily and answered, "Oh, goodness! I went with the blackguardly captain of the football team, and Papa sent Marquette to spy on me." She laughed again. "I didn't even know Marq was there, until the very end when the guy got drunk and attacked me."

"He *attacked* you?"

"Well, he tried, but I put up a pretty good fight, and when I was through with him, Marquette stepped out from behind a tree, or somewhere, and wrenched the guy's arm."

Noah laughed. "I hope nobody's spying on Ty tonight."

Tillie looked up at her husband and smiled into his eyes. "There won't be. He's a great kid, and everybody knows it."

*****

The Casellis arrived early Saturday morning for the first in what Jake and A.J. touted to be the *triple line up* of receptions. Along with Ty, Tillie's nephew, Angelo, and her niece, Gabriella, were graduating that spring, and plans were complicated. They had obligations all over the country, and Tillie wondered how they'd make it to all of the receptions.

Before the pregnancy was realized, Tillie and her sisters-in-law set the craziest plans into motion. Ty's graduation was scheduled for the second Saturday in May. All of the Casellis planned to arrive in Rapid City that morning. They were scheduled to fly to Cambridge, Massachusetts, on Monday, in order to prepare for Angelo's graduation. Shortly after Angelo's reception, the family would fly aboard Petrice's jet to Cape Vincent, where Gabriella's graduation was scheduled for the very next day.

Poor Tillie reeled around at Ty's commencement and at the reception, trying desperately to control her nausea. Unfortunately, there was no way to control the surprise attacks, and there were several times when somebody asked for her, noticing that she was missing again. Noah found his wife in the bathroom, tried to comfort her, and eventually wound up laughing at yet more of her awful jokes.

"Right around Ty's birthday," she encouraged Noah with a smile as he walked her back to the reception after another bout in the bathroom, "I'll be about at the twelve week mark, and this part will go away."

"It just up and goes away?" Noah looked skeptical.

Tillie nodded. "And I'll be *totally* back to normal."

*****

Ty's graduation and reception was bearable because Tillie was in the comfort of her own home. However, the flights to the East Coast proved to be terrible for Tillie. She managed to not *toss her cookies* on the flight to Boston, but when they all got into the rented van and began the drive to Cambridge, Noah had to pull over several times. Once they arrived at the hotel, Jake and A.J. purchased club soda and crackers from the convenience store across the street, and brought the supplies back to Tillie.

Angelo had *two* graduation commencements: one at Harvard, which was extremely formal and long and drawn-out. The other was on Hanscom Air Force Base, where Congressman Jack Goldstein gave the commencement address. Tillie wanted to hear him speak, determined to *tough it out*.

Noah and their children, along with the rest of her family, were amazed Tillie made it through Congressman Goldstein's lengthy speech. However, when the Air Force began their showy flyover above them, she headed for the bathroom.

"You shouldn't have looked up," Noah said, hurrying along behind her.

"I know," she moaned. "Don't remind me."

"Kate has lots of club soda at the reception."

Tillie rolled her eyes. "Oh, that's great. I'm sure that'll straighten me right out."

She made it all the way from the air base to Harvard Square Hotel in Cambridge where Kate and Vincenzo had planned a reception. Many of Angelo's friends were in the Air Force, so there were a significant number of uniformed soldiers in attendance. Also at the gala was Congressman Goldstein.

Gabriella was beside herself with excitement. Her father and his brothers kept a watchful eye on the young congressman, *especially* when he brought her a very suspicious-looking glass of punch during the reception.

Marquette frowned as he and his brothers watched the exchange between Petrice's very young daughter and the Iowa Congressman. "How old is that lecher anyway?" he asked.

Petrice gritted his teeth and answered, "Nearly twenty-nine — a full ten years her senior. And to think I actually had a fundraiser for him. What was I thinking?"

Vincenzo huffed with a scowl, "Apparently you were not."

"Has he asked to spend any time with her?" Marquette questioned.

"None," Petrice answered, "and he will get absolutely nothing. He is far too old for a child as young as Gabby."

On toward evening, Noah noticed his wife was missing again, and he began looking around for her, sending Laura to check the bathrooms, and Jake and A.J. to search the courtyard outside. Perhaps she'd stepped out for some fresh air.

"She's not in there," Laura reported when she returned from the bathrooms.

Noah thoughtfully scratched his chin. She would have never gone back to their room without telling him first. "Well, where could she be?" he wondered aloud.

Jake chuckled, "Hey, Dad, we found her." He laughed, pointing to the far corner of the reception room. Seated beside an artificial tree was Noah's pretty wife. She was leaning against the trunk and had fallen fast asleep, club soda still in hand.

Noah's expression was one of pity. "Oh, she must be so uncomfortable there." He hurried to where she sat, kneeling down in front of her, trying to rouse her without startling her. "Angel," he whispered, taking one of her hands into his own, giving it a soft kiss. "Wake up."

Tillie didn't move from her leaning position against the tree, but she opened her eyes and looked sleepily at Noah. "Oh, brother, did I fall asleep?" she asked.

Noah nodded with a smile. "You're gonna get a stiff neck sleeping there. Why don't you let me help you get up to our room."

Tillie lifted her head and frowned. "I'm wrecking the whole reception."

Noah shook his head and replied with an encouraging smile, "It's been a *great* reception. Nobody even noticed." He helped her to her feet.

Tillie leaned heavily against her husband and began to cry. "I wrecked the whole trip."

"No," Noah chuckled, shaking his head as he put his arm lovingly around her. "It's been a *great* trip."

"I haven't been able to visit anybody or do anything," Tillie whined. "And the kids have been totally ignored. I haven't even seen my nephew or congratulated him. I'm just a big, old fart."

Noah laughed and kissed the top of her head, walking her out of the reception room. "Oh, Angel, it's the baby. It's not *you*."

Tillie sighed with a sniff and nodded her head.

Noah placed his hand over her flat stomach, kissing her cheek as they walked along. "And don't feel bad about the kids, they've been having a great time. Why I think Laura even ran off with a fighter pilot." He laughed at himself, and so did Tillie.

She managed a smile through her tears, putting her hand over Noah's with a sigh. "I can't believe that such a little thing can cause such an upset. Pardon the pun."

"Me neither, and I wish you didn't have to be so sick."

"I wish you could be sick instead," she said with a grin.

Noah smiled and nodded his head, and if he could have traded places with her, he would have.

*****

They flew out of Boston the next day, aboard Petrice's Learjet, and Tillie had to admit she was far more comfortable than she had been on the commercial jets.

Gabriella had been homeschooled her entire life, so hers was a very small graduation. Thirty teenagers had a short ceremony at the church on Kanady Street, and everyone went off to their own receptions.

Elaine had decorated and prepared their lakefront home before going to Cambridge for Angelo's graduation, and everything was ready when they arrived. She prepared traditional Italian food for the Casellis, and *almost* all of them partook in generous portions. Tillie poured her usual club soda and relaxed in the soft furniture of her brother's living room. This was much more comfortable than the last reception, and she drifted off to the hum of the familiar voices.

Ty joined Petrice's son, Michael, and Vincenzo's son, Angelo on the deck. Over the past few years the three discovered their common interest in politics, and a fast friendship ensued.

"So have you made that decision about school yet?" Angelo questioned

Ty shook his head and sighed heavily, replying, "I don't know what's wrong with me, guys. The only thing I know for sure is that I want to play ball for a little while, and learn architecture." He looked at Michael and asked, "How did you decide?"

"Well, I had already been in the Guard for a couple of years," Michael replied. "I've known that I wanted to be in the Pentagon since I was a little kid, so I've kept that as my focus. I always wanted to be a lawyer, like Papa, and I can combine the military with my profession by staying in D.C. and applying for a position with JAG. I wanted to stay in D.C. — I've lived half of my life there you know — so I decided to pick George Washington."

Ty nodded, turning to Angelo as he asked, "How 'bout you?"

"Just wanted to be a pilot," Angelo answered with a grin. "So I made sure I got into ROTC so that I could be an officer." He added with a wink, "And I just got the sweetest assignment in London — spokesman for the American ambassador."

Ty rolled his eyes. " You guys make it sound so easy. Lynchburg wants me on a scholarship, but I don't know how I'd get along there without knowing anybody."

"I bet your dad really hates to see you go," Angelo said, remembering the tears of his own father when it came time for him to go to Harvard.

Michael rubbed his curly head of hair. Suddenly his blue eyes sparkled with an idea. "You know, Ty, George Washington has a phenomenal baseball team. And I'd be there, and so will Gabby. We can hang out."

Ty raised an interested eyebrow. "What about an architecture program?"

Michael shrugged. "I don't know, but Gabby has some catalogues. She could loan 'em to ya. Noah and Auntie could take you over there for a look around."

Ty smiled and shook his head. "I don't know how I can ask her to get on one more plane. She's so sick."

"Well, maybe Papa could fly over you and your dad for just a quick look," Michael suggested. "You know, your dad might be more comfortable with you going to school in D.C., with us and Uncle Marq there. You'd have family around."

"It's really tough going off by yourself," Angelo added. "I hate having to leave Alyssa at Harvard alone for the next two years."

Ty smiled and nodded his head, feeling the strangest, but most comforting warmth in his heart. *You'd have family around....* They considered him *family*.

Chapter 18
June, 1995

Tillie awakened in the darkness of their room. In the dim, early morning light she saw Noah sleeping beside her…*usually he's outa here before I get up*, she thought. Since April, the pregnancy had kept Tillie in bed until at least seven o'clock, or later, and Noah was usually up long before then.

She automatically reached for the soda crackers she kept on her nightstand, suddenly leaving them where they lay — something was different this morning. She lay still in the darkness, listening to Noah breathe…*do I smell cinnamon? And espresso?*

She slipped from beneath the covers, being careful not to disturb Noah, and tiptoed out of their room. The aroma of cinnamon was stronger in the hallway, and it made her smile. She hurried down the stairs and into the kitchen, where she found Rosa just pulling a sheet of fresh rolls from the oven.

"Ma`ma!" she exclaimed. "I could smell these baking clear up in my room!"

Rosa looked surprised. "I am so sorry, Angel," she quickly apologized. "I did not think you would be up so early. Is it making you sick?"

Tillie inhaled deeply, shaking her head. "It's gone, Ma`ma!" she gasped in a whisper. "It's *finally* gone!"

Rosa laughed. "Oh, thank You, Jesus!" she whispered. She looked at Tillie. "Would you like to celebrate with a roll?"

"Is there espresso?" Tillie asked.

"Decaf for Papa, *and* steamed milk," Rosa added.

"I'll have decaf with Papa," Tillie said decidedly. "And a big roll on the side."

It was only a few days before Ty's eighteenth birthday and, right on schedule with her prediction, the morning sickness left Tillie and her regular energy returned. She had just turned thirty-eight and was ecstatic to bounce back to her regular self. She was up before Noah on most mornings, again, greeting everyone in the kitchen when they came down.

Noah helped her paint the nursery a soft yellow, because they didn't know if it would be a boy or a girl. Tillie found wallpaper border at the Sherwin-Williams store, called "Noah's Ark." It was a cute cartoon representation of the Biblical Noah as he loaded animals onto his ark before the forty days of rain. Tillie thought it was perfect, and when she showed it to Noah, he laughed.

They got everything they needed for the nursery at Sears: a crib, a changing table, a dresser and a rocking chair. As a last minute idea, they put a small refrigerator in the corner so that bottles could be kept ready for middle of the night feedings. They bought baby blankets, sheets for the new crib, tiny t-shirts and sleepers.

Mona stocked the nursery with assorted skirts, dresses, shoes and coats, "because it might be a girl," she reminded. Mrs. Romanov knitted everything under the sun, including an Easter bonnet.

Noah and Ty went to D.C. twice. They met with counselors at George Washington University and toured the campus. GW offered an excellent architectural engineering program, and, after Ty's fabulous tryout, the coach was anxious to have him play ball on their team. After discussing it with Petrice and Michael and Gabriella, and praying with Tillie and the rest of the family, Ty decided this was the best college choice. Petrice and Noah secured a nice apartment for the three cousins to share not far from the university.

It was hard for Noah to think about Ty leaving home. He'd been Noah's sole responsibility for such a long time. He still remembered the bawling red-headed newborn, and the nickname, 'Tiger.' *How in the world could that little baby have grown up so quickly — a man, with dreams and ideas of his own?*

Tillie tried to comfort her husband, but she wanted to cry every time she looked at Ty.

"Why does he have to leave already?" she whispered to her father when they were alone one morning. "We are just beginning as a family."

"It is God's plan," Guiseppi reminded. "He designed us to have our children for only a short time. Ty is ready to find his own way in the world. You must let him go with grace and dignity."

Jake was tough about the whole thing, but deep down inside, he already missed his brother like crazy. Having A.J. and Laura around would help, but Ty had always been with Jake.

Ty knew his family was mourning his departure, yet he was excited to go. He confided in Guiseppi one day, "I don't think it will be that bad. I'll be home for holidays and major breaks. Why are they making such a big deal about this?"

Guiseppi took Ty's hand into his own and said, "Because you are their sweetest treasure."

"But they have lots of kids now," Ty argued politely.

Guiseppi nodded. "That is true, but they have only one Ty."

Ty frowned thoughtfully. "Do you think I should go to school in Spearfish, so that I'll be closer?"

Guiseppi shook his head. "I think you should go to D.C., for a wonderful adventure has yet to begin for you."

*****

They had baseball games nearly every night of the week between The Builders and Post 22. Joshua and Mona came to all of the games, watching Guiseppi and Noah coach The Builders through an all-win season. Noah left Guiseppi "in charge" in the dugout frequently, running over to the stands to "check on the girls" and to give Tillie a soft kiss on the lips. He gently patted her stomach, and she gave him a mischievous wink. He blushed and hurried back to the team. It was the best summer of Noah's life, and that was obvious to everyone.

As Guiseppi and Rosa watched their daughter and her new husband, their hearts filled with contentment. Noah was so mindful of the miracle happening within his wife, it touched them to their very souls.

By mid-July, nearing Noah and Tillie's first anniversary, a tiny bulge began just below Tillie's belly button. She could wear only soft, summer dresses as she was unable to button any of her jeans or shorts. She started to feel the first flutters of life within her, and she could hardly believe it.

In the evenings, when they were alone in their bed, Noah would place his hand over Tillie's warm abdomen, waiting patiently for even the smallest of movements.

"The baby is too small," Tillie whispered with a smile. "You won't be able to feel anything for a few months yet."

"I know I feel *something*."

Tillie giggled. "It's your imagination."

"No, it's the baby," Noah insisted.

Jake and A.J. won their All-Stars tournament for the third season in a row, and Post 22 was unbeatable. It was Ty's last year to pitch for the home team, and the fans in the bleachers gave him a standing ovation when he took the pitcher's mound for the last time that season. Ty smiled and tipped his hat, giving the applauding crowd a generous bow. He behaved so much like Guiseppi it made his family laugh.

Tillie's family came to Rapid City for Labor Day. After a short celebration, Ty planned to leave with Petrice and his family to begin school in Washington. Tillie and Rosa prepared Ty's favorites: Stromboli and cannoli for the occasion.

Tillie and Noah's baby was showing quite markedly. Tillie's brothers and their wives were taken aback when she and Noah met them at the airport. The newlyweds looked at least twenty years younger than they had when they last saw them in New York. Noah's countenance was filled with delight, and Tillie's black eyes sparkled in a way they hadn't seen since she was a child.

Changes happened in their children as well. An obvious and intense bond had developed between the four of them. They smiled and laughed as they chided one another and their uncles, aunts and cousins. They appeared to be even *more* content than Tillie and Noah, if that were possible.

Everyone had to have a delicate touch of the new baby beneath Tillie's rounded out dress, and she giggled and laughed when her family took turns giving it soft caresses. It had been so long since there was a new baby born in the Caselli family, no one could resist spending just a little extra time with Tillie.

"I can't believe how young they look," Elaine whispered to her husband as she watched Kate and Vincenzo hover beside Tillie and Noah.

Petrice smiled. "I do not believe I have ever seen my sister so happy. This is what she has wanted for all of her life. God is truly blessing her with this little one."

"We can't come to Sioux Falls for Thanksgiving," Tillie told her parents when they had a moment alone. "Dr. Barnes says that, considering my age and the complications with the twins' birth, he doesn't think I should travel such a lengthy distance at this stage."

Guiseppi nodded in understanding. "I think we will remain in Sioux Falls for Thanksgiving, my Angel. Sam is having such a terrible time and I have been thinking we might be able to coax him into spending some time with us over the holidays."

"It's okay, Papa," Tillie replied with a smile. "We'll be okay without you for one holiday."

"But we'll be out for Christmas," Rosa assured. "And maybe there will be a baby by then!"

"I hope so!" Tillie agreed. "I hope the little bugger doesn't make me wait too long!"

Tillie and Noah, along with Joshua and Mona, and Jake, A.J. and Laura, went to the airport terminal with Ty and the Casellis. They hugged Ty, kissing him, over and over again, until Petrice thought he might miss his takeoff time. They behaved far worse than a bunch of Italians, and it was all Petrice could do to get them to let go of the child.

"I'll be home for Thanksgiving," Ty promised, attempting to back away. "And I'll call as soon as I get there."

Noah broke watching his son backing away, openly weeping.

Ty dashed back to his father, wrapping him in his long arms, smiling into his eyes. "It's gonna be okay, Dad," he whispered. "*Everybody* does this."

Noah tried to swallow away some of his tears, but he couldn't. "I know," he quietly sobbed.

Ty laughed through his tears. "Nobody has a dad like you," he whispered. "And I'm so thankful for you."

"Thanks, Ty," Noah managed to croak.

"When I'm done with this," Ty continued, "I'll come back and we'll work together for the rest of our lives."

Noah nodded, holding onto his son for dear life. "I'm proud of you, Ty," he whispered, finally letting go, allowing him to board with the Casellis.

Ty turned at the gate and gave them one last wave. He and the rest of the Casellis boarded the plane, and Noah and his family watched them leave the runway. Ty would be desperately missed by all of them, but they were happy for him, too. His life and his dreams were just beginning, and there was a sweet thrill about waiting to see what happened next.

*****

Jake, A.J. and Laura began their freshman year of senior high school at Rapid City Steven's. Noah and Tillie dropped them off, and then went over to Maggie May's for a good cry over a cup of coffee. Guiseppi and Rosa were gone for the winter now, and their big house was quiet.

Since Maggie came to know the Lord in the summer of 1994, she stopped serving liquor in her bar. It was only a small restaurant now, but continued to do a booming business being situated so close to the interstate.

She frowned at Tillie and Noah when they came into the old bar, lamenting that their children had gone to school.

"Oh, pull yourselves together. Things could be one heck of lot worse for the two of you," she scolded.

"That's right," Estelle sided with her sister.

"Get out to the mall and buy something for the baby," Maggie went on with a frown. "Go and enjoy yourselves for Pete's sake. Don't be sitting around in this old place, crying about all of the fun you had with your kids." She rolled her eyes and shook her head. "You're pathetic." She snorted one last time, hurrying off to wait on another customer.

Noah and Tillie looked at each other, silently considering their scolding.

Noah was the first to smile. "Well, what do you say we run over to the mall and look at a stroller or something? We don't have one yet."

Tillie smiled with embarrassment. "Okay." She gave Maggie a sideling glance and added, "And let's try to pull ourselves together — apparently we're *pathetic*."

Noah raised one eyebrow and said, "I say we pull ourselves together with a 'Blizzard' over at the Dairy Queen."

"I say I'm in," Tillie replied with a wink.

*****

The days of September stayed warm in the Black Hills that year. Noah went to the office in the early mornings, checked on a building site or two, and was home before noon to spend the rest of the day with Angel. Her little belly grew significantly, and Dr. Barnes said that her measurements were right on schedule with the due date he'd given her.

Tillie was in her studio painting from an old photograph when she heard Noah's boots on the front porch. The front door opened and closed.

"Angel, where are you?" she heard him call.

"In the studio," she answered, noticing he was home earlier than usual today. She heard his boots on the wooden floor leading to the kitchen, and soon he rounded the corner into the studio.

Noah paused to smile. There she was, in her bare feet, dressed in a pair of overalls she'd rolled up to her knees, and a pink t-shirt. He smiled and kissed her, reaching for her free hand. "Come on, I gotta show you something," he said.

Tillie set down her brush and followed him out of the studio. As they went down the hall, a wooden cradle came into view, and Tillie smiled. It was on a tall pedestal, about four feet in height, and securely fastened into place. It was finished in the same stain as their baby's other furniture. It would be perfect to put beside their bed for those first few weeks of the baby's life.

"Where did you find this?" she asked as she put her hand upon the curve of the wood. At her touch, the cradle gently rocked. Tillie gasped with delight, "Noah this is wonderful! I can just reach over and rock the baby!"

"Do you like it?" Noah asked, watching her touch the wooden cradle.

"I *love* it."

"I made it," Noah said with a satisfied expression.

"You made it?" Tillie gasped quietly. "Noah, this is *amazing*."

"Thanks," he said, delighted by her reply, thinking if he were a younger man he'd be doing handsprings. "I've been working on it a little at a time, when I go in in the mornings. I would have given it to you over the weekend, but the stain hadn't dried yet."

She smiled into his eyes, and put her arms around his neck. "Noah, you're awesome and I love you."

Noah put his hands around his pretty, pregnant wife, sighing with contentment. "I love you, too." He laughed and shook his head.

"What?" she asked.

"Sometimes I still can't believe it. My life has gotten so great I just can't believe it. I mean, here you are." He smiled down at her bare feet and saw the pink toenail polish and he laughed again. "Barefoot and pregnant, in the house I built for you. You can never imagine how happy I am. I just feel like laughing all of the time."

Tillie smiled into his eyes, touching his face with her hand. "If ever a life was absolutely perfect, this one is — this one I share with you."

Her stomach was up against him, and he felt the faintest flutter. Noah gasped, placing his hand over her womb and waiting. In a matter of seconds his baby moved beneath his touch and he smiled. Indeed, this was a *perfect* life.

Chapter 19
December, 1995

Tillie, Mona and Laura baked gingerbread men, almond-flavored Christmas cookies, loaves of spiced breads and rolls, and stirred up batches of fudge and divinity to celebrate the upcoming Christmas holiday. Angel's Place was decked out in the most glorious of decorations as they anxiously awaited the arrival of the Casellis and Ty — *and* Noah and Tillie's baby. Everyone, including Dr. Barnes, thought the baby would come early in December, but they were all wrong.

Noah's forty-fourth birthday was upon them, and Mona invited everyone over for dinner.

"So when are them kids out for Christmas break?" Mona asked as she carefully counted forty-four candles on the cake.

"Tomorrow's their last day," Tillie answered with a tired smile.

Mona frowned at Tillie and said, "You look a little done in, Angel. You okay?"

Tillie shrugged. "I've had some heartburn today…and a pain in my side, but nothing I would classify as a contraction. I'm nearly a week past my due date, and that's really an issue with Dr. Barnes."

Mona nodded in understanding. Because of the complications with Tillie's first pregnancy, Dr. Barnes was very hesitant to allow her to deliver naturally. The doctor was adamant that she would submit to a caesarean birth if anything seemed unusual in the slightest during the pregnancy — including going past the due date.

"He'll take the baby c-section day after tomorrow," Tillie continued, "unless the little bugger comes tonight or sometime before midnight tomorrow." She sighed heavily, smiling faintly at Mona. "I'd do anything to get out of having another c-section."

"I don't blame you," Mona said. "My little sister, Charlene, had a c-section. Oh!" Mona rolled her eyes and shook her head. "She *hated* it! Said it was the *worst* thing in the world to have happen to a woman." She gave Tillie's shoulder a pat and said, "Now, just stay put while I go and get everyone. I'll be right back and we'll have some decaf with this cake."

Tillie nodded and watched Mona go into the living room.

Noah was on the couch, sipping a bottle of root beer, watching the children attempting to beat Joshua in a game of Yatzee.

"It's time for your cake," Mona announced from the doorway.

Joshua looked up with a grin. "Come on, kids…let's make sure ole Mona got plenty of candles on that thing."

The children laughed, following Joshua out of the living room.

Noah got up and smiled at Mona as he asked, "I hope you left a few off this year."

Mona shook her head and put her arm around Noah's waist. "I never lie, Noah. There are exactly forty-four candles on that cake."

Noah pretended to moan as he and Mona went into the kitchen.

Joshua was counting the candles on the cake, being closely supervised by the children, and Tillie was still sitting quiet.

Noah saw the strange look on her face and he sat down beside her. "Everything okay, Angel?"

Tillie shrugged, reaching for Noah's hand, placing it over her hard stomach. "I'm hopeful…do *you* think that's what *I* think it is?" she asked.

Noah swallowed hard as he felt Tillie's stomach contract beneath his hand. "Could be," he answered in a cautious tone.

Tillie frowned. "Well *you're* the expert," she quietly snapped. "*I've* never had a baby the regular way. *I* don't know how this goes."

Everyone had heard Tillie snap, and it was such an odd tone for her that they all instantly quieted.

"Angel?" Mona whispered, going to Tillie's side. "Are you alright?"

Tillie shook her head and answered, "That pain is back again…and I'm sick to my stomach."

"What pain?" Noah questioned.

"She's had a pain in her side today," Mona answered.

"All day?" Noah asked.

Tillie nodded, and Noah felt her stomach contract again.

He raised his eyebrows in surprise, looking at her stomach. "That feels like the real thing to me," he said. "And it was only a few minutes after the last one." He took a deep breath and looked into his wife's frowning expression. "All day?"

"All day," she confirmed.

From what Noah recalled with Carrie's deliveries, the babies came pretty quick after the contractions got to be a few minutes apart. He remembered that Carrie's water broke just minutes before her babies were born.

Noah got to his feet, helping Tillie to hers. "I think we'd better go," he said.

"Go where?" Jake asked with a frown.

Laura's black eyes were wide open with surprise. "The hospital?" she whispered.

Noah and Tillie nodded, and Joshua and Mona gasped.

"Well, we should all go together," Joshua suggested.

A.J. nodded. "We can all fit in the Suburban."

"I don't know how much time we have," Tillie said. "And I'm worried about that. I think we should hurry."

Noah moaned, shaking his head as he took his wife by the hand and hurried for the door.

Joshua unloaded the coats from the closet, handing Tillie hers first.

Noah took it from her and offered, "Let me help you with that."

Tillie turned around and started to put her arms into the coat when a splash sounded.

Everyone looked at Tillie.

Tillie swallowed hard. Afraid to look down, she asked, "What was that?"

Everyone stared at the puddle at her feet, but said nothing.

"Noah," she said in a tone he didn't recognize.

He looked at his wife, noticing that she'd gotten very pale.

"Noah," she said again. "Don't lock up on me now. I'm really sick to my stomach. You gotta get me outa here *now*."

"Start the truck, Ty," Noah ordered, scooping Tillie into his arms. "Mona get a blanket."

Ty ran outside, and Mona dashed into the living room for an afghan.

"Should we call an ambulance?" Joshua asked.

"No," Tillie answered. "This will be faster."

Mona appeared with the afghan and covered Tillie's wet legs.

Ty burst through the door and announced, "The truck's started."

"Let's go," Noah said, heading for the door.

In just a matter of minutes, Ty was driving them all down Jackson Boulevard and they were listening to Christmas music on the radio. Tillie was very quiet and that made Noah anxious. He wondered how close the baby was to being born. Perhaps she'd been in labor all day and hadn't realized it.

"You doin' okay, Angel?" he whispered.

"I think so," she answered. "It really hurts."

Noah held her close and prayed.

Jackson Boulevard curved into Mountain View Road, and soon they turned on St. Joseph Street. They were held up at a stop light at the corner of St. Joseph and Mt. Rushmore Road, but only for a few moments, and then Ty turned south on Mt. Rushmore Road. He turned onto Fairmont Boulevard, and the hospital came into view.

"You and Angel go ahead through the emergency entrance," Ty said. "We'll park the truck."

"Great idea," Noah agreed as they pulled into the emergency entrance of the hospital. Joshua jumped out to help Noah and Tillie out of the truck.

"I think I can walk," Tillie said as they exited the vehicle. Noah gently set her on the ground. "It really hurts now," she whispered, taking a tight hold of his hand.

"Oh," Noah breathed as he placed his hand on the small of her back and coaxed her toward the glass doors.

"It's really hard to walk," she whispered.

Noah moaned under his breath, approaching the receptionist. "We might need a wheelchair," were the first words out of his mouth, and the receptionist smiled and nodded. She'd seen Tillie waddling in and had already sent someone for the wheelchair. "And her water broke about ten minutes ago," he added.

"Are you pre-registered?" the receptionist asked as she typed on her keyboard.

Noah helped Tillie into the wheelchair that had arrived, frowning as he answered, "Does it matter?"

"Matilde Hansen," Tillie answered.

Seemingly oblivious to Noah's huff, the receptionist produced a white, plastic bracelet, and put it on Tillie's arm. The nurse from the obstetrics floor joined them. She started to wheel Tillie away, when the rest of their family burst through the emergency room doors, and began to follow.

"Wait for us!" Jake called as he led the charge.

The nurse who was pushing Tillie asked, "Did the whole family come along?"

"Well, we all fit into the truck," Tillie answered offhandedly.

"That's nice," the nurse replied. "We've got a waiting room near your birthing room. They can all wait in there."

By the time they reached the second floor of the hospital, Tillie was very sick to her stomach. She wondered why it was getting worse, but she didn't say anything. Everyone kissed her before the nurses took her and Noah into the birthing room.

"Dr. Barnes is already at the hospital," the nurse said, she and Noah helping Tillie out of the chair.

The moment Tillie stood up, it became black and she dropped for the floor. Thankfully Noah caught her before she hit the hard tile.

"Angel!" he gasped. "Are you okay?"

No answer came from Tillie. She was out cold.

Before he could say another word, a flurry of nurses were around them and they quickly moved Tillie into the bed.

"It's her blood pressure," a nurse said, staying calm as she put a cuff around Tillie's bicep. She put her stethoscope on Tillie's chest and listened. "Heart beat is still good and strong, but we'd better get some ephedrine handy."

Another nurse thrust a pair of scrubs into Noah's hands and said, "You have to put these on."

Noah hustled into the soft, blue scrubs, while the nurses put oxygen tubes beneath Tillie's nose, and checked the progression of her dilation. Flashes from her accident began parading through his head. *Lord, don't take her now*, he silently prayed, *we have so many plans....*

Noah finally found his voice and whispered, "Is she okay?"

Tillie's eyes fluttered and she looked around the room, finding her husband's face. "Wow," she whispered, "I had this really weird dream —" Her voice was cut short as she winced with pain. "Oh, no!" she cried, "this is *for real!*"

"I'm here, Angel," Noah said, taking one of her hands into his own. "I think you passed out or something."

Dr. Barnes dashed into the room, heading for the sink. Hello you two. Are you gonna have a baby tonight?" he asked.

"Pretty quick now," the nurse announced. "Her water has broken and she's fully dilated...blood pressure ninety-five over sixty.

She did lose consciousness and we started her on oxygen. We have ephedrine ready."

Dr. Barnes dried his hands and went to Tillie. He leaned over the bed and looked into her face. "How are you feeling, Tillie?"

"Like I might have to push, but I'm not sure."

Dr. Barnes put his hand upon her stomach, just as a contraction began. Tillie suddenly winced with pain, tightly gripping Noah's hand. She was suddenly terrified. She'd slept through her last delivery. This sort of birth was unknown. *How bad is this going to get?* She looked up into Noah's eyes. "Don't leave."

Noah kissed her cheek and said, "I'm not going anywhere."

"I'm scared," she whispered, trying not to cry.

Noah put his face against her cheek and whispered into her ear, "It's okay. The first part is always a little scary, but it'll get better in a minute. It's gonna go *really fast* now, Angel." And he was certain of his words because he'd done this twice before. With his strong, but tender hand, he brushed some of her soft curls away from her face, noticing that she'd started to perspire. "I love you, Angel."

"I love you, Noah," she whispered as the tears dropped from the corners of her eyes.

He gave her a gentle smile and touched her tears with one of his callused fingers. "It's gonna be okay. I'll be right here with you, Angel."

"That's great," she replied, taking a deep breath. "But you're not partaking — just like with the morning sickness —" Another contraction took her breath. She gasped and frowned at Noah. "I think I'm gonna be sick."

A nurse hurried to Tillie's side with a small bedpan, just in time for Tillie to throw up.

"Blood pressure is dropping again," the nurse announced.

"Then let's hustle," Dr. Barnes barked.

"It seems like it's taking longer than it should," Jake complained as he flicked through the channels on the television in the waiting room.

"Sometimes these things take a while," Joshua answered, pacing back and forth.

Mona was sitting with Laura, paging through a magazine. She looked up at her husband and smiled. "Do you want to pray some more, Josh?"

Joshua sighed heavily and nodded. The family gathered together and they began to pray.

*****

Tillie's eyes flickered open and she found Noah looking intently into her expression. She took a gulp of air, realizing that there was a mask over her face. Instinctively she reached for it, but Noah's hand held it steady.

"Just take a few more breaths, Angel," he said with a serious expression. "You passed out again. But that last push was a doozy. You gotta be just about done."

They heard Dr. Barnes laugh out loud, and then he said, "Is Mama still with us?"

"She's awake now, doctor," the nurse answered.

"You got a baby girl!" Dr. Barnes exclaimed.

Tillie gasped with surprise. She thought for sure the baby was another son for Noah.

"A girl," Noah whispered, kissing Tillie's cheek, looking into her eyes. "We got a baby girl."

"What's her name?" Dr. Barnes asked. "Do you know yet?"

Tears of joy fell from Noah's eyes as he whispered, "Her name is Annie Laurie."

The baby suddenly cried, and Noah laughed through his tears. "Did you hear that, Angel?"

Tillie nodded with a smile.

A nurse tucked the bundled and crying baby into the crook of Tillie's arm and removed Tillie's face mask. She adjusted a tube beneath Tillie's nose and said, "If you stay up and runnin' we won't have to use the mask."

Annie's parents looked down into her little, red face. The baby cried for all she was worth, and Tillie and Noah chuckled.

Noah reached for a touch of the baby's black ringlets. "Look at that curly hair. And she's got a ton of it."

Tillie nodded and began to cry as she looked at the precious life in her arms. "I can't believe it, Noah. Look at how perfect she is." She reached for a touch of the baby's face, softly stroking her with her index finger. She looked at Noah, whose tears hadn't stopped, and smiled into his eyes. "God gave *us* a baby…He must really love us."

*****

A very exuberant Noah joined the rest of their family in the waiting room, and they all got to their feet. He was still in his scrubs, and from the expression on his face, they could tell that everything had gone as perfectly as only the Lord could make it.

"Her name is Annie Laurie," Noah announced, and everyone gasped and clapped, throwing their arms around him, kissing him.

Two old, black women trudged up the hall, and Noah looked at them with surprise.

"Josh called us," Maggie grumbled with a frown, coming to a stop before Noah. "What did you get?"

Noah beamed. "Her name is Annie Laurie."

Maggie rolled her eyes and shook her head, but Estelle giggled.

"They're taking her to the nursery to weigh her and measure her and do the new baby check," Noah went on with a smile. "They're just about finished up with Angel, and she'll be getting to her room, and then we'll be able to see her."

"How did everything go?" Mona asked with a smile.

"Kinda scary," Noah admitted. "Angel had trouble with her blood pressure, and she had to have a couple of shots of ephedrine, but she was a real trooper. It all happened so fast."

"We should probably call her family," Joshua said, looking at A.J., Jake and Laura. "You guys should call the family. You've got a new sister to talk about."

They all looked quite amazed.

Jake whispered, "Our own *sister*…we've got a sister... *together*."

*****

A nurse led Noah to Tillie's room. Hopefully she'd still be awake. She had to be exhausted after what she went through. She was covered in white blankets. A nurse beside her was checking her blood pressure.

"She's just about asleep," she said, looking at Tillie. "Hey, kiddo, your hubby's here." She removed the cuff, hung it on the hook by the bed and smiled. "Pressure's perfect." She bustled out of the room.

Noah went to Tillie, taking her hand into his own. She looked into his dancing, blue eyes and gave him a tired smile. Noah sat down in the chair beside the bed, putting his face very close beside hers.

"You did great," he whispered. "You'll be a tough act to follow."

Tillie grinned and said, "It was that last shot of ephedrine." She chuckled softly, feeling the warmth of his stubbly face against her own, and she closed her eyes. It was the most secure feeling she'd ever known — the touch of his face against her own, and the familiar scent of his Old Spice. "How is she?" she whispered, giving his stubbled face a soft kiss.

"She's still in the nursery. They weighed her and measured her. Now I think they're getting ready to give her a bath. The kids can't wait to see her, and Maggie and Estelle are here."

Tillie smiled and nodded. "How much did she weigh?"

"Eight pounds even."

"And how long?"

Noah chuckled, "Only eighteen inches."

Tillie laughed softly and asked, "Does she have blue eyes?"

"Yes," Noah answered. "And she looks *just like me*."

Tillie laughed again, looking into the dancing, blue eyes she'd loved for so many years. "Happy birthday, Noah."

"Thanks, Angel."

Tillie gave his handsome face another soft kiss, her eyes slowly closed, and she fell fast asleep....

To be continued

EPILOGUE

May, 1998
Rapid City Regional Cancer Care Center

Rauwolf stumbled from the bathroom, dropping his exhausted body onto the hospital bed. *Maybe it would be better to just forget the treatment and allow myself the dignity of death,* he thought. *No one will miss me anyway. Mario's children rarely come around anymore, and my own son isn't even aware of my existence.*

He pulled the covers over himself, hearing a knock on his door.

"Come in."

Dr. Carson came in and stood beside the bed. "How are you doing, Roy?"

"Is this working?"

Dr. Carson shook his head. "It doesn't look like you're going into remission this time. I want to put you on the donor's list for marrow — unless you have any blood relatives — we should try them first."

Rauwolf swallowed and closed his eyes. "I have a son."

A Special Message for the Reader

"I, even I, am He who blots out your transgressions, for My own sake, and *remembers your sins no more*." Isaiah 43:25 **NIV**

While the consequence of our sin has the ability to leave a lasting mark on our lives, the sin itself is removed by God, and sent so far from us that we cannot comprehend its location.

"He does not treat us as our sins deserve or repay us according to our iniquities. For as high as the heavens are above the earth, so great is His love for those who fear Him; as far as the east is from the west, *so far has He removed our transgressions from us*." Psalm 103:10-12 **NIV**

I am so thankful for a *forgetful* God.

God removes our sin, but our flesh, on the other hand, does not appear to have God's infinite ability to *forget*. We are commanded to *forgive* one another, but the lasting mark of consequence is something our flesh struggles against — especially when that mark is inflicted upon us by someone we love. We must make a conscience choice to *forget*.

Tillie was in that very kind of a predicament. She loved Alex, and wanted to forgive him, but she remained fearful that he would return to his wicked ways. When he died, she was faced with the reality of having left so much business unfinished between them. Without truly forgiving her husband, Tillie found it impossible to heal her body completely — as well as her heart.

The apostle Paul was keenly aware of the harsh consequence of his sin against others as he'd been the primary persecutor of the early Church. He regretted deeply what he'd done, but rather than wallow in it, he went forward and gave this advice to the Church at Philippi: "But one thing I do: *Forgetting what is behind* and straining toward what is ahead, I press on toward the goal to win the prize for which God as called me heavenward in Christ Jesus." Philippians 3:13-14 **NIV**

Though Alex was at risk of falling back into his "old self," God had forgotten his previous sin. When Alex died, his place in heaven was assured. Even though Alex had become a real believer, he, like all of us, can fall off the wagon, so to speak. It's pretty easy for a believer to put the "old self" back on, wear him or her for a time, and inflict a little more sin — not only on ourselves, but the ones we love. (see Ephesians 4:22-24)

Paul knew this when he wrote to the Philippians, advising them to always "press on toward the goal," which is Christ. If we take our eyes off of Him for even a moment, we become entangled within the same old web of sin and unforgiveness we experienced before we met our beloved Savior.

If you're reading this and you don't know the forgetful love of Jesus Christ, Beloved, meet Him at the cross today. Ask Him to forgive you. Believe on His holy Name and you will be saved. Find a Bible and read about His love and forgiveness, *and forgetfulness*, and you will be changed.

Hallelujah, what a Savior!

Other Books in The Caselli Family Series:

Book I
The Pretender: A Blackguard in Disguise

Book II
Pit of Ambition

Book III
A Blackguard's Redemption

Book IV
The Gift: The Story of Annie Laurie

Book V
The Truth: Salvatore's Revenge

For future release date information, check out
www.TaMaraHanscom.com

Special Sneak-Peek Preview

Book V
The Truth: Salvatore's Revenge

He slipped past the lit room and moved closer to the door. He tried the knob and groaned. *It's locked.* He tucked his gun into his waistband, reaching for the metal pick he kept in his pocket. With his left hand he held the knob steady, his right hand working the tumblers. At the sound of several clicks, the knob released and the door creaked open. He slipped into the dark room and closed the door behind him. Yesterday he followed Luigi Andreotti to the dock where the Senator's yacht was moored — Senator Caselli had taken Andreotti into this very room.

Jason fumbled in his jacket pocket for his penlight, switched it on and shined it around the small office. There was a glint of something white under the corner of a chair and Jason focused the small beam on it. A paper matchbook. He picked it up and looked at the cover. *Circle Q Bar & Grill.* He frowned as he tucked the matchbook into his pants pocket.

Something cold and hard was suddenly thrust against the back of Jason's neck. He jumped with surprise, reaching instinctively for the gun tucked into his waistband.

"Don't even try it," demanded a deep female voice from behind him. "Just put your hands on the back of your head and turn around. *Slowly.*"

With a heavy sigh, he did as he was told. A light came on and he was face to face with a tall woman in her mid-twenties. Her dark eyes frowned at him through soft black, whispy bangs. The rest of her hair was very short, showing off the diamond earrings dangling from her feminine lobes. She was dressed in an exquisite white, sequined gown, framing her six-foot figure perfectly. She was stunning, to say the least, except for the .38 Special she held in dead aim at Jason's head.

She raised one sultry eyebrow. "Whatcha doin' in here, Pretty Boy?"

Jason swallowed hard, searching his mind for an answer. *Who is she? Does she work for Andreotti or is she one of the Casellis? She looks like a Caselli...except for how tall she is...wonder if she knows how to handle that piece....*

"Answer me," she prompted with a frown.

Jason cleared his throat, tossing his sandy, blond hair out of his eyes. He smiled shyly, attempting to flirt, "I was looking for the bathroom and just got lost."

She nodded at the gun in his waistband. "Try again."

Jason looked down at his gun and back at hers. As usual, he was in over his head. He was out of his jurisdiction and he didn't have a warrant. "I work for Andreotti," he lied.

"And what do you do for him?"

"Security. I'm his body guard," Jason answered, impressing himself with his quick and clever lie. He smiled with confidence.

She sighed, "Slowly, take your weapon and drop it to the floor."

"Listen, Miss, just let me go about my business and I'll be off this boat in no time."

Her face was stern and her eyes bored into his. "Drop the gun, pal."

He thought about refusing, but she was so...*authoritative*. He let out a soft breath and slowly reached for the gun, dropping it to the floor.

She came closer, pressing the barrel of her gun into his temple. Beads of sweat ran down the sides of his face as she reached inside his jacket. Her hand brushed past the badge he kept in the inside pocket, and she pulled it out. She opened the leather wallet, finding his detective's shield: *Jason Patterson, Rapid City Police Department*. She shook her head and made a soft 'tsk' noise. "Good grief, you're a cop," she said, letting out a disgusted breath. "Rapid City, South Dakota?"

Jason swallowed and nodded.

She tucked the wallet back into his pocket and took a step backward. She raised her black eyebrow again and demanded, "Now, you'd better tell me what you're up to, because Rapid's an awfully long way away. Obviously, you don't have a warrant."

Jason took a deep breath and replied, "I followed...I'm doing some investigative work. I thought I might be able to find some information here."

She seemed satisfied with his response. She lowered her gun, stepping back a few more feet. She gestured to his weapon on the floor and said, "Go ahead and pick it up, but holster it."

Jason stooped to pick up his gun, tucking it into the safe shoulder sling beneath his arm. "Can I go?" he asked.

"No," she answered abruptly, lifting the material of her dress to her mid-thigh, delicately placing her weapon into its secret holster. She smoothed out her beautiful dress and looked him in the eye. "I've got a couple of questions for you first."

"Who are you?" he asked.

"United States Deputy Marshal Alyssa Caselli."